Alpine Duty

Henry Melton

Alpine Duty

Henry Melton

Wire Rim Books
Hutto, Texas

WRB

Alpine Duty © 2019 by Henry Melton
All Rights Reserved

Printing History
First Edition: July 2019
ISBN 978-1-935236-72-6

ePub ISBN 978-1-935236-73-3
Kindle ISBN 978-1-935236-74-0

Website of Henry Melton
www.HenryMelton.com

Cover art by HMT STUDIOS Manila

Printed in the United States of America

Wire Rim Books
www.wirerimbooks.com

Acknowledgements

The order in which books are written is not necessarily the order in which they are published. This is an example, written well before most of the Project Saga was fleshed out, but published in story-chronological order. As a result, I have had the opportunity over the years to have many friends and helpers look it over and help me smooth out the rough patches. I have a horrible fear that I'm forgetting someone, but at the very least I need to thank the following people:

Jonathan Andrews, Jim Dunn, Linda Elliott, Cindy Howard, Payne Kenneth, Barbara Knighton, Mike Lynch, Alan McConnell, Mary Ann Melton, and Tom Stock

Contents

The 48-Hour Lunar Day

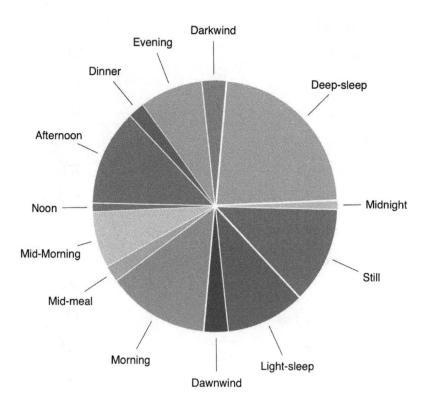

Northeastern Luna

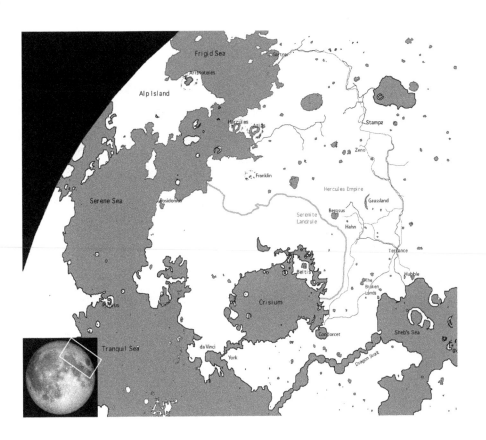

Brothers

Charles looked off at the light of the campground peering through the trees in the distance. Settlers, heading out for free land in the east, were clustered together, their wagons' brightly colored canopies looking like a Freeday morning's display at a Gartner flower shop. Grain haulers were lined up side by side like ships in docking slips. Even the Legionnaires had formed their supply wagons into a tight little triangle, with their muskets stacked in plain sight, ready for action.

Someone, he darkly suspected the commander of the Legion detachment, had requested the two Alpine brothers bring up the rear. The Fasail wagon had no place to set up for the night in the main campsite. All the good places were taken. Before darkwind, his brother Rad had just stopped at a wide place on the trail and walked off.

Charles didn't even know where he'd gone.

"Big brother and his secrets." The burning log in the oxygen-rich Lunar atmosphere was too hot to handle! He tossed it back into the fire and the flash of heat made him turn his face away. It was quickly consumed.

Enough of that! "I hate fire." He only built an open fire because he could. He was no longer an indentured dockworker, forbidden to have any kind of flame.

Across the gully, in the main campsite, there were numerous glowing campfires, but they were all safely enclosed in fire baskets to restrict their oxygen and let them burn safely and slow. He had one, of course, strapped to the side of their wagon, but the need to display a raging open flame just came over him.

He was Alpine. More than anyone, he understood the need to keep fire tightly under control near the great wooden dock works where he had worked.

I'm the only one who understand why things are the way they are!

Except his brother, of course.

"But where is he?"

He shot a dark look towards the Herc settler encampment. Rad was far too friendly with mainlanders.

"He should know better."

...

Seven years earlier, Rad had helped his little twelve-year-old brother walk steadily on the mud-soaked deck of the Herc merchant ship, a grip on his shoulder with one hand, and the little bundle of their only possessions in his other.

Captain Jenner frowned at them. Survivors hadn't been part of his plan. "Billy, take these two below before they wash overboard."

"Sir," Rad said, "our family is at Aristotle. If we could—"

"That's where we're headed," the captain cut him off. He looked down at the little one and sighed. "Don't worry. I'll make sure you're safe."

And they sailed up the coast of Alp Island, until they could see the rimwall of the mighty, cratered city through the endless storm. Muddy ash fell continually, until even Rad was pressed to join the crew keeping the decks washed clear of the stinking gray muck.

Charles was restricted to a shared bunk below, with a tiny slit of a window out onto his devastated homeland. Captain Jenner's crews made several trips ashore, bringing pieces of burned and mud-caked machines back on board. There were no other survivors.

Desperate to find some usable salvage to cover the cost of his expedition into the Burn, the captain took Rad ashore, for a last look at Aristotle.

His brother's eyes, when they'd come back empty-handed, had haunted Charles for years.

"Nothing," Rad said. "It's all gone."

"Everything?"

Rad nodded. Rinsed of the mud, but still soaked, he lay down on the board and turned his face to the wall. In whispers only Charles could hear, he tried to describe it.

"All the buildings are gone, scoured clean. Even the Shrine ... Even the Library."

In his mind, Charles could still see the white city of his birth, ranked in terraces on the inside crater walls. Mostly wooden, there had been a few structures built from stone. Their house had been high up, on the Fifth Tier. Down on the shore of the lake, the First Landing Shrine had been stone. The Library had been carved into the face of the rock itself, as secure from the elements as it was possible to make it.

The reality of the Burn had set in gradually. He'd realized that nothing organic could have survived. The great forests had all turned to ash. The wooden buildings would have gone, too. And, of course, all the inhabitants.

But what could have taken the stoneworks as well?

Whispering, barely stirring the air, he asked, "The ships?"

Rad had nodded silently, and then his back began shaking, his grief for him alone.

There had been two space-capable craft left to humanity. Two mighty beamships had brought the Alpines, and the Library of Humanity, from their old home in the Space Cities, and then rested in the center of Aristotle's crater walls. Rarely, those spectacular metal cylinders lifted off, for visits to the lands of the Hercs and the Serenites. Visits made to remind the mainlanders of the undeniable Alpine superiority.

But if the Burn had destroyed the ships, they would not have gone quietly. Energies that could take the ships into space would have been released in a mighty blast.

A blast that would scour everything from the crater.

Barely sure of his own thoughts, little Charles had whispered to Rad, "The Burn destroyed the ships?"

"Maybe." And that was all he would say.

Charles puzzled over it until the horrible possibility swept over him, too. Perhaps the Burn hadn't destroyed the ships. Perhaps the ships' destruction had triggered the Burn.

Maybe his people had destroyed themselves.

They spoke no more about it, keeping quiet and out of Captain Jenner's sight as the expedition sailed back toward the Empire of Hercules on the mainland, nearly empty-handed.

Charles feared for the future. What would become of them? At least big brother Rad was there to take care of him. And hadn't the captain promised to keep them safe?

The ship pulled into the Port of Gartner, with its massive docks, built in tiers to handle all stages of the great tides. Charles looked to the city beyond, wondering what they would need to do to find their way.

He needn't have worried. They never left the docks.

Jenner counted his money. "Sorry, boys. I have to pay my crew. Besides, indenture isn't too bad. It'll make men of you. Just save your money and you can buy your way out in no time."

It had taken seven years.

...

Nineteen-year-old Charles stirred the ash pile. Even the coals had burned themselves out quickly. Nothing was left but the smell of smoke. He wrinkled his nose and went to collect water from the creek to turn the ashes into mud. It'd never do to risk a spark, even if dawnwind was hours away yet.

The clouds above were illuminated. The Earth had risen, but it was rare to see it in all its glory. He was grateful for enough light to make it down to the water without wasting lamp fuel. They were through the mountain pass, and they'd be following this watercourse for a while.

I don't really need the wagonmaster to tell me which way to go.

The Gaussland Trail was well rutted. If it weren't for the threat of Kimmer attack and Rad's stubbornness, he'd have gone on ahead of the rest. "Better than eating dust."

But the Legionnaires weren't there for show. Single wagons, and smaller trains, had been attacked by the forest beasts with nothing but bones and ashes left to tell the tale. He hoped to see a Kimmer—at a distance. The tales around Gartner had been so fanciful, large flying beasts with huge teeth and claws—not at all like the sober scientific descriptions of animals his father taught.

Probably no one was left in all the world who knew that Far Earth held wonders like elephants, giraffes, and dragons. No one without an Alpine education and access to the Library could have that knowledge.

Charles retired to his covered wagon. It was only light-sleep and the dawnwind was still hours away.

He hopped the two meters up to the transom, climbed in, and fumbled in the dark for a warmball. With a twist, it sparked inside and the ignited wick turned the translucent stone into a ball of light. There was a little holder for the gadget. Unfortunately, the yellow glow showed a mess of wood chips all over the boards.

There on the hammock he had slung for sleeping was a half-finished carving of the Temple of Sheb's Victory. He reached for it too quickly and one of the columns snapped. *No matter.* He hefted it in his hand. He must have carved hundreds of them, all alike, all junk for the pilgrims that arrived at the docks on their way to the Northern Sanctuary. He'd carved temples, ships, busts of the emperor; whatever was popular for the tourists. Skill wasn't required. After two or three trials, Ferd the merchant would tell him it was good enough. "Just make more like that one."

He'd started this one yesterday to kill time, just as he had made all the others to fill the time between work shifts. A few coins for carvings, a few more for errands—and they saved them all. *No more. I've made my freedom. I don't need to carve any more junk for tourists.* He tossed the broken ornament out into the night.

The chips offended him. Should he sweep them up? Or wait until dawn when he'd be trapped in here anyway?

A long bundle wrapped in oiled leather, caught his attention. He knew exactly what it was, even though he hadn't seen it in a long time. He yielded to the urge and unwrapped the intricately worked cylinder of silvery metal.

A big smile on his face, he ran his fingers over the length of the metal, cane-like device. *Father's impulse rifle.* He shook his head. It was Rad's now.

Captain Jenner hadn't given a second glance to the bundle of rags they'd carried aboard his ship. If he had, then he'd have paid for his expedition many times over.

They'd gone hunting that day of the Burn.

Rad brought his father's prize possession—a one-man tractor/pressor beam gun. Rad, to this day claimed he'd gotten permission to use it. Charles wasn't so sure.

Designed for a single soldier back in *oldman* times, it was one of the rarest and most valuable weapons on the face of Luna today.

As the younger brother, Charles had been using another of the family heirlooms—a hand-pumped air rifle, capable of speeding a pellet fast enough to bring down small game.

They'd survived because Rad moved fast, when the sky turned red. There was a lava tube nearby, and Rad forced them in before the explosive burn wave crested over their part of the island.

Charles pressed something that looked like an ornate carving, and part of the metal changed color, displaying numbers, information about its settings and how much power remained in the storage cell. He hadn't worked it in years. Both their treasures stayed hidden beneath the floorboards in their bare sleeping cube on the docks. After their first small hoard of coins had been stolen, they took extra precautions against thievery.

They'd also tracked down the thief, a rummy named Gill, and beat him so bloody that he'd become the best advertising they could get. Don't mess with the Alpines!

The wagon shook suddenly on its leather springs. Charles gripped the impulse gun tightly. Out of the dark, a fist struck him a stinging blow to the head.

"Thief!" he heard, as strong hands gripped his arm and threw him bodily out into the night.

The Winds

Charles sailed through the air like his discarded carving, propelled by his brother's strong arm. He grabbed, but there was nothing to grip. Free fall was only a few seconds—nothing unusual to a dock fighter. He had just enough time to twist like a cat and try to get his feet under him. He almost made it.

Slipping as his foot struck the ground, he skidded unceremoniously to a halt over the gravel. Leggings protected him from a bad scrape, but not from tomorrow's bruises.

Rad Fasail was a huge man framed in the yellow light from the wagon—his twin in muscle and mass. Charles had been on the receiving end of his brother's anger more times than he could count. They were matched. Together against the others of the sweat gang, they'd been unbeatable. For the last two years, more often they fought each other.

Instinct moved muscle and he rolled, popping back upright. Charles launched back toward his brother before he even took in another breath. He'd learned to be quick.

Rad had experience. Charles was quicker in speed and in temper.

Reason was gone. He wanted to *beat* Rad!

He'll eat that word!

His leap was true. Rad, staring into darkness, had left himself unstable, holding the gun with one hand and the wagon box with the other. Charles jabbed his elbow into Rad's stomach and felt him go flying.

"Rad!" a girl's voice cried out. It distracted Charles only an instant, but his brother turned toward the call, spoiling his landing. It was all the edge Charles needed.

Low gravity fighting was all about bracing. If you can't keep your feet under you or put your back against something solid, then all the muscle in the world is useless. Charles grabbed the wagon wheel and used it to put precision and muscle into a double-leg kick. He felt Rad's ribs under his feet as a *Hoof!* of pain escaped. Rad went tumbling and the impulse rifle *clunked* to the ground off in the dark.

Charles gripped the wagon wheel and waited, his mind churning. It'd be a mistake to chase him down, even if it let Rad rest and regain his balance. *Can't let him call me a thief!*

They'd made 'thief' into an insult word during their time on the docks. It'd started with their private quest to recover their stolen coins. Making an example of old Gill, Rad had punctuated it with days of deliberate taunting, letting everyone know where they stood. They'd been new. The crew could've sided with Gill.

In the darkness, Charles was surprised to see a couple of strangers. *A Herc girl.* She'd distracted Rad. Her white dress made her stand out like a tall willowy ghost against the trees.

There was another figure, short, and harder to see. Charles recognized him with a sour taste. It was Grand, the centurion of the Legion detachment.

Rad popped suddenly into view, and began the growl he always voiced before leaping into attack. Charles shifted around to face him, making sure he had the wagon at his back.

"Stop it right now!" Grand yelled, louder than anyone his size had a right to sound. "I've had enough of you two."

Charles saw Rad stop. Cautiously, he stood upright. Grand was a Herc, but he was a Legionnaire, and even Rad showed him respect.

"I am no thief!" Charles shouted.

Rad said nothing, watching the outsiders, just standing his ground.

Grand spoke in a more normal voice, "Fasail, you'd better take care of that." He pointed to the ground, where the impulse rifle was a glint of silvery metal in the weak light.

Charles felt the back of his neck crawl. Grand had seen the impulse gun! Few men could recognize it, but the old soldier might be one. They had kept the secret of the gun's existence all these years, and now someone else knew.

Rad strode quickly over and plucked it up. He looked at Charles with a dead, stern gaze, and then dropped his eyes. Avoiding eye contact with everyone, he went to the other wagon entrance and climbed in.

Charles, still boiling inside, turned on the two, "What are you Hercs doing here?" The girl flinched.

Grand held out his hand toward her, "Come on Maria. Let's leave the idiots to work out their own problems."

Charles burned at that. *Who was he calling an idiot?*

They'd just turned back toward the camp when Rad tossed a small-pack out of the wagon and dropped to the ground. "I'm going hunting," he declared. He picked up his gear and quickly strode away into the dark.

Charles clenched his fists, unwilling to call him back.

Just like Rad to skip out and leave me to take care of the wagon. How many times had he said that we had to work together? We're the last Alpines left, and we can't count on the Hercs. What's happened to him? He hasn't been pulling his weight for a year. It would serve him right if I just let the dawnwind flip the wagon!

Not that he meant it. You learned to respect the winds before you left your crib. Dawnwind was coming and he could no more ignore it than a mouse could ignore a cat's jaws.

His father's words echoed in memory. He'd been tall but slight, an intellectual, not a big, muscular dockworker like his sons had become. Some lessons had branded themselves vividly into his brain.

In his classroom, Professor Fasail lowered the lights and projected a huge image, the primeval Lunar globe, gray and bare and pitted.

"Luna was turning. More time and energy—planet busting energy—had been spent on getting it to turn than had been spent on such lesser tasks as giving it an atmosphere and carving great channels into its surface. Luna has always rocked gently and stately like a pendulum in the gravitational field of the Earth. But finally, human will and the orbital energies of the planets themselves amplified the swings until the ultimate ... happened.

"Shaking with continuous quakes, and spilling lava from its re-heated interior, Luna flipped over."

The image changed to another, with fewer maria, dominated with the mega-crater Oriental, but lit with red patches and streams.

"Across the face of the Far Earth, our oldman ancestors stopped their lives and went outside to see what no human had ever seen before, the face of Farside, hanging in the sky.

"Once started, great tractor and pressor beams that coupled Luna to Mars and Venus were reconfigured to increase the spin. The Project goal had been to bring it up to a 24-hour period like Earth and Mars, but ... the Plague struck, wiping out the very Project itself.

"Luna was left with a 48-hour day—fast enough so that humans and animals could adapt, but not so they could live in comfort."

The projector changed again, to a great ball of clouds, showing none of the surface, but textured with the chaos.

"The sun winds were part of the price—the darkwind *and the* dawnwind. *No one had expected them. The dynamics of a thick atmosphere under a low gravity and slow spin were much different from the banded thick atmosphere in the heavy gravity and 10-hour days of Jupiter. Nor was it like the trades and tropics in the thin atmosphere of Earth.*

"The sun's heat forever expands the atmosphere beneath it, constantly pushing winds toward the night side where it cools and contracts. As the globe spins, every morning heralds the coming of the sun with a blast from the east. Every evening, the sky darkens to the howls of the winds from the west. Midnight and noon bring the still *as winds shift direction.*

"Every life form from pine to pika, from dolphin to dandelion learned to adapt to the winds, or it no longer survives with us on Luna."

Charles loved his father's speeches. The man had been a biologist, but every facet of knowledge was his joy, and his first pupils were his own sons.

The lessons stuck, although it didn't need an Alpine professor to teach them. No human, even those protected behind the crater walls of every major city, could afford to forget the winds, not even once.

Forgetting it out on the unprotected trails was suicide.

...

Rigging the wagon was something Charles could do in his sleep. It was a little harder doing it alone.

A sledge hammer loosened the heavy iron stake that had secured the wagon from the previous darkwind. He would have preferred to have left it and moved everything else, but the flat area by the stream bed where they'd stopped wasn't large enough on the western side.

Poor planning, Rad! Poor planning.

Dawnwind was already growing, and the canvas was popping as it rippled under the growing gusts. The ox was not happy with being moved from his rest, but the animal they'd bought was neither energetic nor temperamental.

"Move, you stupid beast!" Dock work had given him no training for this, and there had been no oxen on Alp. For a moment, he was afraid the animal was deaf, but the canvas snapped louder, and that got its attention.

Gradually, it responded to its traces and pulled the wagon about. Charles had a good feel for the air, and he quickly aligned the pointed tail of the wagon's canopy, the apex of the cone, into the wind.

The stake was tough to drive, forcing wrought iron through layers of streambed gravel, but he put all his frustrations into the swings, something he'd learned to do well.

Port Gartner was the largest port on the northern end of the Herculean Empire. It was the gateway to the northern, called "Spanish", branch of the Gaussland Trail. An overland road went eastward and then down to the southern part of the Herculean Empire, avoiding the Serenite armies that claimed the southern reaches of the coastline.

Gartner wasn't a cosmopolitan center like the twin cities of Atlas and Hercules, but its port was busy enough to keep its dockworkers sweating every day.

North of Gartner, settlement dropped off. Snow and ice permanently limited sailing and farming. There were no seasons on Luna, at least none to speak of, with its axis of rotation almost perpendicular to the sun. The ice fields that stopped northern expansion never retreated.

Some sailors swore that the ice was growing, although that made no sense to his Alpine education.

Charles drove the last stroke and confirmed that the cables were firmly attached. It was none too soon. The wind was picking up rapidly.

He kept his hands on the looped rope that ran around the edge of the wagon. Even in the protected cities, a number of people died each year from being caught up by the winds. Out here in the open, Charles tensed with each new howl.

Only once, in his first year on the docks, had he lost himself to the winds. There'd been ropes everywhere, but he'd made the mistake of reaching for one with his left hand *after* he'd let go with his right.

The screaming blast of wind threading through the wooden structure had chosen that moment to shift, grabbing him and ripping him from the catwalk. He must have blacked out, because he couldn't remember anything until he splashed into the cold water of the bay.

He remembered fighting the winds as they tried to push him ever farther away from the dimly lit docks. After fighting, and losing, as every stroke of his arms only succeeded in slowing the rate he was pushed away, he remembered his father. *You will never beat Luna, Charles. Learn its rules, and then you can survive.*

Charles remembered that time with a grin. He hadn't panicked. "Alpine training," he said later with pride. He ducked beneath the waters, where the winds couldn't reach, and swam toward the docks, only surfacing for quick breaths of air.

He hadn't known he'd made it back to the docks until Rad was suddenly in the water with him, pushing a rope into his hand. Others told him later his brother had been like a wild man, screaming his name and getting them all to spread out on the docks and look for him. Rad had threatened the gang boss, trying to get a boat, when he had been spotted. Rad jumped in after him, trailing a rope.

Charles felt some of the anger fade as he remembered. Rad saved his life many times. They had suffered together. They were brothers, Alpines. There was no one else. Without his brother, he'd be lost.

He checked the ox, settling down with its back to the wind, nestled as close as possible to the protection of the wagon. Charles quickly did the same, climbing into the empty interior to sleep out the dawn.

Dust and Rumors

It's days like today, Charles thought as he swatted at a large biting fly, *when I can almost believe that Father made it all up. How could the human race, the Project no less, wielding powers that defied comprehension, with the will and imagination to remake the whole solar system into a garden—how could they be so stupid as to include flies and mosquitoes in paradise?*

After ten hours on the trail, with the noon still approaching, the air was hot and uncomfortable. The dust of all the wagons before him still hung in the air. The air was different here, on the other side of the pass. He could feel his lips crack from the dryness.

It was Rad's fault. If his lazy brother had been there, taking his share of the chores, he wouldn't have overslept and ended up at the tail end of the line, again. If Rad had been around to take his turn at the reins, then he wouldn't be starved, hot, and seriously in need of a break to go visit the bushes.

I hate being last. His nose twitched with the urge to sneeze. After all, what was there to do on a long drive, but look ahead, imagining the new sights and new places that were just over the horizon? *I can't do that through this dust.* He was lucky to see the front end of his ox. Early morning had been better, with a quartering breeze to blow it off the rutted trail.

I miss the docks, he suddenly realized, a little shocked at himself. The work had been just as mind-numbing, even more, but at least the breeze over the water had been sweet and clean. When the noon still came, and the workload permitted, he could even jump into the cold fresh water and lose his own stink.

Gartner had been a pretty bay. As a privileged young Alpine boy, he had traveled to Hercules and Posidonius with his father. He had seen enough of the world to be able to make some honest comparisons. The harbor was large, as most Herc ports went. It was a flooded crater, of course. Unlike the high, steep crater walls of Hercules and Atlas, the twin capitol cities of the Empire, or even like his native Alp's Aristotle, with its enclosed lake, Gartner was open to the Frigid Sea along the south and west, surrounded across the northern and eastern arc with the high hills of the crater rim. Of course, that made the darkwind even more severe than most ports had to contend with, but at midday, with a break in the clouds, it felt to Charles like he could see forever out across the endless waves.

The ox stumbled and caught itself. Charles brought his mind back to the task at hand, watching the endless rhythm of the rear end of his beast. He seriously considered giving it a name, just so he could yell at it more creatively.

"Charles Fasail!" He looked up, and noticed that there was someone waiting for him on the trail. It was a Herc girl.

"Yes? What do you want?"

She put a foot on the step and pulled herself up to the driver's box. "I'm sorry to bother you, but have you seen Rad?"

He shifted to the side to keep his distance. So, she was the girl from the fight. Rad had probably been talking to her. Just one more example of how crazy he was acting. How many times had Rad told *him* to avoid the Herc girls?

"No. Gone hunting. He'll be back when he's ready."

She nodded, but she seemed in no mood to leave. "I'm sorry Rad got angry with you. I feel like it's my fault."

Charles objected, "Don't apologize for him. It's not your place." Defense of Rad was instinctive. "He's my brother. If we fight, it's our own business. Who're you anyway?"

His abruptness was meant to push her away, but she shook it off. She seemed immune to his rudeness.

"My name is Maria Turner. I'm the daughter of Chess Turner. You may have seen our wagon? It's the black and white one. Rad has been nice enough to help us out the last couple of days." She smiled, and Charles felt the urge to yell at her fade away.

She's irritating. First, she was a girl, that nearly always made him edgy. Living on the docks gave him no experience with them. Secondly, she gave the one answer that would shut him up. It was his father's voice in his head again. *An Alpine should be judged by the help he gives the world.*

More than a biology professor, he was often a preacher. Live the Alpine ideal. Help the world. Bring Luna up from ignorance. The Alpines had no other reason to exist.

It meant little, in Charles's opinion, while being a slave on the docks. Of course he and Rad were helping people! They'd get whipped if they didn't. Maybe not volunteers, but they were certainly helpers.

Charles had an uneasy memory of his father looking down over his shoulder, asking, *What have you done today?*

He had no reason to question Rad. As much as he hated to think it, maybe his brother was just out doing his Alpine duty and finding ways to help these Hercs.

He tasted the idea. It would explain the strangeness. It wasn't something that appealed to him, but maybe his brother was being more conscientious about his Alpine duties than he was.

The girl kept talking, "Rad has been a big help to us. I have a couple of brothers, but they're both too young to help Father with the rigging. I hadn't seen your wagon all day. I was worried."

She looked carefully at his face, trying to read his expression. He felt no need to help her. She added, "I think it is my fault you and Rad fought. I know he intended to get back sooner and help you with the wagon, but I talked him into staying for the Han-meal. Now, you have to handle your wagon by yourself, and it isn't fair. Let me help you."

He had heard of the Han-meal. It was a religious thing the Hercs did every quad—well the farmers and merchants at least. Not many of the sweat gang paid any attention to what day of the quad it was. He shook his head over a half-smile. "No. I don't need any help—although I wish the wagon master would call the noon break."

She shook her head, "But—there isn't going to be one! It was announced this morning. Everyone was supposed to use feed bags for their teams and we would skip the breaks. If we make good time, we could be in Stampz before darkwind."

Charles growled, "Nice of them to tell me about it. I'll have to stop. 'Dusty' down there," he pointed at the ox, "will need to eat, even if I have to do without."

No one was behind him, so he wasted no time, reigning in the ox and setting the brake.

"Let me help. I really want to help," she asked. He just grunted and headed into the interior of the wagon to get a feed bag and fill it with grain. By the time he poked his head out, he saw that she was not going to be ignored. She had already set up the collapsible leather watering trough in front of the animal and was emptying a skin of water into it. The sound of the splashing water made him even more uncomfortable with his other concern.

It took a few more minutes to let the animal drink and get started into his feed bag. Charles really needed to relieve himself, but he just couldn't, not with a girl waiting, trying to help him. *I can't even drive off and leave her.* Last wagon always had to gather any stragglers.

She looked so cheerful and pleased with her efforts. She asked again if there was anything she could do to help.

"Can you drive?"

"Oh, yes. I help drive our wagon all the time."

"Good. I really need to take a break. Can you spell me for an hour or so?"

"Oh, longer than that, if you need me to. Do you want to take a nap?" She was already climbing up into the driver's box.

"Not exactly."

. . .

Charles ran free and easy, his hand feeling the cool metal of his air rifle, and the wind of his own speed cooling his sweat. It was a dirty trick getting her to drive for him while he went on a hunt of his own. But oh, it felt good to get free of that hard dusty perch.

Running across the broken ground filled him with a bubble of joy. It was so new, after seven years of confined city living. He hadn't managed to break out and really feel his new freedom. It had all been a rush; the Match Ceremony with the scribe to break the indenture, the haggle with Amos to get the wagon they'd picked out, gathering the supplies and rushing to the staging field to make the final call.

Freedom was supposed to let him to run away from his problems.

The wagon train had been winding its way through the broken highlands that separated the plains east of Gartner from the Spanish River valley. It had been slow and rough getting this far. The wagon master promised it would only get easier.

As Charles gained altitude, taking a path that headed parallel to the river bed, he could feel a lot of his cares drop away with the dusty air. It was clean up here and he could feel the scent of rain to come. He hoped the wagon master was right about the river. A full day without rain was a rarity, but with cloud tops that could reach hundreds of kloms up into the thick atmosphere, downpours could happen that could scour the whole river valley. The wagons could float well enough to handle a stream crossing, but a torrent would take them all.

A shout in the distance almost threw him off of his pace, and he skidded to a halt. There was no one in sight, just the rocks and the stunted shrubs that occupied every protected low spot. Across the narrow river valley, the dark cliffs lined the other side.

He moved closer to the edge and was not surprised to see the colorful moving wagons below. He couldn't hear anything now—only a chance alignment of the far rock face, reflecting the sound, had made it possible.

When Amos the wagon seller explained to him the reason that the guild required every wagon painted a different pattern, he didn't listen, familiar with the Herc rationalizations. Just another way to pick his pocket, he was sure. But now, he was grateful, because at this distance the canopies were the only visible markers.

His own wagon, with its yellow gold top, was still at the tail end. *But she's closed the gap. Better driver than I'd expected.*

Other wagons held little interest. He could see the Turner wagon, now that she'd pointed out its black and white pattern. There was the wagon master's own rig at the lead, with its red and black bands. He was able to put wagons with faces in a couple of other cases, but he had to be honest with himself, he didn't really care about which Herc had which wagon.

Charles settled himself on a large flat boulder and watched the tiny toys move slowly along their graveled path, kicking up a dust cloud that hung in the air until a rain or the darkwind swept it clean. In the middle of the train, the military wagons looked out of place with their unmarked white canvas tops. There were two ordinary supply wagons and the secret wagon.

First day out, Charles was introduced to the caravan's biggest mystery. One of the Legion's wagons had bogged down in thick mud. Rad had been driving and called him up into the box when their progress was halted by the sight of the half-dozen green-uniformed men up to their knees in gray clinging mud.

The two Fasail brothers would have been content to watch others sweating away for a change, but then, the soldiers' loud and sarcastic leader, Grand, noticed them watching with far too much enjoyment on their faces.

He turned his attention toward them, much to the relief of his own bogged down men and asked, "If you two whales would stop quivering and come help, then maybe we could get back on the road. That is, if there is any muscle buried in all that fat!"

Charles sneered, "I've got more muscle in my right arm than you have in your whole body." It was an exaggeration of course, but not by much.

Grand said nothing, but the tilt of his nose was enough of a statement. Rad looked at Charles and he shrugged. The little man had nothing but a mouth and an attitude to push his authority, but there was something engaging about him. Rad locked the wheel and they climbed down to help.

Quickly enough, Charles learned why the soldiers were having trouble moving the completely shrouded wagon. The secret cargo was heavy—dense like iron or a huge tank of water. They heaved in unison, but although it shifted in the mud, they still lacked the strength to get the leading wheels up over the edge of the pit.

Having been in the business of moving cargo, Charles was quick to suggest, "We need to unload the goods to lighten the wagon."

Grand seemed to ignore his suggestion, frowning as he stared at the surrounding hills. Then with a "Stay put!" he headed off to bully or cajole some more muscle.

Eventually, with three more men, they managed to get the wagon moving again.

Anyone who hadn't noticed the extra attention the Legion was giving that wagon was soon informed. Gossip about its secluded cargo became the number one campfire topic.

Rad, who moved about the Herc campground with much more ease than Charles ever did, told him some of the speculations.

He chuckled about it. "I have never had my opinion valued so highly before. It seems my expertise in cargo handling now carries some weight."

"What do you mean?"

"Well, everyone wants to know what's the big secret military cargo. They're desperate for ideas.

"One theory is that Sheb is finally deciding to buy the loyalty of the Hahn settlement by sending them a shipment of Franklin muskets."

"Against Kimmer or Serenite bandits?"

"Kimmer. Grand tells me Serenite raids have fallen off this year. There's hope that the Two Houses will renew the pact of Sheb the Fourth."

Charles grunted his opinion of that happening. From his Alpine perspective, gained in Lunar history class, the Herculean Empire and the Landrule of Serenity would always be enemies. The Serenites had fixed borders. Hercs had a frontier. Now, without the fear of Alp to lend some stability, more war was foreordained. Seven years of dockside scuttlebutt presented a bleak picture of the state of world harmony and the brotherhood of man.

"So what are the other theories?" he asked, dismissing offhand anything that smelled like the current Herc ruler actually planning for the future of his empire.

Rad grinned, "Other ideas get progressively more interesting. My favorite is that this is a secret shipment of *oldman* weapons to the Southern Palace to keep the Governor from breaking away from the Empire and forming his own kingdom."

Charles laughed, "Who thought that one up? No one is stupid enough to move *oldman* technology along wagon routes! We've only got a handful of Legionaries—the risk is too great. The Herc navy still controls shipping all the way to Condorcet. They would use a four-master or better, armed to the teeth, and if they had problems, the guns would go to the bottom, rather than be used against them."

"Hey, I didn't say I agreed with it, I just like the style of the story. I especially like the idea that giving a rebellious governor more weapons would keep him loyal.

"But you'll love the variant. One noodlehead claims that it's not guns that Grand's men are shipping, but gold."

Charles had a thought, "Is high and mighty Grand listening to all this?"

"Of course, half of the men are watching his face looking for a smile or a tick—looking for clues, but a man who's played poker for a hundred years isn't likely to be read that easily."

"He's not that old."

"I don't know—take a look at his face in a good light. I'd bet he's at least a hundred. There are plenty of rumors about him, too."

Charles wasn't willing to concede his brother might be right, but privately, he resolved to pay a bit more attention to the enigmatic commander.

He sighed and stood up from his break. The wagons were moving out of sight.

Enough speculation! He took this break to go hunting, and that's what called him now. There were more interesting inhabitants of these hills than Hercs!

Goose and Gate

The goose hadn't seen him yet. It was swimming in the small pond, contentedly searching the water below for edible weeds, ducking below the surface for several seconds at a time.

Charles found the flooded craterlet an hour earlier, high up in the hills, part of a hanging valley that spilled a misty white cascade down into the river gorge below. The first flock scattered in panic as he climbed down to a flat rock surrounded by high grasses. The wait paid off when this lone bird landed to a smooth ripple in the still water.

There was a chill in his shoulders that had nothing to do with the temperature. His father had taught him how to hunt. Their last time together had been several weeks before the Burn. He'd huddled next to the water, a small boy with that paternal presence so close behind him that he could feel the warmth. His father had held his impulse rifle, but this was his son's hunt and had to be conducted for the pump gun's limitations.

Charles pumped the lever on the ancient air rifle, carefully moving his body in time with the vegetation around him. A startled goose meant another long wait. He knew the limitations of his gun and his skill. Once in flight, it would be useless to shoot.

Seven years ago, he spent hundreds of hours collecting gravel to find just the right sized grains to use as ammunition. In a leather pouch permanently attached to the stock were two metal sieves. If a grain of rock could shake through the red one but not through the yellow one, then it would work in the gun's mechanism. That had never been good enough for him. Young Charles had matched rock types and hand picked for shape and texture and density. Little iron pellets worked best.

Just as true now as then—he owned a truly unique *oldman* weapon. Not powerful, not even compared to the black powder guns anyone could own for a few shebs, but it was *oldman* manufacture, of some metal whose very name was unknown. His ancestors loved and preserved this tool of another age. He, Charles Fasail, was the one true expert on its care and use, and he used to be a pretty good shot with it.

He pumped twenty strokes, enough to speed the pellet along a flat trajectory with enough force to kill a bird. He moved into an aiming stance with an ease he hadn't expected. Habits came back, using memories he hadn't touched in years.

He estimated the drop and touched the trigger. The *pfft!* of air was loud, but the goose didn't notice a thing. The pellet missed and was swallowed into a *plop* of water.

He held his breath. If the bird had noticed anything, a second unknown noise would be enough to send it flying.

The black-feathered head, with its bright white chin patch, never turned his way, concerned with its bird thoughts and unaware that it was destined for dinner. When it ducked its head beneath the water again and waved its tail feathers in the air, Charles resumed breathing and again started his slow pumping.

He took more time with the second shot, aiming carefully at the head. It was a habit. Something his father once said around the campfire had impressed him; "We all have to live and die, but only people have to suffer." He enjoyed the hunt and took pride in a clean kill. Inevitably, the goose was going to die to feed some part of the food chain. Charles was happy to be that predator, but he preferred to believe that it passed from the cool water into a cool death with a minimum of pain and no suffering. *pfft!*

...

Close. He was surprised by Stampz. Cresting the latest hill, the wall mountain of the crater suddenly became the eastern horizon. Maria whatshername had mentioned that they might reach Stampz Gate before darkwind, but this was only a couple of hours away.

With gutted bird in one hand and the air gun in the other, he looked for a quicker path down to the riverbed. He had to get back. The hunt had taken longer than he had expected, and he needed to be back in the driver's box.

Several times, he'd heard travelers bragging about their view of Stampz Gate over the years. Descriptions varied, but the enthusiasm was universal. He would likely come this way only once and he didn't want to miss any of it.

Stampz itself was officially a Duchy, but it was nothing special. It was smaller than Franklin, Mercury or even Zeno. Grainhauler and trade goods wagons liked to stop here. For settlers, though, it wasn't a popular destination. The free lands farther south like Gauss were the real goal.

The commercial stops like Zeno, Rynin, Terrance and Hubble made the trip desirable for the merchants, and in turn their regular trips made for a broken trail and experienced guides for the settlers. Certainly, the Legionnaires weren't with this trip to make the settlers feel safer.

Charles made it down to the trail and was able to pick up his pace. The gun and the bird made running a little awkward, but he soon got into the rhythm. Low gravity had given rise to a number of new gaits for the human inhabitants of Luna—everything from *rooing,* which was a series of double-legged long distance jumps, to the *toerun,* which had the runner almost face down, bent into the wind, pushing with the toes. Charles settled on a more upright gait due to his load, taking alternate strides in a slow rhythm that ate up the distance more due to the span of the steps than their rate.

Each footfall brought the intimidating wall closer into focus. From this viewpoint, there was no noticeable curve—just a wall at the end of the world. Typical gray stone, it was laced in terraces. In the ridges were garlands of green, the hardy brushes and even some pine that could stand the winds. That part of Stampz was no different from any other crater on Luna. It was the Gate that made it distinctive.

He could see the scar, a great dark crack in the wall, a wound from that time when the Project brought Hell to Luna.

It must have happened late in the change, he thought, when most of the atmosphere had already arrived in the form of an unending stream of man-made comets. There was air, and there were growing seas, and there was a torrent of rain across the whole face of the globe. Most craters filled up, collecting water that had no place to go. To this day, such lakes were common.

I would have loved to be alive in that age—to see it happen.

Luna was under stress, groaning under cosmic forces. Great Project beams were focused on the soil, bedrock and mantle. One beam connected Luna to Mars when their orbits were right, using the energy of the receding red planet to pull one edge of the globe. Another beam, in its season, connected to Venus, using its push against the other edge.

These planet-moving beams were not the only forces at work. There was another, something far older and more intimate.

When Luna was originally formed and caught into its orbit around the Earth, the mutual gravitational attraction caused the moon to settle into an oblong. Now that it was turning, that shape was no longer natural. It began to shift.

Quakes, some triggered by incoming comet impacts, some by a build up of tidal stresses, shook every part of this world.

One day, Stampz shook. A crack formed in its crater wall. The waters came out.

Charles tried to visualize the flood pouring out of the opening in the wall above. He looked again at the land around him, and suddenly, he could see the evidences of the massive outpour all around. Hills were flattened. Lesser craters were erased. The land was instantly shaped into a river valley, bent northward by the higher ridge to the east.

Most of the rivers worldwide were created in such disasters, where the millions of cups of water broke their rims and laid down a drainage system where none had ever been before. Even the lava flows of the creation had been different, bleeding up from the depths to fill the maria.

A feeling like hunger came over him, the kind that brought tears to his eyes. *I would have loved to have seen it.*

The torrent had scoured and enlarged the crack, leaving a gateway into the interior of the crater. Now there was a floor wide enough to pass wagons, as well as the remaining river as it left the bowl of Stampz and headed north to join the Spanish River on its way to the Humboldt Sea.

He could see more detail as his flying pace made the distance dwindle. The face of the crack itself seemed a darker red, more vivid than the rest of the crater wall. Some of that was likely the shadows of the canyon itself, but he had seen enough other rock fractures to know that the colors of fresh surfaces were real enough. A few hundred years were still not enough to dull the surface to that gray uniformity that millions of years of meteoric gardening and unrelenting solar ultraviolet had lent to most of the land.

Without warning, he could see the splash of reds, blues and golds of the wagons up ahead. They were at the Gate itself, but surely he could catch up to his wagon before it headed in.

Above, the opening crack was becoming alive with detail. On the left face, there was a wisp of waterfall that vanished completely into mist before it reached the bottom—an outflow from a hanging valley in the upper reaches.

Dark red differentiated into layers of upturned strata—different basalts that had been ripped from the surface and folded over backward like blankets on a bed by the primeval impact explosion.

Vertical bands, formed by springs, traced down the cliff face, sometimes with the brilliant green of lichen or fern living in the permanent dampness.

A white patch—no two! What are they? Surely, it was too warm here for snow. But maybe there was enough permanent shade...

No. They were moving, and there were more of them. Birds?

If so, they were dropping fast.

Charles watched as they circled down directly over the caravan. They were big, now that he could compare them with the wagons.

Those aren't birds.

The first twisted in mid air just above the wagons and dropped to the ground.

Kimmer! Kimmer in sailsuits!

The wagon was under attack.

Kimmer Attack

No!

Charles began to run. He dropped his trophy without a thought and started pumping the lever.

Kimmer were the demons of the forest, the one hazard of the trail everyone feared. The wagonmaster made a point in inventorying the weapons of the travelers, an inventory the Fasails discretely avoided. He wanted everyone to know that while an attack by the creatures was possible, it hadn't happened in several months and these battles were often one-sided, with a good Franklin musket able to drive off a dozen of the savages.

The guide's upbeat assessment fell a little flat on his ears. Tales had persisted for years about travelers in the central and eastern reaches of the empire having their wagons burnt. Tales of total massacres floated around the docks.

Charles slowed his toerun just enough to look at the sky. A dozen white shapes still rained down on the train. He winced as a bright flash of light and a puff of smoke told the tale. *One wagon down.* He located a glint of gold canopy and dug in with his toes.

No one knew much about Kimmer, other than their mindless destruction and their surprise attacks from the sky.

He glanced up from the ground. There was his wagon—and a Kimmer! It swooped in like a man-sized egret and landed into a run right before Charles.

Charles felt a rock give under his foot, and his balance was gone. He spilled to the right. *Pfft!*

Everything swirled around him as he skidded at high speed into his first battle, on his backside with an unloaded air gun.

Instinct brought him up to his knees, his hands in the gravel, and he found himself facing a Kimmer.

It looked like a man, dressed in a dark leather vest, breechclout and leggings. Something yellow and metallic, like gold was in its ragged hair. Charles felt details sharpen as he realized the Kimmer warrior was turning the barrel of a shiny black musket toward him.

Charles jumped straight up.

Stupid. He knew better. Never jump *up* in a fight. It gives your opponent leisurely seconds to size you up and destroy you.

The Kimmer's inexperience with the gun saved him. Air shook with the boom of the musket. The ground below, where he had been standing, was filled with a sulfurous white cloud of smoke. He was glad he wasn't there.

The savage looked up at him with a brown-toothed grin. He dropped the gun and reached for a belt knife as he loped easily to intercept his landing.

Charles twisted in the air and threw a stone he'd picked up with all the strength of his terror.

It clipped the Kimmer on the head, and it was the savage's turn to stumble on the rocks. Charles landed just as a second Kimmer arrived, a musket aimed his way. Charles kicked to the left and swerved toward the boulder field. He had no desire to confront armed warriors with nothing more than an unloaded pump gun.

Two more wagons exploded into flames. Charles didn't even look back to see if one was his. He didn't try to run more zigzags. He wasn't fast enough to outrun a bullet.

Let them all be bad shots!

The wagon train was bunched up in front of the Gate, confined by high walls on both sides. The fan-shaped flat area had space for only one wagon at a time heading into the Gate. The Kimmer were attacking those at the rear, the only wagons with any hope for escape.

Charles climbed the rock wall quicker than any thick-handed dock-worker carrying an air rifle should have managed. There was a recess in the rocks, a place to hide. Maybe he could find a way to shoot down into the battle … or throw rocks.

He threw himself over the ledge and panted for a few seconds. He chambered the next pellet and cranked the lever.

At the edge of his vision, he saw motion and spun around to train his gun on it.

"Alpine!" It was Grand, in the rocks just above him. Charles lowered his gun and twisted his way through the boulders.

"Get down!" Grand was watching the battle through a sight-hole between rocks. His pistol and powder bag lay beside him. Something in his voice made Charles look closely.

This was the first time he had gotten a really good look at the old soldier since Rad's comment. Charles could see it now. Not only old, but pale.

"Are you okay?" he asked the man. In battle, the old grudge faded away. When he set the pumpgun down, he noted dark wet spots on the rock.

Grand ignored the question and asked one of his own, "Do you have that impulse gun?"

Charles shook his head. Now was not the time to deny its existence.

"Did Rad have it with him?"

"Yes. He went hunting." Resentment came boiling back. *Rad should be here now!* An impulse gun with an Alpine to use it could turn this battle.

Grand kept his eyes on the fight below. A wave of pain nearly doubled him up, but he made no noise. In short breaths he asked, "Can you track him down? Get that gun back here?"

Charles frowned. "What good would that do?" he asked, his eyes drawn to the plain as another wagon exploded in flames. "The battle will be lost before—"

And then he saw it. Kimmer had overrun the legionnaires' position. They stripped the canopy from the supply wagon.

Underneath was one large machine, alien in its shiny metallic lines. Charles stared in fascination. A schoolbook illustration from history class in the third year swam out of memory.

He looked back at Grand in horror, "A laser cannon. You had one of Sheb's laser cannons!"

Grand nodded through his pain. "Stampz was to get it secretly, for defense against the Kimmer. The duke is some relative of Sheb. Somehow, the Kimmer must have found out. They've got muskets, too. Kimmer never had that many muskets before. Something is in the wind."

"Can we get word to the duke's forces?"

Grand shook his head. "Kimmer must have taken the guard posts on the rim. By the time you make the climb and skim for help, the Kimmer would have the Gate secure with that cannon. We will have to destroy it."

Charles flinched as if Grand had struck him. Destroy an *oldman* thing? That went against everything he had been taught since birth. Alpines preserve and restore the old ways. "No!"

He could still remember his Charter. His family stood at the ancient wooden desk, while he stepped forward alone and nervously accepted the scroll from the Administrator and read the oath before the assembled crowd of neighbors and friends come to celebrate his adulthood.

"... and I swear that the legacy of the human family has become my charge and my duty, and that my life is dedicated to restoring that which has been lost..."

Charles shook his head. There must be another way.

Grand waited out the storm on his face. Then he said, "Imagine a Kimmer tribe with a laser cannon, Charles. They hate our building and our settlements. This duchy would only be the first they would burn to the ground. Remember what happened to Alp!"

And Charles did remember. He was there. But no one really knew how the Burn started, not even Rad, who'd seen the destruction of Aristotle first hand. But Hercs believed Alpines did it themselves, tinkering with some *oldman* device. Neither lightning strike nor unchecked campfire could have spread so wide a blaze, they said.

If Rad hadn't forced them to go back to the lava tube, and hide underground while the wave of fire had passed over them on its march to the sea, they would have joined their family and friends in a blazing death.

That memory of a line of fire consuming the world, and then of mud and ash—all that was left of his island nation—that memory formed his deepest nightmares. But it had been no dream.

The exploding wagons brought those memories painfully close to the surface. But to destroy the laser cannon....

He asked, "What do you want me to do?"

"The machine is tough. It is *oldman* and the metal won't even dent if you shoot a musket at it. But nothing stops impulse. It's one of the chemical pulse kind. Two tanks are attached to the rear. They contain gasses to fuel the cannon's fire. The cannon makes these gasses itself out of pure water, but if an impulse gun can punch a hole in the machine where the two tanks connect, then the fires of the cannon escape. The machine explodes like an *oldman* bomb. That's how we took Plinius Island."

The Battle of Plinius Island. Charles thrilled at the name. He hadn't realized Grand was so old. When the Hercules Empire pushed the Serenites off Plinius Island a hundred years ago, they locked in their control of the seas, something they'd kept since. Grand must have seen a lot in his life.

"I will find Rad," he promised. "How will I find you?"

Grand smiled, nodding towards the scene below. "Don't try." Three warriors were weaving their way toward the base of the cliff where they rested. "I'll slow them up for you, Alp."

He picked up his pistol and powder and set them on a rock before him. "Shoot straight when you get it in sight." He dragged himself forward to a firing position. His legs were limp and lifeless.

Charles wanted to say something, but he was at a loss. It really wasn't time for words anyway. He grabbed his pumpgun and climbed. The wall was nearly vertical, but there were finger holds. After a few minutes, he heard gunfire far below. He didn't stop. He was an easy target for all the world to take shots at. A bullet bounced from the rocks several meters to one side of him, and he began to feel safer. No one could possibly hit him at this range.

Halfway up, there was a wide ledge with soil and trees. He paused to catch his breath. Down the way he had come, there was no one in sight. Far below, the wagon train looked like a twisted, dead earthworm, with ants swarming all over it. Ten of the fifty wagons were fire-blackened skeletons.

None of the remaining had the Fasail gold-banded canopy.

He shook his head to clear his eyes. Every thing they'd saved over the years in Gartner, all the sacrifices they'd made, everything had gone into that wagon. He gripped his pumpgun tighter. It was all he had. He snapped the gun up to a firing position and pulled the trigger. The *pfft* was swallowed by the wind. The pellet might never have existed.

They were far away—too far away. *I've got to find Rad,* he thought. He stood up and turned to face the cliff he had yet to climb. It saved his sight.

A flash of heat and light forced him to close his eyes. Stressed basalt rock shattered above where he stood. Red-hot shrapnel rained over the spot where he dropped. He slapped and rolled to shake loose the burning torment.

The second laser pulse hit a tree. A hundred meters of green exploded in a roaring tower of flame. Searing heat washed over him, and then two other trees ignited in chain reaction from the first. Millions of tiny pine needles blazed in Luna's oxygen-rich air.

Alpine Duty

Charles curled into a ball. He could smell the smoke from his own hair and see the light through the flesh of his arm. It was a blast furnace. His mother, his father, died like this.

Two more trees exploded. Each boom robbed him of thought. He clutched at the blackness he could hold tight to his chest.

Rad

"Run Charles! Don't look back at me. Run!"

He could feel the heat on the back of his neck and arms. Rad was faster than he was. He was only a little kid. Why was Rad behind?

The funnel was just ahead, where the runoff from the crater emptied via a lava tube down to the sea. They'd visited it this morning, but now the rocks were red, reflecting the thing behind them.

He slowed and Rad's hand was quick on his back, shoving him on. "Don't stop! Keep going!" He staggered, but he didn't dare fall. Rad wouldn't allow it.

He noticed the shadows as he ran, seeing the elongated dark silhouette of him and his big brother surrounded by a world gone red. They were getting smaller the more they ran. He couldn't breathe. It was getting closer.

Suddenly, the dark hole into the ground was before them and with Rad's hand on his shoulder, they went inside.

There was a heavy wind in his face, and it quickly got too dark to see where to step, but Rad was not satisfied. They had to slow to a walk, but Rad made it a quick walk.

The wind changed to a roar from one breath to the next.

"Down!" Rad forced him flat against the side of the tube. He cut his arm on the abrasive rock.

Deep in the tube, deeper than they had ever gone before in their explorations, there was still light. Where there'd never been more than the yellow glow of a warmball, there was red—reflections of the unimaginable blaze outside, destroying his world.

...

Silence.

I'm still alive. The fire hasn't gotten me. Yet. It had gotten his family and his people. Somewhere, the fire was still out there, waiting for him, too.

His left side was in agony from the burn. It forced him back to the present. He could smell the scorch of his hair, but he could move.

The only sound was the wind and the popping of the remaining embers rapidly being consumed in the rich air. There were no more shots, laser or otherwise. Hopefully, the Kimmer thought he was dead in the fire blast.

Grand… No, best not to think about him, or the others in the wagon train. He needed to get moving.

Creeping carefully on hands and knees, he found a route up. The gap in the rocks was well shielded from the plain below. He could get up and make better time.

Knife-edged pain from the early afternoon winds on his burned skin kept him returning to focus on the problem. Where was Rad?

He'd gone hunting. Charles distinctly remembered him heading off to the southwest. That would mean that he intended to travel in parallel with the wagons, just as he had. Head south, keep to the ridge tops, and just hope he spotted his brother returning before he walked into a trap.

Boys together, they'd thought nothing of hiking the forests of Alp for several days at a time. *If I'd skipped out to go hunting first and knew Rad was minding the wagon, I'd have stayed gone a lot longer.*

But even Rad couldn't miss Stampz Gate, so he should be heading back soon. *I have to get to him first.*

But his gut churned with worry about the laser cannon. *What should I do? I can't destroy it, can I?*

Yes. No!

He could still smell the burned stench of his own hair. Grand had a strong point. The Kimmer were savage beasts intent on burning down the whole world. *They burned my wagon!* Once again, he was reduced to a burned, destitute refugee. The air rifle in his hand, once again, was his only stake in the world.

Unless someone did something, the Kimmer were going to drive that wagon into Stampz and burn the whole duchy to the ground. After that, who knew their intentions?

One thing was for sure, they hated buildings with a religious zeal, often ignoring the people altogether to raze a cabin or shelter to the foundations. Now, they had the power to take on whole communities, and he knew they wouldn't be timid about people getting in their way. Unbidden, he could see people being blasted to ash. He felt a twist in his stomach.

. . .

Red glare from the mouth of the lava tube faded quickly, and the wind dropped to merely a shrieking blast, carrying droplets of water that stung hard from the impact on his skin. It was getting hard to breathe, and Rad again put his hands on his shoulder and herded him—this time back out the way they came.

Before they exited, it was already clear that the world had changed. Light everywhere was a dull red, the sunlight almost totally blocked out by great clouds of smoke.

They walked out into a landscape of ash. They stepped through it and choked, barely managing to breathe the heated, suffocating mix.

Then it started raining—big fat globs of evil gray mud, turning the ground below their feet into a thick river trying to drag them back into the darkness of the lava tube.

. . .

Charles shook off old memories and winced at a fresh stab of pain from his burns. He had to prevent a new disaster. No one would have to go through another burn if he had anything to do with it.

If the laser cannon had to be destroyed, then it was only right that an Alpine should make that decision. *Oldman* machines were their natural charge. It was the Alpine duty to see they were not misused.

The ridge topped and he looked back for Kimmer. No one was following. Nor could he see anyone in the valley ahead. Trees were thick here, sheltered by the bulk of the crater wall. It would give him some cover. It would make finding Rad harder as well.

Forget the laser. Find Rad first.

. . .

The mainland had several differences from his home island. He was suddenly reminded of that by a set of rough claw marks high on a tree, brown sap congealed in the scars. *A bear.* He knew that. He'd just forgotten. His father had commented often enough on his misfortune that a population of *Ursus* had never been established on Alp. His mother, he remembered, had expressed her contentment with that arrangement.

It was harder to think about her. Memories of his father were bright and cheerful. He was a loud, opinionated man who treated his sons as his prime students, always quick to correct sloppiness and quick to let them know how proud he was of them.

But his mother .... She was quiet. He remembered her smell and the warmth of her hugs on the cool mornings when they opened the shutters to the Frigid Sea and wolfed down her hot breakfasts. Their home overlooked the white-frothed waves from the north lip of the crater wall.

He shook off the memory. He'd stopped crying seven years ago. He blinked his eyes clear and took a deep breath. He had to concentrate on the job ....

Rad! There he was.

Bold as a baron, he was walking down the middle of the stream channel with a field-dressed buck draped across his shoulder. *Serves him right. Going after game that size without anyone to help him carry it.*

Charles moved out of the shadows, up high on a ridge above him. He waved and shouted, "Rad! Up here!" But it was too far for sound to carry. Rad continued, head down, burdened under his trophy.

A Kimmer stepped out from nowhere, across from Charles on the far cliff. He looked at Charles, and then turned his attention on Rad below, as he shook out the fabric of his sailsuit.

"Rad!" he screamed, "Look out above!"

His brother continued his steady plod.

The Kimmer stepped off the cliff and began the slow drop, down toward Rad.

Charles screamed again, wordlessly, and started pumping on his air rifle like mad. The Kimmer was picking up speed in his fall.

Charles dropped into a cross-legged sitting position and aimed. There was no time to think about distance and drop. He aimed and took a breath, letting half of it out. He squeezed the trigger. *Pfft!*

The Kimmer was spreading his arms, and the sailsuit billowed, collecting air and slowing his descent. Charles could see him turn in the air, circling down like a vulture. Eyes only for his brother.

Rad stumbled. He spilled the buck. Charles was on his feet, waving frantically.

Rad spotted the movement and looked up where Charles was pointing and gesturing.

His brother saw the white form coming down at him. He pulled the impulse gun out in one smooth motion and with an invisible push, he crushed the attacking warrior.

The Kimmer tumbled, folding up on himself. Gaining speed, he hit the ground hard.

...

Rad was sitting next to his deer, waiting, when Charles finally made it down. The Kimmer was a crumpled bundle, motionless over to the side.

Rad asked, "How many pumps?" He rubbed a red mark on his arm.

"Twenty."

"Fifteen would have been enough."

"Better accuracy at twenty." Charles grinned.

Rad pointed at his attacker, "What was that all about?"

Charles dropped the grin "Kimmer have attacked the wagon train." Rad jerked to his feet. "They captured the Legion's wagon. It was a laser cannon, Rad! Grand sent me to find you and bring the impulse rifle. It is—"

"Maria! Charles, is Maria okay?" Rad looked frightened. Charles had never seen that look on his face, not since the day of the Burn.

"I don't know. She'd been driving our wagon, but I wasn't..." Again, Rad didn't wait for him to finish. He was already pacing quickly up the river bed.

Charles felt like the air was humming, like it did before a big storm. He could feel something terribly wrong, but the only ideas that came to mind didn't make sense.

The body of the Kimmer caught his eye, and to shake the sense of doom away, he took a closer look.

The sailsuit was supple leather, bleached white, thin but strong. It was like a cape, but with straps and thick bone fasteners to secure it to arms and legs. On impulse, he opened the fasteners and rolled the body free of the suit. It was still warm.

There was a small bloodstain on the suit, but it was otherwise intact. He rolled it into a compact bundle and then headed off to catch his brother. There was still a lot he had to tell Rad before he blundered into the Kimmer.

...

They crept up to the side of the cliff slowly, keeping to the shadows.

Surprisingly, most of the wagons were still intact. The scene looked peaceful, almost normal, with people in standard Herc clothes wandering about, getting the wagons organized to move.

They've won! But... no. The truth was more ominous.

Rad spoke what Charles just noticed. "Those aren't Hercs. No women. And look at their hair."

"Kimmer." Charles agreed. "Where are the settlers?"

Rad pointed off to a deep-sided ravine that emptied out onto the flat. Warriors, still dressed like Kimmer, stood waiting with muskets at ready, guarding the entrance.

The wagons began to move. This time, Charles noticed, white Legion wagons led the way. Kimmer, dressed in the green of Legionnaires rode on the first three wagons, muskets in their arms.

What had Grand said? Where did all the muskets come from?

This was unlike everything Charles had ever heard about Kimmer. He was still a little shocked that they looked so much like men. All the tales he'd heard led him to expect smaller creatures, covered with hair like the pictures of the apes in his textbooks. The warrior he had stripped of his sailsuit looked exactly like a human.

And this organization ... this was not the action of unreasoning beasts. Grand, he suddenly realized, had feared what he was seeing below. It was a carefully prepared surprise assault on Stampz, using *oldman* weapons and the best of modern technology.

He pulled his brother back from the ledge where they could talk.

"The lead wagon has already entered the Gate. We need to get up ahead and find a place where we can stop it."

Rad shook his head. "No. As soon as the wagons move into the Gate, it'll be the perfect time to free the settlers. The Kimmer will be down to a token force."

"Rad, you don't understand! That first wagon is a laser cannon, and the Kimmer know how to use it! They are going to burn out the whole duchy. And that's just to start. Grand explained it to me.

"The impulse gun is the only thing that can stop it. And we have to move fast or we will never get ahead of them."

Jaw muscles running up the side of Rad's face tensed and released a couple of times. A distracted look in his eyes that made Charles wonder if he were even listening. Then, Rad shook his head in a quick side to side jerk.

"No, Maria comes first. I have to rescue her."

Charles couldn't understand what he was hearing, "But why?"

Rad spoke carefully, slowly. "Maria comes first. She is to be my wife."

Charles took a step back, staggered almost as if he had been struck.

"You can't do that. She's Herc, you're Alpine, " he stated the obvious. "You marry your own kind!"

There were layers to that sentence that caused a flinch in Rad's tense granite face, but he shook his head. "My own kind," he spoke it like a curse. "Who would you have me marry? Do you know a nice Alpine girl?"

Charles could hear a roaring in his ears, louder than the growing winds. He couldn't understand. He couldn't believe. Rad could not be standing here saying these things!

He swung the air rifle and struck him across the head, cracking the wooden stock. Rad tumbled back, and lay, stunned.

Charles picked up the impulse rifle from the dirt, "Who are you? What are you doing with an *oldman* thing?"

He let the air rifle slip from his other hand. He turned and headed up the crater wall. There was no time to waste. He had to get ahead of the wagons.

Into the Gate

The Stampz crater wall rose steeply to a ridge. Its Gate formed a narrow path all the way through. If he took too long to find his ambush point, the cliff would be so steep and tall that he would never be able to make it down to find a good hiding place.

You shouldn't have said those things, Rad. The Kell sisters were Alpine. Of course, after their kind of indenture, they weren't exactly "nice".

The face of the cliff had a secondary ridge at a lower elevation, so he climbed down to it. He still had to move faster than the Kimmer, and the ridge looked more direct.

Port Gartner wasn't the whole world, and it's not like every Alpine in the world was at home on Alp when the Burn happened. Surely, in Gaussland or Hubble....

He caught a glimpse of the wagon train struggling below. Stampz Gate had a reputation as a hard trail. It was closed regularly when the rains got too heavy and the entire floor of the chasm was nothing more than a river.

The Kimmer fought their animals. They seemed to be using the whips too much, but he was surprised they even knew how to drive. One more difference between the legend and the reality.

It's not as if I'm making up the rules. You were quick enough to lecture me when I talked to Dehear's daughter at the marketplace. And I wasn't even interested in her!

He made quick progress for as long as the ledge held. The rock had split cleanly, fractured probably at the very creation of the crater. He snatched a glimpse of the river below, a giddying view. He was getting ahead of the wagon train. No doubt about it.

Mother would have been against it. Remember when we took that trip to visit the court at Posidonius? You had your mouth open looking at all the girls in their fancy clothes, and she said, "Alpines must always marry Alpines." We all laughed and you turned red.

He lost some time climbing down from the end of that ledge to another below it. Rock climbing was not too difficult. In spite of his size, he was strong enough to lift his whole body weight with one hand, but the gun was difficult to secure.

Don't you remember, Rad, the times when we stood at our family bench in the arena, and chanted the Tenants with all the other families of Aristotle? Surely, you can remember the words you spoke hundreds of times. "And that we may bless the World by our separateness, that we remain a People Apart."

Does all that mean nothing to you?

He'd hoped that he could stair-step down the face of the cliff from one ledge to the next, with nothing more than a little rock climbing. The ledge ended, and there was suddenly nowhere to go. The nearest outcrop was too far, and the face of the cliff too sheer to allow anyone with his skills to climb. If he tried to retrace his steps back the way he came, there'd be no chance he could get ahead of the train. If he stayed here, the shot would be impossible—he was too high.

Charles shook off his one-sided dialog with his brother. He cleared his mind and faced the idea that had been growing quietly in the back of his head.

The far ledge was out of his climbing range, but a Kimmer in sailsuit could leap across that distance in a quick, easy glide.

He unfolded the garment. It looked like a cape, but nothing fastened it around the neck. Only reasonable, he thought. You wouldn't want to choke yourself. There were wide loops of the garment like sleeves that he could fit his arms in, with straps to tighten it across his chest and bands that fit across the palms of his hands to keep it from bunching around his shoulders.

He'd seen the Kimmer dropping down onto the wagon train. He closed his eyes, struggling to remember that vision in detail, but he couldn't make it any clearer. In his mind, he saw a rough image of how they moved their body, but the harder he strained to remember details, the more convinced he was that memory was becoming imagination. Right now, trusting his imagination could kill him.

He frowned, fumbling with the leg straps. He'd released them from the previous wearer of this suit, but how to fasten them? He fit his boots into the folds and tried to tighten the buckles of the straps, but it didn't seem right that it would hold, when the straps came free so easily in his hands.

He worriedly took another look over the edge of the cliff and tried to estimate the distance to the nearest ledge. He'd never been terribly afraid of heights, but now seemed like a good time to start.

He gripped the impulse gun tightly in one hand. What if he should drop it? Would it be damaged when it hit? Could he ever find it again? And would it unbalance him when gliding? He really should make a sling for it or try to secure it inside his clothes.

Like a clap of thunder, a body slammed against him and Charles tumbled out of control off the cliff.

. . .

"Ahhhhhh!" His scream of panic echoed faintly off the rock face spinning past his eyes.

He tried to grab for rock, but it was out of reach. The bright sky, a ribbon of light, swept by, and then he was looking down, where all lines drew his eyes to the rocks below.

His fall was starting slowly, as all falls do, but the sound of the air was changing rapidly.

The suit flipped over his head, *Oh no, the straps have come loose!* But no, he could feel them still tugging with the twisting of the wind.

I've got to stop this spin. The flap slipped free from his face and the whole cloth billowed and tugged hard at his arms and legs as the view of the river below twisted through his vision.

Then, as if he were falling again, he tumbled and the sailsuit slapped up against his back.

Sky, then the dark river below.

He tried to twist his body, just as if he were trying to regain his stance in a fight, and he had some luck. *I'm going to make it!*

Even as he thought it, he could feel his body turning too far to the right. The impulse rifle threw him off balance. The sail collapsed and spilled the air. He twisted again on his back, but the tumble was slower this time. *I will not drop it!*

Sky again filled his sight, but this time, he noticed a dark blot. *A Kimmer! He knocked me off!*

He was hovering above, waiting for gravity to finish the kill.

I'll show him! I'm no Kimmer, but I took Physics 3, Acoustics and Atmospheric Dynamics!

Charles just hoped that Academic Justin did a good job with his ten-year-old self.

He was tumbling slower, but unless he did something, he was never going to be able to hold a steady glide. And he had to do it soon—the drift was slower but he was falling faster, getting closer to terminal velocity. The jerk on the straps was stronger each time.

Center of Mass. Center of Drag. He had to move one or the other.

He pulled his right arm in, and instantly he started tumbling faster.

No. Think! The gun isn't that heavy. It was *oldman* metal and in spite of its strength, it was lighter than wood. *Forget the mass.* The rifle must be spoiling his drag on the right side.

I can't fix that. Spoil the left.

He pulled his left arm in, and the tumble immediately stopped, but now, he was quickly gaining speed as he glided almost head down.

The cliff! His glide was steering him straight toward the rocks. He drew in both legs and suddenly he was in a spin. *Push!*

The spin stopped but his stomach didn't. *The legs!* That was how to steer. A few tentative moves and he was in control. The straps bit into his flesh as he killed the velocity of his fall.

Instead of a ribbon of darkness below, the sand and rubble below dominated his view. *How do you land?*

The silhouetted figure above drove that thought away.

He twisted, and saw a flicker of the Kimmer, moving fast in a spiral, closing down on him. *He's going to kill me!*

Another impact like the one that knocked him off the cliff could send him into another tumble, one too late to stop.

Rage washed out his thoughts. As in all the battles he had fought before, the lust to *beat* him surged up.

He didn't think. He just moved his right leg and flipped over onto his back. While the sail slapped at him, he adjusted the power of the gun, snapped it up and triggered the beam.

An invisible pressor beam lanced out of the device both fore and aft. The aft beam quickly penetrated the rock wall. The fore beam connected microseconds later with the flesh of the Kimmer's left forearm. In that instant, a *Nance-Bate overlap* occurred, and the metered energy from the internal cell of the gun was partitioned by the conservation of momentum. Tons of rock would not move, so flesh did.

Charles spared a half second to see the Kimmer's skillful spiral dive crumple into a falling bundle of sail and skin.

He twisted again, holding the gun securely, and flipped over.

Oh no! The ground was close, very close, and he could do little more than sag into the binding straps, and hope that he could kill enough speed to survive the impact.

Out of the corner of his eye, Charles saw the Kimmer strike the side of the canyon and bounce. A second later, the bird with a broken wing smashed against rocks at the base of the cliff.

Charles had barely time to register that he'd killed him, when he sailed face first into the sand.

. . .

He couldn't breathe. *But at least I saved the books.*

Charles shook his head and spit sand from his mouth. *No. I'm not Charles Grayley.*

He hurt all over. And he could breathe, it just hurt. *And I sure don't feel like a hero.*

Grayley had been his childhood hero after he had seen the play "The Burning of Alexandria" that featured the great scene where the Academic sacrificed his life by blowing out an airlock to keep the Library from burning.

And no one can save the books now. This was the great tragedy that put a lump of black basalt under his Alpine heart. The Burn had spared nothing of the Great Library.

Charles cautiously tested his arms and legs. They still moved, and it was aches, not the sharp pain of a broken bone, that greeted each flexed muscle.

I did land. Not gracefully, but I did it.

He fingered the cloth of the sailsuit. There was potential here.

He started to get to his feet, when he heard the echo of a man's shout. *Kimmer! How long have I been out?*

It was irrelevant. He had to get to an ambush point before they got to him.

His plan had been simple—find a ledge a little above their path and target the tanks on the laser cannon as it passed. That was out. No time to climb and barely time to hide.

The canyon floor was wider here, where the original crack split at right angles for a few hundred paces before returning to its preferred direction. The river, bunching here in high water, left a pile of sand and rubble.

The shouts were coming stronger. They were getting closer by the minute. Where could he hide?

The lead wagon came into view around the near bend of the canyon. At first glance, there was nothing to indicate that this wasn't a perfectly normal detachment of the Legion of Sheb's Heart. The uniforms were correct, and so were the wagons.

But the men were all riding on the outside, hanging onto the rigging. Not a one was inside.

They have hair longer than girls. Like those Fendites. He remembered the minor spectacle when the small tribe came through Gartner on their way to settle in the cold north. *I hope they don't fight like Fendites.* They'd been a close-knit tribe, and several dock workers suffered for it.

Charles tried to limit his breathing, hiding on the back side of the sand bank. If he made any movement, he was sure that they'd notice him.

The lead wagon, as he suspected, had problems turning the team when the trail crossed the watercourse. The river had washed out any obvious ruts. The oxen were probably tired and irritated from the long day's pull, not to mention the battle and the fires. It took a lot to ruffle the calm of an ox, but this driver couldn't see it coming. When the wagon stopped and the left ox did nothing more than lower his head at the whipping, all the other Kimmer dropped off the wagon like fat ticks off a dog.

Soon, the whole train was stopped, and people were walking about, shouting at each other and at the animals.

Charles tried to stop breathing altogether, to stop thinking, afraid at any second one of the crowd would look at the irregularity on the sand and discover him.

He was close enough to really look at a Kimmer face, and to listen to them talk. Maybe they were genetically altered like the legends said, but the base stock was human, not ape, and certainly not bird. Dressed as they were in clothes from the settlers and the Legionnaires, the whole mob of them could walk the streets of Gartner and cause no more talk than any of the other strange travelers that visited that town.

"Get off of those traces! And you! Stop using the whip." One of the Kimmer, a false settler, came up with a bag of feed and got the others to settle down and let the beast regain its composure. After a few kind words and some mouthfuls of grain, a gentle tug on the yoke got the pair moving again.

There was a family resemblance to them; a prominent nose, all had a dark brown hair, skin color something like the Manili.

He was surprised they spoke English like everyone else. The common language was a fluke of history, and he half expected something more primitive out of the savages.

The question is, where did they learn it? They had a strange accent.

The lead wagon had moved less than a few hundred paces when there was a shout, and again Kimmer dropped from the wagons. One was pointing off into the rocks at the base of the cliff. Others were grabbing their muskets.

Oh. They spotted the one I killed.

Discovery of the dead Kimmer caused them all to go silent. It made his skin itch.

Orders were being passed. He could see the hand gestures, but these were hunters, they made no noise.

I'm dead. They'll find me.

He gritted his teeth. He came to stop the wagon. He'd better do that, or this whole effort would be for nothing.

His stomach now hurt worse than before, but not from his fall. It hurt that he was going to die. It hurt that Rad was turning against everything they were. It hurt that he would never find a place for himself.

He shifted slightly, slowly to the right, and the pile of sand he had burrowed into began to stream off. Only seconds remained.

The laser cannon wagon was shrouded behind the canopy, but he bet that they hadn't secured it. They were trigger-happy with it before.

He dialed a minimal pulse and the wagon rang like a temple gong.

From slow systematic searching, the Kimmer were instantly hyper-intent, moving at a run.

Boom. Crack. Someone used his musket at a shadow or an unlucky bird.

He could only wait now. He was only partially covered, and the sail suit was brighter than the color of the sand. Once they looked closer, there'd be no mistaking him.

He debated escape, but there was no way out. The channel of the river ran behind him, but it wasn't deep enough to swim.

Ah. The cover over the laser cannon came off. They had to check on the noise. He dialed up the power.

It was a beautiful piece of metal. It shone in the daylight like a jeweled shrine to the Unknown. He wavered as he tried to aim the gun at Grand's weak point. He couldn't destroy it, could he?

It would be a violation of his oath, wouldn't it? How could he, an Alpine, destroy a remnant of the *oldman* technology and condemn the future of humanity to be poorer for its lack?

Boom. Sand just to his left fountained. His finger twitched and the energies in his hand acted.

Two things happened.

Before him, the laser cannon wagon skidded hard across the dirt and struck the side of the cliff. *Shreeeq!* The sound of its impact and damage reached him about the same time a white cloud started flashing out of the depths of the machine.

Behind him, sand caught in the back beam splashed back, highlighting his position in a great circle of motion. Those not concerned with the fate of the cannon had their eyes drawn to him.

He could see dozens of muskets turning toward him. He rolled back. *Get down. Hide.*

Why didn't it explode? He was almost relieved. He damaged it, but maybe not permanently.

Boom. Boom. Sand splashed like a miniature meteor impact. He dove for the river. It was hopeless, but he had to try.

At least I saved Stampz.

The world turned white. He entered the water as it foamed from the cataclysm.

Rad's Blood

Little Charles held onto his mother's hand to keep from falling. The ship under his feet lurched again as the swells were getting choppy so close to shore.

"Mom!" he called urgently. She led him over to the railing and he emptied his stomach of the little bit of water and biscuit he had managed to eat. The family trip to the continent was not starting out well, at least for him.

He looked up to see his father beside him at the rail, a stormy look on his face as well, although not from seasickness.

Charles followed his father's gaze and saw the man in a long coat and a funny hat. "Who is that?"

His Father smiled down at him, "No one important. It is just an official they have here called a scribe. He will read our letters of intro-duction and the captain's shipping documents."

"Why do they need someone to do that? Can't people read their own letters?"

His father shook his head sadly, "No, strange to say, they can't. Most people over here can't read."

Charles was shocked. He didn't know how to fit that news into his tidy world of perpetual schoolbooks and reading lessons since he was four.

"Well, I can read my own papers," he finally declared.

"I'm sure you can." His father put his hand on his back. His big hand fit comfortably across his neck.

"But you must," he continued in a serious voice, "let those people read your letter for themselves and not try to read it for them. They have a new law here that only scribes can read legal and business papers."

"Why Daddy?"

His father shook his head, "I don't know. I think maybe they are afraid of us."

...

I hurt, Charles thought.

He hadn't felt this bad since the Foshona Temple was being built. One of the minor nobles had discovered a protected crater filled with straight trees, and had shipped huge rafts of the lumber down the Spirit River. The Gartner crew worked four quads, even into the freeday, to get the rafts loaded onto special transport ships to be moved to the site of the new temple. He'd felt nearly dead for days after, but the noble had been granted a better title and more lands.

Even then, the pain had been from exhaustion and overworked muscles. This was different.

He couldn't think well through the pain in his head. It came in waves, peaking every five seconds. And his skin was burned, it seemed. Every time he shifted in his bed, the cloth felt like a lava scrape.

I'm alive, was the second complete thought that he managed. He flashed back to the battle, the white plume, the dive into the water. *Hydrogen gas. Some musket set it off.*

I shouldn't have survived. I am destined to die by fire.

But not yet, it seemed. He suffered another peak in his headache and drifted off to sleep again.

...

Charles started awake at the touch of a wet cloth on his face. It was daylight, filtering through a checkerboard patterned canopy. Maria Turner was holding the cloth.

The pain in his head returned like a gust of darkwind. "Wha..." he tried to speak and tried to move his arm to push himself up, but he was as weak as a blind kitten.

"Take it easy Charles," she spoke softly. He could barely hear, distracted by a constant noise in his ear like a tireless mosquito. He could do nothing more than relax down into the bedding.

"I'm glad you're awake. We've been worried about you."

"Where…" He had to pause. Everything was hard, from trying to move to putting together a complete thought.

She didn't wait for him to finish. "Rad is off with a hunting party, trying to restock provisions for all the people. Half the wagons were destroyed, but most of the people survived.

"We are all grateful for what you and Rad did for us. You will stay with us and we'll get you strong again.

"Rad also said that if you were worried about your… Alpine things?"

He managed a nod.

She smiled, "Rad said that both of them are fine, and that you shouldn't worry about them."

Charles felt relieved. "I don't have… anything else." *Not even a brother.*

She nodded, "I lot of people are like that. But we're doubling up and no one will starve."

He closed his eyes and let the sleep come for him again.

…

Rad's hunting party was gone for two days, and Charles pushed himself to get up and out of the wagon.

He couldn't bring himself to be rude to them. They were doing their best to help him, but he couldn't stand to be pampered like an invalid. Not in that girl's wagon.

The headaches dropped to just an annoyance after the first day on his feet. His hearing was still messed up, but he imagined that it was getting better.

He gave no thought to the bruises from his fall. Bruises were part of his life and they took care of themselves.

The burns worried him. They were Maria's main concern, as well. She treated them every few hours, using what salves she could contrive out of their dwindling food stocks.

There were more than he remembered.

"I was wearing a Kimmer garment when…" he began, when she was treating a burn on his back that he did not remember from the exploding trees.

"Yes, I'll get it," she said, returning a moment later with a folded, scorched and burned sail suit.

"Rad said he found you in the empty stream bed, wearing this and still holding onto your Alpine thing."

He felt a chill as he saw the damage that the cape had taken, burned away in places. His exposed skin couldn't have survived it. Burns that extensive were fatal to anyone. The sores would get putrid, and nothing anyone could do could stop it.

The burns on his skin were more limited—one side of his scalp was bare of hair. His shoulders and several places on his arms were bad. The spots on his back were manageable.

"You look horrible," Maria told him cheerfully. He demanded to see himself in the water.

They went outside and after a flurry of activity, they managed to get him a pot with a few centimeters in the bottom. "I'm sorry, that's all we can spare until the next rain." The matronly lady apologized as she handed it to him. Water, too, was becoming scarce, since the river dried up.

His head was a mess, he saw, with the hair burned away in irregular patches, shiny where the salve was applied.

He handed the pot back, "Here, that's all I need."

He asked Maria, "Can you shave the rest of it off? I'd rather be bald than a spectacle."

She deferred the task to her father, Chess, who was nursing a musket wound in his leg. He seemed happy to do it.

"I'm useless around here until the hunting party gets back," he confessed. "If it weren't for Rad taking the lead here, we'd all be in for empty bellies."

Charles winced as the blade nicked part of the burned area, but Chess noticed it instantly and dabbed the trickle of blood.

"I haven't heard the details of what Rad did."

Chess grinned. "Oh, it's quite a story. I'll be glad to have a story to tell, at least something good from these last few days."

The Kimmer had attacked without warning just as the wagons were forming up for the entrance into the Gate. The wagon master had waited an hour or so for the stragglers on the train to arrive, hoping for one of the Stampz guards to arrive from their lookout up on the crater's rim.

It was over quickly. The savages targeted the Legionnaires and their wagons ruthlessly. None of the soldiers survived.

The wagonmaster and a few of the others had guns, but the bulk of the people were unarmed and put up what defense they could with shovels and axes and whatever they could find at hand.

But the Kimmer were armed with muskets, and it was a lost battle from the beginning.

The Kimmer understood that a loaded gun was more powerful than an unloaded one, and they worked in pairs to contain the settlers. Only a few of the settlers were shot, only enough to persuade the rest to protect the women and children.

They were herded into a canyon and many of the men had their clothes taken.

There they waited, unsure of their fate.

It was hours later, at sunset, when Rad showed up, muskets in hand, having defeated the guards as they had taken shelter from the peak of the winds.

"He told us," Chess continued, "that you and he had split up and that you were going to stop the Kimmer in the Gate, and that we could attack from the rear. By then, you can bet that we were angry enough to do just that.

"Although, I must confess that several of us were a little skeptical that you were going to be able to stop the whole band of them by yourself. I'd seen the laser cannon. I expected to find you dead and the Kimmer already into Stampz."

But they were wrong. They quickly noticed that the river was drying up as they walked. Those in the lead carried muskets, and they were primed and ready when the first Kimmer were discovered.

This time it was the Kimmer who were caught off guard. The first were disorganized. The ones behind them were injured from the blast. The rest were already dead. The settler party moved quickly, with the first priority to collect more muskets. With both sides armed, the Hercs proved more experienced, and were soon the victors. The Kimmer didn't seem to understand the concept of surrender, which was fine with the settlers, still hurting from the losses of the first attack.

"I don't understand what you did to stop them. It was powerful Alpine magic, I understand. But I've never seen such destruction. The lead wagons must have been wiped from the globe."

Charles did nothing more than grunt. He didn't want to explain.

"When the last of the savages were done, we righted the wagons that could be salvaged and corralled the animals that weren't too hurt to pull. It was about then that Rad found you."

They found Charles in the mud, unconscious, and brought him back. He finally woke after a long day when they were beginning to think that he never would.

...

Charles volunteered to be on watch after midnight. He was sleeping a lot more than he was used to, but he still couldn't manage to sleep away the whole night. Neither could anyone else, and that was the problem.

As it was in Gartner, and as it was back in Aristotle, so it was here on the trail, people tended to gather in the pre-dawn hours and socialize. It was too dark to get much work done and everyone was too rested to sleep.

Charles had always been a loner, content with the company of his brother. He couldn't stand the constant attention. "How did you kill the laser cannon?" "How did Rad and you learn to fight Kimmer?" "Do you have secret Alpine magic?" "Did you really fly like the Kimmer?"

That last was a topic he really wanted to avoid. He said yes, once, and one of the kids that seemed to be following him around everywhere promptly stole a blanket from his mother. He tied it around his neck, jumped off a high rock and fell wrong, scraping up his arm.

Better to chalk it all up to "Alpine Magic", and the best way to do that was to keep his mouth shut.

Charles found a relatively sheltered spot where he could watch and listen to the riverside pathway.

He held a musket, not that he was familiar with the weapon. Neither slaves nor Alpine children had much opportunity to learn how to use it. He understood the theory, but had his doubts about the thing.

He was sure he could get one shot off, but he didn't intend to reload. If a Kimmer party showed up, it would be best to get the word back to the camp and get everyone ready, rather than to hold them off single-handedly with a tube of wrought iron that fired its pellets with less accuracy than his air rifle.

He would rather have his pump gun, he felt. At least he knew its strengths and limitations. He hoped Maria's message had been accurate. He couldn't find the gun anywhere, and he wasn't going to arouse interest by asking strangers for help.

It was dark out. Earth had set a few hours before, and except for the faint glow of the campfire over the hill, there was absolutely nothing to see.

He wished for a thunderstorm in the high atmosphere. Often those would illuminate a dark night.

It was so dark that imagined swirls of patterns and lights were a distraction from what he was trying to do. He set himself the task of locating and identifying all the sounds he could hear. Luckily, his hearing was getting back to normal.

There were the moving branches in the early dawnwind. Down below his position, one tree had a major branch rubbing against another, making a loud high-pitched scrape with each gust.

Among the repetitive pops and snaps and squeaks of the trees, there were some other, more interesting noises.

A rabbit, or some other small creature, moved slowly through the underbrush. He could follow its position as it dashed from place to place.

Birds collected on a bush nearby to the left. He could hear them calling to each other. They were probably settling in to wait out the dawnwind here in the wind shade of the Stampz crater wall.

What was that? He heard a strange call, almost like a man.

He'd been fooled before—so many sounds distorted over distance that it could be anything. But he was here to watch, so he moved cautiously, making no noise of his own, to get a better view of the trail.

For a moment, there was nothing but wind noise and the flashes of light-starved eyes. Then one of the lights moved.

He shifted his head side to side, *That light is real.* He picked up the musket carefully and aimed it in that direction.

More than one light. They were approaching.

Then, as if a mist lifted, he could make out details. It was Rad.

Like a giant among the other settlers, Rad was leading the way, carrying a deer on his shoulders just like the other day. There were warm balls lashed to three of the men, casting enough glow so they could hike through the darkness.

It was obviously a successful hunt—they were in good spirits, laughing and talking so loud he could hear them from his vantage point.

Charles itched to go down and meet them, but watching Rad's face, so obviously one of the good fellows of the hunt, the impulse shriveled up into a tight knot and sat at the pit of his stomach.

He was out here to watch, not to play welcoming committee.

The party passed close beneath where he sat, and as they passed, he turned his face away to the black unknown.

...

Dawnwind came, and he rode it out in the scant shelter of his hiding place. The wind was rough but muted by the crater wall. A short rain came through during the worst of it, driving fat drops with speed enough to leave red welts on his skin.

When it was done, the wind dropped to a warm, stiff breeze. He got down and walked around in circles for a few minutes to work the kinks out of his leg muscles. The rain had left him damp, including the small pouch of gunpowder. He had nothing but contempt for technology so fragile that a morning drip could render it worthless.

But the sun was warm, and it felt good to shake the shivers out of his skin. His burns itched, and he knew he had to go back into the camp to get more salve, but he wanted to stay away for as long as possible.

He sat on a rock and tried not to think about Rad. It was hard, and the wind kept causing his eyes to tear up.

The crunch of a foot on gravel alerted him. He turned to face his brother.

"Hello, Charles. It's good to see you up and active."

"Hello, Rad."

Rad held out a freshly roasted slice of venison. "Here, I thought you might..."

The smell of the meat triggered his hunger, but he slapped out and knocked it from Rad's hand.

"I don't want anything from you!" He cried, "How could you desert everything Alpine?"

Rad stood still, silently listening, but his face lost the cheer that had been there seconds before.

Charles stepped up and pushed his chest with both hands. Rad stumbled back and fell.

"Stand up and I'll beat some sense into your head!"

Rad shook his head. Even as he started to stand, he spoke calmly, "It won't change anything. I've made up my mind. I've been in love with Maria for a year now."

A year? The thought stopped him. "Just when were you going to tell me? On your wedding day? Or when you brought your little half-Herc get to me for my blessing? You joined us to this wagon train to be with her, didn't you? You turned our entire future into ashes, all because of her. And not a word to your brother as you wrecked his life?"

Rad stood. He nodded. "Yes."

Charles howled and started hammering blindly with his fists. Rad took it, bracing himself against the onslaught, avoiding none of the blows.

Soon, Charles slumped to his knees, his eyes blind with tears, too tired to hit any more. He didn't look at Rad.

But he wasn't done. "You were born Alpine. You took the oaths. ALL OF THEM. Your blood is Alpine and it belongs to us!"

Rad spoke low, and Charles caught a glimpse of his face. It was gray and tight with his pain. "No, Charles. The Alpines are gone. My blood . . . my blood belongs to my sons."

With that, Rad turned and slowly headed back toward camp.

Charles shouted, "I'm not going back there, among all those Hercs! Send someone out here with my gun, and I'm gone. I have my own future to live!"

Rad didn't look back, but Charles thought he saw a nod.

Soon there was nothing but silence. Charles sat still on a rock.

Rubble

Charles hefted the fullpack and started up the Gate. He felt empty.

Chess came hobbling out on a cane a few hours after Rad left. His oldest boy, Curt, carried the load. They brought the pack and the man reaffirmed his invitation to join them on the trail to Gaussland.

From his friendliness, Charles could guess that Rad hadn't explained the reason he was leaving. He honestly didn't hate the Turners—he just couldn't stand to be with them.

"I am Alpine, and I have business in Stampz," was all he managed in explanation. Chess shook his head and gave him farewell.

When they left, he checked the fullpack. It was much too large for his needs, more designed to carry cargo than just supplies for one man. Inside were food and water and extra clothes, as well as a knife, a coil of rope, and a pouch of burn salve.

Wrapped in fine leather cases were both guns, his air rifle, and the impulse gun. There was a scrap of sailcloth wrapped in with the impulse gun.

On it Rad had written with charcoal, "OLDMAN LEGACY SHOULD BE IN THE CARE OF AN ALPINE. TAKE GOOD CARE OF IT."

Charles cried until his head ached with the strain.

Empty, he fixed his burns, ate a mouthful of biscuit, and headed for the Gate.

Gaussland had lost its pull, now that he was alone. Maybe he had never wanted to be a farmer, after all.

The unexplored lands around him were unappealing, just yet. He had seen enough Kimmer.

Back to Gartner was back to slavery. He'd never take another indenture, but he'd seen the lives of the merchants there. That was not his future either.

He was an Alpine. No more pretending he was just another Herc. Alpines would be a dead people when he was killed, not one second sooner.

He was born an Alpine. He took the oaths. He was going to be a force for the restoration of Science and Literacy. He was going to preserve the *old-man* technology until it was once again the common property of all humanity. He was going to use his skills and his knowledge to help all mankind.

Stampz was his destination. The river had dried up. The explosion must have caused a blockage. They needed to be warned that their Gate was blocked. They needed to get workers out to clear it. Getting the message through was an honorable task for an Alpine. After he took care of that, then he could think out a long-term plan. But for today, Stampz was enough.

The Gate was a channel for the winds from inside the crater, and it was cooler than outside.

There was also the scent of decay. It grew as he walked farther along the canyon floor. Crows were thick in the air, passing overhead in clusters of a dozen or twenty.

It wasn't until he passed the first broken wagon that he spotted a cluster of birds, fighting over the remains of a body.

He reached into his pack and pulled out the impulse gun. He aimed and fired. Dead birds and fragments of a Kimmer body went sailing across the landscape. More birds closed in on the reorganized feast.

Charles vomited up the little in his stomach.

He hurried on, and startled another cluster. They took flight and left the dismembered arm that lay in the dirt.

I have to get out.

The cliff wall was scalable here, so he stowed the gun and started up. Anything to get above the stench and the chatter of carrion birds.

...

The climb was cleansing. He focused his thoughts on finding a good hand-hold and scouting the best route up.

Up was his goal. Luckily, his fullpack, all the possessions he had, was strapped down thin and light. It wasn't much of a problem on the hand-over-hand stuff. Even then, on a break, he took out the coil of rope and secured the pack so that he could pull it up after him.

Looking down, he was relieved to see that distance obscured most of the details. He could see burned wagons, but he didn't search for bodies.

The site of the explosion was what drew his eye.

He had thought the dull red of the canyon walls distinctive before. It was nothing now.

The force of the explosion had shattered the base of a tall column of rock. The slab had peeled loose from the side of the canyon and had buried anything below it under uncountable tons of rock.

The fresh wound on the canyon wall was vivid in its textured colors. There were reds, but also blues and whites and yellows, rocks that had not yet had time to oxidize to the dull red of their neighbors. Now that he could see the patterns so plainly, he could make out their dim siblings in the weathered cliffs. The whole canyon must have been like this when the Gate broke open.

Down at the base, the great slab survived mostly intact, blocking the floor of the canyon. That had stopped the river and caused the rest of it to dry up. A little lake was growing upstream, flooding the entire floor of the Gate.

I wonder if it will flood back into the crater? Most craters had little lakes of some kind, even if they, like Stampz had breaks in the wall to let the water escape. A typical meteor impact left the crater floor lower than the surrounding terrain. But the Gate, he heard, had been cut deeper by the rushing waters gushing out into the Spanish River valley and had left a sheltered valley perfect for farmland. A jewel snatched up by the nobility and granted as a prize to one of their kind.

How deep can it get? He tried to estimate the height of the rock dam, but from his angle, he couldn't guess.

In any case, they aren't going to be traveling that route any time soon. He hoped they had another road out.

The ledge where he rested continued for a few hundred paces, and then he had to look for another route up.

The view was grand from where he stood, but he wished for another sailsuit. If rock climbing stopped being viable, he would have a long hard climb back the way he came to get to safety.

Luckily, the walls were fractured here from the same forces that caused the bend in the Gate, and he was able to get higher, to find another recessed ledge. By noon, he found a walking route to the inner surface of the crater wall.

...

Stampz spread out like a patchwork quilt arrayed carefully around a central peak. In the haze of the distance, he could see a castle at its top.

Charles took a moment to rest and admire the view. In some ways, it reminded him of Aristotle. The view was like that from their home on the north rim. But Stampz was smaller, an agricultural place, rather than a growing city, and its lake was just a wide place in the river, before it exited out the Gate, rather than the vast lake he'd played in as a child.

Big craters, those he'd visited in person, were all very different. As a child, he saw the capital of Serenity, Posidonius, and the twin-city capital of the Empire, Atlas and Hercules. These plus Port Gartner were all harbors, open to a greater or lesser extent to the sea, with the base of the craters flooded. All the buildings and roads and activity clung to the inside of the crater walls, like great, wide stairsteps dotted with white tile roofs.

I wonder if Gaussland is like this. Gauss was a huge crater, touted by the rumors as a protected basin where common people could hold land of their own. Charles knew there was a Baronetcy of Gauss, but he suspected it was little more than the noble's estate.

And if Gaussland was so huge, was it really as protected as people said? Small craters were a good protection against the winds, but even in a deep crater like Aristotle, the winds were pretty stiff if you were too much in the center, away from the walls.

Stampz, by the evidence of his eyes, was protected enough for open farmland. His father should have seen this. Adaptation to Luna, by animals, plants, and men, was his favorite interest.

A successful adaptation was a joy to him. At least from this high up, Stampz looked like one.

He got to his feet. There appeared to be a footpath that led from the top of the crater wall down to the floor. He headed down.

Of course, you could never tell how people lived their lives by looking at their lands from on high. Port Gartner looked like a pretty place, and had a tenth of its population in slavery. The rest were tied to their jobs and routines by debts and strong oaths of other sorts.

Maybe that was why Gaussland was such a magic lure to tired people when they paused to rest. So many people wanted to go, and so few took steps in that direction.

The trail down was an easy walk, as long as he was careful not to go too fast. The vegetation on the slopes was different, as well. The exterior walls were mainly pines and firs, twisted by the winds into shapes protected by the irregularities of the rocks.

Here, there appeared to be more variety. There were white-barked aspens, taller and straighter than most trees he'd seen. Down in a watercourse, where a stream barely as thick as his arm splashed noisily down the rocks, a large boulder made a little pond that hosted a willow and a dozen different scrubs. There were even flowers floating on the water.

It was a tempting spot, but his easy dance down the trail was too fluid and quick to stop. He admired it for an instant in passing and went on.

This slope was a balm to his spirits. Everywhere he looked, some beauty of nature recalled more pleasant places and more peaceful times. If he had to choose now, he would build a little house along this stream and spend his days smelling the scents of this woodland and absorbing the vista below.

Boom. A rock to the left of him exploded. Up ahead, a white puff of gunpowder smoke pinpointed a man with a musket.

…

Stopping wasn't easy. He knew he had several seconds, even if the man were a fast reloader, but he had to have shelter before then.

He turned right, making a curve for a tree that grew up next to a man-sized rock. He skidded and rolled, his fullpack making it clumsy, but he was sheltered before the second shot bounced off the rock with a *bing.*

Charles fished the impulse gun out of the pack. He put his hand on the metal, and an unbidden image of that disembodied arm flashed across his memory.

He yelled to his attacker, "Cut that out! Stop shooting!"

"Kimmer beast! What have you done with my Brady?" The man punctuated his shouts with another musket ball.

Charles could feel the anger building, and he knew he could punch the heart out of the man before he knew what was coming.

A gap between the tree and the rock showed the man, a farmer probably, frantically loading his musket.

He dialed the beam width and set the power.

Charles shouted, "I am no Kimmer! I am Charles Fasail, Alpine! You have no quarrel with me and I have none with you. Stop shooting now!"

The Stampzian didn't stop. He removed his tamping rod from the barrel of his musket and started to bring it up.

Charles aimed carefully, the impulse gun under his arm, the back beam braced against all the crater wall behind him. He triggered it.

Invisible as ever, the pulsed pressor beam lanced out and struck the boulder the man was using as protection. The only noise was a crack, and the boulder split and began to roll backwards down the slope in two chunks.

His attacker danced to the side to miss being crushed and stood open-mouthed as he watched them rumble out of sight. His musket drooped in his hand.

He turned to see Charles, also standing in plain sight, with the shiny metal of the impulse gun under his arm. He asked, "Who are you?"

Charles eased his aim away. "I am Alpine. My name is Charles Fasail. I do not want to kill you, so put your musket down on the ground."

Firefight

The farmer's name was Gwedon. His boy Brady was on duty at the guard station on the rim. He hadn't come home yesterday when he was due.

Kimmer attacks had been especially heavy for the past two years, and Gwedon feared the worst.

"No. If the Kimmer have attacked the guard station, we should not go fight them ourselves." Charles put as much authority into his voice as he could. He had bossed loading gangs and he knew how to use his size to put emphasis in his orders. He feared that the guard station was taken and this little man would step into a trap if he didn't persuade him to go for help.

He fired the musket's load into the air and pocketed Gwedon's powder horn. "Sorry," he explained, "but these things make me nervous." He handed back the musket.

The trail was well marked, and Gwedon was eager to make good time. Charles wasn't used to sustained downhill runs, so he had to call a halt several times. Close to the floor of the crater, Gwedon frowned when he called and kept on running.

Charles slowed his pace. If he had gone ahead to arrange an ambush, it would do no good to arrive out of breath. If Gwedon were just impatient, then the farmer would be the one to collect his neighbors anyway.

He was down to a walk as the trail passed through a glade of aspen and emptied out onto a level footpath between two different cultivated fields. One was high in grass, the other had low plants with white blossoms. He stepped over the pile of stones that marked the fence lines and picked one of the blossoms. It was fibrous and soft, with hard little seeds in the mass.

Cotton, he decided. He had never seen the plant that grew it, but he had loaded many bales of the stuff.

On impulse, he sheathed the impulse rifle and hid it in his pack. If he started fighting here, the whole population would turn on him.

The footpath led to a small village, a cluster of four buildings all on the same side of a larger road. It was the road that led out through the Gate. Gwedon was standing in the road with four other men and one woman. They all looked his way as he approached.

One took off his hat and swatted Gwedon with it. "He isn't a Kimmer, you idiot. Whoever heard of a bald Kimmer?"

The fatter of the men took a step forward, "Ho. Stranger. Gwedon tells us you took his gun from him."

Charles pointed. "He still has his gun. I took his powder." He tossed the horn to the man. "He kept shooting at me."

"He thought you were a Kimmer."

"Probably a good idea. But wrong. I'm Alpine."

"There are no Alpines. The Burn killed them."

"Not all of us." Charles set down his pack. "But we came back down to get help to fight Kimmer, not to talk about my ancestry."

That got all of their attention. Gwedon must not have explained it well.

"I was with a wagon train out of Port Gartner. We were due here yesterday, but as we gathered outside the Gate ...." he told the tale as well as he could, leaving out the laser cannon, his weapons, and his part in it all.

"And before he died, the legionnaire mentioned that they had expected to be greeted by Stampz guards from the rim station, but they never arrived."

An older man, who had kept his peace, spoke, "Jason, send flashes to the duke. Gwedon, go get the Dennis boys. The rest of you, go get your guns and call in the men from the fields."

Like that, the town was deserted except for Jason and the woman who headed into a market building. Charles decided to follow them.

...

He entered the low-roofed building, having to dodge the farm utensils hanging from every rafter. The man was pulling a large chest up onto the bench. The woman spotted him and called, "Jason?"

He frowned at Charles as he opened the chest and pulled out a small book.

"What do you want?"

Charles was mesmerized by the book. He had seen only two since Alp burned. But he said only, "I want to help."

Jason wasn't happy about it, but he seemed rushed. "Okay, come here and help me lift this."

Inside the chest was a large, shiny copper disk with a hole in its center. Charles took it in both hands, careful to hold it by the edges.

Jason took out a shining cloth from the case as well, content to leave the disk to Charles. It was heavy, but nothing he couldn't handle easily.

There was a ladder in the back of the building that led to the roof. It was a bit clumsy to carry the disk up there, but he managed.

On the roof was a wooden contraption that Charles first mistook for the axle of a small wagon, but Jason directed him to set the disk over the dowel that came out perpendicular from the axle. As he did so, he noticed a number of oddities. One wheel of the axle was chained to an eyebolt fixed to the roof. The other wooden wheel sported a large number of holes on the rim. That side of the axle had a large lever affixed to it.

Jason said, "Thanks. You can go back down now."

"I'll stay." Charles suspected that it was a heliograph, something he only knew by definition. He had to see how it worked. And there was the book. How did that fit in?

Jason looked frustrated at his presence, but he didn't look ready to start a fight.

He started moving the machine with the smoothness of long practice. He took a long look at the position of the sun in the sky, and moved the free wheel until the shadow of the center dowel split the angle between the sun and the castle on the central peak in the distance. He then took some small wooden pegs from his pocket and put them in the holes of the rim of the free wheel, limiting the amount it turned when he pushed the lever back and forth.

Charles gradually made sense of what he was doing. The pegs limited the wheel, one end aimed the reflection of the sun directly at the castle, the other direction didn't. On and off. Perfect for sending a code.

When Jason was satisfied with his alignment, he pushed the lever to the 'on' position and waited, peering intently at the castle.

It wasn't more than a minute later that there was an answering point of light.

"Okay," Jason muttered to himself, and moved the lever back.

He pulled out the little book and thumbed over a few pages, set it down beside him and began working the lever. On for about fifteen seconds, then off for about five, on for five, off for five, on for fifteen, then off for a longer time. Then he started repeating the sequence.

Charles picked up the book, eager to see what it had to say. There were few chances for written words in Herculean society. The Society of Scribes had a lock on all business and court records. Unless there was the seal of the scribes written with the words, no other scribe would read it. It didn't exist, officially.

The ability to write, and the skill to read was a closely guarded craft. You had to become a scribe to learn it.

Rad and Charles used written messages among themselves, it was one of Rad's first rules when they were suddenly on their own, but they were careful not to broadcast the fact. There didn't seem to be a law against it, but in a land where laws can be created on the spot by one man, the rule of law was no great defense.

Still, being forced to pay another man to spend long seconds puzzling out a sentence, one he could read over his shoulder almost instantly, irritated him constantly. Charles had no great respect for their skills. How could they develop any fluency, when their only practice seemed to be reading the same rote sentences over and over? Charles had read hundreds of books before he was twelve.

He opened the book. *Oh. Pictures.*

The anticipation that he'd stumbled onto a place where literacy was more common collapsed like a bubble.

The pages were vellum and the binding was crude.

Each page had a picture, a letter and a code. On the 'D' page was a picture of a pack of wild dogs. On the 'F' page was a bunch of trees burning. And there it was, a picture of a wild savage with a bow and arrow—the 'K' page with the symbol '_ . _' written below.

This was a code book for illiterates. Find the right picture and send the code.

He looked up at the castle—a reply was coming back. '. _ _ . _'

Charles thumbed quickly through the pages. At the very end was a table of the alphabet, with the symbol for each letter. *This is interesting.*

He asked, "'A' 'K' Is that the reply code?"

"Put that book down!" The older man poked his head up through the hole in the roof. "Jason, get that away from him!"

...

Charles had a sudden, cold feeling he'd made a big mistake. He was a stranger here, and unknown, and in the middle of wartime tension.

But he hadn't been a zero-caste laborer for seven years without learning something.

Charles closed the book and handed it to Jason before the other had a chance to puzzle out how he was going to take it away from him.

"I am very sorry," he apologized to the man in authority. "I was so excited to see a book that—"

"What are you doing with it?"

Charles hated being interrupted mid-sentence. He paused a long second before replying. "I told you before. I am Alpine. Books are my soul."

The old face looked at him hard, taking in the size of him, and the muscles. Charles stared back, holding in the flash of anger, looking at the permanent wrinkles and wondering just how old he was.

"So you say," he said. "Now get down from here."

Charles did as he was told, not giving the heliograph another look. He understood the physics of the thing. He could build one of his own if he could find the copper to make the mirror. He did wish that he had time to memorize that code table in the back of the book. With a whole alphabet code, you could send any kind of message. A place like Stampz, which could communicate at high speed all across the expanse of the crater, could be defended very well indeed, with a minimum of men. Just how common was this? How come he'd never seen it used before?

Charles wished he knew the elder's name, but instinct told him to keep his mouth shut until he had something to say that they would like to hear.

Outside, men were already gathering, most with guns, others with sharp metal farm tools. The elder had a musket, but also wore a long sword in a leather scabbard decorated with gold braid and the symbol of some beast that Charles didn't recognize.

The man was spending half of his time checking on the weapons of the others and half looking at Charles with a troubled eye.

Everyone was taking their cue from the old man, and Charles felt helpless. No one was going to take his word for anything.

Three more men arrived, all young men about his age. Charles nodded to them. They returned puzzled stares.

"James Dennis," one introduced himself, extending his hand.

"Charles Fasail," he was glad to take it.

"You from the missing wagon train?"

"Yes. It's not coming."

"Kimmer attack?"

Charles reached up and fingered the edge of the healing burn on his scalp. He really needed to use the salve again. "Yes. I lost my wagon. Everything, really."

"Kill any?"

Charles sighed, "Yes." He didn't elaborate.

"Umm."

Charles nodded toward the elder. "Who is he?"

James smiled, "Peterson. Used to be the duke's personal bodyguard. Decided to be a farmer. Hates it."

"Are you two done jabbering?" asked Peterson.

"Let's get going!" urged Gwedon.

Charles picked up his pack. "I'm ready."

"Hold on. I didn't say you could come."

Charles took an extra second to bite back his first response. *I am sick and tired of having people tell me where I can go and what I can do.*

"Sir Peterson," he began, "I have brought you important tactical information. I have fought these Kimmer just days ago. I need to see it through. And you can't stop me."

"He's right. Let's go," Gwedon urged, but no one was paying him any attention.

Peterson said nothing, then turned to the rest of the party and said, "Let's move."

They all started off at an easy lope. Charles fastened his pack and fell in toward the rear.

Before they got to the foot of the crater wall, Charles noticed that there were women herding clumps of children toward the village.

Peterson stopped long enough to give instructions to a woman, to tell the guards where they were heading.

The trek back up to the crater rim was slower than the trip down. The men laughed and talked as they hiked up the trail.

It was plain that everyone had lost friends and relatives to the Kimmer attacks. James Dennis wanted some resistance. "It'll make better payback for Da that way."

"Nah," disagreed Pen Jesson. "I just want them dead. And none of ours hurt."

Gwedon stopped talking altogether as they neared the crest.

Charles worried about their noisy approach, but that changed. In twos and threes, the group broke up and vanished into the trees. They were dirt farmers, but to a man and boy, these slopes were familiar hunting grounds. Charles followed Gwedon.

They circled the cabin that was sheltered behind a pinnacle of rock at the crest. Charles was fearful as they got closer. If no one were there, he would look like a fool.

Movement—a figure in white robes stood in the doorway of the cabin, looking out.

Gwedon made a small noise, like a dog growling low before beginning to bark. But the farmer's bark was loud and left a red hole in the Kimmer's chest. That was good enough signal for the rest. A hail of shots passed through the clearing. Kimmer that Charles had not even seen began dying.

Musket fire from at least two guns came back from the cabin. Charles dropped to the ground. He fumbled for his pack to drag out his gun.

Stampz people didn't wait. They were running all over the place, screaming and shooting. Before he had time to find a good target, one of the boys kicked at the door of the cabin. He fired a blast inside, then ducked and ran.

Off to his left, Charles heard a man give a high-pitched shriek. "They're dead!" he cried. "Kimmer killed them all. Here's the grave."

Gwedon wailed. A noise grew in the back of his throat until it was a howl that echoed from the pinnacle. Torches appeared. Two of the farmers ran up and tossed their flames against the cabin. Fire ran up the sides of the log walls like a red lizard running up a tree. Charles watched with frozen fascination as the flame spread and began to roar.

First one, then several more figures appeared in the doorway and tried to escape the death trap. Muskets fired, cutting them down as they fled.

It was over so quickly that Charles felt as if he'd woken from a dream. The roof of the cabin collapsed in a shower of flame and cinders. The walls collapsed a little later. Then, there was nothing but a stone chimney presiding over a bed of coals. Farmers bent to the task of building a cairn for the bodies.

Gwedon cried, softly, but it could be heard above the popping of the coals. Charles realized he'd not fired the impulse gun even once. He slid it back into his pack, out of sight.

He felt ashamed he had not helped in the fight, but relieved as well. He moved into the pack of men collecting stones and helped build the mound to cover the bodies.

It was something he could do to help.

Shouts, more muted than before, heralded the arrival of ten men in green uniforms. Peterson greeted them and began filling in the sergeant on the fight.

Charles turned back to his chore. He picked up another boulder and carried it to a pile of bodies. He almost set it down when an arm moved.

"Hey!" he shouted. "This one is alive."

He tossed the stone aside and grabbed the arm. He was small.

"It's a boy," called one of the farmers.

Buried under other bodies and protected by them from the blaze was a young Kimmer about twelve years old. He stared defiantly up at the tired eyes that started gathering around him. Their killing fever had cooled and they stared at one another for inspiration.

"What do we do with him?" asked Jason of the guard.

Sergent Jed Tylan shook his head, "You caught him. It's your problem, not mine."

Gwedon rumbled, "Kill him. Then he'll not grow up to kill more of our boys."

"We could take him back," another voice suggested. "Maybe he could be broke to farming."

The object of their debate writhed under their gaze. He was dirty and burned on the leg.

"Right. Jerem Dennis could use another hand."

"No," Charles spoke. His voice was too loud, startling himself as well as the others. "I brought you the news of the Kimmer attack. I found him here. I'll take him."

Duke of Stampz

The Stampz party seemed content with his solution, just as Charles started to realize how crazy it was. He did not want a slave. Nor did he need any responsibilities right now.

But the sight of the boy, covered in soot and no doubt orphaned, triggered too many painful memories. Turning him over to be made a slave was not a thing he could do. *Why didn't he just die like all the others!*

Tylan ordered one of his men to tie the boy. "You can have him later, but we need to ask him some questions."

"Fine by me," Charles said. Maybe he could find a way to back out of it. He could even be gone by then.

Some of the farmers begin to pick up their weapons and turn toward the downhill road. Peterson and Tylan were standing off to the side of the activity, talking military stuff, he suspected. They were likely the people closest to the duke's authority. He still had a job to do before he could leave.

He walked slowly over to where they stood and stopped a respectful distance away.

Peterson frowned and stopped talking. Tylan asked, "Did you want something?"

He nodded. "Yes. The wagon train I was part of has left, not because of fear of more Kimmer attacks, but because the Gate is blocked."

Behind him, Jason the shopkeeper said, "What? What did you say? What about the wagon train?"

Charles repeated, "The Gate is closed. There was an explosion and a rock fall. You will get no more wagon trains."

Peterson shook his head, "We've had rocks fall before."

"Not like this one, I'd bet." Charles motioned them to follow. "You can probably see it from the edge."

He walked toward the canyon lip and found a well-used trail that led to a cliff. He could feel winds coming up over the edge even though it was near mid-day. He moved cautiously forward, and a deep vista opened up. Towards the east, there was a glint of water deep in the crevice. Sunlight, at least near noon, touched the waters and showed the wall-to-wall impoundment.

Jason was the first to speak. "Those murdering savages!"

Charles resolved to keep his part in the explosion quiet. For all his bulk, Jason looked well capable of throwing someone off the cliff.

He turned to Charles, "The wagon train. Is it still on the Porch?"

"No. They've already left for Zeno."

Jason pulled his fingers through his hair and muttered to himself, "We have got to open the Gate. We can't lose all our markets!"

He turned to Tylan, "Jed, you have to call the duke. The Gate has to be cleared as soon as possible. If the word gets out, and all the trains avoid us…."

Tylan nodded, "I'll send a messenger. Or can you use the mirror here?"

"No code for this."

"Right."

Charles added, "One more thing. I was a lot closer to the rock fall when I came through. It's very high. There may be some flooding."

Peterson grumbled, "Flooding? We haven't had any flooding here since the Burn…"

Several of the group looked at Charles. He could guess what they were thinking. He had heard it all before.

The Burn had filled the atmosphere with huge quantities of smoke from the total burn off of the forests that had existed on Alp Island. For at least two years after that, rains had been greater than any in human memory. Refugees from the flooding triggered much finger-pointing at the Alpines.

Everyone knew the Alpines had done it to themselves. They'd dabbled in the forbidden arts and paid the price.

Time and time again, Charles found the fingers pointing at him. Every heavy rain had someone wanting to take out his bad humor on the Fasails. There'd been a few broken bones over it. None his. Lately he just ignored the long looks and mutters. He was tired of correcting their manners.

Charles looked at Peterson straight. He ignored the undercurrent. "If you had flooding before, it will happen again."

"We'll see."

Charles turned and headed back toward the ashes where there used to be a guard station. He didn't want to argue with Peterson. Everyone would be on the elder's side. They were all Stampz and he was Alpine. It was a familiar feeling. Only this time he was alone, there was no Rad to stand at his back.

He noticed a fork in the trail and on impulse took the right. It led to a pinnacle a few tens of meters above, where the battle had raged. It was the highest point around. There were toe holes chipped in the rock to make a ladder. If there was a heliograph here, this would be the place. A quick glance showed no one around, so he climbed.

The top was bare except for a wooden chest and the familiar heliograph mount. He looked in the chest. It was all there. The copper mirror, a cleaning rag, and the code book.

He stared at it for a several breaths, a rising sense of something bubbling in him. It was like the sailsuit. The things called to him. He couldn't resist.

He edged to the side to look for people coming. No one.

Before he could change his mind, he picked up the mirror and put it on the mount. He looked at the sun. That part of the alignment went quickly. Then aim at the castle.

Why don't they respond? He looked at the setup again. *Oh yes. Half way.* He found the pegs and finished the alignment.

There was a glint of light from the castle, and he moved the lever back. *Okay, so what do I say?*

...

Charles worked, composing in his head, the code book in one hand, working the lever in the other.

KIMMER KILLED
POST DESTROYED
ROCK SLIDE IN GATE
RIVER BLOCKED
FLOOD WARNING
SEND WORK CREW FAST

He stopped and after five minutes, there was a reply:

" . _ · _ · _ "

AAAA? What does that mean?

Then there was a long wait. He heard voices as someone passed on the trail below. He held his breath, as if that would make a difference. He was completely innocent. He was doing good. That wouldn't stop people like Peterson from shooting him.

I'm stupid. I need to take it apart and put everything back so they won't know I was here.

He almost did that, but then there was a flash of light from the castle.

" . _ _ · · _ · · · · _ · · · · "

This one is sending faster. He bent down and concentrated on one letter at a time, writing it in the dirt with his finger as he decoded it.

PLEASE IDENTIFY YOURSELF

Charles was pleased as the words formed themselves. He was right. Someone at the castle could actually read and write. This code system could send anything. You could actually talk across great distances. It was a great thing.

But now he had to reply.

He settled his mind, took up the code book and worked the lever.

CHARLES FASAIL AN ALPINE
LATE OF THE WAGON FROM GARTNER
TRAIN HAS GONE TO ZENO
SEND WORK CREW FAST
YOU WILL NEED IT
RIVER BLOCKED TOTALLY

This time the reply came almost as soon as Charles had stopped sending. The sender was also beginning to send even faster, as if he were getting more comfortable with the lever.

JAMES NEELY DUKE OF STAMPZ
GLAD TO MEET YOU
WORK CREW BEING ASSEMBLED
STAY THERE
I AM COMING

Charles rested his hand on the lever. *It is the duke.* In signals or not, the thought of talking to the nobility was unsettling. He thought about sending the news that the laser cannon was destroyed, but whether it was the identification of the other person at the castle, or a reluctance to talk about what might be a sensitive issue, he decided to leave it as it stood.

Now he could put everything up.

He wiped the mirror and put it carefully back into the box. He turned to the table in the back of the book. *I wish I had a copy of this code.*

Unfortunately, there was nothing to write on. If he had a stub of charcoal, he would have sacrificed his one remaining spare shirt in the backpack, but he didn't even have that.

He stared intently at the codes, trying to memorize them. He had good recollection; he had to in a world where everything had to be committed to rote memory—the punishment on a society that permitted restrictions on writing. Still, he was uncertain he could learn them all in one sitting.

And he didn't really have time. Regretfully, he put the book back and closed the chest.

There was no one below, so he stepped off into the air. The fall was only about twenty meters, so he landed hard, but safely. When he stood up. He almost ran into Tylan.

Charles had a grin on his face that he couldn't hide, so he blurted it out.

"The duke is coming. I just signaled him. I hope you haven't sent your messenger yet."

Tylan was startled. "The duke is coming here?"

"Yes, he just signaled. He said, 'Stay there. I am coming.'"

Tylan asked again, "The duke. Coming here?"

"Yes. That's what I said."

He turned and started toward the cabin site at a trot.

Charles followed, "What's the rush?"

Tylan was already shouting orders, calling his men together. He spared Charles only a terse, "The duke has a horse."

...

A horse? What was a horse?

Charles felt a quivering in his stomach. What had he set off?

The word spread instantly through the assembled Stampzians. Rugged farmers, people who had just gone into life and death battle with a shout, risking their lives and winning, these people at a word had become anxious and servile, hurrying to get themselves and the site cleaned up for the duke's arrival.

Charles did a quick inspection of himself, not because he was afraid of their duke—well, maybe partially that—but because he didn't want to be any less prepared than those around him.

. . .

Mother pulled a comb through his hair, fussing at him to tuck in his shirt and to put away the spinner, at least until after the dockside ceremony. He did as he was told, at least perfunctorily, slipping the spinner into his pocket instead of putting it back with his bag.

His mother didn't notice what he was doing, concentrating on getting her own clothes and face perfect. It was unusual. The family had been on three other trips to the mainland before, and his father had made others. None of these teaching trips had been other than holidays for the family. His father did all the work. This time, his mother was intense.

He gave his shirt a second tuck. And after a long internal debate, he put the spinner back into his bag.

When they left the boat, everything was different. A crowd had gathered, and there were cheers when they set foot onto the dock. For a heady moment, Charles had thought that the cheers were for him, or at least for his father. The cheers kept going, and he realized that they were for the man seated in a tall, colorful wagon. He was waving to his people and they loved it.

Charles felt relief that he had realized it before he had made a mistake. It would have been embarrassing to wave and have the crowd ignore him.

There was another moment of panic when he realized that he and his family were walking up to meet this important person. But he looked at his parents, put their smiles on his face and walked where they did.

. . .

Charles realized he had been remiss in treating his burns. Since there didn't seem to be anything likely to happen soon, he found a comfortable rock and opened his pack.

As soon as he opened the pouch that contained the salves, he knew the Turner girl had packed it. Rad was never so neat and tidy.

He shook off the thought and dipped a finger into the stuff. *Bear grease, mainly. Well, better that than nothing.* He applied it miserly to the healing burn on his scalp. Whatever he had now had to last. There was no guarantee that he would get any more soon. He had no money, and from what he had seen thus far, the Stampzians weren't likely to shower him with gifts for bringing them a double load of bad news.

He finished up his treatment and nibbled a bit on his provisions. Inside Stampz, he would be unable to live off the land. Nearly the whole of the place looked cultivated.

The locals were still a hive of activity. How could they expect to keep this up? It would take a long time to get here from the castle.

Almost as soon as he formed the thought, a runner came up and shouted, "The duke is at the wall."

What? Charles got to his feet and walked over to a rise. Down in the woods at the base of the crater wall, he could see something moving very fast along the trail.

The duke has a horse. What is a horse? He struggled with old memories, picture books that his parents read to him.

A big animal, it came to him. *Four legs, wings? A horn?* He shook his head. It couldn't have four legs and wings. His father taught him that. Only four limbs to a critter, unless you were a bug. He didn't know about the horn.

Oh! The royal beasts! He remembered something. The royal family had a zoo of exotic beasts. Horses, something about beasts that always killed themselves.

Animals that can't adapt. He remembered his father's Funeral Lecture, he had sneaked into the back of the classroom often enough to have heard it several times. A litany of Earth beasts that could not adapt to the gravity, or the higher oxygen content, or to the long day, or to the lack of seasons, or to the dimmer light of living at the base of a deep atmosphere, and so died out.

Horses must be one of those. Charles tried again to spot the duke, but the slope prevented him. He walked back to where he had left his pack in a churn of conflicting anticipations.

The thought of seeing, first hand, one of the lost legendary beasts of Earth was exciting. But seeing royalty was an event as well, one that left him uncertain.

As a child, his father had been treated as a welcome guest. After the Burn, Rad and he had been unnoticed dirt beneath Hercs' feet. Perhaps it had been a mistake to come here. This place was well organized. They would have taken care of the Kimmer and discovered the rock fall in their own good time.

What if they don't let me go? Gwedon could call me a Kimmer again, or worse, tell them about the boulder I uprooted with the impulse rifle, and they could believe him.

What were the chances that he could slip away and keep ahead of them if they followed?

He looked around at the scene. Farmers were still doing meaningless tasks like picking up rocks and making a fence around the burial cairn. Others were finding water from some spring nearby and dousing the ashes of the burned out guard house. Guards looked to be practicing some ritual salute.

And there was Peterson, resting with his musket in his arms, looking casually in his direction. They locked eyes for a moment, and then with no change in his unsmiling expression, he looked away.

At least one man here was his enemy. How many others?

...

"Assemble!" shouted Tylan.

Everyone moved. Charles got to his feet, unsure what was expected of him. Too late to run. Too late to hide.

The guards were already in place, and the farmers must have done this before because they formed two lines of equal length on each side of the trail. The guards and Peterson formed a third side facing downhill.

They have left me out! He was not going to go to the tail end of the farmer's line, like the younger son of a landless laborer.

He straightened himself up. He was big, and he had better use that to his advantage. He walked confidently around the outside of the assembled Stampzians and stood a body-length behind Tylan and Peterson. Peterson looked like he wanted to tell him to go elsewhere, but it was too late for that. Charles pulled on confidence that he didn't own and composed himself. He, too, knew how to stand at ceremonial attention.

...

The Central Archivist arranged the children in her class in two rows, twelve girls and ten boys facing each other, and with a word they stopped the laughing and talking.

She stood at the head of the two lines and spoke, "Face." They all turned in unison to face in her direction. She turned as well and called out, "Scholars seek knowledge!"

From behind the large wooden gates, a voice answered, "All seekers of knowledge are welcome to the Library." The doors slowly opened, and the Archivist called to her students, "Fore."

As Student Charles stepped into the darkened entry way, he caught a whiff of a familiar scent. Whether it was the books or the Library itself, this place had a smell that brought a flash of images, far away times, far away places, the friends whose only reality were black marks on yellowed paper, yet no less real than the bodies next to him.

They were inspected, each in turn. Charles held out his hands, and felt the warm, dry hands of the attendant check his own for any dirt or oil. They were then dusted with a special powder that would keep his hands from staining the pages with his sweat.

He then turned to enter the stacks. He was still young, but he looked forward to the time when he could be a Scholar like his father, free to roam through the endless shelves and discover knowledge that had been forgotten.

...

Charles glanced at his hands. Dirt was ground in so deep it looked like part of his skin. When was the last time he had washed them?

Tylan shouted, "All Hail James, Duke of Stampz!" The crowd shouted in unison, "Stampz Forever!" just as the duke and his beast appeared over the rise.

Charles was suddenly deaf to the call and response that continued. He had seen the horse, and its master.

Albino white, the horse was as large as an ox, but formed more like a deer than an ox. Sleek muscles, shimmering with light off its sweat, the horse barely touched its dainty feet to the ground. No horn, no wings, but it had a fire in its eyes that took in the assembled men and gave a snort of offense.

A calm hand patted its neck as he turned and slowed the animal into a wide circle at the opening of the assembly. "Greetings, good people." The duke spoke with a loud voice that, while clear to all, did not sound like shouting. He was dressed well, but not in the finery that Charles had come to expect from nobility among the common people. He looked like his farmers, Charles suddenly realized, but where their shirts were coarse, his were as white as the horse and looked fine, indeed. His vest and trousers were brown like theirs, but his alone had the fine sheen of supple leather.

He circled twice, and then called, "Sergeant, would you please attend." Tylan stepped out and jogged over to the duke. He was handed the reins to the horse, and Tylan gave his attention to walking the beast in the circle.

The duke was young. Rad's age or possibly older, probably ten years older than his own nineteen. Charles felt the people turn to follow the noble as he walked forward, like the magnet drawing iron pellets, their faces and attention on him.

He had smiles for all as he moved between the ranks. He walked up to Peterson, "Will, I see your men have won the day, as I expected."

Peterson kneeled, "For your honor, Sire."

The duke held out his hand, "Rise. Surely there are heroes among them today, show me."

Peterson nodded, and began to tour the duke around the ranks, detailing the exploits of some like James Dennis who had gotten in close and kept the Kimmer pinned down.

Charles glanced again at the horse. Tylan was continuing to walk the big circle, checking the animal on the flank every so often. One of the Tylan's guards broke away from the group at a gesture from his commander and brought a large skin of water over to the horse.

The duke was talking quietly to Gwedon, who was unable to raise his head. He couldn't hear what was being said, but he could see the bereaved farmer straighten a little under the words of his duke.

The duke turned and looked at the care his horse was getting, and then walked with Peterson to where Charles still stood.

Charles tensed, and cursed himself inwardly for showing it. Was he expected to kneel? Some of them did. How was he supposed to act?

He remembered a moment from his childhood. His father before a king. Charles bowed from the waist, as had his father.

The duke gave him a half bow in return, and held out his hand. "James Neely, Duke of Stampz. I believe I have met your father."

Respect

James Neely had attended one of his father's lectures at Posidonius. "And he would be happy to see what we have done with some of his ideas here at Stampz. Our cotton crop is the biggest on record this year."

Charles was pleased and distracted by this sudden change. Peterson's face had changed from open disapproval to neutrality. He was almost tempted to relax.

"My father," he replied, "would have been overjoyed to see his work move out of the lecture hall and into the field. His favorite times on Alp had been trips out into the woods with his classes to see what the real animals and plants were doing."

The duke nodded, "Had other events not transpired, I had planned to spend the summer of '25 attending the Invitational on Alp."

Charles remembered that event, "It was a good session. My father was in fine form." He paused, "I guess it was his best year."

The duke put his hand on his shoulder. "The Burn caused a great loss to all peoples on Luna, but certainly the loss of a father is a unique pain."

Charles had become immune to certain kinds of hurt. He'd polished the skill of shutting down his reactions to anything that would make him appear vulnerable in public. He did miss his father greatly, but that was an emotion for deep in the still of the night.

"Speaking of loss," Charles began, forcing words into an uncomfortable silence. "You have lost your Gate."

Neely dropped his hand, "Yes, a rock fall you said?"

He nodded, "A big one. It can be seen from here."

They retired to the cliff. After he pointed out the size of the fallen slab, the duke was silent for a long time. None other of the party dared talk while their leader was deep in thought.

Charles did not choose to talk either. The man seemed a pleasant enough, but the ways of nobility were an uncharted trail. He had known soft-spoken men who blazed into a violent rage when crossed. Anyone in Gartner could tell tales of merchants who lost fortune and family by attempting to collect the wrong unpaid debt.

It was best to wait quietly, be the obedient menial. There was no such thing as a free man in a land where a noble could raise a finger and everyone would turn against him.

It was becoming evening, and the shadows were deepening in the canyon below. The duke turned to him.

"Alpine. I could use your skill with the helio while the light lasts. Would you send a message to the castle?"

Charles felt his mouth twitch into a smile, "Gladly."

Neely, it seemed, kept a journal with him. He produced a scroll of fine vellum, a thin flexible swath of calfskin rolled on a dowel. He advanced the roll to a blank section and produced a quill pen and a small bottle of black ink. "My own mix," he smiled, "candle soot and cotton seed oil." The duke wrote several lines and handed it to him.

"Send a little slower than you did before. Zed is on duty, and he tends to make mistakes if the codes come too fast."

Charles nodded, clutching the scroll.

He half expected a guard to go with him, but no one followed. Didn't the duke want to ensure that he didn't read the rest of the scroll? *I wouldn't trust a stranger like that.*

He climbed the pinnacle and re-aligned the mirror. It was different, now with the sun almost on the opposite side of the sky from the castle, but he was pleased to see the answering flicker of light when he finally got the alignment right.

He thought about many things as he sent the message, a list of the Stampz dead and an order to the castle guards to send a new group up to the rim to rebuild the station.

His father had a saying. He'd dismissed it as a Scholar witticism when he was younger. "Everything is a test," his father would say, generally when

Charles had complained about his studies being too hard, or taking up too much of his playtime.

He looked at the scroll, the dark spiral of pages unseen. How could the duke possibly know whether he read it or not? Could he even know how those hidden words called to him? He was starved for text. You can't raise a child on expectations of a mountain of books too high to climb, and then starve him for years on rude letters, marked out one at a time with fingers in the dust! He had to read. He could feel an ache in his arms from the readiness to open what was not his.

Everything is a test.

He sighed. There was the flicker of acknowledgment from the castle. He disassembled the helio and stowed the parts. He picked up the scroll, and then headed back down.

...

Charles was invited to sit with the duke and Sergeant Tylan for a dinner on the rocks. From somewhere, a meal of beef, bread and apples had been provided. It was quite good. The height of his culinary experience these past years had been when he had splurged to get food from one of the vendors on the docks who catered to the pilgrims who came to Gartner. Not even the food on the wagon train while he was recovering had been much different from what he had lived on as a dockworker. He knew little other than various types of boiled grains, sometimes flavored with vegetables and fat. Charles wondered if Tylan had sent a runner down to the village the instant he had known the duke was coming, or if that had come later.

He wasn't able to savor the meal at leisure. The duke asked him directly, "We have had rock falls before, and more than once we have had to clear it away before the Gate was usable, but this is something different. Before, there had been quakes. None were the size of this one. Why was this one different?"

Charles had feared this question, and he was almost relieved that it had come out. "When I resolved to enter Stampz and warn you about the blockage, I had to pass along the cliff above it and had some time to think. There was an explosion, which broke the rock at its base, the slab above it was no longer supported and collapsed."

The duke was silent and attentive, waiting. Charles took a deep breath and continued, "The explosion was the result of a laser cannon being destroyed."

Tylan, who had been the silent and attentive subordinate at the meal, gave out an involuntary grunt, as if hit in the stomach. The duke did not visibly react.

Charles returned to the physics, "The cannon had a hydrogen tank which ruptured, and musket fire set it off. I suppose its matrix power cell must have discharged, as well, after the first explosion. The wagon was right against the rock. A blast that intense could have shattered the rock and done the deed."

Tylan looked to the duke, an unspoken question. In that moment, Charles knew that sending him off to signal the castle had been less a test of him than a means to get him out of the way while they conferred about him. His gut twisted.

The duke looked at Charles, ignoring his guard, "The shipment of that laser cannon to Stampz was supposed to provide protection against the increasing Kimmer attacks. That they could have destroyed it before we—"

"No," Charles interrupted the duke (just as part of him cringed at the very idea of interrupting royalty), "The Kimmer did not destroy the cannon." He pushed past a slow tongue that was suddenly terrified of saying more. He made his words distinct. "The Kimmer were ready for it. The wagon train rolled into a careful trap." He turned more towards Tylan, "Can't you see? They took out this guard station so there would be no warning. They attacked from the air when we were all bunched up and had nowhere to run. They captured the Legion wagon the very first thing, and practically ignored the settlers and their wagons except to steal clothes. They dressed up as legionnaires and settlers and started to take the wagons through the Gate with the laser cannon in the lead.

"They didn't want to destroy the cannon. They wanted to destroy you!"

Tylan waved his hand, "That can't be. Kimmer aren't that smart and the shipment was secret. They wouldn't even know how to use it."

Charles touched the burn on his scalp. "This happened when they blasted a tree near me when I was escaping the scene. Their aim was good and they fired several times. They can also use muskets well enough. Don't try to tell me they can't use the cannon, because I know better."

Tylan frowned, "I still don't believe this. Yes, the Kimmer have gotten more bold. I have seen the muskets with my own eyes, so I have to believe that, but this idea of yours of a carefully planned attack to gain the laser cannon is unlike everything I know of them. They attack in small groups. They attack buildings, even if it means letting the people escape. We have always been able to defeat them with better strategy and coordination. Always!"

Charles countered, "I don't know Kimmer. I'd never seen one until the first was aiming a musket at me. But it's very good strategy to take your enemy's most powerful weapon and use it against him. Either they knew, in advance, that the laser cannon was coming, or there was a very smart Kimmer that discovered it during the attack and planned the whole thing on the spot."

Tylan did not answer, and Charles felt no ill will toward him. He had a difficult task, and either revelation was bad news.

The duke spoke, "Sergeant Tylan, I suspect that the Kimmer are capable of more intelligently planned attacks. Perhaps we should discuss this. I would like to see you, the other guard staff, and Will Peterson at my conference room at the still. I would also like to get Snow back to her barn before darkwind. Could you please see that she is ready?"

Tylan rose and bowed. As he left, the duke turned his attention to Charles.

There were just the two of them sitting together. The duke spoke in a low voice. "I am compelled to believe your story. There is only one question that I must have answered before I leave.

"How did you survive the explosion when you destroyed the laser cannon?"

"Luck." Charles decided to be open with this man.

"The sandbar I was hiding behind must have deflected some of the shockwave. I had dived into the river at the moment of the explosion, that also would have deflected part of the shock."

Neely nodded, "Luck indeed." He looked directly into his eyes. "Did your father's impulse rifle survive as well?"

Charles jerked, "You know about it?"

The duke laughed, "He carried that wonder like a scepter of office! I am not the only young student of his that lusted after it. I hope that if you decide to stay with us, that I will be granted a closer look at it."

Charles nodded, daring to hope, just a little, that this man was as honest as he appeared. The fear that the gun would be taken from him ate like bad food in his belly.

"One more question," the duke asked. "Would you stay and help us with the removal of the rock fall? I would appreciate an Alpine's perspective on the problem."

Charles nodded, "Yes. I think I would like that." It may have even been true. He certainly had no other place to go.

"Good." The duke rose, and perforce Charles did also. "Let's go make some arrangements."

...

Charles had trouble sleeping, even though he needed to take advantage of every moment in this rock shelter halfway down the cliff face.

The guard sleeping beside him, whom he only knew as Bomm, had no trouble finding his way into dreamland. He didn't talk much, but seemed content enough to guide him down the guard trails to the base floor of the Gate. They were to be an advance for the party that would be arriving at the rockfall after dawnwind.

Charles looked at the musket that he had been given.

What have I gotten myself into now?

The duke gave orders, sometimes only mild suggestions, and people jumped to comply. *Even me.*

The farmers had already dispersed back to their homes. The guards had begun the process of rebuilding their shelter. Peterson was still there, and must have expressed his disapproval of Charles, because he heard the duke say, "Oh, he is an Alpine, no doubt. I have met others before, and I knew it as soon as he opened his mouth. We have puzzles to solve now, and Alpines are good at puzzles."

Whether those words were meant for his ears or not, it resonated with his feelings. *I am Alpine. I have to be a help to the people around me.* Perhaps the man had read his soul and said just the right words to capture his allegiance. *If so, then he is very good at it, this Duke of Stampz, out here at the edge of the frontier.*

For now, until he changed his mind, he would help Stampz clear the Gate. *It's your mess,* he heard his father say, *now clean it up.*

But for certain, he would have to guard his heart. He had never been so willing to work for another before. *I'm a free man. I can't ever forget it.*

Job Boss

The wind over the water sent a chill that his light clothes did nothing to block. *A lot better now.* The dawnwind swept from the interior of Stampz down the channel of the Gate, blowing the stench of the dead away.

Charles sat high on the slab, facing the new day. *It's going to be cold for a long time.* Unless the winds got warmer before the dawnwind died out, it could be uncomfortable here.

He'd slept very little during the long night. Even placid Bomm had a hard time of it. Only the assurance that the dead were all Kimmer helped the guard doze off. Of course, he woke a few hours later worried about ghosts, but by that time, the wind had shifted and the rot could be forgotten.

Charles looked up at the narrow band of sky, already morning bright.

The Earth had passed across that gap in less than two hours. We won't get any more direct sunlight than that.

The rockfall, up close, had bled away any optimism about his job here. The slab was settled and content. Under his body, it felt ready to sleep for another few million (*or billion!*) years.

Covering the slab was rubble that itself would be a major job to move.

He looked to his left, and saw piles of rock. From the rim he'd thought that the individual rocks were man-sized, but up close he saw them as the house-sized massifs that they were. *How do you move one of those?*

The duke had indicated that they'd moved rockfalls before. He hoped the crew was experienced and had more ideas than he had. If not, the whole project was doomed to failure.

Bomm ambled up and sat down next to him. He blew on his hands and rubbed them vigorously together. "They're coming."

Charles looked harder at the water where the cliffs merged, but he saw nothing. He almost started to ask what Bomm was talking about when there was a flicker of motion, and an open boat came into view from around the bend.

Bomm slapped him once on the back and once again got to his feet. Charles wasted no time pondering Bomm's minor mysteries. He got to his feet, as well. Suddenly, there were things to do.

Small open boats had different needs than the clamshell ocean-going ships he was most used to dealing with. For one thing, an open boat was guaranteed to capsize during the sun winds, so they had to be secured on land at sunrise and sunset.

Unfortunately, there was no convenient dock here on this rocky dam. Charles started walking the slab, looking for some place where the boat— boats, he now saw—could be unloaded, and then hauled up. He hoped that they carried enough rope and tackle to handle the job. Surely, they would.

"Bomm, come here!"

There was indeed a place among the rocks where a rude docking could be accomplished. They would just have to trust to luck that the choppy waters wouldn't slam the hull up against the angular, broken basalt hard enough to hole it.

They waved the two boats, each containing a dozen men and equipment, toward the spot. As the first one drew near, a rope sailed out toward Charles. It was a familiar sight. He snatched the rope out of the air and had it secured without thought.

The men on the boat weren't as comfortable. Charles had to climb aboard and help them get themselves and their equipment unloaded. When he realized that two of them had lost their breakfast in the chop, he had to strain to keep a straight face. The waves on this little lake were nothing, compared to the massive ocean waves that commonly dwarfed the cargo ships themselves.

Soon, however, the boats were unloaded. Charles waited a few minutes, trying to figure out who was the leader of the crew, but then decided to get started anyway. "You there, fasten this rope to the bow." He directed a few others, and soon they were pulling the craft out of the water.

Others, he saw, were busily arranging supplies and tools that had been unloaded from the boat, but most were wandering about on the slab, taking in the size of the task to which they had been assigned. He didn't see any smiles.

Charles knew he had the most experience securing boats against the winds, so he handled that job personally.

As he tightened the last knot, he looked about, still hoping to spot that cluster of people that would point out who was in charge.

No crowd, but he did see a young man about his age, heading down his way, bearing a pair of scrolls and a box. He looked a little young to be in charge of this work crew, but he was the only one moving with purpose.

He came directly to Charles, "Here," he handed the scrolls to Charles, "one is for your use and the other is for reports to the duke."

Charles took the scrolls and the box mutely. He was pleased by the gifts, but he was uncertain about this report business.

One scroll had writing at the beginning.

"Greetings to Alpine Charles Fasail, from the Duke of Stampz. Your crew contains my best masons. I would appreciate a report on your progress to be returned on each of the daily supply boats. Cut off a portion of the scroll at need. Good luck."

Charles glanced up at the people milling around. They were looking at him. That's why he couldn't spot the leader. He was the leader.

...

Okay, if that's the way he wants to play it. He had been set up before plenty of times on the docks. It did no good complaining. You had to beat them using their own rules.

He stared at the faces. They were waiting on him.

"Everybody up on top!" he yelled. He had to get them moving, or what authority he had would bleed out all over the group.

They moved, that was good.

At the top, he talked loud, so everyone would hear over the morning breezes.

"I don't know you, and you don't know me. We don't have time for lengthy introductions; this is a big job."

That got a few nods. He had learned a long time ago, that getting people to do things for you was a matter of getting them to say "yes", and strangely, it didn't matter what they were saying "yes" about.

"A few of you know a lot more about moving rocks than I do." Some nods there, too. "I will be talking to each of you. The duke, in his message to me," remind them of his authority, "called you the best! I want to see that best."

"But we have some grunt work to do first. You all look strong enough to me, so I'll just take you by thirds for now." He waved them into three groups.

He picked the one with his guard, "Bomm! You know how important this is. Take your group downstream and bury all the dead Kimmer you can find." There were some groans from the burial detail. Bomm took command and moved them off.

He spotted the boy who had handed him the scrolls in the second group. He was probably his age, but with a more normal build, so he looked a lot younger. Certainly the youngest of the crew. "You, what is your name?"

"Fal Barrier, sir."

"Well, Fal, take your group and set up a camp. Get all the supplies out of the weather. If it rains, don't get me wet. I get grouchy when I get wet."

He nodded, and that group headed off. He hoped the boy was smart enough to get some experienced help.

Charles walked over close to the eight remaining men, walking as straight and tall as he could, letting them see just how strong he was.

"We're going to get started on the real job—moving rocks. Come with me." He led them over to the north face, where the slab had come loose. The rubble was highest there.

"I want a ramp here, smooth enough and wide enough to drive a wagon up and down. For now," he hefted a rock the size of his head and tossed it over the side.

Soon he had his crew working, but that wasn't the purpose of this group.

"Hey you, what's your name? Help me with this rock."

"So you and George are brothers?"

"How big was the last rockfall you had to deal with?"

"Oh, so you are the expert mason the duke mentioned."

"This is your first time in the Gate? Mine, too. Big, isn't it?"

"No, I haven't been south. I came from the west, Port Gartner."

"Yes. No lie. I am Alpine. My brother and I were the only people left alive on the island when the Burn was done."

"Which of them was best, do you think? Which one would you want to work under?"

...

Charles rested, sitting on a high rock, overlooking the bustling camp. His arms and back ached. He hadn't put in a day's work like this in over a month, and his muscles had gone soft.

It had been a good day, as far as he was concerned. He had talked to everyone, and everyone had seen him working hard. He had been properly deferential to his experts, and he had shown a confident face to all.

If he could just feel some of that confidence himself. This wasn't like unloading a ship. Some of these rocks were not going to move. And the slab . . . .

He shook his head.

Why did the duke choose me? Is it just another ruse to keep me safely out of the way?

It didn't matter. He had to do this job, and do it well. He could be a good job-boss; he had done so dozens of times. It just felt strange that there was no Port Authority beltman looking over his work.

The wind picked up another notch. Soon he would have to go down and trust the night to Fal's handiwork. At least the stench was much better. He never wanted to have to do burial detail again. Seeing the blind maggots wiggle their random scatter from the dead flesh of a man you had killed . . . that had been bad. If there hadn't been people watching, he would have lost his lunch then.

Oh well, everything is a test.

He felt at his scalp. The burns were much better. The hair was starting to come back; he could feel the stubble.

I wonder if I can get it shaved again. A bare head in all this heavy lifting was a blessing. *Cooler.*

...

Greetings to the Duke of Stampz.
Report on the 11th day of Jan on the work at the rockfall.
The camp has been established and the work is in progress. Your chief mason, Bremmer, has informed me that the task of removing the main blockage is impossible. The slab is too large to be budged by all the manpower of Stampz, even if they could be gathered into this place. While I have to agree with his estimation, I am not ready to call off the effort.

It occurs to me that two things are important. The water must not be allowed to back up and flood the fields of Stampz, and secondly, some method must be found to allow easy wagon traffic into and out of Stampz.

To facilitate wagon traffic, even if the slab cannot be moved, I have started work on a ramp that will allow wagons to move over the slab if a way can be found to drain the water.

I have a question that Bremmer had no answer for: Do you have access to metal pipes? With such, perhaps a siphon system could be made which could keep the water drained. The masonry drains that have been described to me would not do the job.

In hopes of better news tomorrow, I am Charles Fasail.

...

Charles walked the camp in the still of the night. *I don't like these reports.* He didn't like what he said in the first one. *Almost lies. There is no way a siphon on that scale would work.* And he had only seen siphons on Alp, where there had been some remnants of pipes brought down from the Space City Alexandria when the colony was founded.

The simple truth was that the job of clearing the rockfall was impossible, and he was going to fail. *What do I say in tomorrow's report?*

Maybe they could tunnel under the slab and drain it that way. He would put Bremmer on that task in the morning.

Bomm walked past, carrying his musket and powder bag.

"Bomm?"

He stopped, "Yes."

"How much gunpowder do we have?"

He patted his bag, "Enough."

"No. How many bags? Is there any powder in the supply tent?"

Bomm just looked puzzled. Charles waved him away. That was something else to look into in the morning.

...

Greetings to the Duke of Stampz.

Report on the 12th day of Jan on the work at the rockfall.

The work of clearing the rubble is continuing. With the exception of three large boulders and the main slab itself, there appear to be no problems in moving any of these smaller rocks.

In mid-morning, I attempted an experiment on one of the large boulders that was resting on top of the slab. It had resisted all attempts to be levered or hauled with the ropes and tackle. I had noticed that there was a fairly tight cavity in the space between the boulder and the slab. I filled this cavity with gunpowder from the camp's supplies and ignited it with a length of rope.

It was an impressive sight. The explosion was loud and reverberated from the canyon walls. One large fragment from the boulder arched through the sky, trailing white smoke, and landed with a splash into the lake a hundred meters away.

The boulder itself rocked back the other direction, and almost stopped. But there was just enough slope on the slab, and it began a slow, crashing roll down the back side and cracked into two pieces when it hit the floor of the canyon.

The cheers of the crew were loud and sustained, and I had to enlist the aid of your guard Bomm to prevent the crew from burning the other two-thirds of our powder to blast the other boulders. I wonder if there is not something in the smell of powder smoke that doesn't incense people to great enthusiasm. I confess I felt it, too.

I walked the site of the explosion and looked very carefully at the effects of the blast. My smiles were a little forced after that. Yes, the blast worked wonderfully on the boulder, and we do have a useful tool to get rid of the others.

But the slab itself was little more than stained by the powder. I have to wonder if the reason that the slab stayed in one piece after the original explosion was that it is natively stronger than the others that did not survive intact.

On another subject, I directed Bremmer to see if a tunnel could be carved under the slab to drain the water. After his first examination, that option does not look easy. While he did discover a spring, which indicates that water is being forced through the ground, he told me that the base on which the slab is sitting is a firmly packed mass of boulders, many as big as the one we moved today.

A tunnel could be built, but it would take a long time, perhaps a year or more, and would require a sustained effort to break through to the other side. There is also the possibility that the large rocks would prevent the tunnel altogether. Bremmer was not confident that he could promise you success on that effort, and he was insistent that I would write his misgivings into this report.

The third possible solution that I will mention in today's report is an uncomfortable thing to write, as it supposes my complete failure to clear this slab or to drain the lake.

However, this idea has occurred to me and I would be remiss if I did not bring it to your attention.

If the lake is permanent, and if no other roadway into Stampz is available, then I suggest that a dockworks be built on this slab. The ramp that this crew is close to completing would provide access to wagons moving into and out of the Gate. Cargo boats would need to be constructed, perhaps with the help of Gartner or Atlas shipwrights, to move the produce of your fields to the docks where they could be loaded onto the wagons.

Thus, your trade could continue, although with more effort and difficulty than before.

On that note, I will conclude this report by Charles Fasail.

...

Charles knew he was taking a risk as he climbed carefully along the cliff. It was deep in the still of the night, and the waters below him were as calm as he had seen them. If he succeeded, there would be considerable risk for his crew, as well as for him.

But he was at his limit. Everything he had tried failed. Even in his dreams, all he could think about was how to move the unmovable.

How far we have fallen! The Project Engineers could have solved his problem in a minute. They had moved worlds! How little it would have been to them to move this little piece of rock.

He dreamed he was back in the Assembly, and he was called to account for his oath. All around him were the faces of his family and instructors. All looked at him with the frown of censure.

Had he preserved the oldman technology?

He could visualize the laser cannon, what remained of it from its explosion, smashed flat beneath the slab.

Had he used his knowledge to help mankind to regain its lost knowledge and power?

In this dream the duke rose to condemn him, *"We had begun to use his father's Alpine knowledge of plants to gain our economic independence and to make Stampz a shining example in the world, but he,"* pointing a finger his way, *"destroyed our markets and flooded our fields and brought us nothing but ruin."*

Had he brought honor and respect to the Alpine people by his actions?

In the crowd that surrounded him, one voice spoke out. It was Rad's, *"Because of him, the Alpine people no longer exist!"*

His father had handed him the impulse rifle. *"It's your mess. Clean it up, Charles."*

He awoke just an hour ago burning with anger. He had to do something.

So now he climbed, impulse rifle in hand, knowing that what he was about to try would not work.

But I have to try!

At last, he reached the ledge he had sought. It was below the level of the slab, but still above the water.

Long-tolerant Bomm had accepted his order to keep everyone off the slab until he returned. He didn't understand, but that wouldn't stop the faithful performance of his duties.

Charles fingered the controls on the impulse rifle. Numbers lit up, just bright enough to read in this darkness. He brought the power level all the way up. He tightened the fore beam to the limit. Concentrate its effect and maybe he could do some damage. He widened the back beam to take in as much bulk rock behind him as he could.

He aimed carefully at a particular spot on the slab and triggered the device. Millions of tons of the cliff behind him were balanced with the hundreds of kilograms in the slab before him during the instant of the *Nance-Bate overlap.* In that fraction of a second, energy poured out of the impulse rifle's power accumulator, following the strangely twisted space into the momentum of the rock, partitioned, as always by the need to balance $mv=mv$.

Something happened. Charles felt it. He listened carefully for a sound over the water, but there was nothing. He glanced at the impulse rifle. *Half the power gone, in one pulse.* He couldn't do that again.

He worked his way back along the cliff in a hurry to check the effects of the impulse. *What if I cracked it? Could we use that as a starting point?*

The whole camp was up and Bomm's orders notwithstanding, many were up on the slab and saw him return.

Gerald, Bremmer's first assistant, was the first to call, "Did you feel the quake?"

"No, was anyone hurt?" He held the *oldman* device where no one could easily spot it.

"Not that bad. Just enough of a tremor to feel it in the rock. Just a quiver and it was gone. We've had worse, it's just that sitting down in this pit with all these rocks over you makes you nervous."

Others agreed. It was indeed nothing, and most headed back to the camp shelter.

Charles headed for his target point. *Nothing.* No crack. No chips. No evidence of damage at all.

He slumped back and lay flat on the rock.

Maybe a little warmer there. That is all.

So not even the impulse gun worked.

"Just a quiver and it was gone."

Nothing he tried worked. Everything was a failure.

...

The supply boat arrived a little later than usual and among the food, ropes and shovels was a roll of vellum. "It is from the duke!" he was told by the boatman.

"I have no doubt."

He took the message to his corner of the shelter and ordered his food to be brought there. He'd not written the day's report yet, and it looked like he had one to read as well.

Probably asking why I haven't made any progress.

The message itself was a little less informative.

"Greetings to Alpine Charles Fasail, from the Duke of Stampz. I would appreciate your attendance at a meeting in my conference room during the Still on Freeday upcoming to discuss the current issues."

Charles penned a very short report. *Now is the time to decide,* he thought to himself as he rolled it up. *If I leave Stampz, no one would stop me.* He had just received a message from the duke. If he told the workers that it sent him on a trip to Zeno, they would outfit him with food and clothes and wave to him as he left.

If he went to attend the meeting with the man, what would he be walking into? He'd seen scapegoats before. It wouldn't help his case one bit that he *had* been the one responsible for the loss of the Gate. If the duke wanted a public villain, then the rogue Alpine was the logical choice.

Maybe Rad was right. Maybe the safest course is to pretend to be Herc and vanish into the new lands.

He heard a voice, and then Fal Barrier came into the shelter carrying his food. He approached with a little nod of a bow and set the bowl on the wooden plank that he had been using as a writing surface.

Then again, if I were a Herc, I would be Fal, bowing as I serve food to my superior.

He made up his mind.

"Fal, call Bremmer here to me, and pack your gear. We are leaving on the supply boat."

He paused with his mouth open for just a second, then nodded and jogged away in a hurry.

The duke wanted an Alpine. I'll give him an Alpine!

Survey

Charles sat on a rock, as he had many times in the last two and a half days, and tried to sketch the scene before him. It was difficult to be stingy with the vellum and accurate at the same time. Luckily, this was the last, and he could afford to use all of his writing surface. At least the ink had lasted. He'd worried at the beginning that he would be reduced to drawing his maps with stubs of charcoal.

Fal worked over the stake, *thunk!, thunk!, thunk!* as he put the marker into the rocky soil next to the road.

He came to where Charles was working and looked over his shoulder. The boy was no longer quite as timid around the Alpine as he had been before. Charles liked it better that way. Having people bow and serve you was pleasant as a change, but he wasn't comfortable with it.

"We're going to lose it all, aren't we?" he asked Charles with a sad finality.

Charles nodded, "If nothing changes. If nothing changes." They had discussed it often enough as they worked. He bent down to look across the sights again, to check where the line of the new lake level would be. He had to steady the floating block of wood as it bobbed in the bowl of water.

Bremmer had made up the sighting bowl for him, and he was pleased with how well it had worked. Charles and Fal had ridden the supply boat with this device and their gear until the first bend in the canyon, and then disembarked. Carefully used, Charles could sight across the aligned nail heads on the float and accurately move the bowl higher or lower until it was exactly as high as the top of the slab. This was the level the lake would soon reach.

From that spot, they sighted farther along the canyon wall to identify another point at that same level.

Charles would then take careful notes, and they would hike the canyon walls until the next bend and repeat the process. All afternoon and evening of the thirteenth, all of the fourteenth, and most of today, Jan Freeday, was spent hiking and peering over the sights, and taking notes.

Twice they had to backtrack to re-measure when a landmark proved to be nothing more than a trick of the light, or an illusion. When the canyon opened up, the full scope of the flooding became clear. It was sobering.

Charles asked, "Fal, where is your family's farm?"

He pointed off to the northwest. Charles said nothing. All of that land would soon be under water.

...

Charles spread out his maps on the finely polished, dark wood table. Neely had several ornamental statues, which he placed with practiced ease onto the corners of the vellum to keep it from rolling up.

"My maps are crude, but the landmarks are accurate."

"No," he objected, "you have done fine work." The praise was a little flat as his whole attention was on the drawings before him. He sighed.

Charles added, "Of course, the flooding won't happen quickly. As the lake spreads out, it will take longer and longer to come up because it will have that much more land to cover."

The duke was silent for another minute as he continued to study. He then commented, "There has been minor flooding before, during stormy seasons. I had been thinking of the problem in those terms. This is entirely different. If the lake fills to your marks, two thirds of Stampz will be gone."

Charles had nothing to add. He had stared at his drawings often enough last night. All he could do was assure the duke, "Unfortunately, the measurements are accurate. We have left the map points here," he pointed at the x-marks, "staked so that you can send others to check our work. We couldn't do anything like a full survey in the time we had, or with the equipment we could make. I just thought that some real facts would be valuable here."

He grimaced, "Actually, I had hoped that my worst fears were groundless and that the flooding would be confined to the Gate."

Neely shook his head. "Our worst fears are never the truth. When the time comes, it will be better or worse than our imaginations. But it will always be different."

He sat back down into a chair next to the table and indicated to Charles to do likewise.

"Charles Fasail, I do believe that you are a continual bearer of disaster." Then he saw the look on Charles's face, and smiled, "No. I don't mean that. You bring me painful truths. They won't be disasters unless I fail to rise to the occasion."

They sat in silence for several long minutes, each consumed by his own thoughts.

Charles finally asked, "Have you read the reports I sent?"

The duke nodded, "Yes, I have them all here. I also have a couple that you have not written, would you like to see them?"

The two short scraps of vellum were practically identical. Following the pattern that Charles had left, Bremmer had written in crude block letters, "14 JAN, WATER IS AT THE 52 MARK."

"Both are dated the fourteenth," the duke commented, with a grin he couldn't quite suppress. "Bremmer has used numbers in his work, but he hasn't used words before. I assume that this is a level of the water height?"

Charles felt his face redden. He nodded, "We marked a good scale on the face of the slab. As the water rises, the numbers should go down. I forgot to tell him to change the date."

The duke waved it off, "I can keep the records here. No harm done." He moved the reports one at a time as he read them again.

Hesitating to interrupt, Charles said, "I have been thinking about the gunpowder explosion."

The man set aside the report, "Yes?"

"If we could chip a hole into the rock and fill it with high-explosive, instead of gunpowder, then perhaps real progress could be made."

"That is not possible."

"Isn't there someone at the Court who could authorize it? After all, someone did send you ...?"

The duke raised his hand and stopped him with a shake of his head. He rose from his seat and Charles followed to a small dark chamber next to the conference room.

"We can talk here." Closing the door and twisting a warmball, the duke said, "I let the cook use the room whenever her little girl starts crying. I am *sure* that no sound escapes here!"

"Do you have eavesdroppers?"

"I don't know, but that is the way to bet. Have a seat."

He set the light into a sconce on the wall. "Tylan knows about the laser cannon. Two others as well. Most of Stampz knows nothing about it. I had promised the people help against the Kimmer, but I had not been specific.

"As far as help from Court, the cannon was it. It was to be a loan, a loan that can now never be repaid. My support in Sheb's circle has always been very meager. I cannot count on any help from them. Stampz must survive and thrive on its own. I have known that since I was sent here.

"As far as your request—high-explosives do not exist."

Charles complained, "They do. I have studied them in Alpine history classes…"

The duke nodded, "Yes, they did exist. But not anymore. Neither Hercules nor Serenity has had them in over fifty years. We never knew how to manufacture them, and the old stockpiles were gradually used up. Any report you might have heard about their recent use was simple mis-reporting, either accidental or deliberate."

He looked into Charles's face, "Unless this is an Alpine secret that you retain?"

Charles shook his head, "No. I am sorry. I wish I knew. We studied it. There is something about nitric acid, but I am not even sure what that is." He sighed. "I was only twelve when the end came. There is so much I never learned."

"When I was twelve, I learned that I was to die." Neely closed his eyes. "My mother came to my room in the middle of the night and packed me a bag to carry. Will Peterson, my bodyguard and Hen Freick, my tutor, took me across the border, and I never saw her again."

Charles was thrown out of his own reverie by the duke's words. "What? Who was trying to kill you? Why?"

The duke shrugged, "Everybody, it seemed. It's a long story. It was inappropriate for me to bring it up. You have my apologies."

"Okay." Charles hesitated. One did not push royalty to share confidences. He collected his thoughts.

"So, no high-explosives." *Back to the topic,* he thought. "Still, if we had good rock-drilling tools, and enough ordinary gunpowder, we could chip away at the slab. It would take time, but if we do nothing, then the floods come."

"Good. We do that. Can you start back in the morning?" The duke seemed pleased that the decision was made.

Charles put up his hand, "No, it's not that easy. I said good rock drills, and enough powder. We have neither at the site.

"Bremmer educated me on the drills. The ones he brought with him are already worn out. The iron is too soft. To drill a rock, you beat an iron rod into the rock, and with each stroke of the hammer, the rock under the tip of the rod has to crush. You then twist the rod to move the powdered rock out of the way, and strike the rod again.

"But if the iron is softer than the rock, the iron will bend and flow under the pressure. That's what happened at the site."

The duke frowned, "Can't we make the right kind of drill? Our blacksmiths are skilled at all types of iron work."

Charles shook his head, "I don't think so. To make the iron harder requires some high temperature process. A blacksmith has to make sure that he never gets his fire too hot. I'm sure you've seen iron that burns—blinding white sparks all over the place. Supposedly on Old Earth, it was easier to melt iron safely, with a lower percentage of oxygen in their atmosphere.

"Franklin Iron Works sells the best tools, and they charge dearly for it. They know the secret, and they aren't sharing it. You could send someone who knows iron to buy the drills there."

The duke looked unhappy when he mentioned Franklin. "I could send you."

Charles laughed and shook his head. "I'm just repeating Bremmer's words. The only thing I know about iron is bar talk from iron placer bums."

"Who?"

"Iron placer bums—the men who make their living by following the rivers and sorting the gravel, looking for chunks of raw iron. Back on Earth, there were places where iron soils were mined and heated until the iron poured out as a liquid.

"We don't do it that way here. If iron can be mined on Luna, no one has discovered how yet. But we do have a rich littering of meteorites all over the place, many of them made of iron. We haven't had an oxygen atmosphere long enough to convert it all to rust, so we can collect it. Blacksmiths can then heat the iron and beat it into tools, wheel rims, nails and such.

"When I was at Port Gartner, there was always a rumor of some valley where a man could collect enough iron to retire rich. Most who tried it never made enough to do much more than buy a stake for another try."

"Charles, you are always surprising me. I have found iron pebbles in the streams before, I suppose everyone has. I just never knew people could make a living collecting them. I see that my education has some holes in it.

"So, back to your plan. We purchase good drills from Franklin, and then we can cut a way through the slab?"

Charles nodded, "Yes, but drills is just one part. We also need gunpowder. Lots of it."

"How much powder?"

"Oh, I don't know. Maybe a couple of wagonloads to start. We have not had a successful trial yet. I don't know how much rock would be blasted away each time."

The duke gave a sad laugh, "A couple of wagonloads! To start!" He shook his head. "Charles, I was lucky to get a half-load two months ago. With all the Kimmer unrest along the frontier, Sheb is rationing out the powder. I know I won't get any more until the month of Apel or later."

Charles felt his enthusiasm bleed away. "We have to have the powder sooner. Apel will be too late. In two months, Stampz will be under water."

...

Light-sleep was the worst part of the day for Charles. That five or six hours after the still and before the dawnwind got strong enough to shut down outdoor activities didn't suit his life. Half the population slept through it. Charles was part of the other half. He did well enough with sleeping through the deep-sleep, that early part of the night that lasted ten to twelve hours, and a three hour nap in mid-morning.

The conference with the duke with its irresolution left his stomach in knots. He walked the corridors of the castle.

The central peak of any crater was an artifact of the impact, part of the splash frozen in stone. The castle had taken the small mountain and built in and around it. The main part of the building was a connected series of courtyards and enclosed apartments that circled the base of the peak. A walkway wound its way up to the top. If earthlight hadn't been muted by clouds, he would have checked up there. It would make a prime location for a heliograph station.

There was evidence all around that the previous lord of the place had a larger household.

The duke is a mystery. He was part of the royal family, if he understood all the ins and outs of the nobility.

He was given Stampz and a free hand in its rule. That meant that Sheb or someone high up was on his side. Someone had agreed to part with one of the rare and irreplaceable laser cannons as a favor to him.

But he couldn't get supplies. Someone had been trying to kill him, and the duke despaired of getting even a full load of gunpowder.

He feared enemies in his own house, or else why the quiet room.

And there is no duchess. Everyone seems to love him, but he strikes me as a lonely man.

A middle-aged woman dressed for cleaning passed through the connecting corridor. On impulse, he followed. A few twists and turns later, he entered what looked to be an eating room.

Guard Tylan was seated at a table working on a stew bowl and bread. He waved Charles to join him.

"Hello, Alp. Come, have a seat. The food is good here."

"Thank you." He sat down and one of the women brought him a bowl. It was good. He hadn't realized he was hungry.

"How is the rock hauling?" Tylan asked between mouthfuls.

"The ones that can be hauled are mostly done. The slab is still stubborn."

"Rumor has it that you tried to shoot it."

Charles had a moment of panic that he was talking about his impulse experiment, but then he realized the guard was talking about his gunpowder blast.

"We moved a big rock with gunpowder. It worked pretty well. I would try it again if we had more powder."

"Yes, you have to be careful. Another Kimmer attack like yesterday's would be bad if the powder was gone."

Charles set down his spoon, "What Kimmer attack? I hadn't heard."

Tylan nodded, "At the rockfall. The guards on the rim saw the battle and tried to send help, but it was pretty much over by the time they got there."

"Was anyone hurt?"

"One of the farmers. Greg Kend—do you know him?"

Charles nodded. He didn't really know the man, but they had exchanged a few words.

"He took a ball in his leg. He came back with the supply boat. The duke's doctor is the best with bullets."

That did little to relieve Charles's mind. If infection set in, the farmer could lose his leg.

"I should have left them better prepared for an attack. I didn't think about that."

Tylan shook his head, "That was Bomm's job. He don't talk much, but he is a solid soldier. No one was killed, except the Kimmer. You can bet Bomm was expecting them to come. What would you expect with all that construction going on? It would attract the Kimmer like flies."

"Then maybe we should stop. Until we can get the right tools, we won't make much more progress on that slab."

He shrugged, "If you think so, then tell the duke. He won't thank you if you get his farmers hurt for no good reason."

Charles sipped more of his stew.

"Everyone seems to love the duke."

Tylan nodded, "Earthlight, yes! There isn't a man here who doesn't know that the duke would call up the whole of Stampz if his child were missing." He pointed to the stew. "You like the food? You think the duke eats well? Well, two years ago, we had a bad crop failure. Not only was the duke starving with the rest of us, but he sold every one of his royal carriages to old Folsin in Mercury for shipments of grain to hold us over until the potato crop came in."

Charles said, "He isn't like the nobility that came through Gartner."

"He isn't like the old Baron, either. There are many who pray thanks at the shrine that Sheb sent his nephew to us, rather than give Stampz over to that one's kin."

"Sheb's nephew?"

"Sure. You think dukes grow on trees? He's Sheb's brother's son. His crest slants the wrong way, but the father acknowledged him right enough before he died. If Sheb hadn't sired a pair of boys of his own, our duke would have been in line for the throne itself."

Charles shook his head, "I was just getting comfortable with him. Now I learn this!"

Tylan chuckled, "Don't worry about it. If the duke likes you, he'll not let you get stiff. A few months ago, he had my father in to teach him to play a better game of Go. Dad could barely speak when he arrived, but they were joking about my baby clothes an hour later.

"I knew that I had to be the duke's loyal man when I chose the guards, but I have never been happier with my choice. If you stay with us, you'll think the same soon enough."

Just then, a boy in the house livery came up.

"The duke requests both of you at his conference room."

Tylan and Charles looked at each other and rose to their feet.

...

The page opened the door to a scary set of faces. The duke sat at his place at the table. Standing to both sides of him were four men. One was Will Peterson, with his perpetual frown. The others were unknown to Charles, although they nodded to Tylan as equals. Tylan moved to join them.

The duke spoke, "Charles Fasail, could you repeat your summary of what we discussed earlier?"

Charles was unprepared to speak to the group—important assistants or nobles by the quality of their clothes. *Everything is a test.*

He nodded to Neely. *Speak to him.* "As we discussed, it is my opinion that without explosives to chip away at the fallen rock slab, the lake will grow to fill most of the land of Stampz."

He related the one experiment with blasting the boulder, and continued to tell of his mapping trip back to the castle. The ministers asked questions. Charles tried to be as honest as possible, but he felt he had to avoid the topic of high-explosives, due to the duke's reaction before. These were probably his trusted circle, but it wasn't up to him to make that decision. The duke said nothing. He just watched and listened to what everyone said. *I wish he would warn me—give me guidelines.*

The questions ranged widely, from questions about the wagon train, to his ancestry, to descriptions of how he was able to map the extent of the flooding. That last had to be done with many gestures and acting out the process until the minister understood.

Then Will Peterson asked, "What caused the rock fall?"

Charles looked at the duke, but there was no help from that impassive face. How much did these men know? How much could he—dare he tell?

He faced Peterson. "I can not tell you that."

"And why not?"

"Some of the story belongs to the duke."

Some faces turned at that, but Peterson was intent on Charles. "That's a convenient excuse to avoid my question. Why I should believe that a total stranger is suddenly loyal to a man he's never met before! I'd sooner believe that you're hiding the story for your own reasons."

Charles felt his blood rush in his ears. He wanted to punch the old man, even more so because the old bodyguard was partly right. He didn't want the full story told.

"I will tell you everything I can, but beyond that you will accept my silence!"

"You'll accept the tip of my blade!"

Charles locked his jaw and stared hard at the old man. He wouldn't start anything, but duke's advisor or no, he would let no man treat him like a child.

He could see Peterson breathe hard and clench his hands on the pommel of his sword. Charles held his stare for a long moment, until he was sure the man was trying to restrain his own temper.

Charles waited until he was confident his voice would be level and then asked to the group at large, "Are there any other questions?" He shifted his gaze to the duke, dismissing the bodyguard.

This time, the duke spoke, "Are you still of the opinion that no progress can be made without additional gunpowder?"

He nodded, "And the drill tools as we discussed before."

"Then will you act as my agent to obtain the powder from the Southern Governor at Condorcet?"

Charles hesitated, not quite understanding what was being asked. He did know one thing, though; he would accept whatever task it was that the Duke of Stampz was offering. He nodded, "Yes, I will."

At the Duke's Castle

The duke turned to one of the men. "Sir George, draw up letters of identification for Charles Fasail, Alpine, acting as Trading Representative to the Southern Court at Condorcet. On a separate scroll, address a letter to Governor Frerick under my seal and bring it back to me for my use.

"Lord Smith, have your ladies prepare a court robe for Charles, make it a big one, and have them pack supplies for his journey. He will be needing it by noon." He turned to the rest of them, "Are there any other comments?"

Only Peterson spoke, and that in a whisper that Charles could barely hear, "Sooner he's gone the better."

"Then be about your tasks, and my thanks for your assistance." The duke rose from his chair, and all bowed and began to leave.

"Charles, stay a moment, we have some things to discuss."

He was glad of that, suddenly realizing that he had no idea what a Trading Representative was. Or, for that matter, how to get to Condorcet.

A hundred questions bubbled up in his mind. His fear was that the duke was going to turn him loose to sink or swim. It was his habit, as far as Charles could tell. Or maybe just his habit with wandering Alpines.

They again walked to the closed room.

"Charles, have a seat." He reached behind a cabinet and pulled out a leather pouch. "I have prepared some things you will need, in addition to the papers that Sir George will provide."

Charles was immediately suspicious of the weight. He opened it up. There was a sizable bag of coins—gold coins.

"That is bribe money. You will need every sheb of it. The Court functions on bribes. A gold sheb is the document that gets you up the next step of the ladder. At the top of that ladder is the Governor, and there are many steps to get to him.

"Your task is to get those wagons of gunpowder and to get them safely back to Stampz. I tell you now that I don't expect you to succeed."

Charles frowned, "Then why send me?"

Neely looked tired, "Because, I have no other idea of how to save my people. I have always trusted your reports, but yours are not the only reports I have gotten.

"Universally, the expectation is that within the year, most of Stampz farmland will be drowned. We have had hard times with bad crops in recent times. I fear what it will be like with no crops.

"I have people working now on new shelters on the rim wall. I have guards looking for smaller craters outside the rim. I can keep my people out of the weather, but I have no resources to feed them. I am faced with the task of sending them away, on their own, to find new lives elsewhere."

The duke looked him in the eyes. "You have one chance in ten that you can see the Southern Governor. If you see him, I can't guarantee that he will agree to help. I have no payment to send, other than the political promises I will detail in the letter.

"But that is still a chance. The gold is not enough to buy a future for Stampz, I must gamble it."

Charles nodded, then asked quietly, "But why me?"

The duke shrugged, "There are several reasons, some that are not your concern. But of all the choices I have, you are most likely to get there, and most likely to return. You also have an advantage with Governor Frerick that none of my people have."

"What is that?"

The duke only smiled.

...

The morning of the first of Feb was a daze for Charles. When the dawnwind calmed, the castle seemed to be filled with people. It seemed that Stampz observed the freeday more than Gartner had. When a given month lasted into the fifteenth day and the temples chimed the freeday, it seemed in Gartner that everyone was deaf. Not so here.

Of the flood of people that had taken the freeday off, many returned to find that their first task was to get Charles Fasail ready for his trip.

Sir George, in addition to his scribal duties, appeared to be the protocol expert, so for two hours he drilled Charles on the proper forms to be used when he finally made it to the Southern Court of the Empire of Hercules.

Charles thought much of the ritual senseless, but he had not been an Alpine student for nothing. Any subject of study could be learned if you had the proper study skills, and those skills had been drummed into every Alpine from birth.

Sir George was surprised when he was able to repeat the forms and sequences after only a quick exposure. Charles was pleased to be able to show off to the old scribe, but he kept his face straight. That was a skill he had learned in Gartner.

When Sir George dismissed him, a girl about seventeen or so was waiting at the door for him.

"Come with me. We need to get your new clothes fitted. The first thing you need to do is take a bath."

Charles was a little irritated, not at bathing, which he frequently did at Gartner by the simple means of jumping off the dock when he had the time, but at being asked to do so. No one other than his mother had told him that.

But he understood the need. He had to keep the official costumes clean until he needed them at Condorcet.

However, he drew the line at needing help, and latched the door behind him. All the women and girls walking the halls were unsettling enough. He didn't need the distraction of having anyone help him bathe.

Clean and dressed in a sarong-like wrapper, he entered the tailor's fitting room.

Mrs. Ryerly was a little older than he remembered his mother, and she had a firm, businesslike voice that put him at ease.

The tailor and her two assistants soon had measuring strings out and snipped and knotted until they had a tray of strings that defined everything they needed to know about him to shape his clothes.

He was given a white robe and allowed to walk the environs of the castle, with strict orders not to get himself dirty.

He agreed, with the silent exception that he wasn't going to worry about the soles of his feet.

Many things that had slipped his attention during the night were suddenly inescapable.

One thing was clear: this castle wasn't the luxurious residence of royalty he had imagined. It was closer to a working farm than anything else.

One entire wing was devoted to cotton processing. He poked his head into one room and had a dozen young girls looking at him, stopping their work at currying the cotton strands with big wooden combs. They appeared to be removing the seeds and building a pile of cleaned and untangled fibers.

The next room was another that appeared to be a storehouse of baled cotton.

Enough cotton to buy food for the whole duchy, if they could only get wagons through the Gate to take it to market.

Down the hill he could see a grain mill, with stables for the oxen that turned the wheel. It was silent and inactive. He remembered the grain wagons from Gartner. *Were they destined for Stampz?*

One building contained a number of young men wielding hammers, smashing a mass of pulp. "It's cotton seed," one explained, "The duke is trying to find ways to use it for something other than just soil enrichment. We can get an oil out of it this way."

A group of children ran past as he walked. One blundered into him, and Charles had to remember that he was a guest in Stampz and refrain from chasing the boy down. Besides, he wasn't dressed for it.

It isn't the docks anymore. That wasn't an attack. I don't have to growl at everyone who bumps into me.

The cotton areas had little fibers of cotton everywhere. Even the grass had a white edge where the winds had collected stray cotton.

The horse called out to the morning breezes with a loud, liquid cry and a snort. Charles stepped over to the pen where a guard was watching.

"Good morning," Charles offered.

The guard glanced his way and seemed startled to be addressed by a large man in a white robe. "Um, good morning, Sir."

"Are you watching the horse?"

"Uh, yes, Sir. It's my shift."

Charles tried to look at ease, not like some official inspecting the troops. "I've never seen a horse before. Do you have to guard her? Does she escape?"

The guard eased up a bit, "No, nothing like that. She's the duke's baby and she knows it. We just have to watch and make sure she doesn't hurt herself."

"Why would she get hurt? I have heard rumors about horses, but I could never understand what the problem was."

The guard tried to explain. "She is an Earth creature." As he said the word, his right hand made the religious symbol, his thumb and index finger forming a circle. "She is too strong for her own good. If she gets too excited, she can jump very high. Problem is, she can't land right. The duke himself told me her brother had landed wrong and had snapped his neck.

"I've got to watch and keep her gentled. It's not going to be on my watch if she spooks!"

Charles nodded, "I would hate to see her hurt. She looks magical."

"She is, at that."

Charles watched the white horse dance over to the highest point in her enclosure and nuzzle the ground looking for grass. It was a graceful creature. If for no other reason than the beauty, he hoped the species would survive.

But he had seen the beast move like the wind, carrying the duke. *If horses could be bred and trained, imagine what fast communication could do for the frontier.* In a day, a courier could take a message from Stampz to Hercules. His trip to Condorcet wouldn't take much longer. For an empire like Hercules that was shaped like a crescent around its perpetual enemy, fast communications could be a critical advantage.

There is only one horse. He hoped it wasn't the only one left on Luna. Parthenogenesis was a word his father taught his students, but the technique to make offspring animals without a natural sire was long since lost.

He started back to the main house and was surprised to see a hand cart being drawn up before the cotton processing area. The cotton bowls in the cart were blue.

He walked up and picked one of the bowls. Yes, the fibers were a pale blue. What was more, the bowl husk and stem parts still in the mix didn't show any blue on them.

He asked one of the men who were waiting beside the wagon, "Do you dye these? I have never seen blue cotton before."

"No. It grows that way. One of the duke's special projects. We collect the seeds from the blue stuff and grow it in a separate patch. So far, it's stayed blue through four crops."

Charles felt his father standing behind him, peering intently at the cotton through his eyes. "How did you get it? Who discovered it?"

The man smiled, "I did, Jess Mendo." Charles shook his hand. "I was picking cotton one day and noticed the color. Good thing I saved it. The duke promised me double price for all the blue cotton I can grow for ten years."

Charles nodded, thinking of other things, old lectures he had heard. "Does the color wash out?"

"No. Never fades. The ladies love to get their hands on the cloth it makes."

Charles looked around in the hand cart. "I notice that some of them look a little darker."

Jess agreed, "I see that time to time. I have tried to plant those seeds separate. But I can't see a difference."

"Does the darker cotton grow in one place, or scattered throughout the field?"

Jess looked puzzled, but answered, "More in patches, I guess. Five plants in one place. A dozen in another."

Charles felt a strange excitement. "It must be a soil difference, then. Try this," he picked up a stick and sketched a square of squares. "In the top two, mulch the soil with tree leaves. In the bottom two, add a little wood ash to the mix. In the right two, add dark mud from the nearest stream bed. In the left two, add sand.

"This will give your cotton four kinds of soils to grow in. If I'm right, you'll have a chance to get a stronger blue in one of them. If you are lucky, you can make two or more shades of blue cotton, and the ladies will really love you."

Jess Mendo peered over the sketch, his lips moving as he tried to memorize what Charles had said. He looked up and asked, "Who are you?"

Charles shook his hand again, "I am Charles Fasail, Alpine. My father was the best expert on plants and animals in the world. I just hope I remember enough to help you."

. . .

"I told you not to get dirty!" It was the tailor's assistant, glaring at him, her fists at her hips.

Charles dropped the stick he had been using to draw in the dirt. He grinned at her, "Sorry. I had to show Mr. Mendo something."

She looked doubtful, "It is time to finish fitting you."

He said goodbye to Jess Mendo and followed her. He had gone only a few paces when he saw a familiar face sitting on a chair in the sun, dressed in a robe much like his.

"I am sorry, but I have to go talk to that man. I know where you are working. I will be there very soon."

He turned before she could protest and headed over to greet the injured member of his crew.

"Greg Kind! It is good to see you."

Kind had been neither a guard, nor one of Bremmer's construction crew, but rather one of the farmers—one whose turn to join in a duchy project came up just in time to add him to the rockfall clearance crew.

He held out his hand to Charles and smiled, "I'm sorry I can't get up, but that doctor would shoot me again if I did."

"No, you stay put. Get yourself healed up. I'm glad to spot you. I had no idea where to look for you. I had to apologize for leaving you and the crew there to get attacked."

"Not your fault. The duke calls and we come running. We all know that. Besides, it wasn't as one-sided as you seem to think. Ever man in Stampz is good with a gun, we have to be."

Charles asked about his family and wished him a quick recovery. Maybe he wasn't a natural at people skills like the duke, but it was something he probably ought to learn.

"I have to leave here later today, so I've got to run. I have some people waiting for me."

"Going to go get us some more gunpowder?" he asked.

Charles asked, "Ah, what. I mean..."

"Not supposed to talk? It's okay. I was just guessing. I was there, remember. And the duke asked some questions. I'll keep my mouth shut."

"Thanks. I'm new to this." *And I'll have to have my story together better the next time someone asks leading questions.*

...

He walked through the door listening to one of the assistants giggling. The other looked flushed and motioned the giggly one to be quiet.

"Girls!" Mrs. Ryerly, the tailor barked, and they attempted to get back to a businesslike level. Charles could see that the attempt was only partially successful.

The clothes, a full court outfit and two additional shirts were almost completed, but they had to do the final fitting with him posing on demand.

Charles removed his robe and relaxed, enjoying the activity all around him. He had nothing to do, and it was something of a relief. The place was clean and organized, and the smell of the clean cloth and the scented women was enough to let him settle into a contented daze.

The giggly one, Clara, was the junior. She handed the tailor and her first assistant, Bertrice, the pins and measuring strings and fabrics as needed.

Charles felt like a dummy, standing motionless and moving his head or his arm as directed. They worked quickly, stepping him into the court dress, and then removing pieces to adjust the fit. Not even his mother had taken so much care of his clothes before. It was something rich people and nobles had to endure, he supposed. Not that it was much of a task.

Bertrice reached up with both hands to adjust his collar, and he breathed in her fragrance. An impulse shot through him, and he was startled by the vividness and intensity of it.

It was almost as real as a memory—the impulse to put both arms around her and hold her to him.

His heart started pounding and the muscles in his arms tingled, as if eager to act out the image that flashed into his mind.

He could feel other parts of his body reacting as well, parts that didn't stay put by willpower alone like his arms did.

She is too close! He struggled to keep his composure, but something must have cued the girls because Bertrice appeared to be turning red and a giggle escaped Clara.

Charles quit being a dummy and turned to the tailor. "Mrs. Ryerly, I was wondering," he asked, "if you have done much with Mendo's blue cotton?"

The lady smiled, "Yes, we have. Would you like to see some of it?"

"Yes, please." Charles took the opportunity to move off the little block where he had been standing and to follow the tailor, ignoring Bertrice and her scent.

As the lady sorted through her hanging sheets of cloth, Charles was breathing deeply, trying to keep his attention on safe subjects.

Is this what the others go through?

It had been easy to be contemptuous of the bawdy tales and crude conjectures of the sweat gang in Gartner. He knew what sex was all about, from listening to his father's lectures. This other stuff he dismissed as just another cultural trait that made Alpines different, and better, than the Hercs they had to live with.

Maybe it's like magnetism. You don't notice it at a distance, but it gets very strong when you are close.

He hadn't been close to very many girls in his life. Certainly not since he had become an adult.

Rad had set limits on that part of his life, and he had never questioned it. *I'll have to set my own limits now, or else I'll end up like Rad.*

The girls were whispering to each other, but he didn't turn their way.

Mrs. Ryerly brought out a sample of the blue cloth. Charles ignored the feeling in his arms and concentrated on the fabric.

"This is excellent. The color glows into the threads." He threw his mind into the experience. He'd been close to the marketplace for seven years. He'd seen fashions come and go. Certainly, Mendo blue cotton had the potential to attract attention.

And thinking about it kept his mind from other things.

The lady nodded, "I have always thought so."

Charles felt the finely woven cloth with his fingertips. "I wonder if it would be possible for me to take a sample of this to the Southern Court. I'm sure it would be very popular and if I could show it to the right people, it might become an important trade good."

The tailor pursed her lips in thought. "I don't know. I would have to get permission from the duke."

She thought for a moment more, "No. The duke told me to find ways to use it. I will help. We don't have much that isn't already spoken for, but I will make you something."

"That would be wonderful."

The rest of the fitting went smoothly. Now that the tailor was his partner in the promotion of the blue cotton, she opened up and began talking about Stampz and its fabrics and other things that might do well in the marketplace.

Charles was happy to listen to her ideas. He was comfortable, he decided, when he was around people who actually knew what they were doing and had something to say. It was almost like Alp. Everyone had been an expert on something, at least in the circle of people in which his family moved.

As they were finishing up, he noticed Clara picking up the little rack that held all his measurement strings like an array of tassels. *She looks nice, too.*

Stop it.

But it feels so good.

"Mrs. Ryerly?"

"Yes, Mr. Fasail."

"Am I correct in guessing that with that set of strings, you could make additional clothes for me without me being present?"

"Yes. We keep a set of measurements for all the people who have clothes made here."

"Good. Don't throw mine away."

It was Bertrice who asked, "Are you planning on returning?"

He felt a warmth spread throughout his body. "It will be a long trip, but I would like to come back. Maybe get a Mendo Blue Cotton shirt made!"

...

By noon, he was back into his old clothes, although his things had been mysteriously cleaned and mended. He had a major panic when he had returned to his room and found his fullpack opened on the bed, half empty.

A quick inspection found the two guns still wrapped in their sleeves, still secured by knots that looked like his own slider hitch. Everything was still in its place except the clothes.

He looked quickly around the room and found them, all neatly folded in a package on the table.

I don't like this. He was not used to anyone touching his belongings, not even if they were just trying to help him.

If you trust a man, does that mean you trust his servants?

He went back to his pack and reexamined everything.

Even after everything proved untouched, he was still angry and ready to fight someone, anyone.

But there was no one around, and he realized that the twitching in his arms and the sense of alertness could be due to something other than imminent battle.

Something like Bertrice's scent and Clara's giggles.

I have got to get out of this place before I go crazy.

. . .

Noon meal with the duke was an organized affair, with twenty seated at the table and a number Charles couldn't keep straight coming in and out of the room bearing new dishes and removing the old ones.

All the ministers were there, as was Will Peterson and a few other people, men and women, whom he did not know.

At first, he felt like a child at a meeting with adults. The only person there he could talk to was Neely, and it was quite obvious that everyone else wanted to be first in the duke's attentions as well.

Charles was full of frustrations. He would rather have eaten a poor man's meal and headed for the south rim. There wasn't anything useful he could do here.

But the food is good.

He ate quietly, listening to the business of a duchy being conducted. Other people watched him, but he was used to that. If his size didn't put people off, then being an Alpine did. His clothes, that of a common man, among the finery and robes of the upper class was probably another factor.

Clothing could be changed, but the new things had not yet been delivered.

But all things brought into the equation, he liked being who he was. If all men treated him with the simple respect he felt from Neely, the world would be a fine place.

He noticed that the pretty serving girl who had been filling the glasses appeared to be nervous. He wondered what the problem was, and then he realized he had been staring at her.

What is this? Am I doomed to drool over every girl in sight?

He casually turned his attention to what the duke was saying about the painting he had seen in one of the Serenite temples at Posidonius.

Alpine Duty

What was that? Charles had traveled to Posidonius as a child, but that was back when the Alpines were on good terms with both of the empires. Travel between the lands was difficult to impossible now. Hostilities had been simmering for years.

The girl finally came around to fill his glass and he tried to ignore her presence, but he could even feel her body heat as she came near. He could only relax when she left.

I need to be gone from here. Maybe alone, on the trail, I can shake this compulsion. Rad, I may have to apologize for what I said.

Heading South

Charles adjusted the straps of the fullpack so it rode comfortably on his back. The final interview with the duke was brief, mainly just a review of the papers. The invitation to a permanent position at Stampz left a warm feeling.

If I have to work as a vassal, Duke James is about the best master I could wish for.

He looked across the green expanse of Stampz and the rim wall that surrounded it. It was a majestic vista, with the pleasant fields and homes spread across its floor.

Then he remembered his task. The flood he had started was going to spread over this whole land like a blue mold covering a pie. Faces flashed in his memory; Gwedon's tears, proud James Dennis, smiling Jess Mendo, blushing Bertrice.

He could not even remember the names of some of the people he had met—people whose homes and future rested on his ability to get that gunpowder.

He set a firm pace. The fullpack was satisfyingly heavy with all the supplies that he'd been given. It rode well enough, but he intended to re-pack everything once he was out of Stampz. He wanted quick access to the impulse rifle if needed.

Oh no. The duke asked to see it, and I forgot to show it to him. It had been in the pack the whole time as they talked. *If he had just reminded me.*

But that wasn't the way with the Duke of Stampz. *If everything is a test, then mark off twenty points on Charles Fasail for bad memory.*

Perhaps that's why the duke sent him with several rolls of vellum and a supply of ink. *"Write it down for me, trivial things as well. If you can find a reliable courier, then send me reports, otherwise just keep them and I will read them when you return."*

The duke probably expected him to forget things. Or maybe he was just starved for things to read.

A low *boom* caught his attention. He slowed his pace, and then stopped. Behind him, he could see a signal puff of white smoke in the air. Two figures were racing to catch up with him.

He didn't have to wonder long what the problem was. He soon recognized the people. The adult was Jed Tylan. The boy on the leash rope was the Kimmer boy he had claimed.

...

The guard smiled as they strode up, "Good thing you heard me. I'd have had to chase you all the way to the rimwall. You forgot your pack animal." He proudly held up the leash on the Kimmer boy.

Charles felt his stomach sink. He had forgotten the boy. A couple of sentences two quads ago, and it had come back to haunt him.

"Jed, I don't know. Couldn't you keep him until I get back?"

The boy had no expression on his face. He stood silently, the rope around his neck. Still in the deerskin he wore when captured, soot stains and all. His skin didn't look much cleaner.

"I really can't keep him, Charles. A couple of my men did the best they could trying to tend him while you were working at the rock fall. But we have new orders now. The duke is sending most of the Guard to scout out possible building sites on the rimwall.

"We can't just lock him up, either. We tried that. He screeches and bites when we herd him inside. Whatever the Kimmer have against buildings is pretty strong.

"Charles, he's your property and you have to take him. If you leave without him, I'll just have to shoot him."

He tried to remember why he offered to take the boy in the first place. *I don't need this.*

The impulse to claim that his business was more important than Tylan's vanished before it was half formed. If the duke wouldn't rescue him from Peterson's attack, he would have even less interest in bailing him out of this particular mess.

He took the leash, but he had a scowl for Tylan.

"It's okay, Alpine. I don't care what you do with him once he is outside of Stampz. The trail down the south face is fairly steep. He just might fall."

Charles growled, "I don't need a slave right now!"

Tylan laughed, "Why didn't you let Gwedon have him? Don't blame this on me." He turned and started back toward the castle. "Don't get your fingers too close to him. He bites, remember. And good luck!"

. . .

The hike along the southern spoke road was fairly tame. The Kimmer seemed content to match his pace. Charles wondered what was going on in that mop-haired head.

The feeling around Stampz was that the Kimmer were a particularly vicious beast, much like the wild dog packs that hunted at the fringes of most cities.

Charles couldn't accept that, not after seeing them up close at the wagon train. They were people, he was sure of it.

But I'm not likely to argue the point in Stampz.

Too many people there would not thank him for that opinion.

He looked again at the figure walking beside him. *He's so thin the winds will just blow him away.*

Red anger started building in his chest. *Not now. I don't want to deal with this now.*

He picked up the pace and shifted into a long, gliding step. The boy had a harder time of it and drifted back. They were approaching the rimwall quickly. Charles could see a glint of light from the little lake far to the east. The water in the Gate had already backed up into the crater. It would be rising soon enough, and some farmer would be regretting having his land so close to the banks. Every day he wasted would add to those ranks. He glanced over at the Kimmer.

The end of the rope was flopping free. The boy was already twenty meters off to the right running as fast as he could for the foot of the wooded rimwall.

. . .

I've got to catch him! He couldn't let him escape, not here in Stampz. He snapped the rope back and it whipped around his arm, an old skill.

If he reaches the woods before I do, I may never find him. He notched up his speed and began a hard run.

The boy was quicker than he was, it seemed. Over this plowed and even land, he was pulling away. Charles moved down into a toerun, balance a little unsteady because of the unfamiliar weight of the fullpack.

Blind as he was with his face down in the dirt, the toerun was a good choice over this flat land. He raised his head every few seconds to check on the land ahead and the progress of his quarry.

I look ridiculous. A dozen people have seen me by now, and the story will get back to the duke.

The boy was fast, but Charles had much greater stamina, and he was gaining. The boy started rooing, and then dropped back into his normal gait. *He's panicking.* Charles stepped up his pace another notch.

The green mass of the rimwall was beginning to separate into individual trees. When the boy looked back, Charles could see wide-eyed fear on his face.

Charles didn't try anything fancy, he just ran him over. He grabbed and they tumbled together. Charles kept his hand clamped around the thin arm until they stopped rolling.

Fingers went for his eyes, and Charles slapped him down hard. For just an instant, the boy went limp and Charles felt a shock rip through his chest. But in another second, the boy started fighting again.

I need to be careful. I could break him in two.

He held one arm and then grabbed the other. Holding both of the boy's arms in one tight grip, he loosed the rope from his arm and bound the boy's wrists together.

"Now get up. And don't try that again."

He checked the knots and pulled the boy to his feet with the rope.

Through the whole chase and fight, the Kimmer boy had not said one word, not even a whimper. Charles knew that most of the Stampz residents thought the whole race was mute. He knew better, but he could see how the impression might arise.

Charles checked his pack, and then started them moving again. They had a lot of backtracking to return to the southern spoke road. His directions to the guard station were from there.

The boy followed quietly again, but they had to keep to a slower pace with his hands bound.

...

The trail down the outside of Stampz was much less well marked than the one up to the Guard station. Traveling was slower, and Charles had enough time to sink into a thorough depression.

The guards didn't actually say that they had observed the escape, but they seemed to be expecting him as they crested the rim.

The leader of the guards was happy to point out the landmarks to the footpath that rejoined the Gaussland Trail. He also looked over his Kimmer "pet".

"I don't think you understand how it's supposed to work. Let me help you strap that fullpack on him. Let him do the carrying for you."

Charles had smiled and let the suggestion pass without comment. He was too soon out of slavery himself to blithely turn the process around.

But if he isn't my slave, what is he?

The question kept coming back as they wound their way down the steep footpath on the south face of the rim.

Charles hoped for a better trail, one that could possibly be worked into a wagon route. Unfortunately, this path was very steep, with some passages that wound through deep cracks in the rock. It could be done. He had confidence that almost anything could be done. But the road building was like the slab itself. It would take better tools, and a better engineer, and just maybe *oldman* techniques, to do the thing.

What am I going to do with the boy?

He had to get rid of him. *I will never make it to Condorcet with him in tow.* He could kill him. It was scary just how easy it would be to snap his neck and dump the body where the birds would take care of it.

Or he could let him go.

But not here, not anywhere near Stampz.

He suspected the little beast would do very well in the forest alone. He would join back up with other Kimmer soon enough. And then he would tell them everything he knew about Stampz, the castle, the guards, where the guard stations were, and even when the guards slept and ate.

Letting him go too quickly would put the people he knew at risk. The Kimmer were not hesitant to kill the Stampzians, that much had been made very clear. He liked the place.

It might be nice to settle down someday. He imagined what it might be like.

An Alpine research farm. A chessboard of little plots where he would grow new crops, or find new ways to grow the old ones better. He could teach the others scientific farming techniques, and there could be a school where he could teach their children how to read and write.

And he saw a wife, smiling proudly at the great things he did, eager to make him comfortable after a long day. Ready to snuggle into his embrace. He saw her eyes and her lips.

Charles knew he was flirting with the same dream that had drawn Rad to give up his very identity, but this was all just imagination, wasn't it? Couldn't he dream a little happiness every once in a while?

Charles didn't notice the rope go slack. When it jerked hard, he was feet high in an instant, then tumbling over hard rock. He felt the cool pain of a blood scrape on his arm.

"Aaagghh! Not again, you don't!"

When he regained his feet, there was no Kimmer to be seen.

...

Charles pulled up the rope. The end was a ragged cut. *The runt picked up a rock, somehow, and cut through it.*

He had to find him. This time, however, there were no open fields. He had vanished into the jumble of rock and bush and tree.

Charles looked in all directions, but could see no trace of him. He jumped and landed on top of a large boulder. Looking down, he might have a better chance.

The land was hilly, which meant lots of trapped water. He could see a couple of swampy patches in one direction. A heavy brush patch extended in another.

There—a bit of motion, and he could see him. He had been invisible in those raggedy clothes as long as he held still.

Charles leaped, twisting in the air so that he would land prepared to jump again. The Kimmer made a dash in the direction of a field of boulders as high as he was. Charles followed quickly behind him.

He lost him. Charles paused, waiting for him to betray his position again.

He's a magician. He could see how the Kimmer could live in the forest and never be seen. They were good at hiding.

He slipped free of the fullpack, ready to move quickly.

There! It was out of the corner of his eye, just a twitch. This time, Charles pretended that he hadn't seen. Slowly, he turned half way in the boy's direction—he kept him in sight without ever staring directly at him. The instant he felt discovered, the boy would bolt again.

He reached into the pack until he felt the hard metal of the gun in its sleeve. He fished it slowly out. He got it ready, with slow motions. It was like the goose hunt all over again, except he was the one in plain view, and his target was concealed.

Ready. He brought it up and aimed.

As expected, the boy jumped up from his hiding place in a blur of energy. Charles hesitated just enough to be sure of his direction, and then fired.

"Ahhh!" cried the Kimmer as he tumbled. Charles set the air rifle down and jumped in pursuit.

With a pellet in his leg, the boy wasn't quick or smooth. Charles caught him easily. He fought with the fast arms, until he had them trapped again.

"Be still!"

When the boy kept it up, Charles slapped him on the blooded thigh. He shrieked in pain.

"Now be still!"

Charles slung the boy over his shoulder and carried him back to where he had left the pack. When he started to struggle again, Charles raised his hand and threatened to hit the wound. The boy stopped.

He re-tied the boy's hands and then checked the leg.

"What is your name?"

There was no answer.

Charles pulled out his knife. "Tell me your name!" He splashed a little water on the blood and poked it with the tip of his blade. The shriek of pain echoed against the rocks. With a little tug of resistance as the pellet edged through the centimeter of flesh, it came free.

Charles calmly let the blood flow freely as he dug through his pack. He fished through the collection of clothing, food and other supplies until he spotted just the right thing, a wad of raw cotton. He slapped the cotton onto the ooze of blood and then roughly forced the boy's bound hands down on top of it.

"Hold that in place and press hard or you will bleed to death." It was a little exaggeration, but he was secretly pleased to see the boy do exactly as he was told. *Ah ha! I knew you understood me.*

Charles rinsed the blood from his own fingers and then fished out some trail biscuit. He flashed the blade a little theatrically as he repeated, "Now, tell me your name."

Darkwind

"Darkwind." The boy winced. "I am called Darkwind."

Charles laughed, "How did you get a name like that?" He watched out a corner of his eye as the white cotton gradually turned red.

Darkwind's face was a mask of hatred. Charles could see the muscles of his jaw work. He reached over and pushed the boy's hands harder down on the wound.

"Press hard! Now answer me."

Darkwind paled under the pain, and he answered, "Sky-beast, I will feed your guts to the Black Ones!"

Charles smiled. "That's better. It looks like the bleeding will stop in a minute. Now answer me, or I'll have to open another hole!" He chipped another chunk of the biscuit free with his blade, and stuck it in his mouth to moisten.

Darkwind was weakening from the pain and the exhaustion of the chase. He answered sullenly, "My father named me."

"Your father has a funny sense of humor. What did your mother have to say about it?"

Darkwind closed his eyes and leaned back against a flat rock. His hands came off the red patch of cotton, but when there didn't appear to be any seepage, Charles ignored it.

"My mother was gone," he whispered, "in the darkwind. My father called it an omen."

As if the wind heard its name, there came a gust of air. There was only an hour or so before it would be too windy to travel, but Charles decided to wait a little longer before they moved. He regretted bringing up Dark-wind's memories. He had some of his own that he would rather stay buried.

...

The guard who pointed out his route from the south rim claimed that a man with a well-adjusted pack and a quick step could travel the 200 kloms from Stampz to Zeno in one day. Charles estimated they had traveled less than a quarter of that distance by the time they had settled in behind a boulder the size of a house to wait out the darkwind.

The lee of the rock was not the best shelter. They would still be pelted by the gravel that got caught in the wind shadow's eddies. Charles offered a blanket to the boy to hide his face from the dust. The boy took it, but with no trace of gratitude.

When the wind calmed, they shook themselves out of the dirt and headed on just a bit into the deep.

Charles watched how the boy moved and decided not to push it. He would need a little more time to heal.

They sheltered behind another boulder, but with the poor lighting of earthlight behind clouds, the best Charles could do was to make sure that there were woods to the dawn side of them. At least that would cut down on the blown dirt and dust of the dawnwind.

Charles found it hard to sleep. Even with the boy's wrists tied to a tree and with a hurt leg, he was a worry.

Darkwind was going to make the overland trek to Condorcet impossibly slow for as long as Charles decided to keep him. He itched to move on. *I could travel in this light. If it were just me, I could outrun most troubles.*

There were hostile Kimmer all through this land. How could he keep the young Kimmer on a leash without drawing them down on him?

Perhaps it would be best to make friends with the boy. He obviously knew how to move in the woods and to make himself nearly invisible.

Charles twisted his mouth into a rueful grin. *Good move to have shot him, tied him up like a dog, threatened him with a knife, and called him names. It ought to be a noon sail to make friends with him now.*

He leaned over to look at where the boy slept.

There was nothing but a loose rope. His fullpack was open and things were scattered over the ground.

Darkwind had gotten loose and robbed him silently while his back was turned!

Charles wrenched open the fullpack. The pumpgun and the impulse rifle were gone.

He peered into the darkness. *There!* He picked up the sleeve that had protected the impulse gun.

He moved in that direction, deeper into the woods. A few paces later, he found the wrapped package that contained the court dress. A hundred steps later, one of the new tailored shirts was caught in the brambles, the cloth torn.

Charles snorted his breaths, anger in his arms. *I'll run him into the ground and teach him what I do with a thief!*

He headed swiftly down the game path, confident that he would have his hands on his scrawny neck any instant.

The path dropped so abruptly that he had to twist to land upright. He put his hand to a tree to steady himself.

His nose caught the scent before his ears reverberated with the growl. *Bear!*

The cloud cap overhead took the bright earthlight and diffused it. As thin as the clouds were, he could see some detail through the break in the trees.

Darkwind was climbing a huge, outsized oak tree. At its base was a jumble of objects he had dropped. With one rear foot in their midst, a monster of a bear stretched twice or three times the boy's height up the tree. A claw swatted and tore bark loose just underneath the boy's retreating feet.

. . .

"Climb!" Charles shouted, conscious that he risked attracting the bear's attention.

Darkwind showed no signs of hearing him; he was too busy climbing as fast as he could. The bear, the largest animal Charles had ever seen, turned his snout in his direction for an instant, then turned back to his real interest. He roared at the boy, and then began to climb.

Paws larger than Darkwind's head found a secure grip on the side branches, and the bear started up.

Darkwind yelled wordlessly in terror and reached for higher branches.

Charles fumbled at his belt. He had his knife, but it was nothing compared to the claws on the beast. *If I only had the impulse gun.* He looked again at the boy. Darkwind was carrying nothing. *Had he dropped it?*

Charles looked back up and felt a sinking feeling. The bear was gaining. It was a heavy animal, but it was well equipped to the task. The massive tree was an easy ladder.

The boy was going to lose the race.

"Darkwind! Take the side branch. The bear is too heavy."

He dashed to the pile of goods at the base of the tree. Much of his food was flattened by the bear's foot, but he only took time to move the stuff in search of the guns. The smell of bear was overpowering. It reminded him of the burn ointment he was no longer using.

Up above, the bear was a rippling mass of fur, splitting the night silence with its growls. It was climbing out on the limb after Darkwind.

What did you do to make him so mad at you? But he knew the question was nonsense. Anything could make a bear angry.

"Darkwind! Where are the guns?"

Above, the boy was too busy to answer. Twenty meters up, the branch was bending under the weight of the bear. Darkwind could no longer climb. He was doing his best just to hold on to the bouncing, swaying branch.

Charles turned his eyes back to the ground. Darkwind hadn't dropped them at the tree. They must have fallen out earlier.

He started back, retracing the path. *Where did the idiot boy drop them? If the bear eats him, it will be justice.*

The light dimmed a little, and he was forced to move slowly—every branch looked like a rifle.

Heavy bear scent stopped him. A rock overhang had been the bear's den. The ground was churned. *It must be here.* He circled the spot, looking carefully.

And there, an extra branch in a thorny bush, was the pumpgun. He grabbed it, and several pellets rattled in the reservoir. He wasted another few seconds looking for the impulse gun before he dashed back to the tree.

He looked up and laughed. The branch was bending and bouncing. Darkwind was a bundle of terror, a knot of rags at the end.

The bear had slowed its progress. Its growls were different now, laced with less anger and more uncertainty. Only the head down, frozen boy, almost in its reach kept him moving.

Charles pumped. The shot was at a moving target and a long way uphill in bad light. He took a deep breath to flush the tension out of his chest. He braced the stock against another tree and pulled on the trigger.

With a *pfft*, the pellet zipped up and chipped bark right in front of the bear's nose. Splinters hit its face. A yelp echoed from above, and the bear grabbed air, trying to move.

Charles pumped rapidly for a second shot, but he never got the chance. Backing up the branch, the bear slipped, and for five long seconds, it fell.

The bear flailed and twisted, but the long drop was inevitable, punctuated with the crack of branch after branch that had little chance of slowing the bear's fall.

The screams of Darkwind, riding the swinging tip of the tree limb high in the sky, did little more than annoy the shaken beast.

Charles edged back into the trees as the great animal shook its head unsteadily and lumbered off, breaking any tree careless enough to get in its way.

...

Charles waited a moment to be sure that the bear had indeed left, and to let his heart stop pounding. Darkwind was still screaming, the pitch of his wail rising and falling as the branch swung back and forth.

Charles turned his attention to his scattered belongings. The fall hadn't killed the bear, and unless he was particularly unlucky, a fall wouldn't kill Darkwind.

If he is wise, he will just stay up there!

The cloud cover thinned, earthlight giving edges to the shadows. It wasn't a pretty sight. The bear's foot had ground the better half of his food supply into the mud. His ax had a broken handle. Some clothes were likewise ground into the dirt.

He made a pile, collecting whatever wasn't a total loss, and with one muddy shirt, made a makeshift bundle to carry it.

The backtrack along the path, with the better light, revealed things he had missed: his second knife, a coil of snare wire, his extra tinderbox, and finally, near the bear's den, the impulse gun.

He shook with relief when he took it into his hands and it came alive under his touch. Weariness washed through him, and he realized just how much he had been running on fear.

The bear scent was strong, so he moved on, back to the original campsite, and began the process of cleaning and repacking.

In general, the things that had been specially packed like the court dress and the papers had suffered little more than surface dirt. The bag of stamped gold coins hadn't even been removed from the pack.

Food would be a real problem. Clothing would take extra time for cleaning and mending. Some things, like the scrap of cloth that had his last message from Rad, were nowhere to be seen.

Hefting the pack, he made one final trip along the game trail to see if he could find anything else.

By the time he arrived at the huge oak tree, he was frustrated by his losses, and the anger was growing as he watched Darkwind make his way back down the tree.

Once his feet landed on the ground, Charles said, "I knew Kimmer were killers. I didn't know that they were thieves, as well."

Darkwind responded, "You killed my father. I will kill you!" The boy stood up straight.

Charles flashed back to a memory of black birds on the canyon floor, the spinning form in a white sailsuit falling past him, hitting the cliff face, the lone arm torn free by the cannon's explosion.

He had killed many. Was one of them this boy's father? How many other boys hated him with good cause?

Charles faced him head on, and asked, "Who was your father? Where did he die?"

He heard an echo in the back of his mind. Someone had asked him those very same words, years ago. He couldn't remember when.

The boy's fists were balled tightly, and his words were hoarse, "White-talon was my father. You burned him at the house-of-death. I know it was you. They gave you the slave."

Charles felt relief. He shook his head. "I have fought Kimmer. I have killed Kimmer. But that day, I did not fight, I did not kill."

The boy's silence was a judgment of unbelief.

"I would never burn anyone. My father died in a blaze, as did my mother. Everyone in the world that I called kin, except my brother, died in that fire.

"My weapons are powerful. I had no need to burn anyone. See this!"

He pulled the impulse gun to firing position and adjusted the spread. He triggered the gun and ripped off a branch of the oak the thickness of a man's chest.

Darkwind jumped in terror as fragments of wood splinters rained down all around. The anger in his face was replaced by openmouthed awe.

Charles barked, "I had no need to burn anyone! I would never burn anyone! I demanded you as my slave because I pitied you as I pitied myself after I lost my parents to the flame.

"It was a mistake. I want no slave. I want no thief! You can stay until after the dawnwind, but then you go!"

Charles turned his back on the boy and headed back to camp.

After a moment, Darkwind followed.

Tumbletrees

The dawnwind peaked with a sustained howl that shifted into a pure tone like one of the large horns they blew on festival days. Somewhere there was a hole in the rocks that was catching the wind just right.

Charles tugged his hand free of the pack, where he had entwined himself into the straps. If anything had moved, he would have been alerted. His other hand had spent the night curled around the hilt of his knife. No more theft. The boy had been warned.

Charles looked around, but there was no sign of him. He was certain Darkwind spent the night nearby, but he'd remained out of sight.

Sleep had come hard and fast, and he was honestly surprised that he'd slept through the still. He must have worn himself out more than he'd thought.

His stomach complained, but he had to ration his remaining food. *Get moving. There could be Kimmer around.* He was still too close to Stampz.

On his own, he made good time. The rhythm of his preferred gliding step made it easy to drift into the same dreamy world where he spent many a day loading and unloading endless bales of cargo.

The trail was well marked by feet that had gone before, although he suspected there were more four- than two-footed travelers making use of the path.

There were signs of erosion, the beginnings of a permanent watershed. His father said that Earth was all watershed. After millions of years, there was no place to be found that wasn't sloping downhill. Charles found the idea intellectually sound, but it didn't feel right.

Luna still had plenty of places where rainwater, once fallen, stayed in the one place until it settled down into the soil or evaporated into the air. Several hundred years, the age of the atmosphere on Luna, was not enough to break through the jumbled terrain that had done well enough on its own before weather had come.

But drainage was coming. The Gaussland trail was one result. Riverbeds made smooth roadways, and the trail was just human-made tracery along three rivers.

The wagon train had started out from Gartner on the first day of the year, heading up the Spirit River, keeping more or less in its narrow valley until they had to make the rough way over Dunsen's Pass.

The Spanish River valley had been a wider and easier trail as they had come down the eastern branch to Stampz.

The footpath he now walked would soon join the main trail again as it turned up the south branch of the Spanish. Somewhere up ahead was the head of that branch, and beyond Barnes' Pass, the Peach River was born.

The Peach was the longest of the three, and it would guide travelers all the way to Hubble.

His crude map indicated that he had to leave the Peach to make his way to Condorcet.

It was there that he had to do his real job—persuade the governor to help faraway Stampz.

He wondered just how important Duke James was in the politics of Hercules. He was the nephew of Sheb. That had to count for something. But why had he been sent to rule such a remote location?

The Hercules Empire was a two-lobed crescent. Its center of power was the twin craters of Hercules and Atlas, major ports on the Frigid Sea. Clustered around them were the major centers of the Empire, such as Franklin and Hooke, where much of the wealth was concentrated.

But Hercules ruled the waves with the best navy in the world. In the past three hundred years, there had been many clashes between Hercules and the land to the south, the Serenite Landrule.

It had been the first Sheb who had started that naval dominance by sailing down to the Crisium Sea and settling the major port city of Condorcet on the southern shore.

With settlements to the south of Serenity, and a naval presence to the west, it appeared that only expansion to the east was possible for that nation.

But there, the land itself had proved unkind. There were no river valleys, no convenient passes to allow easy travel east.

So, it fell to the richer and more populated Hercules to discover the Gaussland trail and begin the process of settling the eastern lands.

Condorcet became the center of power in the south. While shipments overland could be made, it was still far cheaper and quicker to send cargo ships between the northern lands and the southern capital.

Perhaps, thought Charles, being the nephew of the Emperor would mean more at the provincial capital than it would in Hercules itself. He could feel that there were currents in play here that he did not understand.

Once again, he wished the duke would be more open. Just a little more background would go a long way.

...

His path wound up a long rise, and as he reached the top, he paused. *Smoke.* He saw a curl of smoke in the distance. Just beyond there, the land turned a darker green. It had to be the river valley.

Even though he knew that a Kimmer ambush would not announce itself with a fire, he made extra sure that his impulse gun was readily at hand.

He launched down the trail with renewed enthusiasm. Perhaps it was some other traveler, maybe even a remnant of the wagon train. If so, he might be able to negotiate a little extra food. Not having breakfast was beginning to catch up with him.

There was also the chance to talk to someone. He'd been on the trail only a day, and already, he was bored with his own company. It was a strange feeling. He was used to finding great comfort in hiding out in the back of their room just to get away from the babble of Port Gartner's mass of people.

If truth be told, he missed Rad. His brother had always been there: to talk to, to fight, to laugh with. He had no one now, and he would have no one for a long time to come.

This junction of trails was popular, it seemed. There were many stumps, chopped, not gnawed to a point as was usual in beaver country. Off to one side were the remnants of a rain shelter.

The trail turned through a grove of short fat trees, and he spotted the fire.

Darkwind was sitting contentedly on a rock, tending a roasting rabbit spitted on a long curved stick.

The Kimmer boy looked up as he arrived, and gestured an invitation, "Food."

Charles bounced slowly to a stop. Any residual anger drained away as the sweet smell of the cooked meat soaked into him.

I ought to keep on going.

His stomach growled loudly, and the boy restrained himself from laughing.

Charles stomach won.

...

Greetings to the Duke of Stamps Reporting on the Journey to Condorcet, written in the Still of 2 Feb.

Your instructions were to write of things trivial, or I would not have penned a report at this time, as the journey is happening with no great incident. As you are aware, I am traveling with the Kimmer boy who was spared at the battle on the day of our first meeting. While the original intent may have been to have him assist with carrying my load, he has proved more useful as a guide to the lands I am now visiting for the first time.

To state a point that I have not mentioned before, the Kimmer are both vocal and proficient in the common language with no more than an odd tonal quality to their accent to distinguish their speech from that heard in your halls. The boy's name is Darkwind, and while still avowedly the enemy of Stampz and all "Sky-Beasts", as he denotes us, he appears willing to guide me for some days along my travel. It is not my intention to keep him as a slave for longer than that.

My hope is that having a Kimmer, apparently unbound and accompanying me of his own free will, may aid my chances in territories where a man traveling alone would have reason to fear attack by the forest natives.

In addition, he has proved useful in supplementing my food supplies, a necessity prompted by an unfortunate encounter with a bear that depleted my original stocks.

My current position is northeast of Zeno, due to my choice of the eastern branch of the Gaussland Trail at this point. It is my hope that the direct path will speed me on my way since I have no real need to stop at any settlement at this time in my journey.

My wishes for your continual good health.

Charles Fasail, Alpine.

. . .

Charles rolled the vellum back up.

"What is that?" asked Darkwind.

Charles paused, "What?" He had been thinking about Zeno. The wagon train was likely stopped there for repairs and resupply. He did not want to meet Rad again. Not yet. And it was likely Darkwind would leave for good if he approached too closely to a settlement.

"In your hand. What is that thing in your hand?" Darkwind had started to imitate his own habit of talking slowly and precisely when he didn't think he was being understood.

Charles looked at the roll. "This is a report I am making—a letter to the Duke of Stampz."

"It looks like a skin."

"Well, it is a skin."

"Then why did you call it a report?"

"No," *There is no way I can explain this.* "I am sending a message to the man who sent me on this journey."

Darkwind looked down at the roll. He shook his head, "I don't understand this magic."

Charles laughed, "It isn't magic. I just put marks on the skin, and then when I pass a traveler heading back the way we came, I will hand the skin to him, and he will hand it to the duke."

Darkwind looked unimpressed. "Oh. I understand marks. I thought this was part of your magic."

Charles felt affronted. "Not magic, but writing. Writing is more important than any magic you can imagine."

The boy cocked his head, as if to say, *"I won't say anything, but you are crazy."*

Charles asked, "Would you like to see what I have done?" He nodded.

Darkwind moved over to look at the writing by the glow of the fire. He took one look at the report and started laughing.

"What's so funny?" Charles rolled it back up.

"Oh, I thought you had marks on the skin. That's nothing but hacking."

Charles was getting angry. People may have forced him to hide his writing before, but he had never been forced to listen to a half-grown boy laugh at it.

"I don't think you know what writing is supposed to look like."

Darkwind looked at him with a sideways smile. "My father taught me tree-marks. You can't tell me that little hacking looks like anything."

"Of course I can. Just because you can't read, doesn't mean it's not real."

"Prove it."

Charles reminded himself that he shouldn't strangle the boy. If he hit him, he would fly off to the next crater. *Reason with him.*

"Okay, I will read part of it. Listen: 'Greetings to the Duke of Stamps Reporting on the Journey to Condorcet, written in the Still of 2 Feb.'" He moved his finger under the lines, indicating each word as he spoke it.

"Believe me now?"

"You could have made it up."

"No. See this word here. I said 'the'. Here is another one right here, almost exactly the same, and I said 'the' again."

"That's three words, not one."

"No, just one. There are three letters in that word."

Darkwind shook his head, "That's crazy. A letter is a skin, you said so."

Charles sighed. "No. There are two kinds of letters. A letter is a message. But it can also be one part of a word."

Darkwind laughed, "A letter is made of words which is made of letters?"

"That's right."

"Sky beasts are crazy!"

Charles re-rolled the report. "I suppose your 'tree-marks' are better?"

"Sure. The Four Families ... I mean the Kimmer have used them forever."

Charles let the slip pass, "Okay, prove it to me."

Darkwind was up on his feet quickly. He moved to the nearest tree and pulled out a knife. With quick sure cuts, he carved a half dozen figures into the bark.

Charles moved closer. At first glance, he would have ignored the column of marks as the work of animals, like the bear's marking a tree to indicate his dominance, or the marks of a deer's antlers. But now that he could see them fresh, as the work of a man, even a twelve year old man, he could see the intelligence there.

"What does it say?"

Darkwind smiled, "It says 'Here Darkwind and Treekiller camped.'"

Charles was amused, "'Treekiller'? Is that what you call me?"

"Yes. I can't say this 'Charles'," mangling the word, "Your names are like your hacking, they don't mean anything."

"They mean a lot more than you can imagine. You say you want to learn my magic? Well, you will have to learn my writing. My magic is all cloaked in this writing.

"But I want to know more. I want to know your tree-marks. Teach me, and I will teach you. Agreed?"

Darkwind thought a moment and then nodded and grasped Charles by the forearm. Charles's hand likewise closed on the thin forearm of the boy.

What am I getting myself into? What are the Four Families? And where did he get that knife?

...

The trail was starting to turn south. Every time their trail began to follow a watercourse, Charles felt excitement that it might be the source of the Peach. Twice he was disappointed as the trickles led to local, dead-end swamps.

The third didn't look any better than the ones before, but he knew the Peach River must be soon. Charles paced easily, but it was getting late. He had to fight the impulse to press on for another hour. The winds were already picking up and he worried about finding shelter in this barren, flat part of the land.

Darkwind paced easily beside him, not showing a care in the world. It was unnerving how easily they had changed from antagonists to traveling companions. Charles did not make friends easily. He liked the little rat, and the hints of Kimmer culture the boy let slip nagged at him.

Darkwind chose that instant to skid raggedly to a halt. Charles pulled around in a curve and stared back at him. The boy was pointing to the west and shouting something he couldn't make out. He turned in that direction and searched the horizon. There did appear to be something moving off in the upwind direction. Several things.

He moved back to Darkwind. "Green Demons!" he was shouting.

Charles took another look. The twenty or so objects were getting much closer now. They looked for all the world like big, fat trees rolling toward them. *Sometimes natural adaptation is not enough to tame a totally dead world.* His father's words echoed in his head, and he motioned to Darkwind, "Come on! We must find shelter."

The terrain was fairly smooth, unfortunately. There was only the nearby wash, where rainfall runoff had carved a shallow trench in the land. They raced for it.

The bank was steep enough in some places to lie prone, but it was shallow. Each had to find a spot, there weren't any gaps deep enough to shelter both of them.

The task of making vast stretches of the land fertile, especially when essential trace elements are lacking in the soils, has inspired some innovative plants and animals created by the Biogenetic field team that was active on Luna at the time of the Plague.

Tumbletrees! Charles remembered their name.

These giant relatives of the Earth-native tumbleweeds came racing, bouncing and crashing across the land, pushed by the growing wind. By now, Charles could spot the hand-sized thorns that covered all the branches. He ducked his head and shifted lower into the mud, facing down into the sticky slime. They were moving far too fast to dodge, and any animal would be shredded if caught.

The crashing of the branches grew louder, and then there was a flash or darkness and a sting of pain. Darkwind howled.

Charles waited a long extra minute before he raised his head. His first glance was upwind—no more were coming.

Darkwind was still down in the mud. Charles moved to his side. Blood was dripping from a long cut across the boy's back. A thorn had sliced the leather as clean as a razor.

"Stay put."

"I'm going to die!"

"No, you aren't. Your leathers saved you."

Darkwind struggled to get to his feet, but Charles put his knee on his legs and trapped him, while he opened his pack and dug out the last of the burn ointment and the shirt that he had repaired just the night before.

He cut a strip from the bottom of the shirt, wincing at the sound of the rip as he pulled it free.

The cut wasn't deep.

"Quit crying. You aren't a baby." He let the cut bleed on its own. Nothing he could do would get it any cleaner than the blood's own outflow.

"The demons have me. They will eat my soul."

"No, I am using an Alpine spell right now that will protect you." Charles hated the idea of magic, but it seemed the only way to get some ideas into the savage.

When the blood started to coagulate, he smeared the ointment along the wound and had the boy stand up and strip off his sliced vest and the ragged shirt. He bound the clean cotton around his chest.

"We will need to get out of the wind. Get dressed and let's get moving."

Darkwind whimpered when he put his clothes back on over the bandaged cut, but they were quickly ready to go.

Charles jogged up to the nearest rise. There was a field of rocks nearby to the east. The pair headed there quickly as the light deepened in color.

The wind was starting to fill with sand before they made it. One boulder was large enough, so they ducked behind it.

"Ahh!" Darkwind shrieked, and started to run.

Charles grabbed his arm. Through the worsening visibility, he made out the source of the boy's panic.

A tumbletree was wedged between the large rock and its nearest neighbor. The branches thrashed in the wind. Thorns, as if knives on in a hundred hands, jabbed at them.

"Stay here!" Charles yelled at the boy over the rushing noise of the wind. "It can't reach us here. Just stay put."

He forced the boy down and sat beside him, a few feet outside the range of the thrashing. It was a strange sight to see, but he forced himself to be calm. He had to keep Darkwind from panicking and running out into the wind.

One solution to the problem of infertile areas was the tumbletree. A tree was engineered to tap deep into the soil and deposit several kinds of trace elements into its own trunk and stems. When it matured, the trunk was designed to snap off at the base in a high wind. Its round shape let it roll in the winds.

It was built with thorns to catch up any other loose animals or plants in its way—a cruel, but efficient way to have the winds move the nutrients from the rich areas to the poorer.

The Biogenetic team planted many of these trees at the fringes of the dead areas, knowing that over time, these trees would roll into the sterile areas and be snagged by rocks. As they decayed, they would make patches of fertility where new life would grow.

Charles watched the flailing thorns. Some, indeed held impaled branches and leaves. There was even a decayed mass of what might have been a rabbit.

If Darkwind had not spotted their approach, he might be pinned like a specimen to the branches of a rolling tree, heading for some bleak destiny as food for mushrooms.

"Treekiller!" Darkwind was shivering beside him. The boy was frantic with fear.

Charles nodded to himself. He needed to do it. He reached into his pack, where the impulse gun was quick to reach. He pulled it out, setting the controls. A quick glance at the position of the backbeam, and he triggered it.

The tumble tree lifted, as if by a huge hand, and broke into a half dozen pieces. They were suspended in the air for a long clear second, and then the darkwind took them away as if they had never been.

He put his arm around the boy and waited until he calmed down. Darkwind was asleep before the long twilight was done.

Death Pool

Greetings to the Duke of Stamps Reporting on the Journey to Condorcet, written in the Still of 4 Feb.

You mentioned in one of our discussions that you had an interest in settlements outside the bounds of a traditional crater community. I have been on watch for signs of such settlements, and I have met with mixed success.

Now that we have turned south and are following the Peach River, several such communities have appeared. They seem to share several common features, among which are close proximity to the water, direct access to the trail itself, and most importantly, good natural wind protection. Such protection is usually in the form of mountains, although it is rare to have a good mountain to both the east and west of the settlement. Often, the weaker side is protected by large boulders, or in one case, by a thick grove of trees.

But I cannot tell you much more than that as yet, because every one of these small farms and buildings are deserted.

One farm showed clear signs of attack, with the wooden buildings having been burned to the ground. The others seemed intact, but the farmers had left in a hurry. One farm had an extensive set of ditches to carry water from the river to fields scattered among a cluster of small craters. The farm had been abandoned with water running into some fields, flooding them badly. The place must have been deserted for at least three days.

Alpine Duty

> *My Kimmer guide has shown no sign of surprise at the state of the settlements. Whether this is from general ignorance or his prior knowledge is unknown.*
> *Charles Fasail, Alpine.*

...

Charles put away his writing things, frowning into the darkness.

This is getting harder. Why didn't I tell the duke about the tree-marks? I was thinking about it. Why didn't I put it down in ink? That is important information.

He looked at Darkwind, sleeping comfortably on the rocky ground. The boy had been an enigma as they had explored the deserted farmland. He had avoided any buildings by a dozen meters whenever Charles had gone in to check for any inhabitants. In contrast, the irrigation system had puzzled and intrigued the boy. Charles once again appeared magical when he moved the levers that opened the sluice gate to release water from a flooded area.

For all the Kimmer's native intelligence, it was channeled exclusively into the life of a forest savage. Machines and buildings were things to be avoided.

Charles frowned again as he tried to get his mind around a culture that had perfected the sailsuit, and yet could not bring itself to build as much as a lean-to to keep off the rain.

He's sound asleep. I need to look at that knife.

Charles got down on his knees and peered close at the knife secured in a thong at the boy's waist. *Horn hilt—some kind of carving. A tree-mark? Blade looks like hammered iron. Rust all over it.*

It was clearly Kimmer manufacture. Placer iron, heated and beaten into a blade, but without any of the finished look of a Herc knife. Only the hilt showed any sign of craftsmanship.

How had the boy kept the knife hidden from the Stampz guards? Or did he? He was gone for hours after the bear attack. Could he have located a stash of Kimmer goods during that time?

Off in the distance, there was the sharp sound of a branch snapping.

Darkwind's hand reached for his knife, and he was half up, all in less than a breath. Charles leaned back.

For a handful of breaths, the boy crouched motionless, and Charles got the impression that his reaction was pure instinct.

"Darkwind?" he asked quietly.

The boy didn't respond, but in another moment, he had curled back down, and was asleep again.

...

Darkwind vanished sometime during the morning march. Charles looked behind him and the boy was nowhere to be seen.

He slowed to a stop and waited, but there was no sign of the Kimmer. After a few more minutes, he climbed the nearest hill, but the trail was empty.

He's a native to these forests. He has a knife. I'm not going to wait for him.

He remembered the last time the boy had vanished. He was probably up ahead, well fed and happy.

Charles got back on the trail and picked up speed. He felt like running. He felt like outrunning the gloom that had been gathering around him since he started this trip.

The trail was still rough wagon ruts, worse now that they were following the river. Every gap in the hills had a stream bed, some with water still flowing from the morning's rain. As he picked up speed, he focused his attention on finding the right footfalls to push him ahead without tripping him up.

He ran hard for an hour, before he started glancing more and more at the cool water of the Peach River. It had been more than a quad since he'd last bathed, and the sweat was starting to give rise to some chafing.

Charles slowed back to march pace. No sense in wearing himself out. It was still a long trail to Condorcet.

The river started widening. At first, it barely caught his attention. In this irregular terrain, it was common for small ponds to form wherever the water was blocked by old ridges and rises.

But as an hour passed, and the lake kept getting larger, he started worrying.

Surely, this is the Peach? It would be horrible to have wasted days on a false trail.

No. This has to be the one. Straight south, and the wagon ruts aren't just my imagination.

But very quickly, the shoreline bent to the east. He jumped atop a large rock and surveyed the land.

The road split here. One path headed south and had the deeper ruts. The other traced the lip of a shallow crater. The water had filled it nearly to the brim. As far as he could see, there was no spillover. The river stopped here.

...

The eastward trail ran on top of a large natural dam.

Where does this trail lead? He had not heard it mentioned. *Are there more settlements to the east?* If so, they were not, properly, parts of the Empire. The maps he had seen in the duke's chamber did not cover that direction. He could feel a little tug to go east himself. In spite of all the glowing reports of the lands of Gauss, he could feel in his heart that these lands were already owned. Some minor noble was in charge of every cratered settlement along the trail. What must it feel like to be totally free of the Empire? What must it feel like to be your own master, in every sense?

Charles yielded to an impulse and decided to scout out the eastern trail a little before heading on farther south on the main road.

Farther down the trail, the east road dipped to a wide flat area that was washed clean of any hint of soil. *This must be covered in water when the rains are heavy.* He was a little surprised that there wasn't any water over the spillway.

I wonder if it gets high enough to stop a wagon train? Once past the rim, the land sloped away steeply. He could imagine a wagon being swept away to destruction easy enough.

But for now, it looked as if the trail no longer followed the river. If he was going to swim, this was as good a place as any.

He put his pack out in the open on the flat rocks—there was no one around to steal it. He added his shoes and his leather vest to the pile. No sense in getting that stuff wet. The rest of the clothes he wore could do with a little rinse, so he kept them on as he waded the short couple of steps off the rocks until the water was deep enough to swim.

I must be getting old. The water felt colder than it did when he was a kid on Alp and jumped into any passing stream he could find.

The clothes slowed him down a little, but he quickly dropped into an easy sidestroke, enjoying the clear water over his face, rinsing the trail dirt and sweat away in no time at all.

"Treekiller!" He heard a boy's voice.

Charles stopped and treaded water, rotating until he could see Darkwind on the shore. He had come farther out than he had thought. The little figure was waving excitedly.

"Come on in!"

"... pool ... out ..." Darkwind called, but the splash of the water drowned out the words.

"What did you say?" he called back.

Darkwind was jumping side to side even harder. He made each word a shout, "Death. Pool. Get. Out."

Charles suddenly realized that even as he had stopped to talk to Darkwind, he had drifted even farther away from the rocks. There was a current here.

He felt a shock run up his spine and settle in his stomach. The water was pulling him away from shore!

He wasted no more thought on it. He started swimming a strong, hard stroke for shore.

He looked up once ever other breath, trying to keep his bearings. He had fought currents before, and he knew the hazard of losing your way and swimming toward the very danger you were trying to avoid.

Darkwind was his target, but the current was pushing him sideways, as well. He fought back, but he was soon much farther down the shore.

Forget Darkwind. Just get to the rocks.

He swam with a single-minded effort. Survive first. Think about it later.

His elbow struck a rock, and in spite of the numbness of his arm and the pain, he pulled hard and pushed himself up on the rocks like a large, exhausted frog.

He rested, trying to catch his breath, his legs still in the water but one hand firmly on dry rock. He could still feel the faint tug of the current on his feet. *How could I have missed that?*

Darkwind ran up, awkwardly carrying the pack that was larger than he was and his clothes. "Treekiller! I thought you would die. Why did you try to swim in the Death Pool?"

...

Charles stood and faced the lake. The water was relatively undisturbed so near the mid-day calm. But now that he knew what to look for, the whirlpool was clear to see. Across a span of about thirty meters, there was an evident dimple in the water. He watched as a bit of froth and a floating stick circled, closing ever closer to the center. And then they were gone.

That is why there is no overflow. The water has found another way out.

He felt a chill. It was something like the lava tube that had been his salvation during the Burn. Perhaps a crack in the rock that had eroded under the water's flow until it could take the whole flow of the Peach River.

I wonder how wide it is. Did bodies of the unlucky show up downstream, or did they stay wedged until they decayed and were swept away in pieces?

Charles took the pack from Darkwind and dug for dry clothes.

"I didn't know about the Death Pool. You should have been here to warn me."

The boy's face dropped from open friendliness to resentment in a flash. Charles put up a hand, "I'm sorry. I am glad for the warning. It was soon enough."

Charles burned to ask him where he had been, but now was not the time. He wanted Darkwind to stay, and it was a hard thing to keep his tongue from running him off. As much as he hated to admit it, there were too many things out here in the wild that city life had not prepared him for.

Charles told the boy so. "I do not have a Kimmer's skill in the forest. I am big. I am powerful. But it may be a warning word from you that will keep me alive."

Darkwind nodded, but said nothing while Charles dressed and secured his wet clothes to the outside of the pack so that they would dry.

Charles shared a bit of trail bread, and then they headed back toward the south road.

"I wonder where the eastern road goes."

Darkwind answered, "My grandfather has gone that way, along with most of his pack. Someday I will follow to tell my father's words."

"So, you do have family. Wouldn't it be better to go find them now? I lost my family at about your age, but I had an older brother to care for me."

Darkwind grinned, "But then you would have no one to warn you not to pick up snakes or put your hand in a beehive. No, I have time when I am older to find my father's father's pack. It is more important for now to learn the ways of magic."

Words

Travel soon became a matter of breaks, interspersed with the horrible monotony of putting one foot in front of the other.

Charles could not help looking forward to the next meal, the next rest break, the next reading lesson.

Darkwind seemed to do nothing but gripe when Charles attempted to teach him the alphabet.

"I've learned ten letters now, and not one of them means anything!"

"Whiner! I don't know anything but your deer mark and your bear mark. That does me a whole lot of good!"

"You just think you know the deer mark. You still make the sharp stroke like a moose. And still, two things are better than none."

Charles kicked a flat spot on the ground, "Oh, no you don't. You have ten perfectly good letters. You can make a hundred words from that!"

"Prove it!"

"Okay I will!" He took the stick from Darkwind and started writing. *A I DAD BAD CAD BID* … Saying the words as he wrote them. He stalled out at 42.

"That's not a hundred!"

"It's better than two!"

"It's not a hundred. You said a hundred."

Charles was about to retort, when Darkwind abruptly turned to face the south.

Charles looked in that direction too. There was a dust cloud, a small one, just visible over the horizon. He looked back, but Darkwind had vanished.

"HIDE! That makes 43!" He shouted to his vanished traveling companion.

Charles wrote it down with the others. He packed up the loose items from his pack and hefted it over his shoulder. He wasn't worried about other travelers on the road. In fact, he had been disappointed that the land was so deserted. But he did want to be ready for anything.

It was a single wagon, white with a few markings on it. Over the driver's box, there was a simple, stylized fish. Charles recognized it.

"Greetings, fellow traveler!" The speaker was a small white-haired old man with a loud, mellow voice.

"Hello. Where have you traveled from?"

The little man secured the brake lever, and was down from the driver's box like a Pyrenees monkey.

"I am Harriman T. Moore, most recently from Gauss. Which reminds me—have you and your companion had a really good meal lately?" The man had pulled out a water bag for his pair of oxen.

Charles was put off by the question. Had he seen Darkwind?

"Your little Kimmer friend is watching from the bushes over there." He indicated the direction with a casual turn of his head. "Would you two care to share a steak with me? I have extra supplies that were given me by the lovely couple who were my hosts in Gauss, and I will not be able to finish it all before it spoils."

Charles nodded. "I am Charles Fasail, most recently from Stampz. Your offer is very welcome. We have a fire." They had munched on hard trail bread just an hour earlier, but he could not turn down this offer. His stomach would make room.

Charles offered to unhook his team and stake them for grazing. Moore agreed and fell to the task of preparing the meal.

Soon, the little protected turn in the road was filled with an aroma that made Charles feel like he hadn't eaten in a month.

Harriman Moore presented Charles with his platter, still sizzling from the fire, and with a seasoning that forced him to concentrate on every bite.

Moore had prepared three platters, and set one aside on a flat rock.

He whispered to Charles, "Our little forest brother will be out in a moment to join us."

Charles asked, "Do you travel alone? The lands around here are deserted. There appears to be Kimmer trouble at least from here to Stampz."

The old man nodded, "And more trouble to the south. It is as bad as I have ever seen it. But to answer your question, yes, I travel alone. I will have made the trip from Hercules to Hubble and back again three times when I arrive at the city of my birth. I travel among the people and preach the Word."

"Christian? I recognize the symbol on your wagon," Charles offered between bites. He also suddenly realized that Darkwind was with them, working on his own platter.

"You recognize the ichthys? How wonderful! Are you a Christian, too?" The old face was animated, and tears came to his eyes easily. He reached for Charles's hand and held it for a brief squeeze.

Charles shook his head, "No, my people were followers of the Way as much as anyone else. I have been on my own for many years, and I haven't thought very deeply about religion at all."

The old man nodded, "You are not too far from the heart of most of this world. The Way of Earth has a strong pull on most of us living on this moon, with the long lost home planet shining above us at night.

"But how did you recognize the ichthys? I had thought marking my wagon thus was a private whimsy. I have been surprised by the number of people who have known what it represents."

Charles shrugged, "Well, I can't claim that I know all that much. My mother read me some Bible stories as a child, and I recognized the symbol from back then. I really don't know much more than David and Goliath and Noah and the Ark and Daniel in the Lions Den."

"All great stories of faith. Do you know any more? Have you memorized any verses? I must know if you have. It is my life's goal to collect the lost scriptures."

...

"What lost scriptures?"

Harriman Moore put aside his platter and looked up at the passing clouds. "The great holy book of Christianity is the Bible. As far as I know, the Bible that I received from the hands of my father was the only copy that existed on this world. I was not made a Christian by any man. I taught myself to read, and then the words themselves touched my heart and made me the man I have become.

"The words were too powerful to be mine alone. I shared them with people I knew in Hercules."

Harriman Moore looked off into the clouds. He was quiet for several minutes.

Charles felt a sadness from the man. He asked, "Did you lose your Bible?"

Moore nodded, "It was my pride. I thought that I alone was going to bring the Word to all the world."

He looked at Charles. "Do you know what a printing press is?"

Charles, startled, nodded.

"Good, then you will be able to understand my dream.

"In the early days, I was very well known among the people who had become Christian. There was a time when we made great progress in bringing the Word to people.

"I can remember great meetings, when a thousand people would come together and hear the good news of Jesus. Many were saved. There was a great sense of purpose—to bring the Word to the whole world.

"But we were the seed cast upon stony places. We had no depth of soil, and when the sunlight of trials shone on us, we withered."

He set aside his plate. He looked at Charles with a look of confession.

"There were three of us. The three preachers.

"John James Truman could move a tree to weep over its sins. He had a gift for the word that touched every man's secret guilt. To hear that man was to have the red-hot iron of you own conscience burn a hole straight into your heart.

"Then, he told the story. So simple and pure did he tell of Christ's sacrifice, that it was a balm of healing. You had to have it. John James led thousands to the arms of Jesus.

"Now, Kentucky Derby Dale was a man that people loved. He had red hair, a young man's enthusiasm, and a love of living. He won hearts. He could preach for hours, and people listened.

"He talked of the man Jesus. The Savior came alive in his words. After a meeting with Kentucky, your prayers were always so much more personal, talking to the Man you had just met.

"And I was the third. I had no great gifts with words like John James or Kentucky, but I had the spirit in me to preach. It was if God had spoken to me in a dream that I cannot remember. He had asked me to teach his Word, and I cannot do any less than that.

160

"Perhaps people could feel my urgency when I preached. At least, that is what John James told me before he died."

The old preacher shook his head slowly, "I do not understand the ways of our Lord. 'And we know that all things work together for good to them that love God, to them who are called according to his purpose.'

"There must have been divine purpose in the events. John James Truman died of the lung infection. There was a great funeral, and all the Christians in Atlas and Hercules mourned. But the numbers began to trickle away.

"You see, we three were the only source of the Word. I had the Bible, and in spite of repeated warnings from the scribes about its legality, I would read its words to the people.

"John James was a man gifted with a memory that never let go. He had once been a scribe, and had read my Bible for himself. But then, that once was enough. I remember him quoting the Word for twenty years, and never an error came from his lips.

"Kentucky was a newer convert of mine. He asked to study the Word, and he quickly acquired some skill at reading. He concentrated on the life of Jesus. Some parts of the scripture, he copied onto wooden tablets. But he was less well prepared on some of the other parts of the Bible.

"That is my guilt to bear. I should have prepared the boy better."

The old man looked over at Darkwind, working at a pace to quickly empty the platter, bones and all.

Charles asked, "What happened then?"

Moore grimaced, "Poor Kentucky. People loved him so. It was his snare. It became known that at least three women loved him more than they ought.

"Now, you are from the west coast. It is no great thing if a rich man takes more than one wife, but within our little community of believers, this was a great scandal. Kentucky made it worse. He refused to repent of his sins and claimed divine justification.

"It was my sad task to bring the Bible to the Elders of the Hercules church. There we searched the scriptures for two days. In the end, Kentucky Derby Dale left for the eastern lands. In all my travels, I have never heard of him. If he is still alive, I hope he found a place among people who love him still.

"But with the death of John James, and the exile of Kentucky, the great fire dwindled. I was the first preacher. Now I was the last."

...

Moore was obviously distressed by the telling. Charles was sorry for him, for the loss of his friends. He was also embarrassed to witness the display of emotion. It was not something he commonly had to deal with among the sweat gang.

Charles poured a cup of the hot berry tea that Darkwind had provided and handed it to the preacher. He accepted with a nod of thanks.

"In honesty, I was frightened. From the time I was younger than you, every dream I had for the future concerned the expansion of the Word. I was faced with my successes turning to failure. I suppose I panicked.

"I stopped trying to save people, and instead I poured my efforts into trying to make another Bible.

"I had lost any confidence in my own ability. It was the book that mattered. It was the words on the paper that brought people to Christ.

"I convinced the Elders that a great effort should be started to duplicate my copy of the Bible. We gathered all the people of our faith that could read and write. With a great will and good spirits, we began."

He shook his head, "But our people were not scribes. Copying text is hard, especially when we found that half of what we had written was wrong. Before we had finished with Genesis, people began to leave the effort." The old, tired eyes began to get moist again. "I had to watch as a fine old lady burst into tears and left our assembly when we determined that the tablet that she had contributed had too many errors to be added to the work. I should never have forced this task on the group.

"It was then, about ten years ago, that I had an inspiration that I thought would solve all of our problems."

He asked Charles, "Do you know anything about the Alpines—that race of wizards from over the Frigid Sea?"

The Library

Charles mouth quirked up, and he nodded. "I know a few things."

Harriman Moore nodded, "But much of what you have been told is probably false. I was granted a letter of visit. I journeyed to the great library of Aristotle. There I learned that mine was not the only Bible, and that mine was not the only effort through history to preserve the holy words. I learned many things. I was shocked to know that the Bible had not originally been written in the common language, but it had been translated from many tongues. I was allowed to read some of the books in the library, stories that told of great trials, like ours in Hercules, and great victories, in the long struggle for the survival of the Word.

"And I learned about the printing press, and about paper-making. I was inspired. If the ancients could print their own copies of the Bible, why couldn't we do the same?

"There were two men, Alpines, who came to share my idea. They were scholars, of course, and they found in the great books of Aristotle text describing the tools and machines that we had to make.

"It took over a year, while they struggled with the making of the press, and I struggled with the task of making a paper.

"It was a happy time, with my arms up to my elbows in pulped bamboo. I worried about my abandoned flock in Hercules, but the goal was in sight. Making the plates for the press took longer than copying the pages by hand, but when we were done, there could be made a Bible for every man.

"Just as the book itself had converted me, and had brought out the best in others, we could release the divine words of God directly to the people. They would learn to read and feel the power of the words themselves.

"Never again would we force men like Kentucky to be more than they were.

"Seven years ago, our little family on Alp made its first pressing. We produced ten sheets of paper, printed with the Psalms. I carefully packed those first sheets and sailed for Hercules with the grand news.

"You can guess the rest of my tale. With no preacher and no Bible, the church in Hercules had withered. There were still believers, and they still met together, but the spirit had faded. There were now three groups, each convinced that the others were worshipping falsely. Without my Bible, which I had left with the others on Alp, I had no real authority everyone would recognize.

"Then came the news of the Burn."

The old preacher absently rubbed the corner of his mouth. He blinked, and then the smile came slowly back.

"And so I began my travels. I search. Somewhere there is another Bible. I will find it, and then my friends will copy it. If I can still remember all the details, we will attempt to build that printing press. If not, then we will learn the proper way to become scribes. It has all been done before—we can do it again."

...

Charles had listened to the story with growing excitement. It was all familiar. The printing press project had been a recurring topic of conversation in the little scholastic community where he was a boy. Much debate had centered on which topics to tackle, once the original job of helping the Herc print his book had been accomplished.

It was seen by many as a way to open a crack in the scribe monopoly. No one on the mainland seemed interested in reading, because there was nothing to read. The few places where records were kept were already the exclusive domain of the scribes. This unknown religious order seemed like an interesting exception, having produced several non-scribes who could read.

Debate among the Alpines, as he remembered it, was between those who wanted to spread useful textbooks among the mainlanders, and those who wanted to print popular stories and entertaining histories so that they could create a desire for reading among the common people.

Charles realized sadly that the debate was never resolved. The end came first.

"Do you remember any of the people you met on Alp?"

The preacher laughed, "In my work, learning to remember people's names and faces is the first thing you have to do."

"There was an Archivist named Margaret Fasail."

A flicker of understanding came over Moore's face. "I thought the name sounded familiar. Your mother?"

Charles nodded.

"A lovely woman, if I remember rightly." He closed his eyes. "Dark hair, a somewhat serious expression on her face, except when she would suddenly laugh at my mainlander way of talking. She was very interested in my Bible and talked me into letting her test the paper that it was made from."

Charles found that his voice was a little unsteady. "My mother had it for several days, and she read some of the stories in it. It was a red book, about the size of my hand. Thin pages. There was a fish symbol embossed on the cover. She told me that she had borrowed it from a strange man."

The preacher shook his head slowly, "So the living word reaches out again. You have seen my Bible. I am happy she shared its words with her child." He chuckled, "Although I am not sure how to take being called a 'strange man'."

Charles laughed as well. "My brother and I survived the Burn. We were indentured until just recently in Port Gartner."

"But you can read, since you are Alpine?" There was eagerness in his voice. Charles nodded.

Harriman Moore grabbed a cloth and started working very hard to remove every trace of grease from his hands. "Come with me." He handed Charles the cloth.

Inside the wagon, in a heavy chest, the fragments came to light as the preacher laid out his treasure for Charles to see.

"These are the Psalms." Bony fingers gently lifted the large roll of sheets. Printed on both sides in a small print were thousands of words in long columns.

"And this is Genesis," indicating a stack of very thin wooden tablets, covered in hand-scripted text.

"These are the results of my search." There were twenty other tablets, each containing Scripture. "I have the Sermon on the Mount, from Matthew, and the whole book of Ecclesiastes. Here is another copy of Psalms 23, written in a different form. I have pieces of Ruth, Acts, Hebrews and Revelation.

"Back in Hercules, there is a copy of the letters of John and the letter of Philemon. I have good, faithful friends there who are copying them."

Charles checked his hands, remembering the many times he had cleaned them before touching books, then reached out to pick up the roll of paper. It was lightweight, but stiff to the touch. Black letters jumped out to his eyes. "Oh how great is Thy goodness; which Thou hast" ... "Behold, Thou hast made my days as an handbreadth;" ... "Be merciful unto me, O God; for man would swallow me up;"

Charles turned to the preacher, "Could I read some of this?"

The preacher smiled and indicated another trunk that made a good bench. While Charles seated himself comfortably, the man loosened some gathers on the wagon canopy to let in more light.

It was hard reading, but he drank it in. There were so many unfamiliar words, such a different way to talk. Charles soon realized that this was a collection of short texts, each a 'psalm'. This man David was a puzzle. He was a king, and had many enemies. But he was an artist, too, drawing beautiful pictures with his words. And he loved his God.

Is this the same David as the boy with the sling? He read more.

It was in Psalm 45 that Charles abruptly shook himself free of the words. He got stiffly to his feet and waved to the preacher.

The old man was talking with, or possibly to, Darkwind. The boy looked like he was bearing it all in silence.

Charles asked, "Hey, could you help me with something?"

Moore came and examined the passage under Charles's finger. He read quickly.

"This is a wedding song of the king. A princess is being wed to the powerful king, and she is being told to honor her husband and forget her father and her old family."

Charles nodded. He had read it correctly. A pressure started building in his chest. He looked again at the verse that had burned into him: 'Instead of thy fathers shall be thy children, whom thou mayest make princes in all the earth.'

It was almost the same thing Rad had said to him, only Rad had it backwards.

Okay, if you must love a Herc girl, then let her forget her father and raise Alpine children to grace the world. Not the other way around!

...

Charles looked at the sun, and was surprised at the hours that had passed. His reading had cost valuable travel time. *But it was wonderful to be inside a book again, to feel the new and the strange.*

The preacher asked, "How important is your journey south? My quest is sometimes a little rough on my old bones. I have been looking for a young man—someone who could help me in the great task of preserving the Word. I could not ask for better than an Alpine like you. In the big cities, not one man in a hundred can read and write anything more than his own name, and not one man in a city could have worked his way through the Psalms as quickly as you did. An Alpine child was instructed better than the scribes.

"If I could tempt you to come with me...."

Charles longed for such a life. So much of the old man's quest was Alpine in its search for knowledge, and in its reverence for the words.

Harriman Moore was a lively and entertaining man, and there would be travel through the great cities, where he could seek out others like himself.

And there would be the joy of being able to immerse himself into the whole stack of collected writings, to be able to do what he was born to do.

But... it was not his quest. And he had his own obligations. He shook his head, "No, I am sorry, but I have a deadline that I have to meet."

Moore smiled, "I expected as much, but the offer is always open. I should be heading back south by this time next year."

"Be careful," Charles said, "There was a Kimmer attack on Stampz, and the settlements all around Zeno looked deserted. I fear they have had trouble, as well."

"It is the same, downriver," he affirmed, suddenly somber. "I fear our Kimmer brothers are planning something big. You are traveling with one of their own, but be careful that he does not lead you into trouble. Even at that age, the Kimmer are taught the cleverness of the fox and the quietness of the rabbit."

Charles glanced at Darkwind sitting quietly on the stone farthest from them in the campsite. "I have already experienced his quietness. He almost stole everything I own."

He turned to the preacher and asked, "But are you safe? Shouldn't you get to Zeno and wait out this trouble?"

"No, I think not. I called the Kimmer brothers. I didn't speak lightly. You saw the ichthys and recognized it. So did your young friend. I have been on the road for years, and I have met Kimmer many times.

"They are not Christian, but they do recognize the symbol as a mark of power. I am treated as a magician—a man of power among the Kimmer. They will not attack this wagon."

Charles's face showed his skepticism, and the preacher assured him, "It is true. Ask him. Perhaps you haven't noticed, but when you went into my wagon to view my treasures, your status went up in his eyes. If you get into trouble, you might remember that. In some ways, the Kimmer are like children, if they don't kill you first."

He sighed, "Some day, I must turn my efforts to bring the true faith to these children of the forest. The journey is long, Charles."

Charles agreed, and he felt again the lengthening shadows. The day was clearing off, and the sunlight felt warm and good. Perhaps they could travel after the darkwind. The Earth wouldn't set until near midnight.

"Where are you headed next?" asked Charles.

"My route takes me to Zeno, Stampz and Mercury, before I turn toward my home in Hercules. "

"Things have changed at Stampz." Charles gave him an abbreviated version of the problems there, and the blocked Gate.

"So you will not be able to get a wagon into Stampz at all."

Moore looked worried. "This does pose a problem. I had promised to return to Stampz this trip. There are people there who will be expecting me."

"I wouldn't worry. Everyone there knows that the Gate is impassable."

He shook his head, "I know this. But I am an old man, and I have failed so many promises in my life that I cannot take it lightly."

Charles felt a sick guilt at Moore's dismay. It was his fault, after all.

"I do know that there is a guard station that watches the Porch. Perhaps you can send a message to the people inside that you intended to meet?"

He nodded. "That will have to do, if I cannot take the wagon in." He looked Charles in the eyes, "You know I cannot leave the wagon."

His treasures. Charles nodded. He also had some doubt that the old man could make the footpath over the rim, but then again, he suspected Moore was a tougher specimen than he looked. Living on the road for years at a time would keep him a lot more fit than most city people.

"If that is your plan, could I ask a favor of you?"

After he had explained his reports to the duke, the preacher happily promised to hand them to the Stampz guards. Charles helped him pack up his wagon and get his team back into harness. Soon it was time to part.

Harriman T. Moore looked down at him from the high driver's box and said, "If you travel through Terrance, be sure to seek out a girl there. She is in service to Herb Schuler, a grain dealer. A marvelous girl. She is Alpine, too." And before Charles could think to ask more, he called to his team and was moving.

Gods and Angels

Darkwind was gone like a leaf on the wind, heading south as fast as the preacher's wagon moved north. *But...* Charles stood in the middle of the road, his thoughts as stirred as the slowly settling dust. Then he turned to follow the boy.

Darkwind was moving as if demons were on his trail. Charles forced himself to step down hard for more speed. He didn't really want to catch him, but he did want to keep him in sight.

Watch it. I'm chasing a Kimmer boy in Kimmer-controlled land. He slowed a bit. *He will keep to the road. I hope.*

The lightly-settled land felt emptier than ever before. With the people gone, the homestead off to his left felt like old bones.

Where is Terrance, anyway?

The duke had shown him his maps, but there had not been a great need, he felt then, to take the time to copy them. All he needed to know was the quickest route to Condorcet.

But Terrance was probably that non-cratered settlement down at the junction of the Green and Peach rivers. He had intended to take the route to Hahn past Gauss and then southwest to the Crisium coast.

Terrance is a shipping town, not a farming settlement. He said she worked for a grain dealer.

No! He said she was 'in service' to him. Another Alpine-made-slave, I'd bet.

He became conscious of the slow pound—pound—pound of his feet striking the ground. He was making good time, but it was still three long days to Terrance at this pace.

Should I take the time? Stampz needs the powder.

But what if it was someone he knew? *Is she alone? Could I have survived the sweat gang without Rad? Suppose she is alone and has lost hope.*

No! The preacher said she was a marvelous girl, and an Alpine!

I have to go see. I have to help her.

If he went to Terrance, he would have to take the east road and follow the river. It would be an extra day, even if he did nothing there.

And what would I do about Darkwind?

...

As the still advanced and the winds dropped away, Charles was caught by a growing sparkle of light on the water. He looked up and saw the fat Earth emerge slowly from behind a cloud. *It will form a path,* he thought.

Darkwind had appeared as if by magic, shortly before his namesake winds. They'd made a little more time before stopping.

He was glad they'd found a good campsite overlooking the lake. The shoreline had wandered back and forth like loops of a rope laid out on a dock. Even though they were still following the western side of the Peach River, at least for this night, the lake curved almost completely around them. When he'd spotted the lone hill in the center of the bend, it struck his fancy to camp the night there.

He had a lot to think about.

The Earth was setting soon, and the sky was clearer than he ever remembered seeing. A thousand kilometers of air above the land meant that there were always clouds in the sky. Even clear air shaded into haze. But tonight you could see the swirl of clouds and the hint of continents on the face of the planet above them.

The sight, with the Earth's spreading reflection off the water, was something to savor.

Local legend had it, back in Gartner, that a pilgrim who was blessed with the view of the *Path to Earth* would be granted fortune in all his mortal endeavors. He and Rad had seen it a number of times, living on the docks. Of course, they weren't pilgrims, so they couldn't claim the luck.

It was all just the reflection of the home planet in the water, but depending upon the angle of the light and the calmness of the water, that reflection changed in subtle and beautiful ways. In a still, quiet pool, the reflection could be as exact as if in a mirror. But with more wind, more ripples, the image stretched out in the direction of the real Earth in the sky to form a glowing path across the water. No doubt it was a magical sight for the pilgrim—a vision in the water of *The Way of the Earth* that any halfway artistic soul could appreciate.

Charles gave about as little obeisance to the mystic parts of the Way as he could safely get away with, but the image growing on the water before him was something that he could appreciate on his own terms, free from the religion of the marketplace.

His parents practiced the rites of the Way, but he and Rad hadn't had the time for religion on the docks.

Oh, some of it made sense. It was very Alpine to revere your ancestors. The moral parts about how to treat your fellow man just seemed like good sense. Where Charles had problems with the state religion was in the mystic and commercial parts.

I carved the figures with my own hands. I can't pray to things like that.

His father was a scientist. Charles could believe anything, even the mystical, but it had to make some kind of sense.

The impulse rifle in his pack was pure magic these days. Great power in an invisible pulse—what was reasonable about that?

But he used it. He had seen his father use it. He could recite, but he never understood, the physics behind it. It had rules. There were settings to make. It had to be recharged. He had confidence that, if he had been able to live out his life as a scholar on Alp, he could have come to understand it as well as he understood the wind in a sailing ship, or the explosive power of gun powder.

But what was there to understand about paying the priests to strike the gong for you to give you good luck? What sense was there in this light reflection that would give luck to a pilgrim? How would the prayer of a man in a robe help gain his dead father's help any more than the constant memories he already lived with?

The Earth was there, visible and so far out of reach. He loved history. He thrilled at the new insights that he could discover in it. If he could walk across that path on the water and reach the lands of Earth on the other side, he would give up everything to do so.

But that was a fable. He would never walk on the Earth. With the destruction of Alp, and its two beamships, there was no way to ever get there. Why should he make the pilgrimage to the Seven Temples and give the seven offerings as all the truly faithful were supposed to do? How would that get him on a spaceship that didn't exist?

And what of Harriman T. Moore and his Christianity? How did that fit into the picture? All he really knew was that it was a far older religion than the Way, since it came from Earth and was based on ancient writings.

The preacher was someone he could respect, but weren't there good people everywhere?

This Christ, was he a more real god than the spirit of the east wind in the temple at Gartner?

Charles watched as the Earth dropped lower, and the shimmering path across the water broke up into an occasional sparkle.

He should really try to get some sleep. He had wasted many hours today, and he would need to travel hard tomorrow.

...

"An Angel!"

Darkwind's cry startled Charles out of his dream. There was a pleasant memory of blue eyes and scented hair, and then it fragmented and vanished like a handful of dust tossed into the darkwind.

An Angel? Charles strained his eyes upward to the dark sky. The Earth had set, and only a hint of its glow was visible along the far west horizon. He tried to spot the boy. He pulled off his blanket and stood.

The Kimmer was staring hard at the zenith.

Yes! There, in the strangely cloudless sky, was a tiny point of light so small he could make out no detail, no shape. It was as if there was no size to the light, only a place.

His heart beat faster. *An angel!* How many times had he heard the expressions?

"It will be that way until the angels fall."

"Sooner an angel will fall than I'll change my price!"

"The man is as faithful as an angel."

It was the stuff of legends. Here in the wilderness, far from cities and scribes, sharing the night shelter with a Kimmer, it was only right that he should at last see an angel.

Beren Te, his history instructor, had first mentioned them.

When Alp was first settled, the Scholars had discovered the Angel myth. Where it started no one was sure, but every culture on Luna, including the Kimmer apparently, had it. They could only guess what had started it all. On a world with an atmosphere a thousand kloms thick, filled with clouds and water vapor, it was a rare chance when one could actually see a star.

Charles could believe a mythology could be sustained by sightings like these. He appreciated the magic of the moment. He sat quite still, soaking in the feelings.

Darkwind was acting quite differently.

The Kimmer boy pulled off his clothes and laid them carefully on the ground. Then he lay down on them, arms wide, eyes on the angel above. He began to chant.

At first, Charles could make out no sense in the hard rhythm, accenting every syllable, but then it started to repeat. By the third time around he was able to make sense of the words:

"Ac Sept Oh Ro Bert Hend Er Sun!
"Bi Oh Gen Et Eye Cist Tek
"No Ur Sun By Arm Hend Er Sun
"Know his son Strong Arm Er Sun
"Know his son Green Eye Er Sun
"Know his son Fea-ther Er Sun
"Know his son Blood Fist Er Sun
"Know his son Bear Killer Er Sun
"Know his son Ram Killer Er Sun
"Know his son Sun Mountain Er Sun
"Know his son Thunder Er Sun
"Know his son Cool Rain Er Sun
"Know his son White-Talon Er Sun
"Know his son Darkwind Er Sun
"Ac Sept Oh Ro Bert Hend Er Sun!
"Bi Oh Gen Et Eye Cist Tek
"Know your children Er Sun."

Darkwind repeated the chant ten times. Charles listened in fascination. Did the boy know what he was saying? Had any Alpine or Herc heard this before?

This could make all the difference in the world! Beasts of the forest indeed! It all makes so much sense.

Then the boy stood, and turning to face the four quarters of the world, he shouted:

"*Oh Dawnwind, know the children Er Sun.*

"*Here we stand.*

"*Oh Land of Crazy Sun, know the children Er Sun.*

"*Here we stand.*

"*Oh Darkwind, know the children Er Sun.*

"*Here we stand.*

"*Oh Wide Waters, know the children Er Sun.*

"*Here we stand.*"

Then the ceremony was done. Darkwind pulled his clothes back on and came back to the blanket Charles had been letting him use as a bed. Even in this faintest of dim lights, Charles could see the religious glow on the boy's face.

The speck of light in the sky was fading as the rare patch of clear dry air moved off. It winked out. Charles looked back at the boy.

"Er Sun is your family name?" he asked.

Darkwind looked at him with a frown. "If you were not Treekiller the Alpine, I would have to kill you. My family's words are not for sky-beasts."

"Why am I different?"

He shrugged, "You would kill me first."

"Would it help if I promised to keep the words a secret?" *The words, not the truth. That is too important to keep secret.*

Darkwind shook his head, "No. Only Kimmer keep their word, and if you were Kimmer, there would be no need to kill you."

Charles felt a flash of anger, "Know this, Darkwind Er Sun! I am Charles Fasail, an Alpine. You may know that the word of a Fasail, and an Alpine, is true! I keep my promises."

Darkwind was apologetic, "I am sorry. If you were a man, I would honor your word. But Alpine or not, a sky-beast is not a man. Kimmer understand that any beast's honor is to follow its nature. We do not hold a bear in dishonor if it mauls a man—that is its nature. We do not hold a raccoon in dishonor if it steals—that is its nature."

Sky beasts, Forest beasts. It works both ways. Only the preacher had it right.

"And you don't hold a sky-beast in dishonor if it lies to you?"

Darkwind nodded.

"Then why do you kill sky-beasts?"

He looked puzzled, "But they kill us. They drive us from our lands. They make totem-houses. They bring sickness. This may be in their nature, but we don't have to put up with it!"

Charles had no good answer for that. "Then there is nothing I can do to convince you my word can be trusted like a Kimmer's?"

He nodded, "I am sorry. I do like you."

Charles looked away from the boy, collecting his thoughts. Why did he even try? This was just a boy. But it hurt to have his word openly doubted.

"Darkwind, why are sky-beasts not men?" he asked finally.

There was a trace of antagonism in the boy's voice when he answered, "Sky-beasts are different. They can't be men."

"Are you a man?"

"Yes!" The boy was getting irritated.

"Was your father a man? His father? How about Robert Henderson, Biogenetic Tech?"

"Yes, my father, and his father were men. Ro Bert Hend Er Sun was more than a man. How could a man be an angel? Ro Bert Hend Er Sun taught the beaver how to know the seasons. He taught the marmot how to find the valley grass and the bofung."

Darkwind's voice drifted into a chant.

"He and his brother angels made the sun to rise and set. They made the winds. They filled the seas and planned the courses of the rivers. They scattered the seeds that made the first forests. They taught slyness to the fox and gave the birds the freedom of the sky.

"Then from the sky, beasts with the shape of men sent a curse, like a disease, to kill the angels. The sky-beasts confused the totems of power, and made the totem houses places of death.

"The angels cried to their ancestors on the Far Earth, but their powers were gone. The angels died. All but a few, a handful of acorns from the forest. They fled from the totem houses and placed a curse on all such places, that none would ever use them again.

"In their wisdom, the angels knew that the sky-beasts would come to take the world that the angels had made. They warned their children, that they might kill the sky-beasts and keep faith with our ancestors on the Far Earth."

Darkwind's voice, chanting the old tale, shifted and he looked again to Charles. "Ro Bert Hend Er Sun was an angel, the father of my family. When he died, the sky opened and his light was set above the clouds to watch over the Er Sun. We must honor him when his light shines on us."

...

Charles thought about the tale while he lit a warm ball and folded his bedding into a more comfortable seat. It made sense. It was history, trimmed to fit the mind and memory of an illiterate forest boy.

But I have to be careful how I think of him. Kimmer aren't forest beasts. They aren't even gene-tailored versions of men. They are men. No different from Hercs or Serenites or any other of the settlers of Luna.

No different from Alpines. Charles's mouth twisted as if he had unexpectedly tasted a bitterroot.

But what could he say to the boy to convince him that he, Charles, was a man as well.

Darkwind moved his blankets, closer to the glow.

"Then creatures with the shape of men," guessed Charles, "came down from the sky and built houses."

"Yes. They were shunned at first. But when skillful hunters from the family Kimmer were sent to spy out the totem-houses, they were struck down with disease, like the angels. Thus all men knew in truth that these creatures from the sky were not men, but the sky-beasts of legend."

Charles nodded to himself. The Kimmer had never tried to make peace with the settlers. "Are you saying that not all people like yourself are truly Kimmer?"

"Yes. Kimmer are the family who first met the sky-beasts. I am of the family Er Sun."

"Why don't you correct me when I call you Kimmer?"

"What does it matter what sky-beasts call us? Perhaps it is better this way. The sky-beasts know the name Kimmer and that family has almost been destroyed. Thus we must protect our family name."

"Then what do you call yourselves?"

"We are men. What else?"

The little brat! I know the history of Man on Luna, right now, better than anyone in the world. All he knows is his chants.

Charles decided to change that.

"Listen to me. I am going to tell you a story. I don't ask that you believe. I only want you to listen."

He reached into his supplies for some water, and was pleased to see the boy settle himself in to listen. He knew what to say. The story, most of it, had been told him since he first gathered with his schoolmates, before he could even read.

"There are many worlds. You can see the Earth in the sky, and the ground beneath your feet. The world where we live is Luna.

"All men once lived on Earth, but their numbers were many. They killed each other for land and for food. They became wise, and learned the ways of power. But still they fought among themselves. It seemed that they would turn their powers to even greater killings, so great that all might die.

"But there were some men more wise than others. They said, 'See the empty worlds in the sky. Let us take our powers and move them and shape them into new lands for all our people.'

"And so they moved the worlds.

"These worlds had many names. There was Mars, and Venus, and Mercury, and Callisto, and Ganymede, and Io, and Europa, and Titan, and Triton. And closest of all, there was Luna, shining bright in the sky of Earth.

"The task of moving and shaping the worlds was the greatest deed that man had ever attempted. Great men were chosen to wield the powers that could move a whole world like you or I could move a stone. These men became the Project Engineers of the Terraforming Fleet."

There was a gasp as Darkwind heard those words. Charles could see his lips moving, perhaps repeating the syllables of another of his chants silently to himself.

"The Project Engineers put an atmosphere ... put winds, on Mars, and filled its valleys with seas. Forests were planted. The seas were filled with fish. The world of Mars became a garden.

"Now the families of Earth argued among themselves about which families should be given the new lands of Mars. A decision was made, but many were left out, and many were angered.

"But there were other worlds. Peace was kept with promises of more land for all. The brightest world of them all, Luna, was chosen to prepare next.

"Luna was a small world, with no air and no water. It also had neither day nor night. The Project Engineers found oceans of water, frozen as a giant rock called Hyperion around Far Saturn. They broke it into mountains and smashed them onto Luna. With their powers, they spun the new world as a child would spin a stone, giving it days and nights.

"The waters melted, and with their arts, they made air to cover the world.

"Luna was then turned over to special men of the Project, the Biogenetic Techs," he glanced at Darkwind to see how he was taking the story. The boy's eyes were wide. How much was getting through, he didn't know. He was guessing at this part of the story, but the History of the Terraforming Project was solid, documented history. Charles was certain he was getting most of it right.

"The Biogenetic Techs seeded the world with the forests. They brought animals from the Earth, and changed them to be happy in their new homes. They gave some lands to the beaver and others to the bear. They made special fishes for the great freshwater seas that had formed on Luna, since the oceans on Old Earth were full of salt.

"In the sky of the Earth, the world of Luna had become transformed. From a gray world of bare rock, it now showed the blue of the seas, the green of the forests, and the white of the clouds. Luna had become a world in the sky just as the Earth shines in ours. The old arguments raged fresh over who would have this new land, and who would be left out.

"With the people of Earth hostile and ready to return to killing, the great Plague came. A disease more deadly than anything man had known before, it struck every world. Out of a hundred men, only one survived.

"The great powers were turned suddenly to killing as the wise leaders of every people died. Many that survived the disease were killed by their fellows. Every nation blamed the other for starting the Plague, but the beasts that started it all were never found. Perhaps they were killed by their own disease. No one knows.

"The great powers were lost. The Earth became a world of death and killing. The far world of Mars became silent. It was assumed that the Biogenetic Techs on Luna, few in number and cut off from their fellows, were destroyed by the Plague.

"Only in the cities in space, did there remain people with some of the lesser powers. In these space cities, there remained ships that could sail the emptiness between the worlds.

"But the space cities were doomed without living worlds to trade with. On the farm cities, the machines broke. In the machine cities, the food became too poor to keep people healthy, and no one remembered how to make it all work again. Some people left to return to Earth. Without fail, they were never heard from again. No more dared try.

"Finally, the fresh world of Luna called them. Many different peoples came to settle in this world that everyone knew to be empty.

"On the other side of the world, the people of Vesta live. They were the first. Their example inspired others.

"Men from the great space city of Mt. Ural came to populate the lands now know as Serenity. It was these men who first learned that Luna was not an empty world, as strange man-like creatures came out of the forests to kill them."

Charles was watching for a reaction to his description of the Kimmer, and as Darkwind took a breath to interrupt, Charles plunged on with the story.

"New men from the space city of Manhattan came to settle at the twin craters of Atlas and Hercules, with the hope of keeping their rivals from taking over Luna.

"Much later, the rest of the inhabitants of Manhattan settled at York. Alone, the last city in space, Alexandria watched from afar as the peoples of Hercules and Serenity fought their wars, just like the old peoples of Earth. Only now, on this world, the old powers were gone for good.

"No one knew what to make of the Kimmer warriors from the forests. The tales of the Biogenetic Techs were still known, but everybody knew they were all killed by the Plague. Perhaps just as those men of power had changed the animals to live in tune with the new world, they had made new-men that could live more in tune with the Lunar world.

"In any case, these forest savages, who could not be reasoned with and who might not even be real men, had to be fought and killed to keep the new settlers safe."

Darkwind was protesting, "No! You are twisting—"

Charles kept on talking. Darkwind sputtered out his protest, then fell silent. He listened.

"Finally, the last people on the space city Alexandria decided that the lost powers and knowledge of the old times had to be brought to the new world. They planned carefully, settling themselves on the island Alp, becoming the powerful Alpines, forcing the Hercs and the Serenites to acknowledge their greatness.

"But even the wise and powerful Alpines were just men. Disaster struck, burning the island Alp to ashes and leaving only a few wanderers, keepers of the last dregs of the power and knowledge of the ancients."

Even as he spoke, Charles felt the tears in his eyes and knew that his story was doing more to him than it could possibly do to Darkwind.

"And I am Charles Fasail, Alpine."

And he would go to Terrance.

Wisdom in the Flowers

Greetings to the Duke of Stamps Reporting on the Journey to Condorcet, written in the Noon of 7 Feb.

This is the first report of the second series. I have dispatched the first series by a traveler I met on the road, Harriman T. Moore, a preacher of the Christian faith.

In case the first series was lost due to Kimmer attack or other misfortune, I wish you to know that there was nothing of great import in those messages with the exception of the following news: Almost all small communities on the Gaussland trail are deserted due to Kimmer trouble, and my Kimmer traveling companion has proved to be very helpful. His warnings have saved my life at least once, and his forest sense has been in other ways helpful.

Our current position on the trail is approximately the third way from the southern branch to Zeno and the branch to Gauss. In spite of my best intentions, my rate of progress is much less than my first optimistic estimates. Your estimate is closer to the reality.

One other item. Harriman Moore is undertaking a project to copy and preserve his sacred writings. In the course of handing over the reports I sent with him, we examined the vellum that you supplied. He commented that it was the finest quality vellum that he had encountered and that he would be interested in acquiring a supply of it for his efforts, deeming the vellum a more permanent and durable medium than the fine-polished wooden tablets that he is currently using for his transcriptions.

> *He would also be interested in discussing the process he has re-
> searched some years past on Alp for the making of vellum pages into
> the codex, or classic book format.*
> *From your servant, Charles Fasail, Alpine.*

...

The trail branched off to the east, to the crater Rynin, he suspected. He remembered seeing it on the duke's map, but he couldn't remember anything about the settlement there. More each day, he was coming to realize that the Empire was losing its control on the eastern reaches. Maybe there was someone in the upper councils who had a finger on what was happening out here, but he doubted it. He would have felt a lot better about Sheb's control out here if he had seen one sign of Legion presence on the trail.

He is expecting all the local nobility to keep their individual areas under control. But the trail is outside of all their ringwalls. Who controls it?

Darkwind was lagging far behind. He could see him back there, but the boy had no interest in talking today. At least they weren't wasting a lot of time on breaks.

I went too far last night. He has his Kimmer history. It must not be easy for him to listen to me tell him that it is in error.

Charles felt a darkness inside him. *I always push people away. What good does it do to tell people the truth if it just stops people from listening to you?*

...

The trail divide happened before he expected it. One moment he was gliding along the seemingly endless trail with nothing but variations in the size and shape of the riverside rocks to entertain him. The next, he was confronted by a hillside with words on it.

Some bored scribe must have passed this way long ago, for in letters as high as a man, made of hundreds of white stones, someone had spelled out a road sign.

GAUSS - HAHN said one side. HUBBLE said the other.

Charles eased to a stop where the road split. The Gauss route, heading off to the right, away from the river, was the most heavily rutted. *I have waited years to go to Gauss.*

184

The route to Condorcet was that way, past Hahn. It bent south-south-eastward to the Crisium coast.

The other went first to Terrance, and then followed the river south to Hubble. To get to Condorcet from there would take a ship down Sheb's Sea and then overland at the closest approach to Condorcet.

There was no trail on the map from Terrance directly to Condorcet, but surely, I can find a way.

I have to go to Terrance.

He looked back and saw Darkwind closing the distance. It was better that way for him as well. Close to Gauss, there was a much greater chance that they would run into a Legion detachment. He had no delusion that anyone would be likely to accept his word that the Kimmer boy was 'tame'.

Darkwind came in with a rush, breezing by Charles and turning his run into a circle to stop his momentum. "The Beast Marks!" he shouted, in seeming good spirits. *So, the Kimmer have a name for the sign.*

The boy looked again at the huge letters as he slowed to a walk. "Treekiller! The Beast Marks are made up of your letters!"

Charles was happy that he was talking again. "Yes. How many of them to you know?"

They had covered the alphabet, and even some simple words, but Charles had no expectations that the lessons had stuck.

Darkwind was obviously impressed with the size of the sign. Charles suspected the boy had traveled widely in the forest and may have seen this before, but now he could recognize some meaning to it.

"Hand. Gas. Hub . . . Hob-Ly."

"Very good. That one is 'Hubble'. It points to the road that goes down to a crater city by the sea. 'Gauss' is the name of the large crater just to the west. 'Hahn' is another crater beyond it. For people who can read, it tells them which road to travel."

"Do all sky-beasts read?" He was still taking in the size of the letters sprawled across the hillside.

"No. Very few. I can read. The man we met in the wagon."

"White-Teeth," he informed Charles.

He tried to resist the smile. "Some of the leaders of each city can read."

"Then sky-beasts are not as smart as Kimmer. We can all read the marks."

Charles reserved his comments on that. He couldn't see the carved marks in trees as comparable to real literacy.

"Alpines, my people, were all taught to read from a very young age. Great power can be had from reading."

Darkwind nodded wisely. "The words can point your way. Which way do you go, Treekiller?"

Charles glanced down the road to Gauss. Within a half day, he could enter the wide valley that he and his brother talked about and dreamed about. Good protected land, where you could grow your crops; a land ruled lightly by a mere baron, who let the people control their own lives; a land being filled by people like the Turners who wished for a better life and had the courage to go find it; these were all things that drew him.

But there is a girl, an Alpine girl, a marvelous girl in Terrance.

The bag of gold in his pack was a faint reminder of his real duty, but he pushed that back. *I will get to that. I have to check on the girl first.*

"We go this way," he pointed, and started down the road to Hubble.

...

While they waited for the dawnwind to die down, Charles decided to build a little raft to carry his pack. From the looks of the ford, he had hopes that the water wouldn't get too much higher than his chest—certainly there was plenty of evidence that wagons crossed here frequently, but he did not want to risk getting the fancy clothing soaked. He had to move carefully, because the wind was still strong enough to whip spray off the top of the river and soak him through.

Darkwind watched but made no comment. Charles was grateful for the return to cordiality that the road sign had brought, and he hated the thought of another debate over the difference between sky-beasts and forest-beasts. If he got curious, he would deal with his justifications for taking such precautions over mere clothes when it came up.

By the time he had finished and lashed his pack to the rude wooden frame, he noted that Darkwind had fallen asleep again.

I don't know how he can be comfortable, draped over the rocks in that contortion.

But he has the right idea. Sleep when you can.

Charles estimated that he too could catch a short nap without any serious loss of travel time. He stretched out on as flat a piece of ground as he could find and let his eyes close.

The wind stirred the returning hair on his head. It was cold—almost like the sensation of wind on his freshly burned scalp.

He was falling, and the ground was coming up fast. He struggled with the sailsuit, unbalanced by the impulse rifle in his hand. He would not let it go!

A flicker of shadow passed overhead. He looked up. It was Darkwind, sailing above him with ease, waiting for him to smash to pulp on the rocks below.

Anger surged in him. He wouldn't let that little rat watch him die. His tree-marks were nothing compared to real text. How dare he doubt his word!

He pulled the impulse gun to firing position and ripped his arm off.

Darkwind! he cried. What have I done?

The boy smashed against the rocks.

His own sailsuit changed from white to black, and he was just one of a flock of crows spiraling down to pick at the body.

No!

A hand shook him.

Charles jumped.

Darkwind was leaning over him, a worried look on his face.

A dream. Just a dream. But his body shook with the reaction.

"What is wrong, Treekiller?"

Killer. That's me.

"Just a dream," he avoided the boy's face. He stood and looked out over the river. It was almost time to move.

Time to run away.

He rubbed his hand over the stiff, short hair returning to his scalp. He no longer had to worry about that. The burns had healed well. It would soon be back to his normal length. It would be as if the cannon blast, the exploding trees, the explosion of the laser cannon itself had never happened.

But they did. I killed people. I smashed the whole economy of Stampz. I made Darkwind an orphan by what I did. More will die, too. How can they not, when the whole population of Stampz is uprooted because of the flood I made?

I have to fix it. I can't let it all blow away like a bad dream.

He walked over to the pack. Darkwind followed. "Are we ready to cross over?"

"Almost. I have one more thing to do first." Charles reached into the pack for his shaving knife.

Darkwind offered to help, but Charles shook his head. He was a bit clumsy, and it took longer than it should.

He passed his hand over his scalp. He nodded.
I won't forget. This stays bald until I fix my mistakes.

. . .

The trail left the riverbank after a couple of hours, and the change of scenery was a welcome change. Charles liked the rolling meadows. This land was rich grassland, not like the isolated patches of grasses and scrubs of a few days past.

The whole world seemed green and fresh. Only in the ruts of the trail itself was there bare ground to be seen.

On impulse, Charles wandered off the trail and with his low-gravity strides, he sailed like a ship through the knee-high grass.

The scent of the grass, still damp from the morning dew was a little intoxicating. Just moving through it was a joy. A clear mind, sailing through a clean world.

The trail was rising to pass through a gap between a pair of medium-sized craters. On impulse, he shifted gait and raced up the side of the left crater. The grade was a bit steep, but climbable.

In a few minutes, he had reached the lip of the crater wall.

A lake. The floor was much deeper than the surrounding land, and rippled under the morning breezes. The inside walls of the crater were thick with water-loving willows. Riding the surface, flocks of hundreds of ducks or geese were enjoying the protected haven.

This would be a nice place to live. I could build a home right here on the edge.

He visualized a comfortable stone house, level with the protecting top of the crater. He could see himself watching the birds, resting in his chair after a good meal. At the edge of his dream, a dim figure moved gracefully up beside him and put her hand into his.

Charles shook his head. *Someday. Someday when I have hair.*

He looked down at the trail, a knife-cut through the green carpet. Darkwind trudged patiently along. Charles waved. He waved back.

Charles moved on, heading for the pass, just a little way ahead. *I wonder what she will be like.*

. . .

Charles beat Darkwind to the pass, and was stopped cold by the sight that greeted him. His heavy pack rode up on his back as he bounced a couple of times in the soft soil, braking his speed.

Blue flowers spread in large swaths, eclipsing the green grass that had carpeted his trail thus far. The dazzling change caught his breath. It was if he had stepped across a line and entered a whole different world. Oh, there was still just as much grass as there had ever been, but the deep blue blossoms, edge to edge for as far as he could see, rose above the green carpet presenting a blue brighter and more colorful than any sea, certainly more dramatic than the pale blue of the sky when the clouds were thin.

He stepped on down a few hundred paces and plucked a blossom. It was a delicate, succulent bloom made of dozens of smaller ones. The composite was longer than his thumb and included in its pallet a pale white and a range of blues deepening down to a color he had never seen before.

Charles hitched his pack to a more comfortable position and started moving again. The trail was still a cut through the land, and he moved into its ruts, reluctant to damage the flowers, in spite of their profligacy. He looked around, feeling his father's eyes again.

There were differences in the colors, subtle, but in patterns. Here, in their midst, he couldn't make sense of it.

He looked around. There was a rocky ridge—a secondary crater splash of upturned rock that had existed since the craters were blasted into the crust. That would give him a better look.

He raced over to it, guiltily trampling a path through the splendor. He climbed the rocks and soon stood overlooking the valley.

Ah! That's it.

He marveled for a long moment, before a figure crested the pass.

Charles shouted, "Darkwind! Come here!"

The boy may not have heard his call, but he could see him gesture. He made his own dark wet trail through the blue and soon joined him.

"Have you seen this place before?"

"I don't remember. I have seen the water flowers before, but not here, I think."

Charles nodded to himself.

"Darkwind Er Sun, look at the handiwork of your ancestors."

The boy looked puzzled.

Charles moved down to sit on the edge of the cliff. Darkwind joined him.

"I had never seen these flowers before, but as I was enjoying their beauty, the words of my father came to me.

"My father was a biologist. He was a wise man who studied the life of this world. In some ways, he was like Robert Henderson, Biogenetic Tech, the founder of your line.

"He taught me many secrets of this world. Would you like to know a secret your ancestor hid in these plants beneath our feet?"

Darkwind was solemn, and nodded his interest.

Charles spread his hands, taking in the expanse of the blue and the green. "Plants like these came from the Far Earth. But they could not live long on this world. Do you know why?"

Darkwind shook his head, "I don't know."

"The plants could grow and thrive, just as you see here, but there is one thing they could not do, and that is bloom and form their seeds.

"You see, life that was formed on the Far Earth had to cope with, and use the seasons. Do you know what a season is?"

"It is a time, longer than a month. Sometimes the elders mention seasons."

Charles nodded, "On our world, on this Luna, there are no true seasons, but we still use the word. On Far Earth, seasons were a real thing. Every three months, the world changed.

"You know that it is colder up north?"

Nod.

"On this world, we can get colder days by moving north, and warmer days by moving south. On Far Earth, you could stay in one place and the days would get colder and warmer on their own!"

Darkwind laughed, not in ridicule, but at the strangeness.

"These are the seasons: There is Summer, when the days are warmest. Three months later comes the Fall, when it grows colder, and many plants stop growing, dropping their leaves. Three months later is the Winter, and the days are cold. Some plants sleep. Some die, leaving only their seeds to survive them. Then three months later, it is Spring and the days grow warmer again. Plants grow new leaves. Seeds sprout and become new plants. Three months later it is Summer again, and the cycle begins once more."

Darkwind was silent for a moment. He looked at Charles, checking for any hint that he was being led on a false path. He asked, "How could that happen? Why would the days get colder, and then warmer?"

Charles was pleased with the question, but he had an instant panic. He knew that it did, but the why—the how, suddenly escaped him. He knew some of the answer.

"Our world, Luna, spins straight. The Earth tilts. It is that tilt that causes the seasons. But we will talk about that later."

"How can that be?" Darkwind was disturbed. "The Earth is perfect. How can it be tilted?"

Charles put a solemn face on. "We are talking science now. These are the deep truths. The Earth does tilt. I can show you this in the sky tonight. Who is to say that this makes the Earth flawed? Certainly not the ancestors of these flowers below us.

"The Earth flowers used the seasons to tell them when to mature, when to flower and form their seeds, and when to die. When they came here, they were confused. Seeds sprouted and grew, but the plant never flowered and never grew seeds for the next generation.

"Without Robert Henderson and his brothers, these plants would have died out."

"What did they do?"

Charles smiled, "The Biogenetic Techs were clever. With tools that we can't even imagine, they looked inside the leaves and stems, deep into the invisible parts of the plant and discovered what the changing seasons did to it. They discovered that the sap changed in subtle ways when the days grew longer.

"To direct the flowers, the Biogenetic Techs created a disease."

Darkwind looked startled, "What?"

Charles nodded, "A disease. It only affects the plants, not the animals, not us. When a plant gets infected, its sap changes just like the seasons changed the sap of its ancestors. It then flowers, forms seeds, and dies."

"I don't know..." he began.

Charles pointed down. "You can see it for yourself. Look at that patch of blue right there. What does it look like?"

Darkwind peered intently at the long stretch of flowering plants. He almost spoke, but stayed silent.

"What were you going to say?"

"Well, I almost said that it looked like a game trail."

"That's exactly what it is. A herd of deer or something came through this notch. They brushed through the plants, spreading the disease from one to others. Where they traveled, the plants flowered.

"Look closely at all the patches of flowers."

Darkwind looked around the valley. He suddenly laughed, and Charles felt a pang of loss for his own youth. When was the last time he could laugh like that?

Darkwind got to his feet, to better look all around him. "It's true! You can see where the rabbits live. And there! A lion ran down a deer. See how the deer tried to move back and forth, but the lion charged straight. And there, it must have been a migrating herd. See where the plants have turned brown! That means it happened before, doesn't it?"

Charles tried to follow the boy's pointing finger as he painted details into the scene that only a forest boy could see. He was a little awed. He had thought to share his superior knowledge with the ignorant boy. And here he was, his own mouth open as the boy taught him.

Kimmer Warning

It was about noon when the path of the river returned to follow alongside the rutted wagon trail. Charles was hungry. He'd been making good progress this morning, and he expected Terrance to appear on the horizon within a few hours.

A city without a crater. That will be something to see.

Darkwind was far behind, and had been most of the day. Charles was growing comfortable with the boy's wide-ranging ways. He had a knife, and especially out here in the open, no large predators were likely to be able to chase him down. That was one nice thing about humans and low gravity. With the ability to leap far and wide, it was a rare cat that could manage to catch a human in good condition.

His stomach gave another indication that it might be a good time to take a break. He found a nice rock on the edge of the water and unpacked more of the hard trail bread. *If Darkwind were here, I'd send him off to catch another rabbit.*

For entertainment, he watched the energetic perch chase around in the shallows. *Different species. I guess the water is warmer this far south.*

It was strange to be so nervous. *I wonder what she will be like. What will I say to her? 'Hello, I'm an Alpine, too.'*

What if it is someone I know?

That could be a problem. There had been two other Alpines in Gartner, and he had not seen them more than once.

The Kells had been a mother and her two daughters on the return leg of a trip to Franklin when the Burn left them homeless. The tide had turned almost instantly against them, as it had against the Fasails. The hired guide that the Kells counted on for support quickly became their master. Charles knew that the mother had died shortly thereafter.

When Rad heard that there were other Alpines in Gartner, he made a strong effort to meet with them. This was hard to do, being slaves themselves. For close to half a year, they were confined to the dock complex at all times.

Rad was not one to take defeat lightly, so he worked himself into a position where the night foreman called on him to handle the odd jobs that he was too lazy to do himself.

He took advantage of one of those errands to make his way out of the dock area up to the rank of houses where rumor reported the girls living.

It was not a successful trip. Rad had returned under guard, with extra duties laid on for escaping to go visit the brothels.

His report to Charles was short. The Kell sisters were now working as prostitutes, and wanted to have nothing to do with any other Alpines.

"We can't have anything more to do with them, Charles. They feel the shame of what has happened to them more than we can imagine. It was unbearably difficult for them to talk to me."

Charles had to accept his brother's judgment on that, and so for a few years, he did.

He did remember one instance, though, when he had delivered a load of his carvings to the marketplace. One woman in a fine dress seemed to be staring at him as he conducted his business. When he turned to face her, she broke and ran, as well as the dress permitted, until she was out of sight.

It was probably one of them.

Was Rad right? Should we have made a stronger effort to help them?

Of course, from her appearance, any money that he could have given would have been pocket-change to her.

He just hoped the girl in Terrance had a better time of it.

He had re-packed his stuff by the time Darkwind came streaking along the trail in a high speed gait.

"Hey! Darkwind!"

He had not seen Charles, and he was racing as if the bear were still chasing him. The call caused him to lose his stride and Charles had an instant's terror that the boy would crash. It was no joke to smash into the rocks at top running speed.

But young reflexes saved him, and he pulled up to a stop with a minimum of gyrations. Darkwind had an expression of agitation that he had never seen before.

"Treekiller! We must go back."

Charles frowned, "What do you mean? This is the road. Why do we need to go back?" He was eager to get moving forward.

"Treekiller, do not ask. We must go back. We must find another path." Darkwind had a pleading look in his eyes.

Charles felt his neck getting stiff. Terrance was just a few hours ahead. This was the road. What kind of itch had gotten onto the boy's scalp?

"Darkwind, you are going to have to give me a reason if you want me to stop. This 'Do not ask' is not going to convince me of anything. I need a reason."

The boy was breathing hard. He put his teeth on his lower lip, thinking. He fitted the words together, "There will be fighting. There is going to be an attack...on the road ahead. We must not be there!"

Charles stood abruptly, and stepped the distance to him. He could see the boy flinch away, but he wasn't quick enough. Charles put his large hand on the boy's shoulder and made sure he had both feet on the road. "You say there is going to be a Kimmer attack? How do you know this? Are they going to attack Terrance?" He shook the boy. "Tell me now! How do you know this?"

Darkwind's eyes flickered away from Charles toward the road ahead. He put his hand on Charles's arm. "Treekiller. I will tell you. But come, now!"

"No."

They stared at each other for a couple of breaths. Charles could hear the water flow—it felt like everything was flowing away. He was scared. It struck him just how ridiculous he had been, walking through Kimmer controlled lands in the middle of a war. What was real?

"I am going to Terrance," he declared. "If you want to stay in my sight, you will tell me what you know."

The boy shook free of his grasp. "I am Er Sun," he snarled. But he didn't meet Charles's eyes. "I don't betray them for any sky-beast! Go then. Die with the others."

Charles noticed his rage building, but forced his tongue to wait. *Hold it in!* He made his words level and calm. "Darkwind, come on with me. I can make you a disguise. You could look like one of the Hercs. You will be safe with me."

Darkwind started a laugh, but it fell flat. He said, "You think *you* can give me safety? You think the Er Sun have abandoned me? How do you think I know of the fighting? My father's brother watches over me even now! He left me the tree-mark as warning. It was he that thought to learn your magician's powers through me.

"And it is only my voice that kept you from feeling the blade of Er Sun. But no more. Go to your death!"

Then Darkwind ducked to the side and vanished into the rocks like a rabbit.

An impulse to chase him came and went within a heartbeat.

The trickle of sweat sensitized his skin. Charles waited a long motionless moment. If an arrow struck him, where would he feel it?

He believed every word. Darkwind wasn't the type to fantasize. Kimmer had been watching over them the whole time.

What now?

When nothing but the insect sounds of the land came out at him, he turned again and moved toward Terrance. Darkwind had given him leave, in a sense, to go on. He accelerated into a hard run.

...

It was a long hour before a bend in the river and trail brought the high walls of the distant fort city of Terrance into view. A flicker of motion made him turn his head.

Another party. At least three of them. *That makes four groups.* And he didn't know how many were quicker or more cautious that he never saw.

None tried to stop him.

Did Darkwind warn them about my weapon? Or are they just too busy to bother with a single man?

Strange walls grew taller as he approached. The city was much larger than his first estimate. It was a true city, not the village he'd expected. He got to the shadow of the dark gray city before a voice from high above called down. "Stop at the post or you will be shot!"

Charles glanced around quickly and moved to the man-high tree trunk buried beside the road. *Don't start arguing with people holding guns.* At least they hadn't ordered him away immediately.

Logs stripped, trimmed smooth, and stacked vertically three tiers high made a city wall daunting to look at—almost a hundred meters to the top. It could be climbed, he decided, but it would be suicidal if there were defenders on the top like there were now.

He looked carefully at the men he could see, "I have come to warn you. There is a large Kimmer force in the woods. You are in danger of an attack."

The spokesman laughed. "Boy, if you came out just to tell us that, you have wasted the trip. We know they're out there.

"No," the man continued, "Our problem right now is what we have to do with you. Just two days ago a Kimmer came up to the gate dressed up as pretty as the flax farmer he killed to get the clothes. He talked pretty, too. Now what can you do to convince us you aren't another of the same breed?"

Charles was silent for a moment. He was asking himself the same question. But he did not like being questioned, not by Darkwind, not by Peterson, not by these unnamed guards. *Everything is a test.*

Charles took a deep breath. *Okay, who am I?*

He remembered his job. He looked straight up at them.

"I believe you," he called, calmly ignoring their scrutiny. *I'll judge you.*

"That is consistent with what I have seen. That is exactly what the Kimmer tried when they took over our wagon train at Stampz Gate. Have they been using muskets here, too?"

"What are you talking about? Stampz Gate? What do you know about the muskets? Who are you?"

Charles smiled. He had been waiting for that one question.

"I am Charles Fasail, Alpine." He paused. "Currently, I am serving the Duke of Stampz as a Trade Representative to the palace at Condorcet. If there is a man of rank among you, I have Letters of Introduction to the Southern Governor which can serve as my bona fides."

...

It took another quarter hour to get him inside and face to face with the commander of the guard. The man sat at his desk in a tired slump, rubbing his forehead as he attempted to make sense of the papers Charles handed him. Another soldier knocked and entered, giving the commander an easy excuse to defer the problem. How to position men at the lookouts was plainly more important than a lone dust-covered wanderer with grand pretensions.

"Commander," Charles interrupted, "I have come several hundred kloms the past few days and I have seen—"

The soldier held up his hand. "I am sure that you're right that there is Kimmer trouble all along the trail, but I only have to worry about this one city. If you can give me useful information for my job, then I want to listen. Otherwise, I have a hundred men that need my time."

Charles bottled up the disappointment. An ambassador from Stampz meant little to a town under siege. He wasn't going to be able to play that role to any profit.

"Of course, Commander," he said, putting as much good spirits in it as he could. "Let me just point out on your map where I saw Kimmer, and then I will get out of your way."

Terrance

Terrance was a city of walls. Here inside the sturdy, buttressed outer barricades, buildings rose to turn the interior into a multi-colored maze of little canyons. The streets were wide enough for wagon, but all Charles could see as he strolled were the many-leveled fronts of the tall buildings. In spite of the obvious attempts the owners had made to decorate the walls, the limited band of sky made it a dark and gloomy place.

The people look gloomy, too.

The air cooled quickly as evening came, so Charles walked the streets, listening to the fragments of conversation around him. Especially enlightening were the bitter arguments between a pair of shopkeepers who had taken a break from tending shops with empty shelves. Charles bought a pastry hawked as a meat roll, but in fact only with enough meat broth in the mix to give it a tempting smell.

"As far as my family is concerned," complained the man sitting next to him, "the damage is already done. My stock is gone, and Mayor Cathyl's little wooden tokens won't buy me new fabrics when the roads open again."

"You're still eating, aren't you?" argued his companion. "My money is gone too, but we can recover when the Kimmer are taken care of. We have to last the siege. That's the important thing."

Charles nodded to himself. This was a market town, not only for the surrounding farm lands, but for the constant traffic up and down the Gaussland Trail. Terrance was on the main overland trail from Atlas to Hubble, and the Green River Trail branched here for the settlements to the northwest, Hahn and Berosus. Other roads connected Seneca, Liap, and the new settlements to the east.

For merchants, empty roads were empty veins. They were dying.

The hotels were filled, but even there, there were no happy faces. The man looked wistfully at his hard coin, but word had come down from Mayor Cathyl himself that none of the people already staying in his rooms would be turned out until the crisis had passed. The hotel manager was taking vows instead of cash. An apprentice scribe, he told Charles, came in twice a day to keep his records.

"I only hope we live long enough to make them worth something."

The only thriving concern, as far as Charles could see, was the temple. When he turned onto the street facing the wide building with stone columns, the scent of incense was thick. *Someone is keeping the altars heated.*

He could see several people bringing their offerings up to the priest. There was another older couple there who weren't as confident in their ancestors. The man and his wife were sitting on the steps, arguing over how to record their wills.

Where could she be?

Would he recognize another Alpine just by sight? There were no distinctive racial differences between the Hercs and his people. The best he could hope for was something obvious, a family resemblance, or the like.

He peered into open doors and along crossing streets as he headed toward the square where the rest of the refugees of the road were sleeping. He wanted to see a familiar face.

He had more hope for her, now that he had seen the people here. *It is not like Port Gartner.* He liked the place. *I haven't seen a single scribe, and there are lots of lettered signs in the shops. Maybe an Alpine could make it here on skill, rather than as a slave.*

A city guard assigned him a place on the grass where he could lay his bedroll. He was cautioned to keep his valuables hidden. "I am here," he said, "to protect the citizens from you, not you from the other transients. So take care."

His neighbors watched him settle in for the night. Newcomers were the only entertainment around. He watched them back.

There were five wagons, three with families—settlers.

One girl watched him constantly. She looked a lot like Maria Turner. He finally turned his back to them. He had other things to think about than girls and Herc settlers.

The other two wagons in the city square were grain wagons. Written in block letters on the side of both of them was the legend "GAUSS-HUBBLE GRAIN HAULERS". Charles wondered if they were full or empty. He bet himself the Stampz bribe money that the Mayor's guards knew. Riding out a siege was a matter of careful budgeting. The ruler had to know where every asset was and how best to use it.

Charles had no intention of staying long enough to see how well Mayor Cathyl handled it. He had to find the girl, and quickly.

He still had a job to do at Condorcet.

...

Charles hated the inactivity. He listened to the darkwind rumbling overhead, impotent to do more than whip the campfires into dancing spiral columns. There were mountains nearby, to the east and to the west, so the town walls didn't have to bear the full brunt of the winds.

Nowhere in the interior lands, he mused, *seems to have sunwinds as savage as the ones we had at Port Gartner.*

Part of him wanted the sea. The life of the port city was instinctive to him. He spent many an evening waiting like this, watching the waters whip up higher and higher, until the winds drove him inside. In spite of the siege, there was something about being with a lot of people, in a marketplace.

He remembered the Voice.

He had never seen her. She sang from somewhere in the city where he was not allowed, and he knew enough not to express any interest. The marketplace was literally one rung above his world. The other layers of the Gartner cityscape climbed one at a time up the inner wall of the crater. Any interest in a Herc lady from the upper city would bring official notice—official interest with clubs and short-chains.

But the Voice echoed her distant melodies and he hadn't been the only one in that distant marketplace to pause his steps in a vain attempt to make out the words.

There had been Herc merchants that he might have called 'Friend'. *How much effort had I spent to wall myself away from old Feng and Dehear? They had been good people. Just how many good Hercs have I been finding this trip?*

Perhaps it had been a mistake for them to have left for Gaussland. It was not at all like they had planned. *Oh well, Rad has his Maria. Maybe it did turn out like he planned.*

He looked over at the other road refugees. The girl wasn't visible. Perhaps she was sleeping in one of the wagons. He felt a stirring as he thought about her. *No, think about something else. Don't repeat Rad's mistake.*

For long hours, he didn't sleep. It had been a long and stressful day. But he could do nothing but think again about Darkwind and watch the nighttime activities; like the slow progress of the lightman carrying his long pole, lighting the lanterns atop the towers at the four corners of the square.

Terrance, like most cities, never truly slept the long night through. Merchants would always attempt to make the most of the long night. Six hours later, as the still passed, the lightman came again to put the lanterns out for the rest of the night, ending the internal debate over whether to pen a report to the duke.

Sometime later, he finally slept.

...

Charles woke at the bare beginnings of dawnwind, when the eastern sky, in a long bright ribbon between the buildings, was blush red from a sunrise still an hour away. The grain wagon puzzled his sluggish mind. He sniffed and rubbed at his nose.

No, he wasn't in the wagon train. He was in Terrance. He had to find a girl.

He stuffed his belongings quickly back into his pack. It would be nice if he could leave it while he searched, but the warning of the guard wasn't forgotten. There wasn't much he could do until the town woke up, but he decided to walk the streets. Perhaps he would see a sign announcing Herb Schuler's grain market. If not, there was still much within these walls that he might want to see. Moving was better than sitting another hour.

The guards on the walls were the only people awake for the first half hour he wandered. Gradually, more people filled the morning streets. He worked his way down the man-made canyons to the south wall, and then began a return path along an adjoining way.

A flicker of darkness above was his first warning. Like a white leaf, whipped along by the dawnwind, a Kimmer warrior dropped out of the sky. Charles shouted, "Kimmer! Kimmer from the sky!" Across the town, he could hear other cries like his.

Then there was a muffled boom of a gunshot. Charles fumbled for his impulse gun in its pocket. The Kimmer, farther down the street, ignored him, strapping a belt around the folds of his sailsuit. Without a glance his way, the warrior turned down a crossing street.

The impulse gun felt body warm in his hands. He fingered the indicator. There was not much power left. He had neglected the recharging. And now he needed it. Still there was enough for several shots if he were careful.

Terrance was packed. Every available building held guests from the road, farmers sheltering from the raids, and refugees from smaller settlements that had fallen. The shout of *Kimmer!* woke them all. In the span of a dozen breaths, the city changed from sleepy quiet, to screams and gunshots everywhere.

Charles followed the path taken by his Kimmer. From a window above, he heard a shout, "The east gate! They are trying to take the east gate."

Of course! Open the gate and let the others in. Darkwind's rusty blade flashed in his memory. *I've got to stop them.*

He ran harder toward the sounds of gunfire. The gate-house was swarming with people. A half-dozen guards, and as many civilians, fought hand and knife with their own number of Kimmer. Above on the walkway, three guards were trying to pick out the Kimmer from the melee with gunfire. The Kimmer were pushing, moving the defenders back.

Charles frowned at his impulse gun. With people packed so close together, an impulse shot could—probably would—kill more than one man at a time. He stumbled on the cobblestones. He pulled at the straps on his full-pack. If it came to hand to hand fighting, he wanted no hindrance. *I don't want to kill.*

Suddenly, two young women ran out into the street from a nearby building. They grabbed a fallen body and dragged it indoors. Charles froze for an instant.

Jelica? It has to be her. Too young to be Mrs. Haren.

A chorus of shouts jerked his attention back to the battle.

The defenders were falling. Two Kimmer had taken the gatehouse and were reaching for the heavy bar that secured the gate. The guards above couldn't aim at them now. The other defenders were pressed hard just to survive their personal encounters. A third Kimmer left the fighting mob to help with the lock bar.

Charles raised the impulse gun to firing position.

Just then, one of the Kimmer at the bar looked out at him. It was a young face. Perhaps his own age. Maybe a cousin of Darkwind.

Charles gritted his teeth and in a fury reached to adjust the settings on the impulse gun. He raised it again and fired.

A great clatter shook the gate, as if a battering ram had struck it. Charles lowered the impulse gun. He watched as the three Kimmer strained at the bar.

It won't move now.

The heavy iron support that held the bar was bent. He had jammed the bar securely in place with a pulsed pressor beam that had nearly drained the gun. It would take more than a dozen men to free it now.

Their moment was gone, the Kimmer looked to find no way out. More defenders were running down the streets. Gunshot boomed. The sulfur tang of burnt powder filled the air.

The last Kimmer leapt from the walkway, knife in one hand, down into the mass of defenders below. There was a scream. Charles could not tell what was happening, but soon the battle was ended.

He let out a breath he hadn't realized he was holding. He felt numb.

No saving the world this time. Some people lived, others died. And one of those still alive is me.

Charles had to lean close to the wall, as people crowded the streets. There were shouts and cries. A woman shrieked as she discovered the body of her husband.

He resheathed the gun quickly.

A mother held her cluster of five children close to her skirts, cuffing them close as they all cried and looked fearfully at the suddenly dangerous sky.

Several men started collecting the dead. The Kimmer were piled separately. One angry man kicked one of the bodies, "Fall out of the sky, will you? We smashed you! We'll smash you again!" He gave the body another kick.

Another man watched the kicker rave for a minute, and then led him away.

Charles looked at the Kimmer dead, decked out in their decorated and finely worked sailsuits. He moved closer, and found the face that had caught his attention before.

Were you Er Sun? he wondered. *What about the rest of them? Brave warriors all. And young.*

A guard came to inspect the bodies, and to shoo off the ghoulishly curious, like Charles.

At the guard's warning, Charles puffed up like a viper and declared, "I am Charles Fasail, Alpine! I am studying the Kimmer. I need one of these sailsuits to help me track down which Kimmer tribe mounted this attack. Now get over here and help me remove this."

The guard was at a loss, but he obeyed the voice. "We have to burn them. Take the thing if you need it."

Charles packed away the sailsuit carefully, fingering the light-weight, supple leather. *I love this thing.*

He was embarrassed by the lie he told the guard, but he had to have it.

He felt the snap of the straps against his body as the cape caught the wind.

Healer

Charles noticed a guard examining the locking bar support. He picked up his pack and started walking slowly away from the area, never looking back.

Jelica Haren.

The dark eyes, he decided, framed in that black mass of hair, that had instantly reminded him of the girl of seven years ago. She had been fourteen to his twelve.

She is pretty now.

A tug on his pack startled him. He turned, almost stumbling. Red hair and freckles stared up at him. The girl was little. He couldn't tell her age—he hadn't dealt with children well enough to know.

"Rad Fasail, come with me," she said, slurring the name a bit.

"No, I am ..." But she had begun running back the other direction. Charles stared. *What is this?*

A heavy man who had watched the exchange pointed at him. "Hey, that's the healer's girl. You had better catch up with her."

Charles, after a moment, began moving. She glanced back and then kept up her pace. Luckily, she vanished into a building while he still had her in sight. He dropped to a walk. He didn't relish chasing a child through this maze of streets.

'The healer's girl'? Surely, the child is too old to be Jelica's.

The door opened and a strong, strange odor made him take a half step back. Inside was a large room. Covering the floor were nearly thirty blankets holding the wounded.

Moans of pain came constantly from a boy against the far wall.

Many sets of eyes turned toward him. Three women, and the little girl, circulated around the room, ministering to the patients. The youngest of the adults, Jelica Haren, called to one of the gray-haired ladies, "Mary, bring some more of the clove water over to the fire, please."

It was then that she spotted him. Her eyes were as dark as he remembered, but they glistened.

She looks dead tired.

"You aren't Rad. You must be Charles?" He nodded, moving over to snare a stool next to where she worked. She turned back to her task. "You look a lot like your brother. Did he survive the Burn?" Her hands were busy even as she talked, molding a mass of what looked like soggy bread onto the ribs of a man still wheezing from his injuries.

"He survived the Burn," Charles confirmed.

She spared a half-second to search his face before she looked back at her work. "The way you said that made me wonder. Are you two fighting again? That's what I remember the most. That was a long month when I stayed at your house. The only thing I could do to keep you two from fighting with each other was to agree with one of you. Then you joined forces against me."

Charles tried to remember. That had been when he was much younger. There was a flash vision of her sitting at the table with the rest of his family, but it was as quickly gone.

"I am afraid our fighting days are over. Rad has been snared by a girl, a Herc." He glanced at the others. There a few ears in range, but he had to be honest. "He wanted to be a Herc, and I couldn't stay."

"You'll get over it. Nothing could ever keep the Fasail brothers apart." She sounded confident.

He frowned. It wasn't something as trivial as she seemed to think. "Have you become Herc, too?"

Dark eyes flashed, "A slave shouldn't presume to be like her masters. Or haven't you heard."

He drank in her anger. It fit his own so well. His voice was icy, "We were indentured. Dumb strong backs. Dock workers in Port Gartner. Forced to hire a Herc scribe to letter the lines on our own contracts. Why do you think I had to leave Rad?"

She looked back to her work. "At least you had a contract. An indenture ends." She paused and put the back of her hand to her temple. "No, I can't deal with this now," she said, more to herself than to him.

She wiped her hands clean on a towel fixed to the belt around her long, stained dress. "I need your help. As you can see around you, today's battle added a few more wounded. The ladies help, and Heidi runs messages for me, but I need someone who can read and who can understand my notes."

She rose and led him to the next room. The sight stopped Charles dead in the doorway.

Hanging from the high ceiling was a garden. Dangling with their bare roots and wilted leaves were hundreds of plants, each individually hung from rafters above.

"My herb garden," she explained. "When the Mayor ordered everyone into the walls, I had a choice of leaving the garden to the Kimmer and the winds, or to clean and dry them as well as I could." She laughed. "You should have seen it. The Mayor gave me six of the guards to help. I must have gotten the biggest and dumbest of the litter. I had to beat on a few heads before they believed me and treated the plants with care. They started out like they were pulling weeds."

He looked again. So many different plants. Attached to many were yellow strips of vellum. Labels, he guessed.

"The Mayor a friend of yours?" he asked.

She nodded, "You might say that. I saved his life, and about thirty others when the river plague hit a few years ago. I am the healer here. During emergencies, all I have to do is bark and the guards jump.

"But the good times come back, and I turn back into good little Jellie, expert maker of beds and washer of dishes." She didn't even try to hide the bitterness. "I could almost wish the siege would never end." But she shook herself, as if she wanted to rid herself of the thought.

Charles asked, "What do you want me to do?"

Back to business, she showed him her notes. Nearly twenty scrolls were filed in a rack designed for wine bottles. "Here are my plant descriptions. These are recipes for various medicines. The others needn't concern you. What I need is for you to make up the medicines I need. I'm needed in the sickroom, and I can barely take the time to wash my hands between patients. Your help will save two or three lives today."

Charles looked at the scrolls and felt a wave of panic. "But, I don't know anything about medicines."

"Look, Charles. It's all written down. You had an Alpine education. Your parents were scientists. Frankly, you're the only person in the whole

Alpine Duty

town I would trust to read and follow the instructions exactly. You will do it. You're an Alpine aren't you? Alpines serve!"

And he did it.

The day was long, but interesting. Twice he left the workbench to help with new wounded. The attacks were beginning to come more frequently. The wall was strong, but the guards were attempting to take the fight back to the Kimmer outside.

He was glad to get back to the scrolls. Blood had no appeal. And the herb room was the only place where the smell of old blood couldn't penetrate.

There were a lot of new scents he was learning to recognize; mint, garlic (lots of garlic), catnip, and sage. He cut, pulverized, simmered, mixed. But the scrolls were clear, and Jelica's tools and measurement spoons were of good quality. He didn't have any idea why he was making a particular concoction, but the making itself was pleasant.

He had only two visitors in the workroom. Jelica would pop in irregularly to tell him her needs. The other was "the healer's girl", Heidi. She came in and watched him in silence. He couldn't tell if she disliked him, or if she was just a somber person. He smiled at her, but she didn't return it. Some hours later in the day, she crawled into the corner and went to sleep. From the looks of the bedding, the girl lived there.

He looked closely at the sleeping face. No, there was no sign that she was any kin to Jelica. *She couldn't be,* he thought. The girl was too old. He didn't know kids, but she was definitely older than seven, maybe ten. Jelica had been fourteen when she went up on the slave block, and that had been seven years ago, she could not have had this child.

It was a relief. He didn't want that to be true.

...

"I can remember your mother forcing me to drink some horrible soup one time when I was sick. Did she teach you all this herb medicine?" Charles asked.

They had gone outside after the darkwind calmed. It was Charles's idea. She seemed one of the walking wounded herself, exhausted and blood-splattered. He requested, and quickly received, a pot of grish-grash for the both of them and he made her come outside to eat.

210

As she spooned a second helping of the beef broth and crushed wheat meal into her thick-walled bowl, he was struck by her age.

She isn't that much older than I am, but her face already looks lined.

The nearby street lantern gave little light, but Charles sensed that the food and the night air had shaken loose some of her exhaustion.

She is really beautiful, in spite of it all.

Jelica's dark eyes looked off into a gentler past. A smile flickered for a moment. "Most of the herb knowledge came from her. It's funny. She was a doctor, a professional, a scientist. I do the same things she did and I am a magician, a witch."

"A witch?" he asked.

She shrugged, "They don't call me that in my presence, but behind my back...." She took a spoonful of the hot mix and savored the feel of it.

She commented, "I have heard Heidi referred to as the witch's girl."

"'The Healer's girl'. She is a quiet one." He gave into curiosity. "Who is she?"

Jelica shook her head, "No one really knows. She had been living in the streets as a beggar for a year before I took her in. No one claims her as kin. If she remembers her folks, she tells no one about it."

"You took her in? What about your 'master'? What did he think about it?"

"Oh, Herb put up a squawk, he always does. But Jane, Mrs. Schuler, took my side. Don't think the Schulers are bad people; they aren't. Herb bought me as a housemaid for his wife, and it was just his luck that he got an Alpine witch instead. I'm grateful it was they who bought me, rather than someone else."

The bag of gold coin that sat in the bottom of his full-pack came forcibly to his mind. This Schuler could probably be persuaded to sell the "housemaid". To hear her talk of being bought was like vinegar. If only the money were his, he would buy her freedom tonight.

But the money belonged to Stampz. His hand came involuntarily to his scalp. *And my time, as well.*

He was pledged to a task that brought him no joy.

He stared up at the western glow. *What is more important than helping another Alpine in distress?*

She had not asked him for help, but it was plain she had not accepted her status. He had to win her freedom.

"Jelica?"

"Yes Charles?"

"I won't be staying in Terrance long, another day at best. I have a debt of honor to take care of in Condorcet."

She set her bowl down. "No, Charles. It's too dangerous outside the walls. Twice the Mayor has sent men out to get word to the Legion. Both times the parties were destroyed. We're cut off here. Besides, I need your help."

Charles shook his head, "The Kimmer let me come in. I can leave as well." He made himself believe it. *With the impulse gun, I can hold them off. The Kimmer aren't stupid.*

He wanted to tell her his plans, to make promises. But what could he say? That he would buy her freedom? With what, once the Stampz money was gone? And once she was free of Schuler, how would she live? He had nothing, he could offer her nothing better. Would she take his offer as intention of something more serious? He had to think this out. He had to have more time.

He nodded to himself, then spoke, "I will be here tomorrow, then I will have to leave."

But I will be back for you.

Escape from Terrance

Charles gave up and went walking the still. The other refugees had already settled into a routine. He had, too. He had slept soundly during the deep, grateful he'd rejected the offer to spend the night at the hospital.

There wasn't a quiet hour there during the day. Maybe they're used to the moans, but I'm not.

The only noise was from a group of guards changing shifts. No one watching the ladder, so he went up.

"Nice night," he commented to the guard who was resting against the firing wall.

"The devils like their fires," he muttered. He was a big man, bigger than Charles.

In the darkness, it seemed like there were a hundred flickering points of light. The Kimmer wanted them to know they were there, and waiting. But were they real campfires, or decoys to make their numbers seem overwhelming?

Charles pointed off to the mountain to the east. "That is what you really have to worry about." The heights had a number of campfires as well. None of the other mountains nearby did.

"What do you mean?"

"These Kimmer are fliers. With a stiff dawnwind, they can launch themselves off that peak and sail right into here. Isn't it obvious? They did it before. They'll keep doing it."

The guard looked again at the mountain. "There's more fires there tonight than last night."

"You won't be safe," Charles asserted, "until you can take and hold that mountain."

...

"Fire from the mountain!"

Charles got to his feet.

At least someone is alert.

People started hurrying out into the street, looking around for the threat.

"There is one of them!"

A kite, lit by the dawnwind glow, silently sailed across the sky, and crashed against a wall. Its smoldering wick ignited the contents of a clay jar and the wooden structure it hit was ablaze in seconds.

People quickly organized. Fire duty was well rehearsed in a city like Terrance.

Charles started to join the line, but half-way there, he turned and headed back toward Jelica's building. He would be more useful with the wounded.

There were other firebombs, more than a dozen struck inside the city walls. But, by the time the sun had risen above the horizon, it was all under control. Then the burn victims began arriving in force. Only two fatalities, but Charles found himself running low on the aloe ointment and Jelica had him switch to others. Heidi was sent out to locate potatoes, butter, and honey. Charles worked without a break through most of the day. When he got hungry, he snacked lightly on the burn plasters he was making.

Charles walked out a few hours before it got dark. He didn't want to say good-bye, and he didn't want any arguments.

He waited until Jelica became engrossed in her lesson time with Heidi. The little orphan was apprenticed to her.

Charles reserved his opinion when Jelica told him of her hopes that Heidi could learn the Alpine medical skills she herself had learned from her mother.

He hunted down the commander of the guards. But that one had no sympathy with his intentions to leave. Charles demanded to speak to the Mayor.

The Mayor's house was near the town square, in that part of Terrance that had the look of buildings built before the walls. They were lower to the ground, and they looked thick-walled.

"So you are an Alpine?" the Mayor asked.

Charles dipped his head in acknowledgment.

"And why is it you want to leave us?"

Charles indicated his papers on the table, "As you can tell, I have urgent business for the Duke of Stampz with the Southern Governor. I had no intention of staying under your protection any longer than was necessary to check on the good health of one of my people."

The Mayor nodded, "Ah, yes. Our Jelica is Alpine. Our good Commander Darret," he nodded to the guard standing there beside Charles, "informs me that you have been helping her with the medical treatments. Are all Alpines so gifted?"

"Alpines can rise to many challenges," Charles commented, irritated by the man's patronizing attitude. "Right now, it seems the challenge is to convince you that you don't need to worry about my safety."

Mayor Cathyl eased back into his chair, "Commander, was that the reason you refused to open the gate for Ambassador Fasail?"

"No, sir. Your orders were to open the city gates for no one without your pass. I only followed your order."

"And very correctly," the Mayor commended. He turned again to Charles, "You must understand that we are under siege. No one, not even an ambassador from an allied city can be allowed to endanger all of us. The gate must remain closed."

Charles refused to let it drop. "I hear your attempts to send messengers to the Legion have not met with success. I am quite willing to carry any message you might want to send along with my business for Stampz."

There was a short, impolitic laugh from the guard. The Mayor raised an eyebrow.

"Commander Darret, you seem to find the ambassador's plan amusing. Would you care to share your amusement with us?"

"Sir. We sent our best men. The 'ambassador' is a young man and probably doesn't realize that the Kimmer would have him roasted for dark-supper if we let him out."

"Ambassador Fasail, I must tell you that Commander Darret has been fighting Kimmer warriors for more years than you've been alive. He has the experience to know what he is talking about. But even if I could send you to your death with a clear conscience, there is still the matter of the city's safety. We cannot open the gate for anyone."

"Then drop me over the wall with a rope," Charles demanded. "You need have no worries about my skin. I have already traveled over eight hundred kloms through Kimmer-controlled land without trouble. I am Alpine, I can rise to that challenge as well."

The Mayor snapped, "My boy, I think you will find that there are quite a few barriers that won't open for you when you use the magic word 'Alpine'. The city gates of Terrance are one of them. Good evening."

And they were dismissed.

You know nothing about Alpine magic.

Charles left with as tight a control on his temper as he could manage. *Bow at them. Smile. Let them see you fume, but just a little. It stokes their ego. Deep will be here soon enough.*

...

"More lights on the mountain again tonight," Charles commented to Mike Jonsen, the guard he had met the night before.

"The devils do like fire. You got any good ideas what we could do about them?" Mike asked. "I hate to think of what devilment they are cooking up tonight."

Charles shrugged. "It's not as bad as it could be. They have to wait for the middle of the dawnwind before they can try anything. And you know to watch for them then."

"Yes we did. Most of our boys had their muskets loaded, ready to shoot the devils out of the sky. And then they send us flaming firepots! Much good muskets could do against that."

"You need to hold that mountain," Charles said with assurance.

The guard shook his head, "No. We would send half our men to take the place, and then we wouldn't be able to hold it."

"Get a laser cannon and blast the peak every morning. That would keep them too busy to send anything this way." Charles was only half joking.

"Sure," Mike chuckled. "Let's get smithy to make us up one of them things."

"How about sending your own firebombs on the darkwind?" Charles suggested. "That would at least keep them from putting up a big camp there. You could start quite a fire on those slopes." He looked off at the distant lights. He wished the idea back.

Mike waved it away with a shudder, "I liked the laser cannon better. I want nothing to do with Kimmer magic."

Charles chided, "Oh there is nothing at all magic about the Kimmer and their firebombs. I could make those things. So could your smithy for that matter. There is nothing magical about flying through the air, especially if you have a good wind at your back."

Mike was skeptical, "Oh, you think so? I suppose you can fly, too?"

Charles grinned, "Sure I can. I've done it. I've got one of those flying suits, too." He pulled open a side-pouch on his full-pack and extracted the sailsuit. "See this cape? It grabs the wind as you fall and lets you land without smashing yourself into bloody putty." Charles looked around. "Hey, I would put the thing on and show you how it works—except I don't want to get shot as a Kimmer."

The guard put on his thinking face, a frown and a pursed lower lip, then a smile lit up. "Hey, I know what to do. Come over here to the vat tower. I'll send Bobbie down to check on the ammunition and you can dress up there, out of sight."

He backed action to words and Charles fitted the suit and cape over his other clothes. This time, he worked the leg straps until he was confident he knew exactly how they worked.

He talked as he worked on the hang of the cape. The guard wasn't understanding the physics of it. But Charles wasn't trying very hard to make himself understood.

"One thing you have to understand," he said to the guard. "The suit slows down the falling. You can't really fly *up* with the thing. Here let me demonstrate." He took his full-pack and tossed it over the edge of the wall into the darkness.

The guard looked shocked. Charles put out a hand, "Hey, it's okay. I meant to do that. It is part of the demonstration. Now watch this."

He looked down into the blackness, and for a second he wavered.

Everything is a test.

He hopped up on the edge and jumped.

For the first second or two, he panicked, disoriented. *Everything is black!* He spread his arms, trying to catch some air and at least know which way was down.

He was tumbling. He had no visual cues.

Ahhh!

A streak of light flashed across his vision. *The Kimmer fires!*

He arched his back, twisting to hold himself flat against the wind.

Falling in the dark was stupid! I can't see the ground. I can't even see the cape.

Then the ground suddenly swam before his eyes. It was coming up fast. Instinctively, he tried to bend his feet under him. And he hit.

The ground was abruptly sharp rocks. He rolled several meters. He took the brunt of the impact on his left side.

The thing worked!

Rough landings aside, something about the cape had made him sail forward, as well as slow him down. He was well away from the city wall. Now he had to go back and get his pack.

I hope I secured everything right.

He looked back. Up high was the tiny figure of Mike Jonsen peering into the dark.

...

Going was tough, as he attempted to put distance between himself and the city walls while Kimmer and Terrance guards alike were sheltered from the growing dawnwind.

He had to crawl more often than walk, using every windbreak that he could manage.

He worked his way to the riverside, and then lashed his pack to a pair of logs. He drifted with the current some distance south before he came out on the western shore.

I have to be well gone before the light gets full.

He paused to look back.

"Oh, no."

The cloud cap was lit red. Something big was burning in Terrance.

I can't stop. Terrance needs her. They will protect her.

...

Mid-morning, Charles found a resting place. In ages past, when this spot was an airless desert baking in the light of a younger sun, a lava dike had formed in this place. When the rains came, water collected behind this natural barrier. The stream that began in the hills above pooled against the dike, spilling through a notch. The water streamed through, tracing an arc against the sky. At the base of the two hundred-meter cliff, the water struck the rock and filled the canyon with thick mist and a skin-tingling roar.

Charles stowed his full-pack above the ridge and climbed down with just the impulse rifle.

This is ideal. And I need a break.

Down in the noise and the mist, he found a good spot to prop up the gun. Carefully, he activated the charging setting.

The pressor beam projector in the impulse gun switched on, sending its influence out in two conical beams, one deep into the rock below, the other into the sky above, catching the falling stream of water. The setting was mild. Used in its regular fashion, the pressor beam could have turned the waterfall back, but that was not his purpose. Now it simply slowed the fall of the water. Instead of crashing into the ground, expending its energy into noise, mist and fury, the water flowed down, as if following the slopes of some invisible hill, until it passed out of the path of the beam and dropped gently the rest of the distance. All that absorbed energy accumulated into the impulse gun.

Charles watched the spectacle for a moment. He wanted to be sure that he was doing it right. Then he headed back to take a nap. It would take some time to finish the charging. The gun would shut itself off when it was done.

. . .

It was noon, he could tell that before he even opened his eyes. There wasn't a breath of air, and through the haze, the sun shone down on his face strong enough to be a little uncomfortable.

I can hear the waterfall again. The charging must be done.

Charles opened his eyes.

What!

He took in the sight of Darkwind, a grim look on the boy's face, holding the impulse-gun aimed at him. He froze.

"Hello. I see you found me."

"Do not move, sky-beast. I have opened your pack. Why is there the sailsuit of a dead warrior in there?"

Charles had never looked at the impulse gun pointed at him. The featureless tip was a dark window that his imagination raced to open. *How tight is the focus? Where is the power? His finger is on the button.*

Charles forced a smile, "I see you have found my impulse rifle. Did the charging sequence end on its own, or did you force an override?"

Darkwind shifted the aim, following his slightest movements. "Tell me why there is the blood of a Kimmer here! Talk, or I will kill you. I know how to use this. I, too, have killed a tree."

I should have hidden my actions before. The boy doesn't lie. He must have figured it out.

Charles eased back. He couldn't jump fast enough to evade a beam. *Don't make him feel threatened.*

"Darkwind, I did not kill anyone. There was an attack on the city. Many people were killed, but I did no killing!" There were tears at the edges of his eyes as he almost shouted the words, and there was guilt in his heart.

"When the fighting was done, I salvaged the suit. I have used one before. I thought I might need it.

"And I did need it. The leaders of the city would not let me leave, and so I had to jump from the wall in the darkness.

"I did not kill anyone!"

Darkwind watched him silently for long enough for Charles to feel his hand cramp where he had it balled into a fist.

Then, the gun wavered, and Darkwind handed it out to him.

Weakly, Charles took the cool metal into his hand. "Thank you." He glanced at the settings. It would have smashed his chest into a thin layer of red on the ground below him. He set it to safety, and set it down.

He looked into Darkwind's eyes. In some strange way, he felt like a brother. "I watched them fight. They fought bravely and nearly opened the gates of the city, but in the end, there were too many people in the city and too few of them."

Darkwind kneeled down beside him. "Did you fight?"

Charles looked down. He felt the shame he had been pushing away from his consciousness. "No. I have become a coward, I think. Twice now, I have stood silent while a battle raged around me. I have lost the taste for killing."

He looked at the boy helplessly, "There is a kinswoman in the city. I think if she were in danger, I would act. Maybe if the battle came too close to me, I would kill. I don't know. My stomach turns at the memory of the dead."

"We grieve for the dead."

Charles felt black shapes at the edge of his memory. "I grieve for myself."

Sheep Totem Crater

The rusty knife blade peeled back a thin strip of willow bark, marking the fifth bar. Charles eyed the result of his handiwork critically. Darkwind, looking over his shoulder frowned and shook his head.

"No. You marked a bear kill. The tail-mark should go up for a deer."

Charles grunted in frustration and tried the Kimmer tree-mark again. "These pictographs are impossible. How can you memorize all of them?"

Darkwind smiled, "You think your alphabet is easy? I have them all memorized, and not one means anything!"

Charles indicated that his latest attempt to make the tree-mark was ready to be judged. He added, "Having alphabet signs that don't mean anything in themselves is good. That way you can put any kind of meaning in them. The symbols don't cloud the message."

Darkwind shrugged and looked over the tree-mark. He took his knife back from Charles and corrected the mark as well as he could, ignoring the attempt at debate. It had been like this for two days. Charles had been revealing the Alpine magic, mainly reading and reluctantly some instruction on the settings of the impulse gun, but he demanded Kimmer secrets in return.

Whenever they disagreed, Darkwind seemed determined to avoid the arguments they had before. He would only shrug and let Charles's verbal probes stand.

If anything it made him more irritated than before.

Charles wasn't happy about the speed they were making. They took long breaks of necessity. He had not been able to replenish any of his food supplies in Terrance, so Darkwind was teaching him how to eat off the land.

Hunting. Cooking. Lesson times. It's a wonder we have any time to walk.

The woods felt safe and empty. *He's acting carefree. As long as he's with me, I really don't have to worry about the Kimmer.*

"You seem more cheerful today," Charles noted.

Darkwind nodded. "We are leaving the Er Sun lands. I have not traveled this way before."

"I would think you would be sorry to leave your people."

He waved his hand in a gesture that seemed to mean dismissal. "They have their war to fight. They have no time for my words. It is much better to learn the magic."

"I wish I had no more worries than being out from under the thumb of my family."

"Do you have a family?"

"No." *Not anymore.*

"What of that kinswoman you mentioned?"

Charles shrugged, feeling a creep of doom settle over his shoulders. "She is not closely related. Just as any Er Sun is related to you." *I should be making better time. This is a long way to go, and there is no road. I have too much depending on me.*

A lucky Kimmer attack could open the Terrance defenses and put Jelica in immediate danger. And what of Stampz? With the Gaussland Trail closed down, he was their only voice. Their cry for help had to come from him. And then there were others—the small towns, the besieged farmers, the stranded wagon trains, even his brother Rad, they needed someone like him to get the word to the Southern Governor. The Empire had to move some serious forces into the area or lose it to the Kimmer. Even his stated goal of getting shipments of powder for the blasting wasn't innocent. How much of that powder would be used to beef up the defenses of Stampz against Kimmer attack?

I can't tell Darkwind about my quest. If I succeed, many Kimmer will die. So what if it isn't my finger on the trigger. I can't allow the settlers to die either.

He had to be on the trail as soon as possible. "We must take advantage of the hour or two of Earthlight after the darkwind. Even at best it will be a cud or more before we reach Herc-settled lands."

"Cud?" asked Darkwind. "What is a cud?"

Charles's mouth hung open for a moment. Certainly even Kimmer knew that. He said, "C - U - D, from the phrase 'couple uv days'. Two days make a cud. Four days a quad. Seven cuds and sometimes a freeday to a month. Twelve months to a year. Surely the Kimmer count days like that, don't they?"

Darkwind laughed. "No! What a crazy way. Three days make a labor. Two labors and the day of rest make a week. Two weeks to a month, and thirteen months to a year. Twelve regular and the Thirteen Month. That is the sacred way. I would expect a magician to know this."

Charles figured the days in his head. "That makes a Kimmer year longer than a regular year. How do you count the new month?"

"When the Earth hides its face, or during the Dark. Sometimes there is a second rest when the Earth is late."

Charles nodded, "The Hercs do the same. A Dark can only happen when the Earth blocks the light of the sun. That happens only with a new Earth. If the calendar is off, a feast day is announced to get right with the sky."

"'In the sky is wisdom'," the boy quoted. Charles made a mental note to track that down when they stopped for the night. He was enjoying the Kimmer folk-tales he managed to wring out of Darkwind. Each time there was some new insight into this strange people knocked back to savagery on a new world.

. . .

This was a land of small craters. There were pits only a few meters wide, scattered heavily among small circular valleys as wide as a klom. The soil was generally porous. There were springs and small pools everywhere. Darkwind called it the Broken Lands, and the name fit well. It was too broken a land, even, for real streams and rivers.

But the trees loved the place. Charles and Darkwind made a twisty trek through the dense wood, following the animal traces and short watercourses, or hiking along the ridges of the crater walls. Plotting a course wasn't easy. The sunwinds let the trees grow only as high as the nearest windbreak. The land stretching before them was a smooth carpet of treetops. Only a careful eye could make out the circular ridges of stone among the green.

"Darkwind is coming," Charles announced, assessing the stiffening wind in his face. "We had better find a shelter. The inside of that big ring-wall will be good." He pointed to the ridge they could just see. It would be another few minutes, but they should be able to make it with no trouble.

They made the ridge top, Darkwind leading the way, but it took longer than he had estimated. The winds were increasing by the minute.

Darkwind, leaning into the wind, almost crawling, stopped abruptly.

"Keep going!" called Charles, shouting over the wind's howl. The bare rock of the ridge top was not a place to kill time.

Darkwind shouted something back, but the words were lost in the noise. He seemed frozen to the spot. Charles moved up behind him and pushed.

The boy struck back at him, with a doubled fist. Charles slipped, and skidded back his full body length as the wind caught him.

Instant anger flared in Charles as the rough stone scraped at his skin. He pulled himself up on his hands and knocked Darkwind to the ground with his forearm.

Through the darkwind howl, he caught a scrap of the boy's cry, "...tree-mark..."

In the dwindling light, Charles looked ahead. There, incised in the bark of a wind-formed tree, was the old scar of a Kimmer tree-mark. Charles could not read it. And he didn't have the time for a lengthy study. They had to get to shelter at once.

Darkwind pulled back at his touch. Charles didn't hesitate—he put his big hand around the boy's arm and forced him onward.

Three minutes got them to a shelter, where a wide tree-trunk was wedged against a large flat stone. Darkwind was still struggling. Once they were out of the wind blast, his frightened words started to come clear.

"We must go! This is Sheep Totem Crater. It is forbidden!"

Charles held a restraining hand on the boy's shoulder. "You will die if you leave here. The darkwind is roaring out there. Forbidden or not, we are safe here. Sit down! We stay."

The words, repeated several times, finally made their mark.

Darkwind moved to a place where he could sit with the cold rock against his spine and waited.

Charles made a fire, when the wind calmed down enough to allow it. His Kimmer expert was still hot to brave the dark and escape the crater, but Charles demanded to be told the tale before he would let either of them move.

Began Darkwind —
  "Kar-Let Mor Gan mighty hunter,
  Strong arm of Ba Ha San,
  Keeper of white spring land.

  "Labor he tracked pure white ram.
  Thru green breaks up crook'd trail,
  Down where wise trees grow.

  "Father beast flashing hoof,
  Horns at ready life breath hot,
  Great ram took his stand.

  "Up he followed bow and blade,
  Man's arm straight and true,
  White fleece burst red flow.

  "Death cry of Father beast,
  Shattered still of deep green bowl,
  Life breath curs'd bold man.

  "Down from sky twisting clouds,
  Tall and fierce anger dark,
  Sheep Totem shadowed death.

  "Blood red came two Demon beasts,
  Fierce as winds wild as sky,
  Stood over slain white ram.

  "Kar-Let Mor Gan mighty hunter,
  Blood of Angels eye of Man,
  One arrow stopped red breath.

  "Straight as sunlight second shot,
  Sky blood mixed with beast,
  Flowed red 'neath Dark stand.

"Kar-Let strode to Father Beast,
Hide and horn, head and heart,
Claim his worthy kill.

"Words as thunder Sheep Totem,
On sacred soil cursed rock,
Tread no foot of man.

"Magic arms Sheep Totem winds,
Wait o're red stained rock,
Fierce words now ful-fill.

"Death waits in deep green bowl,
Man's foot dare not tread,
Dark Totem pledges harm.

"Praise hunter Kar-Let Mor Gan,
Man bold and strong,
Son of Angel Ha San.

"Struggled with dark Sky Totem,
For his claim and worthy kill,
Sky-blood shed by Man's arm.

"Kar-Let Mor Gan, mighty hunter,
Strong arm of Ba Ha San,
Keeper of white spring land."

...

By the glow of a low fire, Darkwind's face was intense. His eyes were wide and his nostrils flared quickly as he rejected Charles's suggestion that they investigate the crater.

"My father was White-talon Er Sun. He was a great hunter. He taught me the words. His name was sung. But he braved the curse of Angel Chung.

He and ten others. Then the sky-beasts killed them all. I alone was spared. I will not stay here and die. The angels will not smile on me again."

Charles nodded. *I can't make him come, but I can't just walk away from this place. What kind of history does it hide?*

Charles picked up his impulse rifle and slipped it over his shoulder. "Okay," he said. "Go. But wait for me. I won't be too long."

Darkwind picked up the full-pack.

Charles snapped, "What are you doing with that?"

Darkwind's eyes didn't focus on him, as if he were something the boy didn't want to look at. He said, "If the Sheep totem kills you, I could not come back into the crater to get it."

Charles didn't know whether to snarl or laugh. "Well you will just have to do without it then. I will be bringing my own pack out. You just wait for me. Okay?"

Darkwind nodded, "I will wait one day."

"It won't take that long. This is a *little* crater."

Darkwind shrugged and slipped out around the rock and scampered up the ledge. Charles watched until he was out of sight and shook his head.

Superstition. He's a smart boy, but with all this nonsense in his head, I don't know if he will ever shake loose of it.

Charles had to start a warmball before he had gone too far into the pocket crater. By its light, it was clear that there was more to Darkwind's terror than pure nerves.

The trees on the bottom were large. They were also well marked. Tree-marks, hundreds of them, covered the giant trunks. Some of them were so ancient that only a faint irregularity in the bark testified to ancient marks. Charles could read none of them, but he could make out the spiral curve that meant "ram" or "sheep" again and again. The trees formed columns along side a well-worn path. He slid his thumb along the strap that held the impulse gun and put his foot to the path.

The tops of the trees, hardwoods mostly, formed a canopy that faded into the darkness of a cloudy, lightless night. It was cool and the light was dim. The roof was held up by hundreds of sturdy columns. On the ground, there were only younger trees, little or no grass, no bushes. There was only a thick carpet of dead leaves underfoot.

The path was fairly straight. Once it twisted off the left to avoid a large fairy-ring. The head-sized orange mushrooms were past their peak bloom. But the shriveled caps made a ring five meters across. It was the largest he had ever seen.

He spotted what he was looking for. But it took him a couple of minutes to realize what it was.

As the ground began to climb toward the central peak, the tree canopy thinned. The ground-hugging plants made the most of the limited light that would filter in during the day. The path became just a narrow trace among the bushes.

Charles pushed aside a low-hanging branch and stared at the sheep totem.

...

His eyes ached to close, and he moved with a tired slouch as he walked out of the crater into the morning light.

Darkwind appeared from among the trees. "Treekiller!" He reached down to a stash and came up to meet him bearing a clump of bofung.

Charles accepted the sweet chewy treefungus and set down his pack. "Darkwind, I am tired. I will need to sleep for a few hours, and then we will need to be moving on."

Darkwind looked timid. He ventured a question, "Did you see the Sheep Totem?"

Charles smiled and nodded. "Yes. It's a big thing." He pushed the pack up against a tree and leaned back on it.

"Did it speak to you?"

Charles had already closed his eyes. He waved his hand. "Later. I'm exhausted."

Serenite Patrol

"Is a man responsible for all of the consequences of his actions, even the ones he can't foresee?"

Darkwind frowned at the question.

"You have turned into a shaman since you saw the Sheep Totem. You keep asking whadivs."

Charles smiled. It was getting harder to force his face into that shape. The world seemed to have turned into a green and gray endless road, and the only thing that he enjoyed doing was talking to this little forest innocent.

"Come on. I want to know the Kimmer wisdom. Is he responsible?"

Darkwind tossed aside the rabbit leg bone and used his rusty knife to cut free another chunk of meat from the roasting animal on the spit.

"If a warrior spreads his arms to the clear air and is caught by downdraft, he is dead whether he could see it or not."

"Ah, but that's different. Of course a man must suffer the consequences of his actions, but is he responsible?"

Darkwind shook his head, "You hurt my ears with all these questions. I have to go up the hill for a minute."

"Why?"

Darkwind looked away, avoiding his eyes. "I have to ... I have to make a tree-mark."

"What kind of tree-mark?"

He was obviously impatient with the questions, "Okay! There is a visa tree there! I have to leave my mark."

"Okay, of course you have to follow the customs." Charles got to his feet to follow. Darkwind hesitated, but reluctantly turned toward the tree.

The visa tree was a broad-trunked variety of hardwood that Charles couldn't identify. The bark was covered with carvings, much like what he had seen in Sheep Totem Crater.

Darkwind located a clear patch, and with quick, sure strokes, carved a tidy icon that featured a spray of rays from the left side. "This's my mark—the darkwind. We need a better one for you, too." He thought a moment, and then tentatively marked a half-dozen strokes. "Treekiller."

Charles could see the root of the icon, a tree, with something else. He shook his head. *I wish I could read these.* They were much more than the simple pictures he imagined. Darkwind could read complex messages in them. *How do you draw a complex idea, like love or truth?*

"Darkwind, what is a visa tree?"

The boy gestured toward the tree before them with a smirk.

"Be my apprentice, Darkwind. We must exchange information. What is a visa tree?"

"You ask too many questions. Answer one of mine."

"Done. Just explain the tree for now."

He sighed, "A visa tree is a marker. We are entering the lands of the Family Chung and we must put our marks to show our respect to the Angel Chung."

"The Four Families. That would be the Er Sun, the Kimmer, the Chung, and the … Ha …."

"The Ha San."

"Right. Like the warrior at the Sheep Totem."

Darkwind nodded.

"Do you fight? Don't you trust each other? Why the visa tree?"

"You talk. I have seen sky-beasts fight each other."

Like Rad and I. Yes, I'm not one to criticize.

"I am trying to understand the Kimmer, not to change you. This is our pact. I will tell you about the sky-beasts and the Alpines. I really want to know if the Four Families are friendly, or are enemies like the Hercs and the Serenites."

Darkwind put away his knife and started back down the hill. He said, "My mother was Chung."

Charles followed, waiting for him to continue.

They packed up their gear, and exposed the buried fire to let it flare up and die out.

"The Four Families have fought over lands many times," he finally said. "It was the Chung who changed the wars ten generations ago."

"Angel Chung was the wisest of the spirits of the people. They were always small in number, but even during the Eastward Push, they worked to spare the bloodguilt.

"Frames of pure white wolf pelt were taken to the edge of each of the Family's lands, and a feast was declared. It was to be the first of the Thirteenth Month's.

"During the last month of each year, blades were sheathed, food was shared, young daughter's of each Family were married to the warriors of another.

"Before the sky-beasts came, the Thirteenth Month was a time of great rejoicing and great mingling. But now, even during the Thirteenth, warriors must carry their weapons and hide their steps.

"My father told me of the trek my mother made with him across the deep forests, hiding from the great wagons and sky-beasts with guns, until they reached the crater of my father's family.

"She lived two years there."

Charles felt the silence grow louder. He hefted his pack. "We need to get moving. Come on."

Darkwind trailed behind for several minutes before catching up.

...

The Broken Lands gave way soon to a broad valley. The sparkling springs gathered their trickling waters into the noisy beginnings of a river.

A scarred magnolia, with thick, spreading roots, straddled both sides of a small creek. They were able to use the roots as a footbridge.

From close narrow traces along the bank of the creek, they passed on to wider trails where hoof marks of a hundred deer so churned the soil that not a leaf of grass had survived. They spent darkwind and the first sleep in a grove of water birch on a small island above the lazy waters of the river.

"Answer for answer," Darkwind declared. "You owe me an answer."

Charles nodded, smiling. *More than one. I've been pushing the kid.*

"Where are we going?"

Charles smile dropped.

Is it time to lie?

He thought a moment before deciding how to start.

"Kimmer warriors attacked a wagon train that was heading into Stampz. They captured a great weapon."

Darkwind was silent. Charles couldn't read his expression in the darkness.

"I was with that wagon train. I fought the Kimmer, and the great weapon was destroyed. In its death, fierce energies were released, and the gateway into Stampz was blocked by rocks."

He deliberately paused, but no denunciation came. He continued.

"The ruler of Stampz placed a task on me. It is my duty to go to Condorcet, a great city on the Crisium Sea, and plead for help to remove the rocks that have closed off Stampz.

"Do you understand?"

Darkwind asked, "Did you kill many Kimmer?"

"Yes. They were brave warriors and I killed them."

"You should compose a song of their battle. I will take it back to my people when we are done."

Charles breathed out a little of the tension he felt. "Darkwind. I am sorry that I killed your people."

"Do not talk about this."

"But I need to ...."

"I don't! Don't talk about it!"

...

Charles awoke when he heard a voice in the distance. Darkwind, sleeping against the trunk of a pine, flickered awake and vanished with no sound.

Charles moved slower, shaking the fragments of dreams away.

Serenite accents. What are they doing this far east?

The group of men in dusky-red garb moved into view in the morning light as they walked spread out on the rubble of the riverbed.

Charles stood, and muskets leveled in response. "Halt where you are," came the command.

He had no desire to do anything else. You can maybe dodge one musket, but eight of them wasn't odds he liked.

"Strange," he said, with as much composure as he could manage. "I must have missed the Condorcet road. I was sure I wouldn't reach it for another half day."

The leader moved closer, "What is your name and what is your business here?"

He felt the strange rhythm of the sentence and the half-dropped syllables of words like 'bisess' and recalled the spires on the tops of buildings in Posidonius. He must have been nine when they made that trip.

"I am Charles Fasail, Alpine. I am on a diplomatic mission from Stampz to the Southern Court at Condorcet. I expect you to respect my neutrality and leave me to complete my journey."

The leader had no marks of rank on his clothes, so Charles added, "I need to know to whom I am addressing. What is your name? What is your business here this far east into Herc territory?"

"Vlad Demerich. And my business is my business."

The other soldiers were quickly picking through the campsite. Charles knew that his pack was next.

"Please! Let me show you my papers. I have letters of introduction that will confirm my story." He reached for his pack from the nearest soldier. Demerich nodded, and Charles took it. Reaching inside, carefully ignoring the guns, he dug out the leather pouch that contained his papers. He dropped the rest of the pack carelessly at his feet.

"Here," he opened the pouch and sorted through the papers and handed him the most ornate of the letters. Hopefully the appearance would be enough to impress the man.

Demerich set down his musket and looked over the paper.

"Do you want me to read it?" Charles asked.

He was looking over the seal, and then held it sideways. He looked up at Charles, and nodded.

Charles took the letter and started reading the stately sentences that said little in a lot of words. Demerich nodded wisely as he recited.

When he finished, he added, "So, you can see that I am Alpine, and thus a neutral. You must not hamper my journey."

"And why is that?

Charles held himself as straight and aloof as he could manage. His best hope for leaving here with person and possessions intact was to make these roving troops afraid to bother him.

He began to recite pieces of the story the Duke of Stampz had told him.

"Didn't you understand what I said? I am Alpine. Alpines are off limits.

"King Petron himself, sitting at the Council of Maury not twenty years ago pledged his domain to respect the persons and property of any Alpine traveler in his lands. If you hold me, you will be violating the word of your king."

"But an ignorant foot soldier wouldn't know about that would he? Oh, stop waving those papers at me. I probably believe most of what you are telling me. But you have to admit it's strange to spot an Alpine in these woods, especially one traveling with a Kimmer."

"What are you talking about?"

"Oh, don't act so surprised. We may not know our letters, but even Vlad Demerich can see there were two people sleeping here. And one was a Kimmer."

Charles knew he could neither confirm the man's words, nor could he deny them. He stared his best haughty glare, and prepared himself for more verbal run-around.

Demerich finally laughed, "I envy you, Ambassador. Traveling here to there, speaking knowledgeably to the great ones. It would be nice to have the ear of someone in power, someone with the key to the gold bin. I'm sure you haven't been sent out on your task as empty-handed as I have. Everyone knows how it is in places like Posidonius and Condorcet and Hercules. Not even an Ambassador can get a hearing without enriching a few petty officials. It is so different for me. I am sent out into these wilds with barely enough coin to feed my men."

Charles nodded, "Yes, it's often difficult."

The rest was haggling over the price.

Charles just hoped the man was an honest crook.

After some low-voiced words, and a blind search in his pack, Charles came up with ten coins.

"That is most generous," said the man. "Until this moment, I had grave doubts about your Alpine neutrality. But now, I can feel safe in my instincts and assure you that you can go about your business."

After a pause, the man walked off to join his men.

Charles could do little but fume at the loss of funds, and feel a little relief that the guns weren't discovered.

Darkwind popped out of the trees a little later. "They are gone up the trail."

"Bandits!" Charles was fidgety with held-in fury. "That crook took half my bribe money! I needed that gold."

Darkwind grinned, "What do you need it for?"

Charles glared down at him. "To talk my way past thieves like him!"

Darkwind ventured, "Then it was very bad of him to take the money that was meant for him."

"You bet. The money was meant for bigger thieves. I never planned on a Serenite patrol out this far east. These lands have been on the Herc map for forty years at least. If they'd been Herc Legionnaires, I would have let them take us—escort us, to Condorcet. He wasn't even patrolling his own lands. Maybe he was a thief at that."

"He had eight muskets pointed at you."

Charles winced. "Yes, and I couldn't get to my pack for anything. The sergeant had his gun on me every minute. Maybe he was a big enough thief for the money after all."

Darkwind laughed and turned toward the way west. Charles followed.

Condorcet

Charles dreamed of the sea. When he woke in the still, he felt its presence.

Darkwind remained in his motionless sleep; so quiet that Charles couldn't detect his breathing.

It must be the moisture. I know the sea is close.

And if the sea was close, so was the southern court at Condorcet. *And I'm not ready yet.*

Everything is a test, and he wasn't prepared. *What do I do with Darkwind?*

Charles lit a warmball and looked at the boy. There weren't any obvious racial hints in his face and his skin. The wide range of people that had lived in the space cities, and thus the settlers of Luna, meant that you were likely to encounter any flavor of the old races of Earth, especially in a port city. The only distinctive peoples he had seen had been from small isolated settlements where the limited gene pool of that family had stamped its mark on the current inhabitants.

But the boy's accent is distinctive. Anyone who had contact with the Kimmer was a hazard to the boy, and in the southern capital, there were sure to be many soldiers that might fall into that class.

Charles poked him awake. Darkwind looked up questioningly.

"We have some decisions to make."

...

It was the first of Apel by the time they entered the palace. Darkwind sat quietly on the stone bench and scratched himself under the unfamiliar white shirt. Charles restrained the urge to smile. The boy had borne up well through all that Charles had thrown at him over the past two days.

The transformation from Kimmer child of the forest to Herc servant boy was not without its traumas.

He'd spent the first thirty minutes trying to convince Darkwind that he should wait safely in the woods until he completed his business in the court. He'd known Darkwind wouldn't agree, but he had to make the case.

Next came the costume. Luckily, there was a bear-damaged shirt Charles was able to cut down to his size. His stitching was crude compared to the ladies from Stampz, but it looked tidy enough for a servant.

They cut his hair—not as much as was common for a Herc, but enough so that he wasn't obviously a forest runner.

Then came the bath; that took awhile.

Charles nodded at the result. Darkwind looked enough like a Stampz farmer boy that they should have no problem.

If he can only handle the waiting.

They were in, appropriately, a waiting area. There was nothing to do as they sat on the cold, white stone bench in an inner courtyard. There was only a pair of green-shirted guards in attendance, each trying to be more statue-like than the other.

Charles noted Darkwind's glance his way, and struggled to compose his thoughts. *I have to give him a good example.* But it was hard. A lot was riding on this meeting.

If Darkwind could handle the stress of entering come the palace, then he should be able to maintain the calm of a real diplomat.

The little rat is braver than I am.

Kimmer culture apparently sat on foundations laid back during the Great Plague. All buildings are likely sites of disease. Disease became curses. Add to that personal tragedies like his father, entering the Stampz guard house for tactical reasons, and then dying in the attack.

I would be a believer in the curse if I were in his shoes.

Darkwind was staring up into the sky. Charles followed his gaze. It was an impressive sight. The clouds above, layer upon layer, leading the eye to infinity, dwarfed the palace. He could feel comfortable with clouds. It was good to focus on things that put the city into perspective.

Condorcet was huge, even for an Alpine who had traveled the world as a child. It must be even more impressive for a Kimmer boy.

It had taken them a whole day of travel to reach the palace grounds, circling the great basin harbor. Their road brought them into a flood of foot and wagon traffic, refugees and businessmen, making their way along the coast road. They'd felt like twigs racing along in the swirl of a mountain stream, caught up in a current. They went where the others went. If the crowd moved slowly, they did the same. They'd walked the road through a trio of small villages. The bewildering variety of houses had Darkwind twisting and turning to see everything.

Darkwind watched with wide eyes as everyone from dogs to adults to small children walked in and out of the buildings freely.

"The world is different here," he told the boy.

Darkwind nodded emphatically. He whispered something about 'The Song of the Angels' and 'The Wisdom of Chung', but Charles couldn't follow what he said, and in the crowd was not the place for that discussion.

Nor was this courtyard. There'd been no time for explanations, nor any additional coaching once they made their way into the corridors of the palace. Charles took a cue from the duke and assumed that everything they said would be reported.

In addition to ever-present guards, there were layers upon layers of secretaries and ministers and assistants and even an ambassador. Charles was quite sure that his status as a trade representative was not likely to open very many doors in this place, although two of the officials had expressed interest in the Mendo Blue Cotton scarf that he wore knotted around his neck. They listened with interest to his sales pitch, but that did not help any with his primary task, speaking with the governor.

He did have two advantages in his struggle, however.

Every one of those assistants took a little of his coin. Not for themselves, it was understood, but to 'grease the wheels' for the next person in line.

Charles and Darkwind turned their heads in unison as the door opened. The assistant something waved them in. In a hurried voice, he coached Charles in the words he was to say.

He even glanced down at Darkwind. "You stay back next to the door. Don't move or say anything."

"James is mute," Charles said quickly.

The man said "Oh", and then dismissed that from his mind.

They stopped before a great double door of black stone laced with white crystals. The man went in, and then a minute later, opened the doors for them.

Darkwind eased to the side of the doorway, playing to perfection the role of the invisible drudge.

The assistant something bowed from the waist to the man seated at a large desk.

Charles followed his example, as did Darkwind. The governor, a gray-haired, large-framed man, growled as he hunted among his papers, not even looking up at the people who had entered his office.

"Your Excellence. This is the young man whom I told you about. He has come from far Stampz to talk to you."

"Umm." he muttered, "Dooley, go get me another ink-pot."

The assistant bowed again and left.

There was a long silence. Charles waited, knowing his role was to be silent until addressed.

Then, the governor leaned back into his high-backed chair. More to himself than anyone else he muttered, "Well, I can't get anything done until Dooley gets back. You there," he looked finally at them, "you have a minute."

Charles made a quick bow. "Your Excellence. I bring greetings from the duke of—"

The governor interrupted, "Yes, yes. I saw your papers earlier. I'm sure the little bastard told you all the correct things to say. What did he want from me?"

Charles took a breath, and then stated, "Gunpowder. Three wagonloads."

"More Kimmer problems, eh? Can't the boy keep out of trouble even in the back woods?" He shook his head. "His mother's blood."

Charles continued, "He could also use a man skilled in explosive work. The powder is needed to blast a giant slab of stone that has blocked off the only wagon trail into the duchy."

The man frowned and shook his head. "No, times are too uncertain."

"The Duchy of Stampz faces an economic catastrophe," his voice started rising, "if it cannot clear its access to the trade routes. If you would—"

"I made my decision, boy." There was a touch of boredom in the voice. "I believe your time is up." His eyes turned back to the papers on his desk.

Charles shifted his stance, anxious to get his words through. "Your Excellence. I also have news about the Kimmer attacks all along the Gaussland Trail. Terrance has been trying to get—"

"Boy," the irritation in his voice was plain, "are you now setting yourself up as an ambassador to all the eastern lands?"

"No, but there have been attacks—"

"Neely is a clever bastard, sending an Alpine. Well, tell him his ploy worked. You did get an audience with me. He would remember that I was the one who pushed through the treaty at Maury and I was honor bound to grant an audience to any Alpine who requested it. But my patience only goes so far.

"Ah! Here is Dooley now. He will show you the way out.

"Good day."

...

I have failed.

Charles walked with a flat-footed plod as he was escorted out of the palace. Unsurprisingly, even the official who was most interested in acquiring his scarf missed his promised meeting in the hallway after the audience.

I failed to get the powder. I failed Stampz. I've killed it.

Out on the street, he realized that Darkwind was still at his side. Still a mute.

"Come on Darkwind, the quest is over. Let's go find something to eat."

Instinctively, he headed toward the docks.

"The city is dusty," offered the boy.

"Lots of traffic," Charles agreed.

"People are like a stampede of wild oxen. Back and forth, full of noise, beasts stamping in the dust and bellowing."

Charles tried to smile at his brother of the road, but he couldn't make his face move like that. "Kimmer are poets."

"Sky-beasts have flat tongues."

Charles didn't even try to object. He hadn't the energy.

It's Apel. For two months, the rains have had nowhere to go. The flooding must be well underway.

When they reached the markets, Charles surveyed the extent of his cash.

"They must have a well-developed sense of smell in the palace."

"Why is that, Treekiller?"

"Because they managed to take every last one of my coins."

"Does that mean we can't eat?"

Charles frowned, "No. But I'll have to do some trading."

I can at least do that right.

Darkwind found a fence with a wide stone cap and rested while Charles moved into the mass of stationary and wheeled vendor stalls.

Every piece of his clothing, and every bit of camp gear he traded away was like a piece of himself whittled away with a ragged knife.

But I'm keeping the scarf.

After several trades, he parted with the fullpack itself, moving the anonymous wrapped guns and the bare essentials of his camp gear into a worn small-pack he purchased for almost nothing.

He jingled a few red coins in his hand. "This will feed us a couple of meals at least. That fullpack was getting to be more trouble than it was worth anyhow. A smallpack is more appropriate for what I have to carry. Come on. There's a lot to see."

It was mid-afternoon, with just a hint of the winds to come, when Charles waved to a man pushing a food cart. They ate on the bridge that arched high across the mouth of Little Circle Harbor. Darkwind picked a hot moist chunk of smoked salmon and popped it into his mouth.

Darkwind frowned down at the three-meter high waves that rolled by beneath the railing every half minute, but he was being too grown up to complain about it. The sea and boats were a world the Kimmer knew little about.

What have I taught him that's good for anything? He wanted to learn the ways of Alpine magic. Well, I've shown him that an Alpine is only good at destroying everything that he touches.

Darkwind turned his eyes to the far shore.

He pointed, "Treekiller. That is the road we came in on. What is that village?"

Charles looked. He was tired, but he had to answer the boy's questions. He owed him at least that much.

"I don't know what it is called. Right around here," he indicated the thickly clustered white-walled, red-roofed buildings that circled the eight-klom wide central harbor, "is Condorcet City proper. Across there," he pointed across the bay, "are a dozen little villages. I am sure these people know their names, but nobody else does."

Darkwind licked his fingers and shook his head. "So many people. Everyone eats dust here. They must be crazy."

"No. Not crazy," Charles disagreed. "There's work to do here, and people can make a living. Condorcet is more than just a harbor to shelter the ships from the winds. Natural and man-made meteor impacts in the ancient days carved a giant trench from the Fertile Sea south of here east to Sheb's Sea. Condorcet sits on the bridge of land that divides Crisium from that waterway. It's a gateway to the eastern lands. A short overland trip can cut out two or more days sea travel around the York Peninsula. It's no accident Hercs built their southern capital here."

"They're still crazy to live here." Darkwind pointed across the waters, "Forests are just over there. I can see them."

"No good. People have to live where the work is. Kimmer can live under the trees, because their work is hunting and gathering the food of the forest. City work is different. I was in a city like this, only smaller, for many years. I lived in a cold little room that leaked when the storms came. The floor was built of warped lumber and I slept on a pile of castoff sailcloth. And for all that luxury, my brother and I paid half of everything we earned. All because we had to live next to the docks, where the work was."

"But you left. You went to the forests. Why don't they?"

Charles saw the earnest young face looking to him for answers.

And I don't have any answers to give. I don't know anything anymore.

But still he waited. Charles could tell that the boy was worried about him. He sighed. *Make up something.*

"There are ties," he began, "that bind a person to one place, or to one person. More ties than you can imagine. A year ago there was a binding on me that made me a slave to carry burdens to and from ships like that one." He tossed a sliver of wood off the bridge and they watched it flicker and drift its curved path down to the low sailing barge passing below.

"I shook off that binding. But still bound to my brother, I set across the continent to find me a place in the forest. A girl took my brother from me. Once that binding was gone, I realized I really didn't want to own a piece of ground like I had thought. I don't know where my place is, but it's not a farmhouse.

"Another man, a powerful man, trusted me to do a great task for him. That was a binding, too. It brought me here."

He clenched his hand into a fist. He looked across the waters in the direction of the palace. Although it was hidden from view by the rim wall, he could still see the stone walls of that place.

He shook his head. "I failed my task. I was too small a fish. To them I was nothing more than a dockworker. It was worth a minute of their time to take my gold, but not to listen to my words."

He turned to look down at the face of the boy. "But that's not your problem. Nor mine anymore. If they want to ignore their own interests, if they want to condemn their own eastern lands to destruction... what can I do?"

He struck the dark wooden railing with his fist. The sting was almost pleasant.

I'm talking to myself. He sure puts up with a lot from me.

"Come on, Darkwind. We still have one last coin to spend before we can shake off the dust of this place and head back into your forests. I still have bindings on me but none of them tie me here."

The York Invasion

"Alpine marvels! Come see ancient artifacts of the wizards across the sea! Come see actual magical machines of the lost race!" A young man shouted to the passing foot traffic along the waterfront. He was dressed in a bright red leather vest with yellow lightning bolts emblazoned across the front. He wore a full beard, powdered to make him look older and stood on a small platform before a tent illustrated with all manner of machines.

"Lost race, eh?" Charles spat on the ground. "He makes me sound prehistoric."

"Ah! Gentlemen!" The hawker turned to them. They were the only ones who stopped. "Come in and see the marvels. Machines of the great wizards. Only a copper sheb apiece."

Charles fingered his chin in thought. "I don't know. What kind of machines do you have in there?"

"Well, sir! I don't normally tell this to everyone who passes by, but I have a hemostat and even one of the legendary framistats. There is a differential gear and its stereopticon.

"The Alpine Historical Preservation Commission, of which I am a founding member, has spared no expense in sending numerous expeditions to the fire-blasted isle of Alp to gather the wealth of that lost race. I am sure that the boy will find it a priceless opportunity to see the magic Alpine machines. There is nothing like it anywhere in this part of the empire."

Darkwind opened his mouth to speak, but Charles put a restraining hand on his shoulder and said, "I am curious about these expeditions. I have heard of a trip to the north shore, near Aristotle?"

"Why, yes. That was Commission. I myself was on that voyage. A hundred men searched the fire-blasted city. We were there within days of the great Burn and our search lasted months."

"I don't suppose you found any survivors?"

"My dear sir! I can assure you, no one survived the Great Burn. The Alpines and their magic are gone, save in the remains of their machines, like the marvels behind these walls. I am sure that the boy will find it a priceless opportunity to see the magic Alpine machines. There is nothing like it anywhere in this part of the empire."

Charles shook his head. "I am afraid we will have to forego the pleasure. We have only a single coin between us and there is more to see."

"Ah well, I do understand. Not everyone is interested in the marvels of the past. However, for an intelligent man like you, let me tell you of a marvel of the future. Yes, a marvel of your future—one you can be a part of.

"The Alpine Historical Preservation Commission has learned great secrets from their expeditions. Plans for a great flying machine have been drawn up. Riding the sunwinds, this great machine can fly men and messages across the waters. Not the insignificant eight kloms across Little Circle. No not even the fifty kloms across the great Condorcet harbor. But the full six hundred kloms across the whole Crisium Sea to the far ports of Lick or Petronsky, or even inland to the great city of Macrobius. We lack only sufficient cash to build this great machine. Your single coin could make you ten or a hundred as an investor in this great advance for mankind."

"Lick, Petronsky, Macrobius. Those are all Serenite cities," Charles pointed out.

"And they are all cities serviced by our great merchant fleet. When was the last time Hercules and Serenity fought, truly? These are modern times. Trade and economic advantage are the politics of today, just as explosives and warships were the politics of the past. Just think what an advantage this flying machine technology will give us here in Condorcet! And you can get in at the very beginning. Your coin will buy your share in a fortune!"

Charles smiled, and out of the corner of his eye, he saw Darkwind had caught on to the fact that he was laughing at the costumed entertainer.

He asked, "Do you have a drawing so we could look at it? I would hate to shell out good money for something I haven't seen."

The hawker was quick to comply. He spread out the sheet of rather inferior vellum showing the elaborate diagram. There was indeed a flying machine depicted. It was a bat-winged affair with the tiny figure of a man riding at the front.

Darkwind tugged at the his sleeve then whispered in his ear, "It won't fly, Treekiller. See the chair. It would nose-dive."

He nodded, and whispered back, "And the launching ring. With a wind pulling at that, the thing would corkscrew. It is pretty, but it'll never fly like that."

To the showman, hovering close to make sure that they wouldn't hurt his picture, he said, "Thank you for the opportunity, but I think we had better keep our coin for now."

When they had walked on, Darkwind asked, "Why didn't you tell him you were Alpine?"

He shrugged, "The man was a fake. Would he love me any more if I called him a liar to his face? Still, that flying machine idea was interesting. I would like to see somebody try it for real."

"They would need an Er Sun to fly it."

Charles laughed. "You mean a sky-beast wouldn't know how to fly a sky-machine."

Darkwind looked up at him with an open face. "Of course not."

...

They watched a man make large flowers from pieces of rope, to sell to the passers-by. Another drew pictures on the ground with colored sand. Vendors sold fish, fruit, and trinkets from far ports-of-call.

Charles poked Darkwind and pointed to a wandering amateur scribe, lettering people's names and selling them on scraps of vellum.

Darkwind nodded, then turned his attention back to an old man who seemed to be surrounded by a double-handful of children.

He was talking to them, and as he talked, he took out a pecan from his pouch and began tossing it into the air. Soon he added another, then another. Before long, he had a dozen of the nuts flying high above his head.

"Juggling," he was saying as his hands kept the string of brown objects circling, "was an art of Old Earth. And one that didn't survive the move to the Space Cities. After all, what use is it to throw something into the air if it never comes down again." The children laughed.

"Of course," he said, as his flying hands cracked one of the nuts and sent the kernel into his mouth, all without dropping the tempo of the circling nuts. "Here on Luna, a good juggle can help out if you don't have big enough pockets." He cracked another nut.

Darkwind looked back at Charles.

"What is wrong?" Charles asked.

Darkwind pointed, "He mentions those 'Space Cities' of yours."

Charles shrugged, "Of course. You didn't think I made them up, did you?"

Darkwind didn't answer.

As the juggler finished up his act, Charles joined him.

"How about a story?" the juggler was asking his dwindling audience. "Who will listen to the story of Admiral Sheb's journey of discovery into the eastern lands? How about the great war between the Space Cities? Listen to a tale of riches when—"

"Good storyteller!" Charles interrupted, when it was becoming plain that people were interested in the juggling, but not the stories. "We might be interested in a story. The boy and I are travelers here, and we'll be gone tomorrow. Do you have a tale of Condorcet?"

He showed the single coin.

"God bless you, Sir! I was afraid that I was going to have to juggle again. My hands are too old and stiff for another show just now." He rubbed his hands together, massaging the fingers. "And yes! I know the true history of Condorcet.

"Come sit on the bench. The winds are getting frisky early today. Condorcet has always been plagued by quirks of the wind. Some say that Roger Spinnaker, the original founder of this city, was driven here, out of control, by the fierce darkwind that turns the waves of Crisium into the finest white froth.

"I doubt the story myself. The Rocks of Athena, in the mouth of the great bay, are not known to be gracious to careless sailors. I think Spinnaker did some tale-spinning himself to make Condorcet seem heavenly ordained as the next Hercules. He was granted discovery rights to the land when he returned. It was his glowing praise of this bay that eventually caused so much Herc settlement here.

"Of course it helped that the land was every bit as fertile, and the harbor was every bit as magnificent as he portrayed it to be. Herc settlers came and stayed. Herc merchant ships soon followed to trade. And of course, where there are merchants, the Serenite pirates always follow.

"Spinnaker barely started his dynasty, when a pirate armada from da Vinci appeared and conquered the city. Yes, these red slopes became a Serenite city in one stroke. The oppressive rule by the pirate lords lasted fifteen long years, and the city itself developed a taste for vice that it hasn't entirely lost to this day.

"The Herc fleet, when it came, sparked a bloody rebellion. Blockaded inside the harbor by Hercs, the pirate ships were holed by catapulted stones launched from the heights above." He pointed to the rimwall above them. They could just make out the stone fortifications. Black cannon muzzles showed.

"The people dedicated themselves, promising that never again would the hated Serenites take Condorcet. They built gun emplacements at the mouth of the bay, and several other places to insure that no fleet would ever have a chance to take them.

"Of course, they couldn't know what would happen to them later.

"The years that followed were prosperous. Known the world over as a safe harbor for Hercules, the port became the natural center of power here on the Crisium shores. Herc influence stretched far north and for a brief time, Crisium was entirely a Hercules lake. Young Captain Sheb made his first mark in the world here, putting down the Serenite resistance in the far ports on the other side of Crisium.

"It was the same man, now Admiral Sheb, who sailed up the Dragon Strait to the unknown sea that now bears his name. He discovered the mouth of the Peach River and his reports opened up the Eastern lands to the ever-growing numbers of Herc settlers.

"Condorcet was enriched by these new lands. Merchants, not the army, built the road south to connect to the Dragon Strait. People could then avoid having to sail around the uninhabited mountain lands that formed what we now call the York Peninsula."

The storyteller paused to settle back against his stone bench.

Charles found that he was enjoying the story more than he had expected.

The man's accent is wrong, and he doesn't look like anyone I've ever met back on Alp, but he talks so much like a scholar.

"It was the Yorkmen who turned this tide of prosperity back," the storyteller continued.

"Just like the originial Herc settlers, they came from the great Space City Manhattan. Five thousand newcomers were ferried in a great beamship to York, on the southern shore of the da Vinci Straits. Armed with five laser cannon and hundreds of smaller space weapons, they claimed all of the peninsula and kicked off the small settlement of Serenites that lived there.

"Condorcet was not happy with their new neighbors. The land they claimed was part of the original Spinnaker grant, and they appealed to Hercules for help against the brash newcomers. Our people sent a small army overland to take the city, but York's beamship proved too formidable and they had to wait for the fleet.

"While Condorcet waited, the Serenites struck. Landing troops in a disguised merchant ship, they held the people of York hostage and took possession of the great armory of space weapons and the beamship itself.

"In this one stroke, the Serenites gained military supremacy of the whole world. Gun for gun, they had armaments to match the best that Hercules could bring to bear. And they had the beamship."

Charles had started to tense, and Darkwind noticed his attention. He put his hand on the long bulge of the wrapped impulse gun.

Charles nodded at his unspoken question.

The boy is listening, and learning.

"The Serenites did not hesitate to use their new power. With all York as hostage, the pilot of the beamship was theirs to command. Their fleet, minus two ships to hold York, set sail to conquer all Crisium.

"Condorcet was their first target. Merchant ships spotted the fleet coming, and we prepared for battle, but laser cannon on their ships soon had all Condorcet ablaze. Surrender was soon coming.

"After Condorcet, Delmotta surrendered. Others soon followed. When the Herc fleet arrived, at long last answering Condorcet's plea for help against York, they sailed into a Serenite Sea.

"Ah, but it was Admiral Sheb in the flagship of this relief fleet! Expecting trouble in the da Vinci Straits, they'd slipped through during the night.

Their first hint of trouble was the Serenite gunboat rounding the Athena rocks and flashing laser cannon fire at them.

"But Sheb was not paralyzed by the surprise attack. They too had laser cannon, and they were well-trained in its use. Return fire burned the Serenite's sails and rigging. Another blast holed him at water level. Before darkwind, Condorcet was back in Hercules hands.

"But the troubles were not over. The Serenite fleet had been using the beamship to coordinate its far-flung fleet operations. Barely had dawnwind died, when it appeared high in the sky over this very harbor. Sheb's first laser blast singed the high-flying ship. Damaging its controls, the ship shot straight up, shattering the clouds with a thunder that could be heard hundreds of kloms away. It was never seen again. Perhaps somewhere in the far reaches of space, it flies yet.

"With the beamship gone, the battle for control of Crisium was evenly matched, with two fleets, each armed alike. The Serenites were close to their homelands, but the great Admiral Sheb more than made up for that. Long and costly battles finally settled the boundaries we have today. Hercules owns the southern shores, Serenity owns the northern."

Charles felt his heartbeat race. The York invasion had been little more than a footnote in the history he had learned as a child—nothing more than a trigger for the pivotal war that had changed the fate of the continent. *This is the missing piece!*

"When Admiral Sheb returned to Hercules, the tales of his battles, and his victories made his climb to the throne possible. Under his hand, the Atlas/Hercules Alliance became the Hercules Empire.

"Now when Sheb the Second came to power—"

I know all that.

"Thank you for the story." Charles interrupted, leaving Darkwind with an open mouth. He flipped their last coin toward the man. The juggler plucked it out of the air instantly. Charles apologized, "I would so much like to hear more, but the boy and I have many kloms to travel."

Darkwind had to hurry to catch up as Charles strode purposefully down the street.

Where was that cloth merchant?

"Treekiller, where are we going now?"

Charles didn't answer. He looked at the sky. *There is still time to make a few kloms before dark.*

Charles found the section of the market that specialized in fabrics. He waded in, waving the scarf.

"Look up! This is Mendo Blue Cotton! This is the only sample of this marvelous new fabric in the entire southern lands."

He had heard sales pitches for enough years that it flowed out of him naturally. He was soon surrounded by interested merchants. Darkwind stood well back, watching it all.

"Choose two of your best experts to examine this. I am sure you all have clean hands, but this is a unique and valuable piece of cloth."

The questions were soon coming fast and furious.

"No, from Stampz. Believe me not even Far Earth has a cloth like this."

"This cloth has been examined by several members of the court, but I resisted their offers because I know that you good merchants deserve a chance at it."

"Yes, if you have a scribe among you? See this paper is my introduction to the governor as a trade representative from the Duke of Stampz."

"No, I cannot take any orders yet. The Kimmer unrest, you understand. This is the only piece of Mendo Blue Cotton you will see for some time. I will be happy to take the names of any merchants back to the duchy."

"No. Coin. Lots of it. I used up all my funds in the halls of the court."

Laughter.

There were several offers, and considerable internecine barter before Charles traded off the scarf to a trio of vendors. As he walked away, he heard them intensely debating which of the great ladies of Condorcet would pay the most for the item.

Beltis Island

"Where are we going?" Darkwind asked.

"North."

"Why?"

Charles spit out his part of the exchange quickly, as he had a dozen times since they left Condorcet.

I can't tell him. I've got to do this on my own.

"I don't want you to follow me," he told the boy as they paused long enough to ride out the darkwind in a village common shelter. "I'll take you as far as the forest road back to Gaussland. From there, you can find your way back to your uncle. My road is north and it is no place for Kimmer."

They traveled by earthlight for as long as the road was good. Charles bade him good-bye where the road branched. But Darkwind was waiting for him beside the road two hours and many kloms later.

"Go!" Charles yelled.

"No," Darkwind replied, quietly.

"It's dangerous up ahead. The Serenites might kill you on sight."

Darkwind shrugged, "Then take me back to the Peach River. I am bound to follow you. I did not think to learn the ways of a magician ... of an Alpine with no risk."

Charles spread his hands in exasperation. "I can't baby-sit you all the way back to your uncle! Time is running out. I have to go north."

"Then, I will go north." Darkwind set his lower lip firmly.

Who is in charge here? Does he think he can just wait me out?

There was a long tense silence, and then Darkwind asked, "You still owe me answers. Why are we going north?"

Charles could not answer, although the justice of the request bit into him. He turned away and headed up the trail.

The road turned gradually westward, following the curve of the mountains that defined the coast of the Crisium Sea. It was a stony path, with the sound of the surf often heard distantly to the left.

Trees came and went with the windbreaks. The winds over the sea grew to terrible force and nothing that grew could bear its fury. They made good time, traveling during the still of the night by earthlight, but the sunwinds cut deeply into their travel time.

Just after dawnwind, Charles was not surprised to spot the eight men in dusky-red uniforms walking ahead of them.

Other than a brief warning, "Don't talk." Charles gave no indication he saw them. He certainly made no effort to hide.

As the rear guard raised a shout, they slowed to a stop and Charles raised his hand. "Good morning, Sergeant Demerich!"

"Ah! Ambassador! What brings you out this way? Are you done with your business so soon?" Almost unnoticed he signaled a pair of his men to check out the trail south—just in case this was the herald of a Herc force.

"My business was the speaking of words to important ears, and that I did. I was done, so I left. I was told this was the road to Gem." He paused and inspected the dust-covered troop.

"Now that you bring up the subject, what are Serenites doing on roads the Hercs consider their own. General Howerd was interested in your presence, when I mentioned it in Condorcet."

The expression on soldier's face turned sour. "You discussed us with him, did you? What else did you talk about?"

Charles let his gaze wander, not meeting his eyes. "Oh, this and that. The Kimmer troubles along the Gaussland Trail. The muskets I saw. Minor things. I am sure you would be bored by it all."

Demerich looked like he had tasted sour milk. He looked over at Darkwind and Charles could read his quick assessment of the boy in the white shirt.

If the soldiers had any curiosity at all, they hid it well. They seemed far more interested in savoring the break from their march.

Sergeant Demerich sighed. "You are a trial to me, Alpine. You know I must take you to Beltis now. You and your boy."

"Well, I am afraid I haven't a single coin to persuade you otherwise. Thieves cleaned me out. Would you believe it—a lot of people in this part of the world take bribes!" Charles proclaimed it in all seriousness.

If they catch me at this lie, the job will be a little more difficult. But he won't hold it against me. Demerich is an honest crook.

Demerich sighed again and gestured for them to lead on.

. . .

"Beltis is a great island," Charles told Darkwind as they sat in the boat. "It rests almost touching the northeastern coast, and it makes the strait into a long twisty waterway, full of fjords. This is undisputed Serenite land."

That last sentence came out with a little more foreboding than he had intended. He had no reason to worry the boy any more than necessary.

I'm acting just like a Herc. I don't trust the Serenites. I say I'm not one of them, that I am Alpine, and neutral, but am I any different?

"They have better forests here."

Darkwind had his hand clamped onto the side of the boat, and looked longingly at the green in the distance.

I recognize that look. The water is a little rough.

"What do you think about the people?" he asked, hoping to provide a little distraction.

"I don't know. There are a lot more of those red warriors than there were of the green ones in Condorcet, but the mothers and the children all look the same. The dogs in the streets look the same. The market we passed looked like the other one. All sky-beasts look alike, as far as I can tell."

"Some day I'd like to visit your people, and see how they live."

"It's a boring life. I've enjoyed traveling with you much more. I'd enjoy this time if I knew what we were doing!"

Charles looked at the little ferry they rode in, heading for an unknown period of captivity or worse.

"I am sorry to've brought you into this. I tried to warn you off."

"Just tell me what you are doing. I can help."

Charles shook his head. "No. In this case I don't think you can."

After a pause, he tried to soften it. "I have done some things that have hurt others. I tried to fix it, but I have failed. I now have one last chance to make things right. To do this, I have to be Alpine, nothing else, nothing less. If you can help me, I'll ask, but it's really my duty and my geas that I must follow."

Darkwind digested it, and then nodded, "Okay, then teach me. We haven't had any lessons in days." He pointed off to another boat. "What does that say?"

Charles looked at the ship pacing them in the gradually slackening morning winds. Barely visible on its side was the vessel's name.

"Okay, what is your guess. Sound out the letters."

"Mar-ia. Isn't that another name for sea?"

"Yes, although it can also be pronounced Mah-REE-uh and is a girl's name."

There was a pool of water on the deck near them, and they spend some time drawing out the letters of words on the wood in slowly evaporating characters.

Charles had him write out the names of people in his family, correcting the spelling where necessary.

The ship was noticeably slower as the winds died out. A few of the boats had oars to help, but at least on their boat, the captain let out an angry shout when the noon calm descended, stopping them dead in the water. They were within clear sight of the forbidding docks of Beltis, the headquarters of the Serenite Navy in Crisium.

These were crowded waters, with a hundred ships visible from where they waited. Darkwind pointed them out, guessing at the names. Charles helped, when he was too far off. There was the Nadejda, the Luba, the Rusalka (that one was painted with the image of a strange creature, half woman and half fish.) There was the Tatiana, the Lena, the Svetlana, and the Natalia.

There were many more. Some of the bigger ships had names Charles recognized, like Pushkin and Lenin, great soldiers in the Serenite histories.

"A lot of the little boats are named after girls," Darkwind commented in disgust.

Charles nodded, "In history, for some reason the Serenites have a tradition of naming their ships with male names, but I have noticed the newer ones are often girls. I can imagine naming something I loved after a girl."

Darkwind considered what he said. "I don't know. My father had a knife that he loved. He called it Samson, a 'he' name."

Charles laughed. He shook his head, "I am sorry. Yes, indeed, knives are different. But there is a reason for that."

"What is the reason?"

He hesitated, and then said, "I will explain it later." *Maybe.*

…

They tacked against the gentle western breeze, coming to rest at a huge dock. Built like a staircase of mammoth proportions, the deep steps provided moorage at all stages of the towering Crisium tides.

Darkwind muttered, "They must have cut every tree on the island to make this thing."

Charles looked up. There was nothing but reddish-gray rock. The cliff rose like a frozen waterfall from the waterline up, and up, and up. It took a clear eye to see the moving dots at the top as men, making their rounds on the castle wall.

He stopped in his tracks a few steps later, watching a tiny platform, loaded with sacks, being raised via a hoist and a very long rope. He muttered, "I am not sure I would like to ride that."

A red-shirted guard answered, "You don't get to ride. You walk."

And so they walked. The stone staircase was long and twisted back and forth as it worked its way up the cliff. They had to step single-file through the narrow channel. There were no rest breaks either.

Several times, they passed through vat stations. The tanks were filled. There was wood for the fires.

Darkwind asked, "Do they think this place will be attacked? That's crazy. No one could fight his way up this path!"

Abruptly, stone cliff became stone walls. There were great square holes, deep windows. Then, a wonderful sight, the last step.

The top floor of the naval fortress of Beltis was a green courtyard so like that at Condorcet that Charles almost expected the green-shirted guards with the dead faces to appear—not that there weren't enough soldiers about.

A pair had nothing to do but watch them. They were herded to a bench and told to sit.

Charles whispered, "If anyone asks you a question, wait for me to answer it for you, but if you have to talk, remember you are James Dennis from Stampz, the place where I got you."

Darkwind barely had time to nod when the messenger came back and ordered them to their feet. They were led through a labyrinth of small corridors, dotted with wooden doors all made the same. Some of them were decorated with drawings of ships or animals. One in particular was a vivid tiger-head painted by someone with real skill. Darkwind mumbled some words, but they made no sense. Some were letters mixed with numbers. He looked at Charles but he just shook his head. *Later* was the unspoken answer.

They were taken to a door just like the others, except it was positioned at the end of a corridor. Darkwind reached up and clutched his hand. Charles gave it a quick squeeze, *He is inside a building again.*

The messenger knocked. They waited.

"Vaideete!" the man inside called, after a moment.

They were led into an office, well lit by the large unshuttered window overlooking the harbor below.

Charles was immediately captured by the walls. His eyes scanned the books, the maps, and the ship-models that adorned the room. He had to force his attention back to the owner.

The man sat at the desk, reading a scrolled message. He was old enough to show considerable gray hair, but he had the look of someone who could fight his own battles.

He chuckled at what he was reading and waved the messenger off.

"Have a seat," he referred to the text, "Ambassador Fasail. You too, boy." He continued reading for a moment, and then rolled it back up.

He looked them with a broad smile, "I am Grand Admiral Bardin, of the Crisium Fleet. Also Count of Littrow, but I am beginning to forget what my lands look like."

Charles attempted a polite laugh, but he was afraid it didn't register.

The admiral continued, "Let me assure you that this inconvenience will be as brief as we can make it. Serenity has always held the diplomatic courtesies in great respect."

He tapped the scroll. "Believe me, I gave no orders to detain you. My scout tells me you are a very difficult man. He let you go once, but you made it impossible for him to do so a second time."

Charles cocked his head and raised an eyebrow. "I was under the impression Demerich was illiterate. I had to read my travel papers to him."

Bardin laughed again. "He told me that. Captain Vlad Demerich is the product of the finest military school in the world, the Naval Academy at Posidonius. If I may be so bold, every Alpine I've met has assumed everyone else is too stupid to come in out of the wind! He simply played the role you expected of him."

Charles was honestly embarrassed. He'd been playing a role then, but he had made that assumption. He was too used to illiteracy. It had become prejudice.

However, I'm still playing a role. Don't let it drop.

"It's a shame," he said finally, a smile breaking through the neutral expression he cultivated, "that we had to play charades like that. I had on my best arrogant diplomat mask to overawe the ignorant minor official. If we had it to play over again, I would've liked to talk to the man. The Serenite Naval Academy was not unknown on Alp. When your people upgraded your standards—when was it? Ten years ago? It was then a topic of conversation in academic circles. By the way, are you related to the Admiral Nicolas Bardin?"

The admiral's face flickered through suspicion, and then gave into pleasure. He said, "The founder of my line. There has been a Bardin here at Beltis since it was built. My family has served Serenity well. But I sometimes wish old Nicolas had been as political a man as that Herc Sheb he fought. Then, perhaps, I would be sitting on the Red Throne myself. It was his doing that this very city was established for all time as land of the Serenites. My name carries quite a bit of weight in Crisium. How is it that you knew it?"

Charles smiled and shifted himself in the chair to make himself more comfortable. "Alpine schools drilled history into us—especially those crucial turning points that made the world what it is today. My instructor agreed with you exactly. He taught us that the Crisium War was the trigger that turned the governments of Hercules and Serenity from their old inherited ruling councils into the monarchies we have today. During the crisis in Serenity, the name of Bardin was a prime contender for that power. What minor change back then would have put King Bardin on the throne instead of Tellis?"

The admiral smiled and nodded, "My mother would love talking to you. She loves nothing more than telling everyone how much better we would all be with her son as king. It is positively embarrassing at times."

The man shook his head at some private thought, and then he sighed and picked up the scroll again. "Ambassador, the current situation—the unrest in the back country—requires me to inquire where you are heading."

"Did the report from Demerich tell the purpose of my visit to Condorcet?" There was a shake of the admiral's head. "Well, let me explain. This 'Trading Representative' is just a bit of a favor for the Duke of Stampz. I did some engineering work for him when an explosion..."

He went on to tell the whole story of Stampz's need for blasting powder and his trip down the Gaussland Trail to present the request to the governor. On a hunch, he included the laser cannon, but not his part in the explosion. He didn't even mention Darkwind.

It was important to appear honestly neutral, even to the extent of spilling an important piece of information like the destruction of a laser cannon.

Finally, after he was done, the admiral rose and called for their escort, "I am sorry, but I must delay your return trip for a few days. However, I assure you that Beltis kitchens can boast much tastier food than you can eat out of your pack. The matros will prepare a room for you and your boy."

Charles bowed and said, "To be honest, it will be pleasant to spend a couple of days indoors, out of the weather for a change. Might I ask another favor?"

"What is that?" Bardin was carefully polite.

"While I was in Condorcet, I listened to a street bard tell his version of the Battle of York. You have an impressive historical collection here." He gestured toward the books and maps. "I wonder if you would let me do some reading. You may laugh at our pretensions, but we Alpines get irritable if we don't have anything to study."

Bardin laughed, waving his hand to encompass the shelves, "Of course, I would be honored."

...

Charles carefully fished out a couple of coins as they walked behind the attendant. He clicked them together in one hand.

The matros half turned his head. Charles smiled, and asked, "Do you know of any rooms with windows? I need a good light to read the admiral's books."

Lessons of the Past

Charles returned to their room after walking the high wall. He lit another lamp—he was well supplied by the matros.

It wasn't how I planned to spend the cotton money, but an extra coin every now and then makes all the difference.

Darkwind was still missing. He was glad that their status as paying guests, rather than simple prisoners, meant that there was no official interest in the boy.

But where has he gone? Surely, he wouldn't have scratched his tree-mark on the door if he had intended to leave.

Charles made sure the door was open a crack, and then headed back to his table. No matter what he was up to, Charles still had work to do.

He opened the fragile paper codex carefully. The logbook he was reading now was one of a few written in paper, and for that he had mixed feelings.

Paper seemed popular before literacy was controlled, back when the cheaper, but less durable material was ideal for the transitory text of merchants. The making of it was one of those skills that couldn't compete in the day to day struggle of populating the new world.

Vellum, which was a natural variation of the preparation of hides, a skill that would always be needed, was the inevitable media for writing in such times. It was a lucky side effect that vellum seemed to last forever.

If the preacher ever attains his goal of building another printing press, then paper-making will have to be perfected again.

Charles had taken to the habit of hunting for any unusual or memorable words and phrases from the Serenite books and saying them aloud, and writing them down in his notes.

He still felt a twinge of guilt about abandoning the reports he owed to the duke. It was his vellum and ink he was using.

But it was handy to show the grand admiral when he called me.

The spur of the moment meeting had been a couple of days before, when apparently Bardin had a spare moment and decided to check on his guest.

It was just the right evidence to let him know I'm a harmless eccentric Alpine.

...

A couple of hours later, the door edged open. Charles didn't look up from the book, but asked, "You have been out a long time. We missed mid-meal."

The boy settled himself on the thick rug that was his bed, by choice.

"Why are you reading all these old things?"

"I told you that before. Did you forget, or are you just trying to avoid telling me where you went?"

"I remember your words. You want to understand the minds of the Serenite soldiers during the Crisium War. But why must we be prisoners for the sake of curiosity?"

Charles didn't answer. There was no use in debating that point.

"I still would like to know where you were. I was worried about you."

Darkwind looked away, "I was watching the ships."

"For eight hours? I took a walk around the wall looking for you just before the mid-meal bell." Charles set down his quill and looked at the boy.

"I'm safe here. A Kimmer boy dressed up in city clothes isn't. There are too many people here—too many things that could destroy your disguise. Kimmer are treated as dangerous beasts in these cities. I don't want to lose you to an ignorant guard."

It was clear Darkwind was agitated. He didn't take rebuke easily.

The silence dragged out until Charles sighed and picked up his book. "Would you like a reading lesson?" he asked.

Darkwind nodded and took the book and began reading where he pointed.

"Day twenty-eight. Stahrshee Pamoshshneek Drusk on watch. Hatch raised at third glass. Under sail. Fourth glass. Invader ship spotted off port. Helio sent to flagship."

Darkwind paused in his slow, awkward recitation and asked, "The Serenites called the Hercs 'invaders'. The man in Condorcet called the Serenites 'pirates'. Who is right?"

Charles smiled wide, "Kimmer call the new people 'sky-beasts'. The settlers call the Kimmer 'forest beasts'. Who is right?"

"And Alpines call everyone they see 'ignorant illiterates,'" Darkwind bit back, angry. "You didn't answer my question!"

Charles was shocked by the outburst. He dropped the smile.

He said calmly, "What do you want me to say?"

"I need to know... I mean, do you like the Hercs better than the Serenites? You did 'ambassador' things for Stampz. Are the Serenites bad? They've kept us here in this place. They won't let us go free. But you don't seem angry. The Hercs at Condorcet made you angry. Who is good?"

Charles shook his head, "I am Alpine. Alpines are neutral. It was that way before I was born. At first, I stuck to that claim because I was trained that way, but now I mean it. It makes my life easier. There are some men I hate and some I like. There is no one who can say to me, 'You must like him, he is Herc', or 'You must hate him, he is not'. I lived for seven years in a Herc city. That made me hate the men who stole those years from me. But I had to live as a Herc. I learned what that is. I can understand a Herc's loves and hates much easier than I can a Serenite's.

"But I am neutral. I will not judge the Serenite people, nor the Hercs. And now, I cannot judge the Kimmer either. Each is a people fighting for a place to live on this world. Each came from the sky. Each will fight and kill to keep its lands. It that good? Is it bad? I don't know. It's the nature of people. I don't have to judge. I don't have to fight. I don't have to kill. So I won't."

Darkwind frowned in thought. "What if," he said after a moment, "you had to choose between someone you liked and someone of your own people?"

Charles frowned, "An Alpine?"

He shook his head, "I don't know. I have so few friends. And there are so very few Alpines." He thought about it. "When we were on the Gaussland Trail, I abandoned you to go find an Alpine I didn't know. But I can't say that I really liked you then." He smiled. "That's a hard choice for anyone. And it's something you have to decide for yourself because you have to live with it all your life."

Darkwind stared down at the book glumly. "It's too easy for you. I want to be a neutral too, but I can't."

"Then do what you have to do. Don't worry about what other people say. You're a man. In my homeland, we had a ceremony for children about your age. My parents took me to the library, the place where we kept all the books of the ancients. There, I had to read aloud the history of Alexandria, the great city in the sky. I read about our people, the sacrifices we made, and the hope we hold for all mankind. It was then that I became an Alpine, charged with all the responsibilities and duties of our people.

"One thing sticks in my mind after all these years. My father took my hand and told me I was Alpine, not because I had said the words and read the books, but because I would do the duties of an Alpine. I would act."

He put his hand on Darkwind's shoulder, "You are like that. You aren't a man because of your age. Not even because your father is dead and you are on your own. You are a man because you make decisions like a man. You decide your own life. You act."

Darkwind didn't turn his eyes up to meet his. He stared down at the book in a haze of thought. He fingered the edge of the page absently. He sighed.

"Treekiller," he said, "there are Kimmer here. I saw them down on the harbor two days ago. Today I hid in a box and rode the hoist down to see them closer. Serenites loaded many guns and bags of powder onto a boat for them. Five of my people were on the boat. They talked with the Serenites like old friends. The guns were a gift, they were not bought with furs or meat."

He looked up, his troubled eyes searching. "I want you to tell me, as a man of wisdom, an Alpine—is this a good thing I saw?"

Charles opened his mouth to speak, but stopped.

I was right. The Kimmer uprising was pushed by the Serenites.

But what is the right answer for Darkwind?

After a moment, he closed his eyes and tilted his head back, blocking out the distractions of the present moment.

Charles reached back into his old memories.

"There was a time, back on Old Earth, when two nations fought each other to claim the new lands across the sea from them. One of the nations was more clever than the other. It made friends with the natives of the land and taught them to make war against the other nation."

"Who won?"

He shook his head, "I don't remember. I only know that the natives lost. A hundred years later, the land was settled by the people from across the sea.

"It is plain that this alliance between Kimmer and Serenites will not do the Hercs any good. It explains much. The Hercules settlements all along the Gaussland trail are being forced back into their stockades because the Kimmer are fighting with musket and powder."

He drummed his fingers on his forehead as if to make the brain work harder. "It's easy to see what the Kimmer want. They get weapons and support." He opened his eyes and looked at Darkwind. "Why did your people, your father, start the latest fights with the sky-beasts?"

Darkwind shrugged, "We've always fought them. Some of the men returned from the Thirteen Month with the new guns. It was reason enough, especially when the men from across the pass came to tell us of their victories. Then, there was a tale that the wagon train was carrying a magic weapon of great power. There would have been great feasting and many words added to our family's tale if the victory had been ours."

Charles nodded. "Someone finally broke the long silence between the Kimmer and the sky-beasts. Perhaps someone like that Demerich person. A deal was made. The Serenites would supply the weapons if the Kimmer would attack the Hercs. Under that pressure, the Herc settlements would retreat behind their walls, leaving the forests free to the Kimmer and their new Serenite friends. Soon, the Serenites will move.

"Perhaps they have already started. Demerich was patrolling Herc lands. The Admiral is keeping us confined to the fortress so that we can't pass on any reports to the Hercs. It all points to a major Serenite attack to conquer the Gaussland settlements. With that done, the eastern lands will be cut off from communication with Hercules except by sea. With a little luck the Serenites could own all of Crisium and the eastern lands within a year."

He cocked his head to one side as another thought hit him. "If this is Admiral Bardin's plan, he just might get his Red Throne after all."

Darkwind asked, "What about the Kimmer?"

He frowned, "The Kimmer. When the Serenites move in, they can either use the Kimmer as hired troops, or they can turn against the Kimmer and fight them."

"Kimmer would never fight for sky-beasts!" Darkwind protested angrily.

"At least not on purpose," he agreed. "But fighting the Serenite military is not going to be as easy as harassing the settlers."

He shook his head, "Surely the Serenites won't want to fight two enemies. They must have something planned to keep the Kimmer happy while they—"

Darkwind interrupted, "Treekiller, not so many words! Is it good for my people?"

Charles sighed. "Serenity is using the Kimmer to fight for them. When this fighting is done, there will be many Kimmer dead and the land will belong to Serenity. It is not good for Kimmer."

"Then I must warn my people."

"Warn them of what? You want to tell them it is bad to take free weapons? Would your uncle believe you?"

Darkwind's face twisted in unpleasant thought. At last, he said, "No. There is no one who would believe me. But there must be something I can do. I must not be unfaithful to my people. I cannot sit on a rug and eat the food of land-stealers!"

The Alpine drummed his fingers on the table. "Darkwind, it's dangerous for you to believe what I tell you. I'm a sky-beast and I've fought and killed warriors of the Er Sun. Think, and do what your mind tells you is true."

Darkwind looked up, "You have a plan?"

"Yes. If the Hercs are warned, then they will attack the shipments of guns. Some Kimmer may be killed, but the war would be directly between Herc and Serenite. Kimmer would no longer be caught in the middle."

"The men I saw taking the guns might be killed if I act to warn the Hercs?" Darkwind asked.

"Yes."

"My people would hate me for acting against them."

"That would be very hard to bear, if you acted just because I told you to," he agreed.

There was a long pause. Darkwind looked away from his eyes.

"Tell me," Darkwind asked, "why we came to this place."

Charles felt a shock go through him. He ached to take the boy into his confidence.

But he answered slowly, "No. My reasons for silence have not changed. My duties are not your duties. You have to decide your own course whether you trust me or not."

Darkwind's face darkened in brief anger, but it quickly became thought-ful. "I must act," he said. "But we have to escape this place."

"You rode the hoist down. Could I do that?"

The boy shook his head, "The boxes are small. You are too big. And I think a guard might have spotted me. He warned me away while I was replacing the lid."

Charles frowned in thought. "And there would be the problem of get-ting a boat to the mainland." He looked at Darkwind, studying him closely. "There might be a way. But it will depend on you."

Riding the Wind

"Are you sure it will work?" whispered Charles as they watched the guards leave their posts to seek shelter from the growing darkwind.

The boy crouched beside him laughed, "I am son of White-Talon Er Sun! I was born to this." His words were barely audible over the growing roar of the wind.

Charles glanced across the top of the stone wall to the darkening far shore. His eyes dropped to the white froth of the harbor waters. The darkwind was building, unhindered for hundreds of kloms over the waters of Crisium.

I ought to call this off. I can't let Darkwind risk this. What a load of nonsense I fed him! His people chose their alliance. I just want safety for Jelica and Rad and the duke. This is my problem, not his.

Far below, the roar of the surf broke through the howl of the wind. He edged closer to the wall, until he could see the docks. Most of the smaller vessels had been hoisted above the waves. The rest were secured in wide webs with long lines running in all directions. Not a sail was showing. Most ships appeared capsized as their closed hatches gave little to distinguish superstructure from hull. The whole harbor was buttoned up for the fury of darkwind.

Darkwind tapped him on the shoulder. He shouted over the winds, "It's almost time."

Are you sure? This is crazy! But the words stalled on his lips.

The boy checked the folds of his sailsuit as the wind whipped the white fabric, popping and snapping, almost pulling him from his feet. Darkwind Er Sun made it from the sheets of his bed, cut and stitched from the plans drummed into his memory by his father. The white cloth was laced with dark

271

ink lines tracing the bird talon that had been his father's symbol. Charles felt the same buffetings on his sailsuit, marked by blood and the patterns of a warrior who had not survived. The wind was hungry for him. He began mumbling pieces of the litany Darkwind had chanted for him while they had made their preparations. *Too slow; pray for speed. Too fast; salute the wind.*

His guns made him stiff, and it worried him. At least they were in pouches. He wouldn't have to hold them this time. Everything else, even his notes, his fancy clothes, his official papers, all were discarded.

Suddenly, the howl of the wind over the fortress battlements began to screech like a dog being slowly impaled on a spike. Darkwind tapped him on the arm and pointed.

Just as the boy had predicted, the high-speed winds meeting the cliffs mounted the obstacle, tortured into a giant vortex leading high into the sky. It was plainly visible in the dim light, a moving snake of angry air climbing endlessly into the night.

Darkwind did not wait. With a shout that Charles could barely hear over the wind, the boy leaped high with all his might. The hungry column of wind swallowed him instantly.

There was a spinning bundle of white, climbing quickly—then he was gone.

Charles felt his arms lose their strength, his stomach burned sour. The vortex danced hungrily before his eyes—a snake of pure violence. He shrank from it. There had to be another way! He couldn't abandon his things. He had been wrong to think he could. He needed more time to study.

Darkwind is gone. He will expect me.

Charles focused his attention on his arms and his legs. *Bend and swing. One. Two. Go.*

And he jumped.

He gritted his teeth. Thinking nothing, he stretched his arms wide. *Oak-leaf; Mount the sky.*

The vortex grabbed him. He tumbled. Sour stomach heaved. Warm vomit—but even that vanished instantly into the spinning void. Charles yelled, spinning, screaming into the sky.

After an eternity, the sky spit him out. There was a pop, a pain in his ears, and he was falling, falling in the clouds.

The quiet, after the roar of the vortex was chilling. But he could see the whole harbor stretched out below him.

Tuck your head; kill your spin.

The darkwind was all around him, but now he was falling with it. The violence was hidden. Tossed as a leaf in the gale, he felt none of the wind. Far above the white water, he could see none of its fury.

Charles stretched wide, holding the pose Darkwind had taught him, bending his body just a little to slide closer to the green and gray of the far shoreline.

In the air, there was no sign of white. He strained to focus, to spot another white bird in the sky. *He was ahead of me. And lighter weight, the vortex would have pulled him higher. Don't worry about him. He is the born flier.*

...

The cliff was growing larger. A block of gray stone, traced with lines of green where the forest had secured a toehold, it rose out of the dark churning waters below. Hands of white spray sent fingers of mist high against the rock. The sea wanted to claim it for its own. Charles felt a wisp of wetness against his cheek. The fury of the sea was reaching even his height.

But how high was he? He looked closely around him. The cliff was nearer by the heartbeat. Clear and crisp, he could see individual trees, the long vertical traces of waterfalls, the folds of the rock. But the crest of the ridge, with its proud pines whipping in the wind—it was *above* him.

I will never clear it!

He looked the cliff over frantically for some place where he could land. But it was hopeless. The drop was vertical, bare rock down to murderous surf cutting its teeth on the granite. He was too high to reach the water.

Paralyzed by inexperience, he watched in fear as the stone approached. He flapped feebly with his arms, knowing it would do no good at all.

Suddenly, he was breathing water. The very air had turned to a cold, wet fog. Then it stung, as a hard rain hit him in the face, welling *up* from the fury below. The straps jerked hard on his shoulders. His knees were bent, as he couldn't hold his legs straight against the updraft, roaring in his ears.

Grab the wind! Ride it! He strained to put his sail wide into the vertical storm. The darkwind had to surmount the cliff. He was going with it!

Then, as suddenly as it had come, the sky-lift quit. He was over, out of the updraft. The great mass of a tree slid quietly below him. Then another, only closer this time. He stretched his glide. His eyes searched the twilight forest for a place to land.

The terrain favored him, for a time. Past the ridge, land sloped downward. His glide kept him above the waiting branches for long minutes. Then, the land flattened into a valley. A secondary ridge was ahead. It was time to land.

The sky-glow flickered off water. A stream, nearly invisible in the darkness, ran parallel to the ridges. Charles shifted his weight. Down under the protective barrier of the ridge, he was no longer a feather in a storm. He could guide his flight. If he couldn't find a clearing, a wet landing would be a good second choice.

Abruptly, there were lights below. Trees fell away from the stream and he was over a strip of farmland. He fought the instinct to change course. It was more important to baby the glide. A cluster of houses came and went.

His ears strained for a shout, but he heard nothing. His altitude was gone. Reluctantly, he bent his knees and moved his arms forward. The sailsuit ballooned as it caught more air in the slack. Speed died, and he began sinking rapidly. The flat field below him was quickly underfoot in a springy shock of dusty wheat stalks.

He bounced, rolling into a ball. His sailsuit was all around him. He pushed it clear of his face.

There was a single light, motionless in the distance. The far away howl of darkwind was the only sound. His own rough breathing and his pounding heart were the center of his world.

I made it.

He shakily pulled himself to his feet, wincing at the noise he made in the dry stalks.

I really made it!

A shift in the wind brought faint voices his way. He fingered the straps on the sailsuit. There were trees a few hundred meters away. Time to hide. Soon enough, he would need to find the road to Condorcet. Darkwind would find him, he was sure. But right now, he didn't want to be found.

Especially not dressed in the sailsuit of a Kimmer warrior.

Into the Broken Lands

Charles shivered. The sailsuit and his guns made a tight bundle on his back. Everything he wore was soaked, and tiny hailstones rattled the leaves of the green-totem tree where he hid.

He kept his eyes on the southern road below. Darkwind would meet him there. *If he isn't lost in the sea, or killed in a bad landing.* The boy said he was a born flier, but how much experience did he have? *Skill didn't save me, just dumb luck.*

Or he might have been picked up by a patrol.

The woods were thick with Serenite soldiers. *Well, at least in this wet, they won't be shooting anyone.* The rain had barely subsided when a troop of thirty or more had passed nearby, heading northward. Several hours later another troop passed by as well, this one bringing a wagon.

Nearly a hundred soldiers on this road during the night. How big is this invasion force? How far have they moved? With a feeling of certainty he could not shake, he nodded to himself. *They will strike at Terrance first.*

He got up and paced the protected waiting place. *I have to get moving. A warning too late is useless. If the Governor doesn't put his troops on the road immediately, he will lose the whole frontier.*

Where is that boy!

It was a long, long night.

When the dawnwind began to pick up, he pulled out his knife and marked the tree with his symbol, Treekiller, and a pointer to the south.

I will leave the instant the wind slacks off.

. . .

He began running. The road south was a gamble. He had to keep a clear eye ahead. It would be safer to stay in the woods, but speed was essential. He had to reach Condorcet quickly.

And then what? Walk up to the Palace and tell the Governor, "I know you threw me out before, but listen to me this time."

What else can I do?

Nothing I can do. Nothing I can dream of doing will stop an army. Only another army can do that.

Darkwind trusted him. He was a silly little boy.

Running on an empty stomach. Stop thinking about it!

He couldn't have brought food, and there was nothing to eat on the road. *Oh, wait. Maybe there is.*

He waited until the road bent gently and then cut across through the woods, looking for the signs Darkwind had shown him.

There! It was bofung. He broke off a shelf of the chewy fungus and savored the sweet taste. Kimmer could eat on the run. He would have to use their skills if he were to make it.

Twice, he dodged into the trees again to avoid Serenite troops. Once, maybe, he was spotted, but there was no follow-up.

A little farther, he spotted a merchant wagon being held by a Serenite patrol.

They aren't attacking south, but they want to keep the word from getting back to Condorcet that a major invasion is happening.

...

He tripped.

He had been running in a daze for hours, off the trail, dodging back and forth among the trees.

Even with a low energy jog, he'd run himself dry.

He crashed into the mud of a small stream, and lay still, the only sound his ragged breathing.

I am dead. It's just as well. I was crazy to think anyone would listen to me.

He closed his eyes and the world went black.

...

Charles Fasail, Alpine awoke, angry at the buzzing of a mosquito. It wasn't fair to have to suffer this annoyance when you were dead.

But he knew he wasn't dead. *Just wishful thinking.* He could hear the surge of his pulse in his head. He could feel the ache of exhausted leg muscles.

He was even thirsty for the water that was trickling across his feet.

I'm just better off dead. My brother betrays me. I betray the duke. What good is an Alpine that brings nothing but destruction to everything around him? No matter how sweet my dreams, it all turns sour.

Charles tried to will himself back into the blackness of unconsciousness, but the rock pushing against his rib, and the annoying mosquito wouldn't let him go.

What am I trying to do? Go warn the Hercs. And why? So, they will stop the Serenites.

But why should I do that? I don't see any moral superiority to the Hercs. Why should the people in the eastern lands fare any worse under the Serenites?

Charles felt his tears trickle down his face. *It's not fair! Why should I have to be the one to stop them? Can't I just for once sit back and let everyone else live out their own destinies? It's too hard!*

A sharp sting on his arm—he slapped at the mosquito.

Everything is a test. If I've got enough energy to swat at a mosquito, then I have enough energy to act. I am Alpine. I will act.

Painfully, he levered himself upright. Hunger pangs shook him. He cupped a handful of muddy water and drank. Every movement was a new pain.

The invasion is wrong. Darkwind's people will be caught in the middle. Conquered people will be new slaves, just like the Alpines. It doesn't matter if they don't have the name—if you can't choose to walk away, you're a slave.

Everybody that headed out onto the Gaussland Trail walked away from the heavy hand of west coast nobility. I can't let them suffer what I did.

He took one painful step after another.

Move slowly. Find some food. Don't be an idiot again. It is more important to get there than it is to move fast.

...

Charles trudged through outlying villages, only casually aware of the stares he drew. He knew he must look like a dirty giant in tattered clothes, but he didn't care.

When he spotted a pair of soldiers in green uniforms, they turned toward him just as he headed their way.

The argument was heated. He demanded to be taken to the palace and to speak to their commander. They wanted him gone. The roads were full of people escaping the Kimmer attacks. The city guards were being pressed to keep order. When Charles walked away, they were pleased to let him go.

...

"Get out of here, beggar!" shouted the guards at the Palace. If they recognized him as the man they escorted out days earlier, it must not have made any difference.

"Listen to me!" Charles shouted back. "I have to speak to General Howerd. The Serenites are invading."

Everybody in the area of the entrance seemed to have something more important to be doing. People were walking away in all directions.

The guards put up with him for only a few minutes before he was faced with the muzzles of well-polished muskets.

Charles backed out into the street. Being right was no protection against bullets.

Several boys waited until the guards went back to their posts and then raced out into the street. Gleefully, they picked up rocks and pelted him with them.

He roared at them like a bear and took a couple of steps in their direction. The boys squealed in terror and in fun and scattered.

...

Charles Fasail sat on the bench and watched the vendors push their carts along the waterfront. He was starving. The aroma of juicy hot fish just a few steps away kept his mouth watering and his stomach churning. His eyes drifted over the crowd, unconsciously trying to spot a Kimmer boy dressed up in Herc clothing.

Down the road, he could see the fake Alpine show and the juggling storyteller. Only now his attention was more on the nuts the man was eating than on his words. He nodded when the juggler drifted his way.

"Back again for another story I see!" proclaimed the man, smiling.

Charles shook his head, "Sorry. If I had a coin, I would spend it on food. Besides, I am trying to tell a story, not hear another one."

"Oh?" The juggler shook the wide sleeves of his costume to straighten them out. Abruptly, he waved his empty hands in the air and caused a pair of nuts to appear magically. He tossed them lazily into the air, as if to start juggling, but bumped them over to Charles.

Charles grabbed them and asking no questions cracked them and devoured the meat. The juggler sat down beside him.

"Tell me," he asked, "this story you are trying to tell—is it exciting?"

Charles smiled. It was painful. "You want to hear my story? I warn you, you'll be the first. No one wants to hear this."

The juggler fished out another nut for him. "You aren't a skilled storyteller. A trip to the fish market can be entertaining if told right."

Charles told him the story of their trip north into Serenite lands and their discovery of the Serenite trafficking with the Kimmer, and of the Serenite army on the move. He also mentioned their escape from the Fortress Beltis.

The juggler listened with a frown. "You say that you and this Kimmer boy flew from the fortress wall off Beltis Island to the mainland in sailsuits during the darkwind. That would be great drama if you could make people believe you."

Charles cocked his head and grinned. He unslung the bundle on his back and unwrapped the sailsuit before the astonished eyes of the juggler. The storyteller's thin fingers reached out to trace the fine markings on the suit. "Tell me," he said with excitement in his voice, "where you got this."

So, Charles told him about his travels from Stampz through Terrance to Condorcet. He enjoyed the look on the man's face.

He kept the story simple, leaving out all reference to his guns and kept all information about Darkwind to a minimum.

"Then this," the man touched the sailsuit, "came from a Kimmer that was killed in an attack on Terrance. This is his blood. Did you kill him?"

Charles shook his head. "No. I haven't killed a Kimmer since I began traveling with Darkwind."

The juggler sat back on the bench mumbling something to himself. After a moment, he turned to Charles. "Darkwind, I like the name. We can use it."

"What do you mean?"

The man straightened his sleeves again, eyeing the sailsuit. "I can tell your story so that people will want to listen, want to believe."

"You can get an audience with the governor?"

"No!" he shook his head. "I tell stories to *people,* not to those royal busybodies at the palace! You came here to tell a story. Do you want it told or not?"

Charles thought about it. These were the people who would have to suffer the consequences of the coming war. If he couldn't warn the officials, maybe he could at least warn the common people.

He nodded. "Okay. Tell them."

The juggler put out his hand. "Give me the sailsuit."

Charles frowned. "Why?"

The man didn't take his eyes from the suit. "Because I need it to make the story believable, and because it is my fee for telling your story. Won't it look great! A genuine Kimmer sailsuit, stained with Kimmer blood. And the story! High adventure. An Alpine hero fighting his way from the pirate castle and flying in the sky with savage Kimmer. They will eat it up!"

Charles frowned, "It sounds to me like you are going to make enough money off my story as it is. Why should I pay you a fee?"

The man in the performer's robes smiled and spread his hands, "This is the way of the world. But I am a generous man—I will buy you lunch!"

...

Charles fell asleep easily that night in an inn on the road out of Condorcet. His stomach was full, he had a dozen copper shebs, and he had listened to another telling of the York invasion before he let the juggler have his story and the sailsuit.

He hated to give up the sailsuit. *That's why he parted with the coins. He would steal the story anyway.* Once the bargaining had started, he realized there were many ways to make better money in Condorcet, but it was more important to get the story told quickly, and believed.

Sleep was long and deep lasting, not only through the deep-sleep and the still but up into the beginnings of dawnwind as well. Then, overworked muscles and strains of other sorts had their say.

Dreams came and went.

He was chased through an endless forest, his lungs on fire for air. The road branched and Darkwind called at him from the left. Jelica called from the right. The Presence behind was overtaking him. He could feel its hunger. Then a great voice came from the sky, demanding the Word.

When dawnwind peaked, its howl waking him from his sleep, Charles felt every ache and every strain, but he knew he was on the right path.

. . .

Charles discovered two things during the first hour on the morning trail north.

The Herc army was active. The faces of the legionnaires he passed were awake. They looked at him closely, as they looked closely at everyone on the road. Soldiers in Herc green scanned the ridge tops as if they expected to see something there. It was officially business as usual. But the refugees had increased. The men with the guns knew that something was happening, even if they weren't being told what.

Charles was glad. Neutral or not, he hated to see the Hercs caught empty-handed. Maybe the storyteller would do some good at that.

The second thing Charles discovered was that the coast road was a ridiculous way to get to where he wanted to go. The map in his head was still good and with nothing to carry but his guns and the clothes on his back, there were better routes.

The land around the great Crisium Sea formed a series of great ridges, the frozen shock waves of a meteor impact great beyond comprehension, an event older than life itself on Old Earth. Unnumbered smaller crater impacts had churned the landscape in the eons since, but the ridges still dominated the land. Charles found a trail through the forest, following the path of generations of deer and buffalo and antelope, taking advantage of their instinct for finding the easiest routes.

He knew where he had to go—the Broken Lands, as Darkwind had called them. His path fell into a cycle. He would head east, following the animal traces over the pass into the next valley. From there he would follow the stream courses north until a churned patch on the bank told of another route east.

A feel for the trees and the land was telling him that he was nearing the route he had taken with Darkwind, when wagon tracks caught him by surprise.

Oh no! Serenites.

Frustration and rage churned his stomach.

Not here! They can't take this away from me, too!

The water was muddy. The stems of grass bent by the wheels had barely begun to straighten. They must be very close.

Charles flowed quickly into the concealing shade of the trees. Darkwind had talked about tracking and how to read the land. Charles put it into practice.

From the prints, he could tell that there were two wagons, and over a dozen men. The flower imprint in the dirt where they had stacked their guns confirmed that they were soldiers. The chopped vegetation told him that this was the first wagon following this route.

I have to get there first.

He stalked them. It took an hour until he had them in sight. From the darkness under the trees, he watched the red-shirted men make steady progress up toward the pass. The impulse gun was in his hands. He was tempted to slow them down. A broken wheel would be easy.

But he decided against it. They were still a dozen kloms from Sheep Totem Crater. These were the Broken Lands. They might pass by and never suspect what it held.

Charles moved quietly, alive to the possibility of Serenite scouts moving in the trees with him, safeguarding their party.

He followed a circling path that took him well clear of the new road.

A Kimmer tree-mark pointed the way for him. His heart beat louder as he made his way over the rim, into Sheep Totem Crater.

An ancient tree scarred with old knife marks showed the trail he'd followed before. He noted gratefully that the trail was no more disturbed than when he'd left it.

Down into the shaded pocket crater he ran. The path was light under his feet. The twist in the path, where there had been the fairy ring last time, alerted him. He slowed up.

There in the glade, just as he had seen it before, was the Sheep Totem. Tall and smooth, shining as no metal he was familiar with, was the key to his hopes—the lost beamship of the Battle of York.

Sheep Totem Test

Charles knew what to do. He'd rehearsed it hundreds of times in his mind.

The beamship resembled nothing more than the flashlight he and his brother had used as children, before the Burn. He vaguely remembered the two beamships in Aristotle. They'd been off-limits to only a few trained people, but he remembered them as silvery, and fatter. This metal cylinder was fifty meters tall and a dozen meters wide. It was a giant tower of clean blue metal. Only its presence in the midst of a grove of giant dark green trees kept it from dominating the scene.

Circling it, like a giant version of the mushroom fairy ring, were dozens of white stones. Charles cautiously moved up and sat on one of them. Feeling curiously at one with the Kimmer chieftains and wise men who must have sat thus, he stretched out his hand toward the cylinder.

The instant his fingertip passed the critical distance, the air shook with the voice.

"HALT AND STATE THE PASSWORD!"

It was just as he remembered it from that day when he left Darkwind and come here alone. Only then, he'd been stupid enough to ignore the command and took another step forward. A pressor beam had slapped him instantly several dozen meters into the bushes. Only good luck let him land cleanly.

In retrospect, the careful positioning of the stones and the well-marked border circle should have told him something. But his thought at the time was that it was some Kimmer religious marking.

Charles smiled. *Religious, yes! If you don't follow the markings religiously, you'll be dead.*

"The Trident and the Blood!" he called. It was the battle cry of the Serenite navy during the York Invasion.

"STAND BACK. UNAUTHORIZED PERSONS WILL BE REPELLED."

Charles sighed. He hadn't really expected to hit it on the first try, but it would have been nice. That other day, after he had picked himself up off the ground and let the world stop spinning around his head, he had tried random guesses for nearly a day.

There was no way to guess how many Kimmer had sat there and tried their guesses as well. But somewhere in the memory of the robot brain of the beamship, was a word or phrase that was the key to its secrets.

And he had the advantage. That password was set either by a Yorkman pilot or a Serenite naval officer. Somewhere, in the books and records of those times he had painstakingly read, was the clue. He had a hundred prime candidates on the tip of his tongue. All he had to do was try them. One at a time. He sighed again.

...

It was a long day. The rigid formula was tiring, far out of proportion to the effort he put into it: Put out your hand. Wait for the response. Shout your word. Listen to the rejection.

With unwanted ears within an easy walk, there was the added uneasiness every time the ship spoke in its tree-shaking voice.

Charles took several breaks, partly to convince himself that no matter how loud the voice was, the dense forest and the crater walls themselves would prevent the sound from carrying far. He also set some rabbit snares, using twigs and rock like Darkwind had taught him. He missed the coil of wire he'd stupidly left in the fortress.

By the time the sun had set behind the crater walls and the wind had risen to a howl, he had acquired one rabbit for supper and had discovered three hundred and eighty-four words that were not the key.

Perhaps I need to try some more York phrases, he thought to himself as he tended the small fire near the ship. He kept it well controlled in fear of the gusty eddies and whirlpools of wind that were the extent of the darkwind, down here in the bottom of the crater.

He'd finished the last of the Old Russian phrases he knew. But perhaps it had been the Yorkman pilot, not the two Serenite officers, who had set the password after all.

Charles banked the coals when the winds began to die out.

He had to go look for the Serenites. He felt their presence—something evil in the dark behind him, waiting for him to sleep.

It will be so different, if I can just find the key word.

He was certain that nothing short of a laser cannon would break through those metal walls. Even if the machine could no longer fly, still he would have a safe haven where he could rest. There were secrets of great power inside. That was his hope, and his fear.

If he could get the machine to work, he could single-handedly restore the greatness of Alp. With a beamship, he could call the scattered members of his people back to their homeland. They could reseed, rebuild. With a beamship, they could have a defense without match.

But it would take time. He frowned. There were no armies of exiles he could call, just a handful of people. Some, like Rad, might not come. Was it even possible to rebuild an Alpine nation from the few remaining? Even without opposition?

For there would be opposition. He had no doubt about that.

What would Serenity or Hercules do if either of them knew the York beamship still existed?

They would kill to get it. Or failing that, they would do everything in their power to destroy it.

Possession of this very ship had undone the conquests of Sheb the First. There was nothing very different today to prevent it from happening all over again.

Am I up to fighting the whole world for this?

It was a lovely dream. A small group of Alpines returning to their island to establish themselves once again as the cream of the human race. They could even take the beamship back into space.

The Space Cities were still there, waiting unchanged from the day they'd been abandoned, holding secure the old secrets. Wasn't this what drove his people? The dream of restoration?

Yes. I will fight for it. Restore the ship. Restore Alp. Restore the human race. It's what I have to do.

...

At the rim of the crater, standing in the dark, Charles discovered he didn't have to go hunting for the Serenites. The wind-scoured rock of the crater lip was the highest point of land. His view from there was excellent.

Due south, about five kloms away, the tips of the trees were alight from the glow of a large campfire.

They will miss me, but not by much.

If this was to be a new road for the advancing army, it wasn't going to be good enough. Hunting parties would be sure to find this place. If not tonight, then before the season was out, the Sheep Totem Crater would be in Serenite hands.

Charles headed back down the trail to the stone shelter where he and Darkwind had slept before. He needed sleep, but his mind was on fire with worry.

I have to find the key! Then fly it out of here secretly, so no one will know of its existence.

His worries shut off instantly, when he heard a sound from within the darkness. He slipped the impulse gun from its sleeve. The fight might start now.

There was no sign of motion. There was no light down in the shelter. The sound had been human, but was he really sure?

Could he risk a light? Where was the Earth when you really needed it?

Well, he thought, *if you can't see them, then they can't see you either.* He silently removed his sling and then like a Kimmer, he took silent steps.

At the opening, he smelled the air. Human, and rank. Then came the sound again.

"Treekiller." It was Darkwind.

...

"You make too much noise, Treekiller. Ba...," the boy's voice slurred off into silence.

"Darkwind? Are you okay?" Charles asked of the darkness.

There was no answer. He fumbled without sight until he felt the dry brush bed and the hot, burning hot, skin of the boy on it.

Charles fished his tender box from his pocket and quickly had a fire going. The light didn't help Darkwind's looks. The boy was unconscious, and feverish, but there were other problems as well. One arm was scraped. The worst of the wounds were puffy, red, and oozed infection. One foot was bare and blooded.

It looked as if he'd walked many kloms that way. His whole body seemed shrunken. He was dehydrated, and probably starved.

There was little Charles could do in the dark with no medicines, but the short exposure he had to Jelica Haren's hospital had left some marks. He forced a little water down Darkwind's throat. The wounds he cleaned and dressed with strips of cloth from his shirt that he washed and baked over the fire.

But Darkwind's fever raged as hot as ever. "You are a real Alpine now," Charles mumbled as he held his water skin to the boy's lips, "You are burning to death like the rest of us."

...

Darkwind woke in the still of the night. He nibbled little of the rabbit and even less of the cheese Charles had brought from Condorcet. He drank more water. He was too tired to talk, and he quickly drifted off to sleep again. Charles watched over him as the boy's body jerked and twisted, playing out in miniature his nightmares.

What had he been suffering while I was pitying myself in the mud? I haven't the right to sneer at the forest-beasts ever again.

Darkwind ventured a smile when he woke again in the pre-dawn hours. "Do your people," he asked with a voice that was weak and hoarse, "sing songs of their great heroes?"

Charles thought a moment. He remembered his father, and a few wild times around the campfire. "A little," he said. "We aren't as good at it as the Er Sun."

"We need one." Darkwind closed his eyes and leaned back into the dry rustle of his bedding. "What a flight! No one has flown so far. No one has flown so high!"

"You didn't have any problem with the cliff?"

"What cliff?" Darkwind asked absently as he re-lived the memory.

"On the mainland."

Dreamy eyes opened. He shook his head a little. "No. I was in the clouds. I was high. High! No Er Sun has ever flown such a wind. Clean and powerful. No mountains to slow it down. I thought I would fly forever."

"How did you get hurt?"

Darkwind's mouth twisted at another memory. "I got wet. The clouds are wonderful, except when the rains come. I think the wind was tired of me and decided to twist my tail. Old Darkwind himself pulled the air out of my sails and dropped me."

He shook his head. "If he hadn't had mercy on his namesake...."

"You have a rough landing?"

Darkwind tried to laugh, it turned into a gut-heaving cough. After a minute, he gasped a breath, and then continued, weaker, "Blind landing. In the dark. In heavy rain. I didn't land; I flew into the mud. I hurt my arm. I was like the dead until morning. Red-shirts spotted me. I led them a chase. Still leading...."

Charles put a hand on the boy's shoulder to keep him from dropping back to sleep, "Serenites. You had Serenites chasing you?"

Darkwind smiled, only half conscious. "Led them a chase. Couldn't shake them. Chased for days. But I remembered Sheep Totem. Sacred place. Won't find me here." He snuggled against his bedding and slept.

Charles stared into the fire. Hunters finding him in a few days was just wishful thinking. If the Serenites had been following Darkwind the whole time, then they must still be coming. Coming straight to the Sheep Totem Crater.

...

There was only one logical thing to do; backtrack Darkwind's blood-stained trail and make a false path off into the forest for the pursuers to follow.

Charles considered it for two minutes.

Instead, he carried the still-sleeping boy down to the circle of stones and made him as comfortable as possible beside the firepit.

Charles was sweating as he finally seated himself on the cool granite stone and put out his hand.

I can't keep him alive. I don't have the skills. But Jelica could. If only I could carry him to Terrance! But there's no time. But the Serenites… they're moving a whole army through here. Would they spare the medicines for a sick Kimmer boy?

"HALT AND STATE THE PASSWORD." The voice sent a hundred wings skyward.

"Admiral Nicolas Bardin." He'd exhausted his ideas based on the York theory. They were a footnote to history; the fourth settlement wave, the trigger event of the Crisium War. But they were quickly conquered, twice. And just as quickly, they were assimilated into the Hercules Empire. They left very few records of themselves. Charles knew more about their story from the old Alexandrine history of their mutiny, as taught in Alpine school, than he did from any contemporary records.

But he knew the Serenites. He knew their names and their personal histories. Charles had already tried out their slogans, their official codes, their ship-to-ship heliograph abbreviations, anything he could think of. He had already verified that the two officers had not used their own names, Captain Van Peter or Ensign Don Menzel.

So now, he was working down the whole chain of command. Maybe they weren't above a little subtle flattery.

But the beamship's voice spoke the same old phrase that meant failure, "STAND BACK. UNAUTHORIZED PERSONS WILL BE REPELLED."

Now try it without the title, "Nicolas Bardin." He had to try it in all combinations. A computer brain gave no points for partial success.

…

After an hour, Charles broke from his efforts and checked Darkwind again. The Kimmer boy was awake and alert. His eyes followed Charles's moves with a strange intensity.

"What is it?" Charles asked.

"You talk with the demon of the totem."

Charles shook his head, "No. That isn't a demon." He didn't want to waste a lot of time explaining. But he didn't want the boy to be upset either. "The Sheep Totem is a beamship, one of the sky-ships that all sky-beasts came in. Even the angels used them. This one is still alive. Remember the story you told me? The red demons were just red-shirts. But they had told the ship to wait for them."

"And when Kar-Let killed them, there was no one to speak the magic word," Darkwind finished for him.

Charles was surprised, and pleased at the boy's quick perception. "Yes. I had to get into the fortress of the Serenites and read their books ..."

"To learn how the old red-shirts thought. You told me that. You want to guess the magic word. Do you think you can do it?"

Charles shrugged. He didn't want to say. Speaking the truth would put a name to defeat; it would force him to make a hard decision. "If I don't find the password in a few hours, the Serenites will find it." He avoided looking into Darkwind's shiny, feverish eyes.

"Can I help?"

Charles opened his mouth to turn him down and tell him to rest. Instead he said, "Yes. You were there at Beltis, too. Any idea you have, tell me."

Darkwind nodded and sagged weakly, his eyes closed.

Charles gave his hot dry hand a squeeze and turned back to the task.

...

"General Stradov." But that wasn't it either.

"Who is that?" came a raspy voice. Charles started. He hadn't realized Darkwind was awake again.

"It was the name of a Serenite warship. They tend to name their warships after heroes."

"Or girls."

Charles shook his head, "No. Their warships ...." That thought died as another took its place. "Maybe you have an idea there."

He put out his hand. When acknowledged, he said. "Marta Menzel."

That wasn't it. He tried the other officer's wife, "Tatiana Peter." No luck there either.

"Marta." The computer said no.

"Tatiana."

For a long breath, there was no response from the brain of the beamship. No warning.

With a surge of almost unbelief that he had cracked it, he shouted, "Hey!" Instantly, it came.

"STAND BACK. UNAUTHORIZED PERSONS WILL BE REPELLED."

What! It wasn't right. *Maybe partly right? What was her maiden name?*

"Tatiana Minkeskey."

It was quickly rejected. *It likes 'Tatiana'. Maybe I jinxed it with my shout.* He tried it again, just the one word.

Again, the ship's computer accepted the name, for a moment. Then, when there were no more words of the magic phrase coming within three seconds, it gave its warning.

A phrase. Tatiana something something.

"Tatiana loves Van."

There was an audible click, then came the voice, "PASSWORD VERIFIED."

On the wall of the beamship before him, Charles saw a line widen and become a door.

An open door.

Discovery

Inside the door was a tiny room. Charles gave one glance back at Darkwind. The boy watched. There was a smile of encouragement on his face, but he couldn't hold himself up.

Charles stepped inside.

Magically, the outside door closed behind him and a second door opened, into the interior.

The light was strange, bluish. His eyes watered. His lungs tightened.

There is something wrong with the air. But almost as soon as he thought it, a cool wet breeze stirred.

It is very dry in here. Bone dry. As he stood for a minute, trying to make sense of the large room, he noticed his skin itch.

The place was alien. It was white. All white. The floor was white. The walls were white. The strange pattern thing, a metal net as a ceiling was white, as was the room above him, which he could see through the strange ceiling. There was no lamp, but there was light, like on a heavily overcast day.

Charles nodded, gradually making some sense of what he was seeing. It was somehow familiar. *A cargo ship, but with the cargo gone. An empty storeroom.*

The room was circular, like a great cheese. The room above was just like it. *And that is the ladder.* The isolated rungs were built into the wall, with an opening in the ceiling large enough to crawl through. He put a hand on a rung. Smooth metal, painted white. He climbed. *How do they get the cargo out the door? Are there other doors higher up? Or does the floor-ceiling move?*

The ladder appeared to stretch the whole length of the ship. As he climbed past the second floor, he understood the layout. *It is symmetrical. Two storage compartments on either end. And something else in the middle. The engines? The control room?*

The central room was closed off by another door. There was a handle, a metal bar like a shorter rung of the ladder. He grabbed it and turned. The door shifted in, then slid sideways.

A mummified corpse lay against the wall. The tidy blue fabric of his uniform made the decayed, dried skin of his face even more horrible. Charles forced his attention away.

The control room was a wonderland of colored lights. More came on as he watched. In the silence, he could hear the faint whoosh of circulating air, stirring dust that must have lain like the dead, still for generations.

There were only two chairs, back to back, facing the array of indicators. One of the tan chairs was stained. He looked over at the pilot. There was a stain on the blue uniform.

Yes. They shot him. In the back.

Cautiously, he moved over to the other chair and eased into it. It was stiff, like old cold leather, unused to a body.

A dark panel directly before his eyes lit up. It was filled with words and numbers and strange indicators like carpenter's rulers with pointers to the marks. His eyes caught some of the words; power, pressure, strain, access, temperature.

But there were others that made no sense; quad-phase, delta-thet, cirrance. Some of the numbers changed slightly. It was dizzying. *What is important?*

As he looked over the command displays and controls, careful to touch nothing, he suddenly noticed something very familiar. Down beside the controls, in a metal pocket, was a book.

He pulled it out, his heart beating suddenly faster. It was a gray, cloth-wrapped book; identical to the Serenite naval logbooks he had studied in Beltis. He opened it slowly, wincing as the first page broke in his hand. It was paper, very brittle.

The first page was the commissioning orders from Admiral Bardin to Captain Van Peter. It gave him command of the beamship "Pride of York". The first logged order by the new captain was to rename the ship the "Tatiana".

Charles began to suspect that Van Peter had been much in favor with the Admiral after they'd captured the ship. He wondered why.

But there was another mystery that demanded his attention. He carefully located the last entries of the log, the last day.

. . .

Ensign Menzel had taken the ship up, lifting from the field at the temporary headquarters of the Serenite fleet at Delmotta. Then the Yorkman, Pilot Davis, had taken over the controls. Their route for the day was the big circle, stopping to deliver coded message rods to the ship captains at Eimmart, Condorcet and York.

They made one stop at Eimmart, and then the Captain took over the controls while the Yorkman explained how to check their altitude and airspeed from the instrument readings.

Pilot Davis took over the controls again after the period of instruction. He predicted arrival at Condorcet in fifteen minutes.

It was there that the record changed from a precisely penned account to a hasty scrawl. Wording was terse. "Condorcet sighted. Laser fire from unknown ships. Yorkman at controls attempted to flee. Refused to return. Executed."

After that, it was a busy day. Both Serenites knew how to fly the beamship, but the York pilot had done something to cause the ship to climb high into the atmosphere. They managed to stop the climb, but when they did, the land was far below, the landmark details they had used for navigation now lost in the haze of distance and clouds.

The Serenites spent the whole day settling down to a lower altitude, and then hunting for a familiar place in a world of forest. When darkwind approached, they finally settled the beamship into a protected crater to wait out the night. They went outside to check for any damage to the ship.

And then they had the supreme bad luck to walk out in sight of an expert Kimmer hunter.

. . .

Charles hesitated, and then reached down to pick up the dead pilot. He forced himself to concentrate on superficial things; how lightweight the body had become, how to maneuver the stiff, probably brittle mummy through the doorway, where to put it out of sight. He found a place on the storage floor one level up.

He hated to do it. He was squeamish. But he didn't want Darkwind to see it. Not yet.

The boy's hot skin had the welcome feel of life. Darkwind squirmed in his arms as he kept twisting his head for a better look as Charles carried him up the ladder to the control room.

He put the boy in the clean chair and gave him a sip of water.

The life is burning out of him.

Back to the logbook. It was a prize. Everything Pilot Davis taught the Serenites was written down. He fought the temptation to read everything. Time was scarce.

He had to make it fly. He didn't let himself think about the possibility that the beamship, like so many other of the old machines, could be flawed, broken, or out of power. The lights, the indicators, even the circulating air spoke of some life. He hunted in vain for some indicator that could tell him how much longer this life would last.

One lesson caught his attention. He set the book down and put his fingers on a set of buttons. The panel that had been displaying the numbers suddenly turned into a window to the outside. He moved the buttons and the image shifted to the side like turning your head. In a few seconds, he had 'looked' in all directions. It was dizzying.

Other buttons caused the trees to come closer. Fascinated, Charles caused the viewscreen to magnify the image until he could see ants crawling on the bark.

Another key brought the scrape of branches and the rustle of leaves to life with a suddenness that caused him to jerk his hand away from the buttons. Darkwind stirred, but did not awaken. He checked the logbook again and managed to turn the volume down to a comfortable level.

...

Charles ran his finger along the old words in the logbook. The instructions seemed clear, but he was nervous, unsure. It was just like the first few minutes alone in Jelica's workroom, trying to make a medicine by rote.

But back there, the worst thing that could happen was a spoiled mess, here... I just don't know.

But he was sure sudden death was possible. He had no intention of flying this machine by trial and error. There was so little tolerance for error in a machine fifty meters tall.

A faint voice made him turn to check on Darkwind. The boy was asleep. Unconscious might be a better word.

Then the words came again—a shout in the distance.

It's outside! He turned to look at the viewscreen. His fingers moved on the keys and the image flowed past.

Then he spotted them. Coming down the trail, past the mushroom fairy ring, was a party of four men. They wore the dusky red of the Serenite forest scouts.

Is the door open?

He didn't know. Nor did he have any idea how to lock it.

How did Van Peter set the security system? Surely, that is written down here somewhere? He changed the password!

But there was no time. Outside, one of the scouts spotted the ship and shouted. They began to spread out, moving quickly to surround it.

No time! Sweating, Charles moved over to the board with the letters on the buttons and spelled out the command words. Words and numbers appeared like ghosts over the image on the viewscreen.

He put his hand on a large handle and squeezed.

Noise, like an avalanche, like a falling tree, like an upset beehive—noise loud enough to cause his ears to itch filled the control room.

The viewscreen showed the trees falling away. Charles let out a breath. The rim of the crater was suddenly visible, until it too fell away.

"We are flying!" he shouted.

He glanced at Darkwind. The body was still. He stared at the boy for a painful eternity, until he saw the motion of a shallow breath.

He's alive. I have to get him to Terrance.

Help

Charles looked out the viewscreen and saw nothing but the haze of distance. *I've got to stop—get my bearings.* His finger hunted unsteadily over the buttons. He hit one, and then felt his throat choke up.

A noise, like the buzz of a single giant bee, sounded in his ears. *That was the wrong one!* The muscles in his arms tensed, but a second passed, then another. He forced a breath as he realized that he hadn't killed them. *Let it pass. Figure out what caused the buzz later.* He forced himself to find the right button and press it.

Words appeared over the viewscreen image. Several of the numbers were changing rapidly. *Three kloms high! I have to stop climbing.*

He grabbed the logbook, tearing another of the brittle pages. *Where did I read that lesson?* He glanced over at the screen. Four kloms high, and they seemed to be gathering speed.

"Oh help," he muttered.

"Please state the subject you need help on."

Charles jerked at the voice coming out of the walls. He clenched the armrest of the chair firmly in his right hand and settled himself back down. *It's the ship. The ship talks. It can listen, too. I knew that. It had to—to understand the password.*

He opened his mouth, and after clearing his throat, he said, "How do you stop?"

"Please clarify. How do you stop what?" It was the same voice. But now much quieter, it sounded almost feminine.

"How do you stop the ship?" Charles asked.

"Which do you mean? Stop the engines in principle, stop the engines with commands, stop the motion in principle, stop the motion with commands, stop the voice in principle, stop the voice with commands, or stop some other attribute of the ship?"

Charles smiled. *All of them!* But he contented himself with asking about the steering commands first. Only when he had started them flying level east toward Terrance did he indulge himself with more questions.

It was delightful (and frustrating!) to talk to the ship. Charles knew about computers, from his schoolbooks. But he had not realized how empty they were inside. It had the personality of a textbook—all information and no humor. But the ship was a treasure house of information. Every time he phrased a question too loosely for the ship, it gave him a list of possibilities. The hints of knowledge in those suggestions let him know he would be a long time listening to it all. The scraps of information he gathered in those few minutes enabled him to cool the cabin down for Darkwind and to reassure himself that they wouldn't come crashing out of the sky. At least not soon.

Only the amazing images on the viewscreen could have possibly kept him from a non-stop question and answer session.

On the forest floor, four kloms below, the landscape was alive with soldiers and wagons. The group that had passed near Sheep Totem Crater had been only one small group of the massive invasion. As streams collect to form rivers, these parties were collecting into an army. As he passed silently overhead, (Ship said that this far from the ground, the tractor-beam pulses that grabbed the air and pulled it around the ship were made so fast that they could not be heard) he was glad for the altitude. He didn't trust his ability to dodge cannon balls. Not yet.

Scanning ahead, he finally spotted the confluence of two great rivers. It had to be the Green and the Peach Rivers. He began to settle lower.

Terrance was still under siege, but those weren't Kimmer below. Arrayed like a giant spider's web in rings outside of gunshot range, soldiers and supply wagons and siege-machines were turning the wheat-fields to mud. It was the Serenite Army.

...

The walled city was still intact, in spite of the large blackened area near the east gate. But from the air, the twisty maze of narrow streets and the square roofs of the buildings gave the place the appearance of an ornately carved table resting on a patchwork rug.

Charles brought the ship to a halt directly over the central square. He needed to land in a clear spot. This was a likely place.

When he had lowered to one klom, the magnified videoscreen showed people, both in and out of the city, beginning to point his way. *No way out of it now. So much for the idea of keeping it a secret.* Charles looked over at Darkwind. There was no choice.

He adjusted his view to pick a landing spot. Not twenty meters from where he had slept under the watchful eyes of the Gaussland Trail refugees, there was a place that had no wagons or buildings on it. It was covered with people, but Charles had confidence that would change as he got closer.

Bing! Charles looked up. *What was that noise?*

Bing! Bing, bing.

They are shooting at me!

He scanned the walls below. There were a half dozen guards loading their muskets and defending the town. *They can't touch me,* he told himself for reassurance. *This is* oldman *metal.* A second volley hit again, ringing the walls like kids throwing pebbles at a washtub.

Below, the people were scattering in panic. Charles kept his fingers resting on the buttons. One man tripped and fell. But he got back to his feet quickly.

Then, he was even with the tops of the buildings. The strange buzzing noise he heard when he had left the crater returned. Outside, the winds the ship created whipped the dust and cobblestones into a raging storm. Even the regular clang of gunfire was drowned out.

Then the fury died. "Cirrance to standby," reported the voice of the ship.

The gunfire doubled, as if the general populace joined in.

Charles looked with the viewscreen out at the lethal greeting he was getting. Not that he blamed them. Anything coming out of the sky was likely to be an enemy. But there was no way he would be able to open the door and go out into that.

"Help," he asked the ship.

. . .

Charles looked out over the scene, his hand over the keyboard. He spotted Mike Jonsen, the man who had helped him escape the first time, fumbling at his ammunition pouch. He had the sound turned down, so he could only guess at the string of words he was spewing as he frantically prepared to fire. *Probably blaming it on the devils again.*

It was startling, even though he was protected inside, to see the muzzle of the musket aim towards his face and fire in a puff of white smoke.

Charles stabbed at the keyboard and shouted at the guard.

"WOULD YOU CUT THAT OUT!" It was a giant voice. Charles continued, "WITH ALL THE ENEMIES YOU HAVE OUTSIDE YOUR WALLS, IT WOULD BE A GOOD IDEA TO SAVE YOUR AMMUNITION FOR THEM. I AM CHARLES FASAIL, ALPINE. I AM A NEUTRAL. I AM NOT YOUR ENEMY, SO STOP SHOOTING AT ME." The shots dwindled off.

I have their attention. I might as well use it now.

"I WANT JELICA HAREN, THE ALPINE HEALER TO BE TOLD THAT I AM HERE. I HAVE NEED OF HER ASSISTANCE."

...

Charles tapped a button to kill the voice. "Ship, do I have to be in the control room for me to give you orders?"

"No. Anywhere within the interior. Reception outside is limited to approximately one hundred meters, depending upon acoustic factors."

Charles quickly arranged several short command words, and picked up Darkwind. He carried him down to the double door and left him lying there where he could be moved in a hurry.

This place could quickly become my prison.

With others ready to take his place in an instant, he could never let his guard down. He could never leave the ship unattended. He could never let anyone inside that he couldn't trust. The ship took his orders because he had passed the security test the last commander had left, but Charles had no illusions that it was in any way loyal to him. The only security was direct possession.

It could get unpleasant. He had found a place to relieve himself, but he had only a handful of food and one water skin.

A quick glance at the viewscreen showed a man approaching. He was waving a white truce flag. It was Mayor Cathyl.

Charles ran his tongue along the inside of his teeth. He didn't trust that man. Or maybe he just didn't like him. But he couldn't ignore him.

He dropped quickly down to the door. "Open."

He stepped into the little room. The inner door closed behind him and the outer one opened.

The smell of gunpowder and too many people assaulted his nose. Even though it was daylight, the natural light looked muted and dim.

"Good day, Mayor!" he shouted. He stepped into the opening. They could still shoot him. It was a risk. He gambled that the Mayor thought more of politics than tactics.

The Mayor took a step forward, "Good day to you, Ambassador. My apologies for the gunfire. We didn't expect you."

Charles smiled, "No harm done. I see you have acquired a few more enemies since I was here last."

The Mayor acknowledged that with a grimace. He nodded toward the beamship. "And you have given up traveling by foot."

"Yes. It is a bit faster this way. I'm in a hurry. Have you sent for Jelica Haren?"

He nodded. "Are you hurt?"

"No. But my apprentice suffered a fall. He has a bad fever. Terrance has the best medical aid in the world."

Mayor Cathyl said, "Terrance has the most enemies as well. Jelica has been very busy since you left us. Have you noticed the changes?"

"You mean the Serenites? Yes, I have. And this isn't all of them. Terrance appears to be just the first target in a major invasion. They intend to take the whole eastern lands. There is a line of supply wagons that stretches all the way to Delmotta." As he spoke, something of the animation faded out of the man's face. He had been looking for hope. Charles had dashed it.

Just then Jelica appeared, rubbing her hands on a bloodstained apron. Charles waved to her. She craned her head to look up at the top of the beamship. She looked down, "Charles! You brought this here?"

He nodded. "Come on in. I have another patient for you." She hurried in through the door. The Mayor moved to follow her, but Charles whispered the door closed behind her.

"Charles. What is this?" She looked at him with suspicion.

"A beamship." He smiled and shrugged. "Formerly of York, then a warship for the Serenite navy, then a religious totem for the Kimmer, and now a courier ship for the Alpine government in exile."

She frowned at that last, "You?"

"Me," he nodded with a grin. "You want to be the government next? It has its moments."

But then the inner door opened and Jelica's attention went immediately to Darkwind. She knelt down beside him and put her hand on his neck.

"Who is this?" she asked.

"His name is Darkwind. He's my apprentice. Will he live?"

She shook her head, "I don't know. How long has his arm been like this?"

Charles told her all he knew, including the escape flight that caused it. She seemed unimpressed by the adventure.

"He is Kimmer, isn't he?"

"Yes. And they are as human as we are."

Jelica didn't answer. She shook her head, checking the pus-stained dressings.

"There will be trouble over this," she said. "But it can't be helped. Come on, help me get him to the hospital."

Charles helped her lift Darkwind and carry him into the little room, but he said, "I can't leave the ship and I can't let anyone in. Your Mayor would kill for this ship. I can hear it in his voice."

Jelica stared at him with hard eyes. "You blame him? No one in Terrance expects to live much longer."

"What do you want me to do?" Charles asked angrily. "Fight the whole Serenite Empire by myself? Kill them all? I don't even know if the ship is armed! I just barely got it to fly. I could evacuate you and your people. I will, if you say the word. But what if someone tried to take over the ship? It could kill us all just as quickly.

"Besides, aren't Alpines supposed to be neutral? Do you want me to give that up? If I could fight for Terrance and the Hercs, who would ever respect Alpine neutrality again?"

Jelica shook her head and shouldered the frail body of Darkwind. "You have your problems. I have mine. Open the door. I have patients dying out there."

Charles gritted his teeth and said nothing but the curt command, "Open."

Mayor Cathyl had to step back to let Jelica pass. Charles was ready to kick him out if he tried to force his way in. He would enjoy that.

But the Mayor's eyes were drawn to Darkwind. He put up his hand. "Hold! That's a Kimmer!"

Jelica stopped and turned to face him. "He is a sick boy."

The Mayor was not listening. "I will not have a Kimmer in this city! Throw him over the wall."

Charles put his hand on the impulse gun and pulled it out where it could be seen. "That boy is my apprentice. He is under Alpine protection."

The Mayor turned to face him. His face glistened with sweat and the lines of his fury made it a demon mask. His voice dripped with hatred. "'Alpine protection'! That buys you nothing in my city. The Kimmer is crow bait. I want him out."

Charles raised the impulse gun. "Try it and you are dead."

The Mayor's face was gleeful, "And then what? Can you kill us all?" Charles looked around. He had no sympathizers. Every eye had a weary look, as if they had been staring into death for too long.

The man continued, "And what if you *do* kill us all with that stick? What loss is it to us?"

Charles felt himself slipping down a mental pit. He took a deep breath.

Abruptly, he felt the pressure slip away. The decision was made.

Charles put a sad smile on his face. The words started to bubble out of him, "You are a sorry lot of people here! Do you think so highly of your revenge that you will commit suicide trying to kill an innocent boy?

"Alpine protection I said! Alpine protection I mean! If that means Terrance has to find a new Mayor to replace the one that got splattered over the grass, then so be it. If it means, stopping the Serenites so that my apprentice can get his medical treatment in peace, then so be it. Alpine neutrality never meant letting ourselves get shot at."

It took a second for the meaning of what he said to sink in, but then the Mayor asked, "Stop the Serenites?"

Charles shrugged, "If my apprentice is being treated here, of course I will have to protect the place. That is only logical. Alpines protect their own."

He then let his voice shift lower, "But if you can't tolerate the presence of a Kimmer, then I will *take* him *and the Alpine Healer, Jelica Haren* and go find a safer place for his treatment."

Mayor Cathyl composed himself fast. It was the politician who spoke, "I must apologize for my ill temper. We have all lost friends and relatives to the Kimmer. If this one belongs to you—a *tame* Kimmer, then I am sure our Jelica will be happy to treat him, here."

Charles looked pained, "Mayor Cathyl, please! She should be called 'Healer Haren'."

He nodded, meekly.

Charles decided to quit while he was ahead. He stepped back out of the doorway and closed the door. He quickly dashed up to the control room and watched the Mayor order two men to help carry Darkwind off toward Jelica's hospital. All over the central square, every eye was on the Alpine beamship. He had become their hope.

Battle of Terrance

Moving numbers on the screen caught his eye. He stared at them, like the flickering flame of a candle, while his mind darted here and there. *I could try to scare them off.* He gave a half laugh. *But then, they might not go.*

He picked up the logbook. There were lessons for flying, for spying, for setting the security guard. *But I could get all that from the ship itself. Was the York pilot trying to keep his guards ignorant? Did he know about the ship's helps? Strange if he didn't. I found it easily enough.*

"Ship. What did the York pilot, Davis, do on this ship before the Serenites took it over?"

"The question is too broad. Limit your question." *Sometimes I don't think you really know how to talk after all.* "What were this pilot's duties?"

"Lieutenant Mark Davis held the position of co-pilot. A duty roster was not logged."

"What other crew were there?" he asked.

"During the period of York authority?"

"Yes."

"Captain Hans Robertson was pilot. Technician Frank Bruce was gunner. Technician Earl Bentin was power systems engineer. Sergeant Larry—"

"Wait a minute! You said a gunner. What does a gunner do?"

"A gunner maintains and uses a gun."

Charles moved forward in his seat. "What *specifically* did the gunner on this ship do, as his duties?"

"First, the gunner keeps a log of all service operations on the gun. Next, he monitors the energy usage and reports to the captain—"

"Wait. What gun?"

"'The M29883F3 strain-cooled, direct-tap, 5643 angstrom, weapon-grade, atmosphere use, laser cannon is designed for anti-structure usage where the mass of the structure precludes the use of tactical T/P devices.'"

"Where is it?" Charles asked, almost whispering.

The screen blanked out. Then in glowing green lines, a drawing of the ship appeared, with all the interior walls outlined. One odd-shaped region near the center of the ship was lined in blue. Charles puzzled over the image, trying to visualize the rooms. *There is the control room. Why does it look so small?*

He looked around at the curved walls and compared it to the floors below. *Why, this is only a third of the floor!*

"Ship, how do you get to the blue area?"

"Through the access hatch."

"What is that?"

The image on the screen cleared and was replaced by another drawing. The ship's voice stated, "It looks like this."

Charles looked around and spotted it. He went to it and found the handle. *It doesn't look like a door.* But the handle moved, and the hatch unsealed.

Inside the cramped engineering area, mounted in a man-sized metal casing was a machine marked, "M29883F3 Laser. Danger. Authorized service only." It had three lights; TAP COOLING STANDBY. All three were glowing green.

...

There'd not been a word about a laser cannon in the logbook. He felt a little more respect for the York pilot. Charles had not understood the man running from a fight. *But it wasn't his fight.* And now he could see him in a different light. He'd been a man in slavery to the enemy, playing a waiting game, doing just enough to keep them from gaining the full power of the ship. He taught them simple rote commands, and hid the true potential. The Serenites were using it as a messenger ship when it was a potent weapon. *And I need it as a weapon.*

Charles shook his head. He flipped on the exterior viewscreen and was greeted by a crowd of worried onlookers. He had the sound off, but he could almost hear them talking to themselves, asking each other, *What is wrong with the Alpine? Why doesn't he move?*

"Voice on. Attention everyone! Please stand back. You could be hurt by blowing dust." He waited for a count of three and said, "Voice off." Outside, people were scattering. He gave them a half minute, then lifted.

The city walls dropped from sight to reveal a stirred ant-hill of human activity. He shifted the view. Puffs of white along the top of the wall and scattered through the army on the ground outside told of a battle already well underway. Terrance was surrounded. Lines of troops circled it two ranks deep, more in places. Siege-machines, looking like wooden pull-toys from his view, were being wheeled up to the city gates. Charles noted a body lying beside the road, like a dead ant. Then he saw others. *No coincidence. I bet I triggered this.* An ache of depression promised future regrets. *But I have no choice.*

He took a deep breath and stopped rising. The ship hovered, its great tractor-beam projectors grabbing great chunks of the atmosphere and blowing it downward. Charles didn't understand how it worked, but luckily, he didn't have to.

His eyes lit on one of the siege-machines, a great battering-ram, carved from a giant tree. It looked three meters across. *It's getting too close. That's as good a target as any.*

Charles spoke the command word and glowing lines appeared like a spiderweb over the viewscreen image. He moved the large fat button carefully until the machine was centered in the heart of the web. "Fire," he spoke, his eyes fixed on the target.

It exploded. Even with the sound off, the blast shook the ship. A great cloud of steam took a moment to dissipate. When it did, Charles touched the controls and averted the view.

No! I didn't warn them.

The heat of the laser cannon had turned the green wood of the log into a bomb. It had shattered, killing dozens of soldiers near it. Even the mighty wall of Terrance looked scarred by the blast. All gunfire stopped, as both sides stood in shock.

So, I have both Kimmer and Serenite deaths on my shoulders.

The white puffs of musket fire began again. *They aren't being scared away. I knew they wouldn't be.*

Charles moved the ship, positioning it near the next siege-machine. He deliberately waited, hovering just out of musket range, before firing. *The smart ones will run.* Most did. He fired.

The blast was as violent as the first, but there was less carnage. *This is the way to do it. Break their tools, but let them escape.* He drifted to the next one. He had less of a wait. The men on the ground needed no prompting to run.

Three down, he thought when the steam cloud billowed up and the seat under him shook with another explosion.

Up on the slope of a nearby hill, a cluster of men were working frantically to move a wagon. *What is that?*

Their actions seemed different from the passive actions of the ground troops who were finding their firearms useless against the thing in the sky.

Charles moved the magnification up. Just in time, he was able to watch as the soldiers pulled the canopy from a glistening *oldman* weapon. *A laser cannon. Just like the one at Stampz.* And it was being aimed at him.

Charles wasted no time. He adjusted the web over the weapon, just as he watched the ground crew align the cannon at him. *Maybe I should dodge.* But he didn't. "Fire."

The screen flashed. He squinted and looked aside as the white glare of the explosion washed out all detail in the view.

His heart beat loud in his ears. *What did...?* Then even his thoughts trailed off as the ship bucked. There was a shove. His hands instinctively grabbed at the armrests of the chair. Then the ship shook under him again.

The screen was dizzying streaks of motion. He grabbed at the controls. He pushed the image, centering it again. Above the hill, a ball of yellow fire climbed high into the sky, trailing a column of smoke behind it, like a giant dandelion blossom for the angels.

On the ground, trees were flattened. A dozen or so were arrayed around the spot where the wagon had been—like toothpicks laid out in neat order. Of the wagon, the laser cannon, the ground crew—there was no sign. The blast had consumed them. For a span of a hundred meters all around the blast point, nothing moved.

I survived something like that? Like never before, he appreciated his luck. "That was quite an explosion. Ship, are you intact?"

"There has been no damage. Fragments of rock struck the hull, but the hull is tough."

I didn't even hear it. "What would have happened if they had shot us? Would we have exploded like that?"

"No. The explosion from a destroyed beamship of this class would be significantly more powerful."

Charles shuddered. His hands were shaking, and his arms felt too weak to hold them up. "How big would it have been?"

"The blast would have flattened the forest for a radius of ten kilometers. The city would have been destroyed. A firestorm would result. The sound of the explosion would be heard for many hundreds of kilometers."

A Burn. Just like Alp. Pilot Davis, I am sorry I ever thought you were a coward. You saved all Condorcet, and you paid for it with your life.

Charles shook his head, to clear it of the image of that fireball. He adjusted the controls, aiming the viewscreen at the ground. People were picking themselves up. He sighed. In spite of all the people he had killed, it was still a respectable army.

He pushed a button and looked at the numbers. Before they had taken off, their energy number was 40, with a string of digits after the decimal. It was still 40 and some. The laser didn't drink energy as badly as he had feared. *I still have an army to stop. I had better do a good job of it. This is too hard. I'll never be able to do it more than once.*

"Come on, Ship. We have some work to do." There was another target, a large supply wagon.

...

He rose slightly higher, to avoid having the possibility of cannon balls striking the ship. He looked around at the deployment of the army. It was an impressive group. Many of the siege machines would have had to have been constructed close-by. They were too large to transport on the new roads the Serenites had recently cut.

One group, on a mountain slightly to the east caught his eye.

Kimmer. What to they think of all this?

He steered the ship over to where they gathered. He had to make every effort to keep them out of the mess—for Darkwind's sake.

"Voice on. People of the Four Families!" he called. "I had no bloodguilt with Kar-Let Mor-Gan, and I want none with you. This place is under my protection. Leave this place of death in peace."

He watched them for a moment, talking to each other. If Darkwind knew the tale, then these certainly would. Some might even have sat at the stone circle. They would recognize the Sheep Totem.

They began to leave, down the back side of the mountain.

"Voice off."

I just wish the Serenites were as reasonable.

...

The destruction of every wagon and siege-machine in the Serenite forces took more than an hour. He was slow and methodical, partly to give the soldiers time to escape the target zone and partly to drum into them the powerlessness of their position. He spotted many soldiers fleeing into the forest.

His last target was a big tent. He had spotted it earlier. It was the headquarters of the invasion force.

He moved the ship slowly up to the tent. He could see the officers below. Some were making their way out of the fire zone, but some were standing their ground.

"Voice on. This is Charles Fasail, Alpine." The tiny figures on the ground stopped moving, waiting to hear what he would say next. *I have got to say it right, or Alpines everywhere will pay for my mistakes.*

"The Serenite army has attacked this peaceful settlement without warning. Alpine nationals and dependents have been placed in jeopardy by your actions, forcing me to act against your tools of war."

He paused to keep his voice cool and composed.

"Threats to the safety of Alpines will not be tolerated. Invasions must give ample warning or they will not be allowed to succeed.

"I now suggest that you return to Serenite territory. You are many. You will start to get hungry shortly. I can assure you that there will be no supply wagons coming. Go home and try your invasion some other day—*after* you make a proper declaration of war."

He closed his eyes. "Voice off." That last comment about hunger came straight from the heart, or the stomach. He commanded the ship to rise another klom and head west.

Final Chores

In a wrapped cloth, he had bread and cheese. He finished the last of it quickly, just in time to spot a group of five wagons. The viewscreen quickly showed up the dark red uniforms. He fired a blast into the road twenty meters in front of the lead wagon, to catch their attention. "Voice on. Get clear of your wagons. I am going to burn them. You have one minute."

Five quick laser blasts turned the train of wagons into a fiery worm. The middle two quickly exploded—gunpowder shipments.

He shook his head, *Three months of work to try to get wagonloads of powder, and I burn them up.*

After five minutes, he turned the voice back on and gave them a brief version of the sermon on the protection of Alpine nationals. Then he moved on. The smoke rose high behind him, marking the forest fire he had started.

It was a pattern he repeated many times in his slow flight back toward Beltis. The fires started to prey on his mind. They bothered him even more than his violent crusade for declared wars. Oh, his position was logically sound, but it didn't sit well. He *admired* the Serenite invasion push, from a historian's perspective. The man who put it altogether, probably Admiral Bardin, was a genius. He deserved his victory.

And Charles was taking it away from him because a Kimmer boy needed medical care. *And because of that look in her eyes.*

...

The sun was well past zenith when the glint of the sea heralded the approaching coast. He stopped at the edge of his viewscreen range.

I have to do this right. Fortress Beltis, like every major Herc or Serenite naval port, had laser cannon defences. *I have to go in, destroy the ships, and get out before they can get a single shot off.*

He had the advantage of surprise. He'd been flying faster than a man could get back with the news of the disaster.

Viewscreen turned up full, he noted the positions of a half-dozen naval cargo ships wavering in the heat-haze. He talked over the power setting of the laser with Ship. He wanted to set the ships on fire, not to blast them into oblivion. His was a war against their machines. *The fewer deaths on my conscience, the better. I know what my nightmares will be for the* next *seven years.*

He was ready. He dropped from his observation altitude to the height he'd last flown across this harbor. It would be harder to hit him that way.

The cliff dropped out from beneath him. He was over the water. Three buttons on the console, and a web appeared over a ship. "Fire." There was a flash, and flame across the water. He moved the target spot. "Fire."

He adjusted his flight path. The rush of blood in his ears was starting again. "Fire." "Fire." "Fire."

The last target was on the screen when the tower on the Fortress heights flashed a brilliant yellow.

"Jump!" he screamed.

Ship had been told what to do. It wasted no time. Charles felt an itching sensation throughout his whole body and the ship rang like the lowest note on a giant horn. They rose three kloms in as many heartbeats. The downwash from the ship spawned an anti-cyclone in the middle of Beltis harbor, swamping ships and making a huge wave that drenched the docks on all sides. *They were fast!* Charles punched keys that sent him off north. The cloudbank offered his only possible hiding place.

As all detail vanished in the white mist, he thought, *Oh. The scouts at Sheep Totem. They could have helioed back to Beltis. They were ready for me.* He adjusted the flight path so that he would curve back toward the mainland. *Their good luck that they missed me.*

Well, at least he was done. He wasn't going back there. His official Alpine position had been stated enough. The Admiral would get the message.

He wasn't going to do any more fighting. Hercules surely was on the move. *It's their fight now.*

Charles picked up his water skin. *Not much.* He drank it down.

From ten kloms up, the forest below looked like a great patch of bofung, green and lush in the morning sun. Sometimes he could make out roads, where men had cut a path in the tree line like a fingernail mark.

Some valleys were black. In every case, the fires had started at the bottom, where the roads had been, and had burned up to the crest of the hill. Whether the rains had stopped them then or whether they would have burned out on their own, he didn't know. *But they are all out. The forest will reclaim its own.*

From this height, he couldn't see anything as small as the Serenite soldiers, but he was sure they were down there. He hoped they couldn't see him. *More people who hate me.* At least they could not pursue the war. With no supplies and no ammunition, there was no way that they could hope to win against the entrenched settlers. They would have to get back to their lands before the Herc army arrived, finally.

Charles felt a flush of anger. *Fat and lazy Hercs! You deserved to be invaded. I am not sure I did you any real favor.*

The rivers, like blue ribbons stretched across the green, guided him to Terrance. The high-walled city sat like a tinderbox in a cross-marked field. He stopped several kloms off and settled to a better altitude. Under magnification, he could see the walls still unbreached. He imagined that he saw motion, guards on the top of the walls.

Clearly visible, even at this distance, were the blast marks from the bigger explosions. Smaller black spots showed where wagons burned. *Terrance is safe. The army is gone.*

He felt annoyance at himself for thinking he had done any good. Yes, he had stopped the invasion. But who knew what the side effects were. *Was a man responsible for the unforeseen effects of his actions?* He hoped not.

I have enough guilt over the ones I can see.

He felt himself trying to think about Darkwind and Jelica and the future, but he couldn't do it. In a few days, he would come back and check on them.

He moved north, following the Peach River. The pattern of muddy waters and clean, where the smaller streams emptied into the larger, fascinated him. It was a whole different way to look at the world, from on high. He liked it.

. . .

The Gaussland Trail was an insignificant line through the trees, when compared to the river. It was still deserted. He wondered what the traffic would be like when the region was back to normal. The Kimmer were still heavily armed, although he suspected their supply of ammunition would dry up. Isolated Serenite groups would be active, he was sure.

He played with the viewscreen controls, hunting the far horizon for the crater walls of Gauss. He wanted to make an appearance, but *just* an appearance. Rumors would be all over both empires within days. He wanted no one to think he'd been destroyed in the raid on Beltis. Alp was back. He wanted that word spread. He had a people out there, working as slaves and servants. *They needed hope. They will need a place. A place for the freed servant to go to find his people.*

A patch of white, down on the forest floor caught his attention away from his daydreams. He magnified the image.

There was a rainbow of canopies. A wagon train was making its way south. It was a small group, only twelve regular wagons, and two that looked different, perhaps grain wagons.

One canopy, with a black and white checkerboard pattern, drew his attention. He took the magnification to the limit. *Is it them?*

He hit the buttons, and started dropping. He played with the viewscreen, keeping that wagon centered. As he got closer, he noticed more details.

It was the Turner wagon. He focused on the driver. It was Maria.

So intent was he on getting a clear image of her, that he was startled when she turned. She looked straight at him. Her eyes opened wide and she yanked on the reins. The team stumbled to a halt. She turned back and yelled something into the wagon.

Charles glanced at his altitude. He was still too far away to hear what she said. He continued to drift lower.

Rad Fasail climbed out of the back of the wagon and stared up at him. Maria climbed down from the box and he put out a hand to reassure her.

The other wagons were stopping as well, but Charles watched with a burning sensation in his eyes as Rad put his arm around her, comforting his girl in the face of the unknown.

Okay, Rad. Maybe you made a good choice.

He commanded the ship to stop in its drift downward.

"Voice on. Wagon train. Warning. There has been a major battle at Terrance."

Maria started at his voice. She looked at Rad questioningly. Rad, too, had recognized the voice. His mouth was drawn up in a look of puzzlement and worry.

Charles continued, "The Serenite Army has moved into the area. They were persuaded to stop their invasion push, but scattered bands of soldiers will be fighting in isolated places."

The people on the ground were talking, turning to each other at the news. All except Maria and Rad. They still had their attention fixed on the sky.

"If you run into any problems, let them know that you are under the protection of the Alpine government. Yesterday, they learned to respect that."

One. Two. Three. "Voice off."

Charles watched his brother carefully. The ship was hovering, waiting. All he had to do was wave him down, signal him somehow, and he would land. Rad was his brother. His only blood tie in all the world. The Alpines had a Kimmer boy, a little Herc girl of unknown heritage, they could make room for Maria, too.

Just make one sign that you want me.

On the ground, Rad and Maria talked. The words were few, and the gestures were full of emotion. They never let go of each other. After a moment, Rad and Maria turned back to their wagon.

Rad glanced back over his shoulder at the ship. He waved. It was a wave of good-bye.

"Voice on. Good-bye. Good luck to you." He slapped a key on the console and the ship lifted, heading north. The viewscreen was a blur of green. He had to wipe his eyes on his sleeve to see where he was going.

· · ·

He saw Gaussland, finally, from the air. How many years had he dreamed of the place? How many travelers in Port Gartner had talked about the great land of opportunity, great expanses of free land for the taking?

It was a pretty place, a large crater containing smaller ones, with a large lake on the eastern edge. There were orderly patchworks of fields, patterns of little villages with larger towns at the gateways through the mountain ring. On the lake were two tiny specks of white on the blue—sailboats. This would be a pleasant place to visit, someday.

· · ·

One lone wagon worked its way north, a half-day by wagon out from Zeno. Charles eased the ship down, landing it in a wide place in the road. The old man driving didn't even pause. He rode up to the ship and was getting out of the driver's box even as Charles opened the door.

"Good evening, Harriman," he called out.

"Charles, Charles Fasail, is that you?" The little man was on him in a minute, grasping his hands and saying, "It is good to see you."

Charles drank in the man's cheer. It warmed him up inside.

"Can I beg a meal of you?" he asked. "I'm starved!"

The preacher fixed him a feast of rich lamb stew and baked apples. They talked together for hours. They talked of the past and the future. They talked of brothers and friends. They talked of duty and peace.

Much later, the first hint of the night breezes told them that they each had a shelter to find. When Charles lifted, it was with a warm feeling. He was accepted, by one man at least.

...

Stampz still looked like a picture book as it grew in his view. But it was a spoiled picture. A good third of the patchwork lands were under water. The central rise was almost completely an island, with only a strip connecting it to the rim walls. It looked peaceful enough, from high in the air.

As he settled lower toward the castle, he saw that much had changed. A tent city had grown around the castle.

The darkwinds were beginning, so he had to move quickly to get down to a protected place. There was still an uncluttered courtyard inside the main castle area. It would do.

As he landed, the Duke of Stampz appeared at a nearby doorway. The corridor was filled, as others reacted the same way.

The gate opened to a cloud of dust and gravel as the beamship settled in the courtyard. The sound cut off abruptly.

A door at the base of the giant cylinder opened up and Charles stepped out.

"Greetings, Your Excellency. I have returned."

The duke gaped, "Charles?" He looked up at the metal tower. "Charles Fasail?"

He smiled, "Yes. Your Trade Representative to Condorcet? Remember? I have come to report on my trip." He stepped forward. The door of the ship closed silently behind him.

Charles made a short bow, the said, "Oh, I should tell you. I have recently declared myself… 'governor'? Yes, 'governor' will do. Governor of Alp. May I beg a few moments of your time?"

The duke was quick to overcome his initial reaction. He put out his hand and gestured toward the gate. "Yes, of course. I would be greatly interested in an account of your travels, Governor."

Inside, Charles was granted chance to clean himself up for the first time in days. Bertrice, whose scent had followed him all the way to Condorcet, brought him a fresh shirt. She ducked a quick bow and darted away almost before he could thank her. It had been tailored to his size.

The duke seemed not too surprised by the general Kimmer uprising and he was only mildly angry as Charles told him the whole Serenite plan for the takeover of the eastern lands.

The duke nodded, "I had expected something like this. Did you know that I was raised in the Serenite Landrule? My father was Duke of Franklin, the brother of the King. But my mother was a daughter of the Serenite Royal House. When I was acknowledged, it was quite a scandal. But I was educated as the duke's son, in the heart of Hercules society. I've always known that the vigor has gone out of the Empire. Maybe something like this will shake them up. I take it that you did something dramatic. You speak of their invasion in the past tense."

Charles nodded, and gave a brief description of his actions and his justification.

The duke looked pained. "Oh, Admiral Bardin will not like that. You have made quite an enemy. Don't be surprised if he gets the Red Throne in spite of his failure. He's been on the verge of it for twenty years at least. A good threat, like you, might do the trick."

It took some of the good cheer off the evening, but Charles recognized the truth in the duke's assessment.

"I'm sorry that my original purpose failed," Charles apologized. "I doubt that anyone at the palace really listened."

"Oh, they listened," said the duke, "but you have to understand that Stampz is a political bad wind. I sent you there as a gamble. I didn't expect their help. I'm afraid we are right back where we started."

Charles put up his hand, "No, I have brought help. It is sitting out there in your courtyard. If you would care to pen a little trade agreement with the government of Alp, I think we can take care of your problem in the morning."

"Trade agreement?" the duke asked, with a little suspicion. "What kind of a trade agreement?"

"Oh, nothing much," Charles said. "I'll be needing food staples, farming materials, occasionally some special things you might have to send off for. But primarily, I need a safe port, where I can do business without fear of being shot out of the sky. I need the cooperation of a man of honor."

The duke shifted in his chair. Subtly, they were no longer friends chatting, but nations negotiating. He asked, "And what would Stampz get out of this, aside from your help in the morning?"

"We will have to work that out, you and I," Charles said cheerfully. "As of this moment, Alp is broke. But we have great potential."

...

The morning was bright and clear. Charles took the beamship up in a glow of good feeling. He folded the vellum copy of their agreement into the logbook. The government of Alp was recognized. Now, all he had to do was find a population, and to do his part of their bargain.

He hovered high above the canyon. The lake that had grown up behind the dam was deep and blue. *But it must go.*

There were no on-lookers. He had made sure of that. With too much energy here in one place, it would be too easy to kill someone by mistake.

"Ship, recall the discussion we had about splitting rocks."

"Recalled."

Charles had first intended to blast the slab with laser fire, but Ship had given him some unpleasant estimates. Basalt doesn't explode like green wood. It absorbs too little moisture to do other than chip off the upper layers of the rock.

Fortunately, Ship knew of other techniques.

The beamship positioned itself high over the canyon. The altitude was critical. When a *Nance-Bate overlap* occurred, energy was partitioned evenly to all the mass within the spread of the beam, but divided between the fore and aft beams such that conservation of momentum was maintained. To give any kick at all to the slab, the forebeam was narrowed down as tight as Ship could focus—a small patch of stone in the center span of the slab. The aftbeam was spread wide, to encompass as much of the mass of the atmosphere as they could manage.

For an instant, the length of time the beam traveled from the ship down to a meter or so into the rock, the main beam generator coupled its energy store into a colossal push, and just as instantly terminated.

"Ship?"

"First pulse engaged."

A great crack, like the sound of lightning directly overhead, shattered the quiet of the canyon.

Charles scanned below, but the view below was obscured by a dust cloud. He played with the view, and located the sight he had hoped for.

Part of the slab had moved, not much, but there was definitely a crack all the way through the immense stone. He moved the aiming point to the left.

"Ship. Hit it again."

"Second pulse engaged."

He was prepared for the effects this time, and had the view focused right where he wanted it.

Rock was moving. Under the pressure of the torrent of water, a center span of the slab was being slowly pushed out of the way. Three months of water were impatient to be on their way.

He repositioned the aim. "Ship. Hit it."

It happened. A center span of the slab was fragmenting and tumbling out of the way. The water was moving and its force was not giving the rock any place to stop.

The gap is big enough for at least one wagon. That's enough.

"Ship, let's move."

. . .

He set down quickly on a ledge well above the Porch. He raced down the ladder and out the door. He wanted to *see* it. Not just on a screen.

The air and ground shook as he ran out the door. He stepped closer to the edge—just in time to see a blast of air and mist surge out of the opening. Trees along the riverbed bent under the wind. They never had a chance to bend back.

Seconds behind the air, came a wall of water. It looked a hundred meters tall, a churning brown mass, carrying stones, trees, anything that had settled or grown in the Gate since the first time it had been flooded out.

The blast of mist reached him, drenching him all over. He was grateful he'd chosen a high vantage point.

Down below, a forest was being uprooted by the spreading surge. It would be a long time before it grew back.

Homeland

Charles landed the ship on the mudflat of the receding lake. There was a party going on. Charles stepped out of the ship and was caught up by eager hands and carried to the table where the duke was doing his best to get his fine clothes muddy—like a kid in his worship clothes, joyous in release.

"Come on Charles!" he yelled. "I have a dozen ladies here wanting to fill you a plate. I hope you're hungry."

...

The party lasted all morning. Periodically, all the big men would grab the tables and move them down to the water's retreating edge. The children splashed in the muddy waters and got horribly dirty. Charles ate until he was stuffed. Everyone had a great time.

A man in simple farmer's clothes came and stood next to the table where Charles sat watching the Stampz people play. When he didn't move on, Charles smiled at the man. He smiled back. After a moment, it finally occurred to him that the man wanted to talk.

"Hello," he said. "Did you want something?"

The man bobbed his head. "Wanted to show you." And he turned and walked off toward the water's edge. He glanced back at Charles, to see if he was going to follow. *Why not?* He levered his long legs over the bench and got up to see what the man wanted.

He led Charles over to a muddy, squarish stone that had just been exposed by the dropping water level.

"This is the cornerstone of my land," said the farmer. He pointed out where his plot of land stretched. Out in the water was a mound that had once been his house. The farmer shrugged off that loss. A house could be rebuilt.

"I have my land back. I wanted to thank you." He took Charles by the hand. Charles could feel the strength in that calloused grip. There was a sparkle in the farmer's eyes.

...

The duke eased himself back in his chair. "What I don't understand is why you're trying to bring back old Alp. You have the power to build yourself any kind of nation you wish. Is it an appeal to attract the scattered Alpines, like yourself? What's wrong with the Kingdom of Fasail?"

Charles shook his head, "No. If I were the only one, I would still be Alpine. It's more than blood. It is my soul. Would you give up Stampz for Franklin?"

There was a flicker of old memory in the duke's eyes. "No, not if I have any say in the matter. I am building something here."

"So am I." Charles looked across the way where men had just finished stacking his supplies in the little room between the inner and outer doors of the ship. He got to his feet. It was time to go.

"Where are you going?" asked the duke. "To pick up your people?"

"No," said Charles. "Not yet. I think I am going to visit my homeland. It has been long enough. I think I will do some planting."

He walked over to the ship. When the door closed after him, the people around moved back out of the way. The winds and the buzz began. The beamship lifted quickly into the sky and headed off to the west.

THE END

Look forward to **The High Quest**, the next chapter in the **Lunar Alpine Trilogy**.

If you want more books like this, consider leaving a review on your favorite online bookstore or review service.

If you're interested in what came before the
terraforming of Luna, then choose the
Earth Branch of the Project Saga:

Star Time
Kingdom of the Hill Country
In the Time of Green Blimps
Captain's Memories
Humanicide

CPSIA information can be obtained
at www.ICGtesting.com
Printed in the USA
FSHW011115280619
59458FS